TW

VIRGINIA COUNTIES

Where the
Western Migration Began

BY

JOHN H. GWATHMEY

AUTHOR OF

LEGENDS OF VIRGINIA COURTHOUSES, LEGENDS OF VIRGINIA
LAWYERS, JUSTICE JOHN, THE LOVE AFFAIRS OF
CAPTAIN JOHN SMITH.

INTRODUCTION BY
JOHN STEWART BRYAN

ILLUSTRATIONS BY
ELMO JONES

Originally published: Richmond, Virginia, 1937
Copyright © 1937 John H. Gwathmey
All Rights Reserved
Reprinted, by arrangement,
Genealogical Publishing Co., Inc.
1001 N. Calvert St., Baltimore, Md. 21202
1979, 1981, 1997
Reprinted from a volume in the George Peabody Library
of The Johns Hopkins University
Baltimore, Maryland
Library of Congress Catalogue Card Number 79-66025
International Standard Book Number 0-8063-0861-3
Made in the United States of America

Epigraph

A people which takes no pride in the noble achievements of remote ancestors will never achieve anything worthy to be remembered with pride by remote descendants.

—LORD MACAULAY.

Introduction

The names of the counties in Virginia, as it has been often remarked, give a very good picture of the changing lines of sovereignty in England. As the names of the kings, queens and royal princes were exhausted the royal governors and later the great citizens and governors of Virginia were called on to designate these subdivisions of State authority.

It was not by chance that the counties in Virginia run from Elizabeth City and Princess Anne to Lee. This phase of county names has been traced before; it has remained for Mr. Gwathmey, who is already established as a student and expositor of Virginia history, to enter more deeply into the twelve counties where Western migration began.

Those who have followed Mr. Gwathmey's previous works may be assured that in this study he has shown scholarship and research, and has added to a clearer knowledge of Virginia.

JOHN STEWART BRYAN.

Contents

List of Illustrations

Twelve Virginia Counties

York River Basin Westward

HIS book is the story of twelve Virginia counties, an effort to preserve their half-forgotten lore and to furnish a record of the people who have lived in them.

Why, it may be asked, were only twelve counties chosen? It was for the reason that most of the leaders in the settlement of Kentucky and the Northwest Territory, and perhaps a majority of the families who first settled west of the Alleghanies were from these counties. In view of these facts, an especial interest attaches to this comparatively small Virginia area.

From them have gone a number of men whose fame has been spread upon the pages of history, and with the outstanding characters this volume is only incidentally concerned. Their biographies have been written. But there were hundreds of others, men of noble achievement in more limited spheres, whose names deserve a place in the literature of their State, and the story of a dozen counties must, of necessity, be largely the story of the men who have lived in them.

The winning of the West is one of the glorious chapters in American history and, fortunately, it has been ably recorded. Comparatively little, however, has been written of the gradual but determined westward movement of population within the bounds of Virginia before the mountains were reached. It covered a span of many, many years. The principal avenue of this advance was through a narrow strip of counties, and it had its beginning in the basin of the York River.

To write of the following Virginia counties is to write of the ancestral homes of a very large percentage of the early Anglo-Saxon population of the great West: Gloucester, New Kent, King William, Hanover, King and Queen, Essex, Caroline, Goochland, Louisa, Orange, Albemarle and Augusta.

Dr. Thomas Walker, who was the leader of the first band of Anglo-Saxons who set foot upon Kentucky soil, in his expeditions of 1748 and 1750, was born in King and Queen and lived in Albemarle.

Judge Richard Henderson, who moved to North Carolina and headed a land company which purchased half of the State of Kentucky from the Cherokee Indians and was the employer of Daniel Boone, was born and reared in Hanover.

Andrew Lewis, who in 1774 won the battle of Point Pleasant and broke the power of a great Indian confederacy, was from Augusta.

George Rogers Clark, known to historians as the Defender of Kentucky and Conqueror of the Northwest Terriory, was born in Albemarle and reared in Caroline.

Thomas Jefferson, whose efforts made possible the Louisiana Purchase, was from Albemarle.

Meriwether Lewis and William Clark, of the celebrated Lewis and Clark Expedition to the Pacific, were respectively, from Albemarle and Caroline.

Nathaniel Massie, founder of Chillicothe, Ohio, was from Goochland.

[2]

Henry Clay and Joseph R. Underwood, at one time colleagues in the United States Senate from Kentucky, were from adjoining counties in Virginia, Clay from Hanover, and Underwood from Goochland.

Zachary Taylor, Mexican War hero and President of the United States, was from Orange.

Many of these leaders, and others who could be named, transferred their residence to the West. Many of their relatives and friends followed them to the new country. In the case of George Rogers Clark and his younger brother William Clark, practically the entire family connection in King and Queen, King William, Caroline, Goochland and Albemarle counties followed them to the West.

It was not altogether a coincidence that such a small area in Virginia played such a large part in the settlement of the vast regions west of the mountains. Population followed the land grants, and the innate love of the soil of the English-speaking people was an important factor. For many years after the Jamestown Colony was planted in 1607, the settlements hugged the navigable river-courses. Men finally obtained grants in the outlying sections of their counties and their sons cleared away the forests and settled upon these lands. As population increased, new counties were formed.

Finally the Valley of Virginia was reached and parceled out in vast grants to men who were interested in inducing settlement upon their lands. Tracts were granted along the Ohio River which eventually played a large part in the settlement of the valley of *la Belle Riviere*. Enormous grants to men in eastern Virginia were made as far west as the Mississippi.

[3]

The usual compensation for past services of soldiers in the Indian campaigns, the French and Indian War and the Revolution was land in the new country, and hundreds of families gathered together all their household belongings, their livestock and their slaves and moved away from their Virginia homes. Their usual route in the early years was over land northwestward to the Monongahela River, down to the Ohio in boats, and then down the Ohio. Also they traveled through the Blue Ridge at Rockfish Gap, and through the Alleghanies at Buffalo and other gaps. Many settled first in Kentucky, then moved northward across the Ohio River.

When English colonists first started making their way over the mountains, they met sharp resistance from the French, who, by virtue of early explorations claimed all of the Ohio valley. They had their chain of forts, and still further sought to strengthen their claim by sending an expedition down the river in 1749 to plant lead plates in the banks of the Ohio. One of these was found almost a hundred years later at the junction of the Kanawha and the Ohio, and is now in the museum of the Virginia Historical Society.

The Treaty of Paris in 1763, which ended the French and Indian War, as well as the Seven Years War in Europe, acknowledged that all of Canada and the Ohio Valley belonged to Britain. The territory west of the Mississippi belonged to Spain. But it came into possession of France in 1800 through European diplomacy, and thus the Louisiana Purchase of 1803 was made from France. Later, when Florida was acquired from Spain, Texas was ceded back to Spain, but became a part of the United States in the period of the Mexican War.

Long before the conclusion of the French and Indian War, in fact in the very year 1749 when the French were busily building forts on the Ohio, the Virginia government was granting vast tracts to land companies which later had much to do with settlement, after the British and their Indian allies had been beaten and the country made reasonably safe for residence.

For a period of more than thirty years just preceding the Revolution, Augusta county embraced West Virginia, the western part of Pennsylvania, Kentucky and all that region to the northwest of the Ohio and extending to the Mississippi then known as the Northwest Territory. Maps of Augusta showed the Great Lakes on its border, and Kentucky, Ohio and Illinois were once Virginia counties. French or no French, there was never a time when the Colonial Government at Williamsburg wavered in asserting its claim to all of this region until after the Revolution when Virginia donated it to the newly-formed United States.

Strange as it may seem, there were no Indians in Kentucky. That is to say, there were no tribes resident there when the settlers first arrived. That fertile and beautiful country was a neutral hunting and battle ground for the tribes of both north and south. The absence of resident tribes had something to do with the rapid settlement of Kentucky when it once set in.

However much or little heredity of blood affects the lives of human beings, it is generally agreed that tradition plays a very large part in shaping human destiny. Much is expected of the man whose forbears have been

[5]

honest, upright and courageous men and women, and as a rule he puts forth an effort to live up to the traditions of his people. Hence the printed page is not written in vain if it bequeathes to later generations a better understanding of those which have gone before.

Formal history must, of necessity, overlook many events usually considered of minor importance which, nevertheless, form the undercurrents of history. In telling the story of these twelve Virginia counties, effort is herein made to preserve as many as possible of the vanishing traditions of their past, with the thought in mind of an eminent essayist, who said: "The perfect historian considers no anecdote, no peculiarity of manner, no familiar saying as too insignificant for his notice, which is not too insignificant to illustrate the operation of laws, of religion, and of education, and mark the progress of the human mind."

The story of the heroism of generation after generation of young men and women who married and left the parental firesides to build homes for themselves farther and farther back into the upland wilderness has never been adequately told, nor is it attempted here. They braved many dangers and withstood many hardships, developing a hardihood and moral fiber which is the rich heritage of their descendants.

This book is an effort to preserve what can be preserved of the history of a dozen old Virginia counties whose soil was perhaps the most important of all channels in the flow of Anglo-Saxon civilization from the thirteen original Colonies into the vast empire west of the Appalachians which now constitutes the larger part of our Nation.

Gloucester County

GLOUCESTER COURTHOUSE

Gloucester County

F the eight original shires into which Virginia was divided in 1634, six were to the north of James River. Five of them, Elizabeth City, Warwick, James City, Charles City and Henrico, were along the north bank of the James, Henrico including territory on both sides of the river. The sixth, Charles River, embraced the lands along the Charles River, shortly thereafter called the York. It was from this shire that Gloucester County was formed, the exact date of its formation being indeterminate. First reference to Gloucester as a county was in 1651, and it had been formally opened to settlement in 1649.

In telling the story of the sturdy Virginia people who lived in the counties between the Rappahannock and the James, Charles River Shire may well be used as a point of departure. From it were formed Gloucester and New Kent, and then began the gradual establishment of counties to the westward, as the people made their way slowly to the headwaters of the rivercourses and finally transcended the mountains. The tidal streams afforded the principal means of transportation for many years and the bottom lands were fertile.

The history of the first permanent English settlement in America is the history of the people who inhabited those lands which became the eight original Virginia shires; the story of the pioneers in territorial expansion is largely the story of succeeding generations who lived in the early counties and gradually pushed back the Colony's frontiers.

Vast were the grants of land in the York River Basin to immigrants direct from the mother country, and many were the families from the original shires who moved into this region, but it should be borne in mind that many years elapsed before there was any appreciable movement of population away from the rivers which had been first discovered, and the conquest of the upland wildernesses was largely the work of younger generations born and reared in Virginia.

The region which is now Gloucester County played a conspicuous part in the very beginnings of the Jamestown settlement, for this area was the heart of the empire of the powerful Indian Chief Powhatan. When Captain John Smith first visited the savage monarch in 1607, Powhatan had consolidated his eastern Virginia tribes and moved his seat from Powhatan, on the James where Richmond now stands, to Werowocomoco, on the banks of the York in Gloucester.

The Indian village was on land which later became a part of the Page estate, Rosewell, and when the estate was divided and the manor house Shelly was erected, the new place was called at first Werowocomoco, but it was later called Shelly, because of the vast number of oyster shells which had been left there by Powhatan and his people. The village stood on the north side of the York, about twenty-five miles below the confluence of the Mattaponi and the Pamunkey, which form the York.

It was here that Captain Smith was led a captive before Powhatan, after having been paraded for many weeks to the Indian villages as far north as the Potomac, and it was here that little Pocahontas, asserting her inherent right as a princess of her tribe, saved his life in one of the most dramatic episodes of all American history. Werowocomoco was the scene of many interviews and *rencontres* between the settlers and the savages, and it was here that Powhatan was crowned with due ceremonies, which had their ludicrous aspects, at the will of King James of England. The village was burned by Sir Thomas Dale in 1612.

After the return of Captain Smith to England in 1609, John Ratcliffe and a party of thirty made an expedition to Werowocomoco with the hope of being as successful as Captain Smith had been in obtaining corn from the Indians, but the entire party met death at the hands of the savages on Gloucester soil, with the exception of two. One made his escape through his own devices and the other was shielded by Pocahontas. Nearby, until very recent years, stood a chimney which was supposed to be the remains of Powhatan's house, built after the arrival of the Colonists by workmen from Jamestown. A whole volume could be written about Werowocomoco.*

On April 18, 1644, when the second great massacre was perpetrated by Opechancanough, the aged brother

---

*Dr. Alexander Brown, in his Genesis of the United States, locates Werowocomoco further up the river on Portan, or Purtan Bay, largely basing his belief on a map drawn by Robert Tindall in 1608. On this chart "Poetan", which may have come from the name Powhatan, was about eleven miles from West Point. There is a very interesting discussion of the location of Powhatan's seat in Gloucester in the *William and Mary Quarterly*, Volume X, which proves pretty conclusively that Powhatan's Chimney was not built by the Dutchmen sent by Captain John Smith in 1609 to build the Indian chief a house. "Comoco" meant meeting or assembly place, and the name Werowocomoco was doubtless given because it was the meeting place of the Werowances, or chiefs.

of Powhatan, the settlers were better prepared than in the massacre of 1622, when the colony was in a fair way to be entirely wiped out. Open warfare continued between the Colonists and the warriors of Opechancanough, who in 1644 was so old that he had to be carried into battle on a litter. Opechancanough was captured at the site of what is now West Point and shortly thereafter was treacherously slain by his sentry at Jamestown.

On October 5, 1646, a treaty of peace was arranged between the English and the Indian chief, Necotowance, who had succeeded Opechancanough. According to this treaty the Indians were permitted to inhabit and hunt on the north side of the York. Two years later the Burgesses decided that "it would no longer be unlawful" for the white people to settle in what is now Gloucester after September 1, 1649. Prior to 1649 a number of grants of land in Gloucester had been made, but it is hardly probable that there were many white settlements.

The earliest known grant was to Augustine Warner in 1635. Argoll Yeardly patented 4,000 acres in Tyndall's Neck in 1640. Thomas Curtis, John Jones, Hugh Gwinne and Richard Wyatt took up tracts in 1642; James Whiting in 1643; John Robins in 1645; Thomas Seawell in 1646; Lewis Burwell and George Read in 1648; Richard Kemp and Francis Willis in 1649; John Smith, Henry Singleton and William Armistead in 1650; and John Page and Thomas Todd, the founder of Toddsbury, in 1653. Thereafter the grants were many.

Still to be seen in the county are mulberry trees

which are scions of the trees planted by the early colonists when an effort was made to create a silk-producing region. The royal robes used in the coronation of Charles II in 1660 are said, probably truly, to have come from Gloucester in his majesty's Colony of Virginia. Certain it is that King Charles, who was a capable judge of such matters, wrote in 1662 that he found the silks from Virginia of as fine quality as those from any other British possession.

On Poropotank creek in 1663 occurred what was perhaps the first serious difficulty between masters and servants in the Colony. The indentured servants of Gloucester county plotted an insurrection. The plot was matured and would probably have resulted in a wholesale murder, had it not been for a servant named Birkenhead, of Purton, who betrayed it and as a reward was given his freedom and a gift of tobacco.

Many of the incidents of Bacon's Rebellion took place on Gloucester soil. Because of intolerable depredations of the Indians in 1675, the General Assembly raised an army of 500 men, which was disbanded by the governor, Sir William Berkeley. The citizens, seeing their country left defenceless, formed a volunteer army and chose Nathaniel Bacon as their leader. Very properly, he applied to the governor for a commission, but when Berkeley dallied long in granting it, Bacon and his volunteer army proceeded against the Indians. Back of these events was an open clash between the royal governor and the House of Burgesses.

As soon as Bacon marched away against the savages, Berkeley denounced him as a traitor and his followers as mutineers for daring to march against the enemy without his excellency's sanction. Berkeley collected a force and proceeded up the James River against Bacon, who was meantime waging a very successful campaign against the Indians. Incensed at the governor's actions, the settlers nearer Jamestown rebelled, and Berkeley gave up his expedition against Bacon and returned.

Later, Bacon went forth again at the head of an army, with a commission duly executed; but again Berkeley dissolved the Burgesses, retired into Gloucester county, declared Bacon and his followers traitors, and assembled an army. Bacon, hearing of this, marched into Gloucester, defeated the governor and drove him across the bay into Accomac.

When the governor rallied his forces and again made his way into Jamestown, Bacon laid siege to the town and drove Berkeley on shipboard. It was during this siege, however, that Bacon contracted a disease from sleeping in the trenches, which brought on his death at a home in Gloucester. A casket supposed to contain his remains was buried by his followers at Poplar Springs Church of Petsworth Parish, five miles northwest of Gloucester Courthouse, but the casket contained only stones, and Bacon's body was buried secretly. Berkeley returned to power and was relentless in his persecutions of Bacon's followers.

Historians are agreed that Bacon and his adherents were patriots rather than rebels. They fought for free representative government in 1676 subject to the general control of the mother country, while the patriots a hundred years later established a free government independent of Great Britain.

Gloucester Point, formerly known as Tyndall's Point

and at one time as Gloucester Towne, was the site of a fort in 1667, and it was here that Bacon led his forces across the river in his expedition into Gloucester against Berkeley in 1676.

It was a Gloucester man, John Buckner, of Marlfield, clerk of the county, who brought the first printing press into Virginia. Buckner printed the laws of 1680 without license, for which he was reproved in 1682 by the governor, Lord Culpeper, and his further printing was prohibited.

In 1676 Gloucester gave a speaker to the House of Burgesses in the person of Augustine Warner. The civil officers of the county in 1680 were Lawrence Smith, Matthew Kemp, Thomas Ramsey, John Armistead, Philip Lightfoot, Thomas Pate, John Mann, Thomas Walker, Richard Young, Lewis Burwell, Henry Whiting and John Smith. The military officers were the same, with the added names of Augustine Warner, Francis Burwell, Richard Booker, Robert Peyton and Symond Bueford.

It is remarkable how many men Gloucester sent to the King's Council. Many who are unfamiliar with Virginia Colonial history think of Virginia's legislative body as consisting only of the House of Burgesses. The Council corresponded roughly with the House of Lords or Senate, and was the upper house of the General Assembly.

Members of the Council from 1607 to 1624 were named by the Virginia Company and, during the Royal Government which succeeded, were appointed by the Crown on recommendation of the Governor.

They were the Governor's advisers in executive matters, and land patents were issued with their "advice and consent." The Council constituted the General Court, which was the supreme court of the Colony, and also had legislative functions as members of the upper house of the General Assembly. The same persons exercised executive, legislative and judicial functions. Their concurrence was necessary for all laws, but they originated no money bills, as is the case with the United States Senate today.

Members of the Council almost uniformly held the higher offices, such as secretary, auditor, etc., and often were county lieutenants, that is commanders-in-chief of the militia of their own and adjoining counties.

Following are the names of Gloucester men who served on the King's Council, with the dates on which they were sworn in: George Reade, 1657; Augustine Warner I, 1660; John Pate, 1670; Augustine Warner II, of Warner Hall, 1677; Matthew Kemp, 1681; John Armistead, 1688; Henry Whiting, 1690; Matthew Page, of Timberneck, 1699; Lewis Burwell, of Carter's Creek, 1702; John Smith, 1704; John Lewis I, of Warner Hall, 1704; Robert Porteus, of Newbottle, 1713; Mann Page, of Rosewell, 1714; Peter Beverley, 1719; Lewis Burwell, of Carter's Creek, 1744; John Lewis II, of Warner Hall, 1748; John Page, of North End, 1768; and John Page II, of Rosewell, 1773.

Members of the House of Burgesses were: 1652, Hugh Gwinne, Francis Willis; 1653, Abraham Iversonn, Richard Pate; 1654, Thomas Breman, Wingfield Webb; 1655-56, Thomas Ramsey; 1657-58, Lieutenant-Colonel Anthony Elliott, Captain Thomas Ramsey; 1658-59, Captain Francis Willis, Captain Augustine

Warner; 1659-60, Captain Francis Willis, Captain Peter Jenings, Peter Knight, David Cant; 1663, Captain Peter Jennings, Captain Thomas Walker; 1666, Adjutant-General Peter Jenyngs, Captain Thomas Walker; 1685, Colonel John Armistead; 1693, Captain James Ransom, John Baylor; 1696-97, James Ransone, Mordecai Cooke; 1702, Peter Beverley, speaker, Mordecai Cooke; 1706, Peter Beverley, speaker; 1710, Peter Beverley, Nathaniel Burwell, Ambrose Dudley; 1714, Peter Beverley, Ambrose Cooke; 1718, Henry Willis, Thomas Buckner; 1720-22, Henry Willis, Nathaniel Burwell; 1722, Giles Cook; 1723-26, Giles Cook, Henry Willis; 1727-36, Francis Willis, Lawrence Smith; 1740, Beverley Whiting, Francis Willis; 1742, Beverley Whiting, Lewis Burwell; 1744, Beverley Whiting, Samuel Buckner; 1745-49, Beverley Whiting, Francis Willis; 1752-54, Beverley Whiting, John Page; 1755-68, John Page, Thomas Whiting; 1769-75, Thomas Whiting, Lewis Burwell.

Conventions of 1775 and 1776: Thomas Whiting and Lewis Burwell.

It should be borne in mind that until after the Revolution Mathews county was a part of Gloucester, the new county being formed in 1790 and named for Col. Thomas Mathews, a gallant Revolutionary officer. It was from that part of Gloucester which is now Mathews county that the last royal governor of Virginia was driven.

Lord Dunmore, who had taken refuge on a British warship and carried on depredations on Chesapeake Bay, finally camped on Gwynn's Island, the British gunboats anchored nearby. General Andrew Lewis, in command of a force of Virginians, erected a battery at Cricket Hill and opened fire on the British fleet on July 9, 1776, forcing the British to embark and sail away, taking with them Lord Dunmore, who never returned to Virginia.

The Gloucester militia organized promptly with the approach of hostilities with Great Britain, with Warner Lewis, county lieutenant; Sir John Peyton, colonel; Thomas Whiting, lieutenant-colonel; and Thomas Boswell, major.

Captains from Gloucester known to have served in the Revolution were Gibson Cluverius, John Camp, Richard Matthews, George Booth, Jasper Clayton, John Hubard, John Whiting, John Billups, Benjamin Shackelford, John Willis, Robert Matthews, William Buckner, John Dixon, Richard Billups and William Smith.

Lieutenants were Samuel Cary, Richard Hall, John Foster, James Baytop, Thomas Buckner, George Green, William Sears, James Bentley, Edward Matthews, John Billups, Dudley Cary, Hugh Hayes, Churchill Armistead, Philip Tabb, John Foster and Robert Gayle.

There was much activity in Gloucester in the closing months of the Revolution. In the belief that the Americans planned a vigorous attack on New York, Sir Henry Clinton ordered Cornwallis, in command of the southern British army, to take a position where his troops could be reinforced. Cornwallis chose York and Gloucester counties for the concentration of his forces.

About two miles north of Gloucester Point, Colonel

Banastre Tarleton, commanding the cavalry of Cornwallis' army, fought an engagement with Choisy's French force and Virginia militia on October 3, 1781. The Duke de Lauzun's cavalry charged Tarleton, who was forced to retire to Gloucester Point, where he was surrounded by French and Americans. Later in that month, when Cornwallis found himself checkmated at Yorktown, he tried to break through the blockade and cross the river at Gloucester Point, but a storm favored the Americans, and the British were forced to surrender on October 19.

Due to the loss of all the early records of Gloucester county, very little is known of the part its citizens played in the War of 1812 and the Mexican War. During the War of 1812, the county was subjected to incursions from the enemy ships. More than once the hostile British fleet could be seen in the Bay. The militia were under arms to defend Gloucester's shores under the command of Colonel William Jones. Captains were Catesby Jones, Captain Baytop and Richard Jones, of Lowland Cottage. The Gloucester Horse, under Colonel Skaife Whiting, saw service at Hampton.

Gloucester Point was an important base for Federal troops in the War Between the States. The place was fortified by the Confederates in 1861 but was occupied by a Union army in 1862. Col. Ulric Dahlgren, after an unsuccessful raid on Richmond, was trying to make his way to Gloucester Point with the remains of his command when he was killed in King and Queen County March 2, 1864. There was a lively skirmish at Gloucester Courthouse January 29, 1864, between Confederate and Union cavalry.

In the clerk's office is a carefully prepared roster of the men from Gloucester who wore the Gray. The county sent five companies of infantry and three of cavalry into the War Between the States. Officers from Gloucester were as follows: Company A, 26th Virginia Infantry: Joshua Garrett, lieutenant, captain, and promoted to major May, 1862; B. M. Page, 1st lieutenant, promoted to captain May, 1862; D. P. Barnett, 2nd lieutenant, 1st lieutenant May, 1862; A. W. Wright, 3rd lieutenant and 2nd lieutenant; and W. L. Enos, 3rd lieutenant.

Company B, 26th Virginia Infantry: Captain P. H. Fitzhugh, promoted to major in 1863; First Lieutenant S. B. Shelton, made captain in 1863; Second Lieutenant Joshua W. Roane, and Third Lieutenant John T. Gwynn.

Company E, 26th Virginia Infantry: First Captain, John T. Perrin; Second Captain R. C. Byrd; First Lieutenant James M. Nicholson; Second Lieutenant Robert Berry; Third Lieutenant Edward Thurston; Third Lieutenant John Llewellyn.

Company F, 26th Virginia Infantry: Captain William K. Roane, promoted to major in 1864; First Lieutenant Achilles Rowe, made captain in 1864; Second Lieutenant James Davis; and Third Lieutenant Billy Rowe.

Company A, 34th Virginia Infantry: Captain T. B. Montague, resigned in 1862; First Lieutenant William J. Baytop, killed at Seven Pines 1862; Second Lieutenant Phil Yeatman, resigned; Third Lieutenant William apW. Jones; Captain Thomas Robins, killed at Hatcher's Run; James N. Stubbs, lieutenant in 1862, captain in 1863, and major in 1864, on General Magruder's staff.

Company A, 5th Virginia Cavalry: Captain John W. Puller, promoted to major, killed at Kelly's Ford, May 1863; Captain J. B. Browne; First Lieutenant J. C. Baytop; Second Lieutenant W. P. R. Leigh; Third Lieutenant E. A. Leavitt; and Third Lieutenant T. J. Clopton.

Company C, 24th Virginia Cavalry: Captain J. K. Littleton, later retired; First Lieutenant Robert T. Sears, made captain; Second Lieutenant Guy Samuel, made first lieutenant; Third Lieutenant Alonzo Atkins, made second lieutenant; Third Lieutenant George S. Shackelford, made second lieutenant; and Third Lieutenant Jerome Spriggs.

Company D, 24th Virginia Cavalry: Captain Thomas C. Clopton, later resigned; First Lieutenant John H. Sears, captured by the enemy; Second Lieutenant W. V. Heyward, captured the day before the surrender; Third Lieutenant R. H. Hudgins.

Referred to as attached to other commands were Major-General William B. Taliaferro; Surgeon Phil A. Taliaferro; Major Peyton N. Page; Captain Edwin S. Taliaferro; Captain William Perrin Kemp; Major Thomas S. Taliaferro; Major Warner T. Taliaferro; Colonel Powhatan R. Page; Chaplain William E. Wiatt; Lieutenant A. V. Wiatt, C. S. Navy, commanded gunboat *Buford;* Lieutenant-Colonel Fielding L. Taylor, killed at Crampton Gap, Maryland, September 1862; Lieutenant William Basye; Captain Joseph S. James; Captain Peter W. Smith, C. S. Navy; Surgeon W. D. Chapman; Captain John L. Hibble; Captain

Charles E. Yeatman, C. S. Navy; Captain Thomas Jefferson Page, C. S. Navy; Major John Eels, killed in Loudoun County; Captain T. J. Page, Jr.; and Colonel Decatur Thurston.

While he was not born in Gloucester County, Lieutenant Catesby apR. Jones, who commanded the *Virginia* (*Merrimac*) in the celebrated engagement with the *Monitor,* was of the Gloucester family.

HOMES ARE INTERESTING

Gloucester County in the early years was dotted with fine colonial homes where hospitality was dispensed with free hand. There was much wealth. Isolated as Gloucester has been all these years, the people of today retain very largely the traits of their ancestors and there is not a section anywhere to be found which is more pleasant to visit. There is now a network of good roads throughout the county and fine highways connect it with all parts of the State, but until comparatively recent years the people were much hemmed in, and lived according to the traditions of their forefathers, little influenced by the outside world.

Rosewell, the ancestral home of the Pages, was in Colonial times the largest dwelling in Virginia. It stood as a stately reminder of the magnificence of the past until the present century, when, as was the case with so many of the old Virginia mansions, it was destroyed by fire. For over a hundred years it was the home of the Pages and many of the great men of the country were there entertained, especially during the period when it was the seat of John Page, governor of

Virginia. It was a great cube of ninety feet, and four stories in height. In this house was a mahogany stairway which could be ascended by eight persons abreast.

Warner Hall, on land granted Augustine Warner in 1635, was built in 1674. Nathaniel Bacon stopped here during his campaign against Sir William Berkeley in Gloucester in 1676. The later house, built about 1740 and destroyed by fire in 1849, has been beautifully restored. On the place is the tomb of Mildred Warner, grandmother of George Washington.

Eagle Point is the ancestral home of the Bryans and was built by John Randolph Bryan, a namesake of John Randolph of Roanoke and educated under his care. He married Randolph's niece, Elizabeth Tucker Coalter. In more recent years the lovely old place was a prized possession of Joseph Bryan, Richmond publisher and philanthropist, who was born there.

Marlfield was the home of John Buckner, clerk of Gloucester County and the man who brought the first printing press into Virginia and was censured by Governor Lord Culpeper for certain of his publications.

Until the War Between the States there stood a brick house at Gloucester Point which was built by the Thrustons. This home may have been built by Charles Mynn Thruston, but more probably by his father, for he was born in 1738. Charles Mynn Thruston was a remarkable character. When only twenty years of age he acted as a lieutenant of Provincials in the campaign which resulted in the evacuation of Fort Duquesne. He later studied for the ministry and was a Gloucester clergyman until his removal to Frederick County, where he preached until the outbreak of the Revolu-

tion. He ardently opposed the Stamp Act and addressed the people with much eloquence and exerted himself
in procuring arms and ammunition. When hostilities
actually commenced, he threw aside the gown, raised a
company of volunteers and joined Washington in New
Jersey with the rank of captain. He made a bold
attack upon a strong Hessian force near Amboy and his
arm was shattered by a musket ball. He was later made
a colonel and after the war rose to a judgeship and
was a member of the Legislature. Still later in life he
moved to New Orleans, where he died in 1812.

White Marsh, one of the most picturesque homes of
the county, was the residence of generations of Whit-
ings, Rootes, Prossers and Tabbs.

Timberneck, overlooking the York river, was the
seat of many generations of Manns.

Gloucester Place was at one time the home of President John Tyler.

The Lewises, kinsmen of Augustine Warner on the
maternal side, came into possession of Warner Hall,
and also owned Severn Hall, Belle Farm and Lewis-
ville on the banks of the Severn.

Sherwood was the beautiful home of the Seldens on
Ware River, afterward passing to the Dimmocks.

Level Green was the seat of the Robins family in
Colonial times.

The Cottage, one of the oldest homes in the county,
was built by one of the early Throckmortons.

Wareham was the ancient homestead of the Cookes
and it was here that Governor Berkeley repaired during his quarrel with Bacon.

Clifford was the Kemp homestead; Goshen the

Tompkins' and Perrin's; Glen Roy the Smith's; and the Shelter was the residence of John Tyler Seawell.

The Rectory, at Gloucester, was for forty-five years the home of the Rev. Charles Mann.

Toddsbury, a magnificent place of great antiquity, was the original home in Virginia of the Todd family, descending to the Tabbs. It was built in 1722.

Belleville was built by the Booths, later passing to Warner Taliaferro.

Burgh Westra and Dunham Massie were owned, respectively, by Dr. Philip Taliaferro and General William B. Taliaferro.

The Exchange and Newstead were Dabney and Tabb residences, and Waverly was the home of Gerard Hopkins.

Church Hill was another Taliaferro place.

White Hall was built in Colonial times by the Willis family. Afterward it was a Byrd home.

Hesse, one of the oldest homes in Gloucester, was the seat of the Armisteads. John Armistead, of this place, was on the Council in the latter part of the 17th century.

Carters Creek was the early seat of the Burwell family. It was here that Thomas Jefferson and Jacquelin Ambler came to court Rebecca Burwell soon after their student days at William and Mary. Upon one of its gables, in iron figures, is the date 1692, and there are tombstones in the Burwell burying ground dating as early as 1654.

Among other old places were Elmington, Whiting and Tabb; The Exchange, Dabney; Midlothian, Deans; Hockley, formerly called Cowslip Green,

Taliaferro; Severnby, once a part of the Eagle Point estate, Withers; and Landsdowne, Thruston.

Concord, on York River, was the birthplace of Robert Porteus, whose son became Bishop of London.

John Clayton lived at Windsor. He was a noted botanist and was clerk of the county for fifty years.

Of the three Colonial churches of Gloucester county, two are still standing—Ware and Abingdon. Ware was built about 1693, and the original building of Abingdon church was erected about 1655. The present building was completed in 1755.

These two Gloucester churches are fair examples of the two forms of architecture generally employed in Colonial times. Ware is rectangular and Abingdon is cruciform. Apparently all of the earliest churches were rectangular, Bruton Parish Church in Williamsburg, erected 1710-15, being the earliest existent specimen of the cruciform type.

Under ecclesiastical law every Colonial church in Virginia was erected due east and west, with the chancel in the east end, and the main entrance at the west end. The pulpit was never placed in the chancel. In the earlier churches it was on the north wall, perhaps for the reason that according to a belief among the early Jews, intimated in the Psalms and in the Book of Jeremiah, when God spoke to man He spoke from the north. So the clergyman, in conducting the usual worship and in preaching, stood on the north side between God and the people.

No Colonial church had any provision at all either for heating or for artificial light. Members of the congregation wore their wraps to keep warm in winter.

There were no lights because the law forbade meetings at night. Every householder was expected to remain at home after dark to protect his family. The weekly church service was the one opportunity for scattered neighbors to meet and discuss neighborhood affairs and the wider aspects of Colonial politics. There was a time set during the service for official notices, the reading of Governors' proclamations, new laws and other matters of importance.

Popular Spring was the church of Petsworth Parish. In 1694 the original Petsworth church was abandoned in favor of this church, which was considered the finest in Virginia. It was here that the followers of Nathaniel Bacon in 1676 interred a coffin supposed to contain the remains of their leader, but which in reality contained only rocks. His body was buried secretly for fear of indignities at the hands of Sir William Berkeley.

In that part of Gloucester which is now Mathews, there were many fine old homes. Among them may be mentioned:

Isleham, the Peyton home. Sir John Peyton, although born in Virginia was a baronet, but nevertheless he was an officer in the Gloucester Militia and was a true patriot.

Poplar Grove was built by John Patterson. From this home came "Captain" Sally Tompkins, one of the most beloved of Virginia's daughters, who devoted her time and fortune to nursing the sick and wounded soldiers of the Confederacy.

Ditchley, originally a Singleton home, later became the residence of Dr. Prosser Tabb.

Seaford was the oldest residence of the Tabb family, and Auburn was still another Tabb place.

Green Plains was the home of the Roys.

HOME OF MANY NOTABLE MEN

The men of note who have lived in Gloucester have been many.

Mathew Page married the only child and heiress of John Mann, of Timberneck, and moved to Rosewell. Their son, Mann Page, built Rosewell in 1725.

John Page (1744-1808) was a Revolutionary patriot, member of Congress and Governor of Virginia. Because of his high character and piety it is said his friends wanted him for Bishop of Virginia even though he had never studied for the ministry. He was an intimate friend of Jefferson, who often visited him at Rosewell.

Lewis Burwell II, of Carter's Creek, was a man of wealth and member of the Council.

Lewis Burwell III was president of the Council and acting Governor. He was educated at Cambridge and was noted for his learning.

It was his daughter Rebecca who was beloved by both Jefferson and Jacquelin Ambler, who had met her during their William and Mary College days. Ambler won, and from this union came the wife of John Marshall.

Lewis Burwell IV, although educated in England, espoused the cause of the Americans after his return and was a zealous member of the Revolutionary conventions.

Dr. J. Prosser Tabb, an eminent physician, acquired the old Singleton place. His wife was related to the Lees and when he built Ditchley he named it after the Lee homestead in Northampton.

General William B. Taliaferro, a gallant officer in the Confederate army, lived at Belleville and, after his marriage, at Dunham Massie. He was an eminent lawyer and statesman.

Thomas Dixon, the author, lived a part of his life at Elmington.

Thomas Todd, a wealthy planter and merchant, lived at Toddsbury. He died in 1676.

Thomas Read Rootes, a noted lawyer, acquired White Marsh from the Whiting family after the Revolution.

One of the most distinguished of Gloucester's sons was Dr. Walter Reed, one of the great benefactors of humanity through his work in making possible the virtual elimination of the scourge of yellow fever.

COURTHOUSE IS COLONIAL

Gloucester courthouse was erected in 1766 on the site of the previous building destroyed by fire. It is a lovely building both inside and out and is typical of a different form of Colonial architecture from the arched form, so popular in the public buildings earlier in the 18th Century, of which King William Courthouse is an example. The porch, with its white columns at Gloucester, was added after the Revolution. The records have three times been destroyed by fire, the last of which was in the evacuation of Richmond.

The debtors' jail, which stands near the courthouse, was built prior to 1754, and in that year the county surveyor was ordered to lay off 300 square yards where the prisoners were to be allowed liberty.

In 1769 the town was laid off, and was called Botetourt.

COURTROOM, COUNTY SHRINE

In the courtroom are forty-eight portraits and seven tablets, and it is among the most interesting interiors in Virginia. Following are the citizens thus memorialized:

Dr. Thomas C. Clopton, physician, member of the county court and of the House of Delegates.

General William B. Taliaferro, (1822-1898) of Belleville, who was a captain in the Mexican War. He commanded the Virginia State forces at the time of the John Brown raid. He joined General Jackson in the Valley in 1862, commanding a brigade. Was wounded in the operations against Pope. Was in the Battle of Fredericksburg, then served the rest of the war period in the South with the rank of major-general. He was a prominent lawyer and highly respected citizen. (There is a second portrait of him in the courtroom.)

Augustine W. Robins, of Mt. Pleasant, was one of the justices and a member of the House of Delegates.

Judge T. R. B. Wright, who lived in Essex, was circuit judge of the circuit including Gloucester. His portrait also is in the courthouse at Tappahannock.

John S. Cooke was clerk of the county, 1870-1887.

Judge Wyndham Kemp practiced law and was county judge.

Arthur Landon Davies was county clerk for forty-four years prior to 1837.

Warner P. Roane, was a member of the Legislature and of the county court.

Colonel P. R. Page commanded the 26th Virginia Regiment, C. S. A.

Dr. Walter Reed, to whose memory a tablet also is erected.

Judge James M. Seawell, judge of the Superior Court.

Captain J. B. Browne commanded a company and was sheriff.

Major P. H. Fitzhugh (in uniform) served with the 26th Virginia Regiment and was a member of the county court.

Samuel B. Chapman was one of the clerks, serving from 1887 to 1896.

Warner Throckmorton Taliaferro was born at Church Hill and lived at Belleville. He was the father of General William B. Taliaferro and a prominent planter and member of the State Senate.

Captain John Newstead Tabb (1845-1920) was a gallant Confederate soldier, member of the Legislature and Commissioner of Revenue.

Joseph Bryan's portrait bears the following inscription:

"C. S. A. 1862-65. Born at Eagle Point, Gloucester County, Va., August 13, 1845. Died at Laburnum, Henrico Co., Nov. 26, 1908."

He was a son of John Randolph Bryan and Elizabeth Tucker (Coalter) Bryan. He joined the army very young, most of his service being with Mosby, and was wounded twice. He completed his education after the war at the University of Virginia, which he had left to join the service. He practiced law first in Fluvanna County, then in Richmond. He was known particularly as a philanthropist and scholar and engaged in many business activities. He was head of the Richmond Locomotive Works and later general director of the American Locomotive Company, and widely-known Richmond publisher.

Major James N. Stubbs (1839-1919) joined the Gloucester Artillery (Red Shirts) for duty in the Signal Corps and rose to the rank of major. He served much of the war in Texas. He was an able lawyer and served for many years in the Senate and House of Delegates.

William K. Davis was one of the justices.

Lieutenant Philip Tabb served in the Revolution.

Judge John Bacon Clopton was a circuit judge.

Lieutenant R. D. Miller served in the Confederate army.

Maryus Jones was a distinguished lawyer and orator. He was commonwealth's attorney of Gloucester, later moving to Newport News, and was mayor of that city.

William apW. Jones, brother of Maryus Jones, served in the army and was a commissioner in chancery.

John R. Carey was clerk from 1837 to 1867.

John Sinclair was a justice of the old county court.

William Robins Stubbs was one of the justices.

Major Thomas Catesby Jones was a Confederate officer.

James Dabney was sheriff of the county.

Jefferson W. Stubbs was one of the justices.

Augustine Warner, known as Speaker Warner, was a member of the King's Council and speaker of the House of Burgesses.

Captain Thomas C. Robins commanded Company A, 34th Virginia Infantry and was killed at Hatcher's Run.

Colonel William Jones was a Confederate officer.

Rev. A. F. Scott was one of the justices.

M. B. Seawell was a lawyer and served as commonwealth's attorney.

Major John W. Puller was a Confederate officer.

Lieutenant William J. Baytop was in the army of the Confederacy.

Judge Warner T. Jones was a county judge.

Miss Cornelia E. Thornton was the first American Red Cross nurse to lose her life overseas in the World War.

Captain Thomas A. Robins was a Confederate officer.

Benjamin A. Rowe was one of the justices.

Col. William apCatesby Jones, soldier, lawyer and commonwealth's attorney of the county.

Colonel George Wythe Munford was Secretary of the Commonwealth, clerk of the House of Delegates and author of the Code of 1873.

John T. Seawell was commonwealth's attorney, member of Legislature and Secession Convention.

Commodore T. J. Page (in uniform) was a noted officer in the Confederate States Navy.

Edwin Broaddus (1801-1881) was one of the justices.

Lieutenant-Colonel Fielding Lewis Taylor, a gallant

Confederate officer, was mortally wounded at Crampton Gap, near Antietam, in 1862.

The seven tablets in the courtroom are no less interesting than the portraits. Back of the bench is a marble tablet bearing the following inscription, known to have been penned by Major James N. Stubbs:

"This tablet is erected by the Gloucester Monument Association to the women of Gloucester County, Va., during the war, 1861-65, whose pious ministrations to our wounded soldiers soothed the last hours of those who died far from the objects of their tenderest love; whose domestic labors contributed much to supply the wants of our defenders in the field; whose zealous faith in our cause shone a guiding star undimmed by the darkest cloud of war; whose fortitude sustained them under all the privations to which they were subjected; whose annual tribute expresses their enduring grief, love and reverence for our sacred dead; and whose patriotism will teach their children to emulate the deeds of our revolutionary sires. November 7, 1904."

The following tablet, with its curious abbreviations, is quoted verbatim:

"Hon. Matt. Page. Mem: of King's Council and of orig. Bd. of Tr's William and Mary Coll., Va. B. 1659. D. Jan. 9, 1703.

Hon. Mann Page. Mem: of B's Council. B. 1691. D. Jan. 24, 1730.

Hon. Mann Page II. Mem: Bd. Trs. Wm. & Mary Coll. B. 1718. D. ——

Hon. John Page (North End) M. K's Council. B. 1720. D. 1780.

Robert Page (Broadneck) B. 1722. D. 1768.

Hon. John Page, of Rosewell. Mem: of King's Council; Va. Conven's; Com. of Safety; of Congress; Lt. Col. in Rev. War and Gov. of Virginia. B. Apl. 17, 1744. D. Oct. 11, 1808.

Hon. Mann Page (Mansfield) Mem: Va. Conven's and Congress. B. 1749. D. ——

Hon. Mann Page (Shelly) B. 1766. D. Aug. 24, 1813.

Francis Page (Rugg Swamp) Han. Co. B. 1780. D. Nov. 5, 1849.

John Page (Shelly) Soldier in War of 1812. B. Mch. 7, 1789. D. Jan. 31, 1817.

Th. Nelson Page (of Shelly) B. Oct. 5, 1792. D. Oct. 1835. Mann Page (Greenland) B. June 9, 1794. D. Jan. 1841.

Th. Jeff. Page (of Shelly) Capt. U. S. Navy. Com. of La Plata Explor'n Exp'n. Commodore C. S. N. B. Jan. 8, 1808. D. Oct. 26, 1899.

Fran. Nelson Page. Major U. S. A. B. Oct. 28, 1820, D. Mar. 25, 1860.

Powhatan R. Page. B. 1822. Killed at Petersburg, Va., June 17, 1864. Col. C. S. A.

John Randolph Page, M. D. Sur. C. S. A. Prof. Univ. of Va. B. Aug. 10, 1830. D. Mar. 11, 1901.

Richd. M. Page Capt. C. S. A. B. Nov. 20, 1838. D. Mar. 8, 1901.

Peyton N. Page. Maj. C. S. A. B. Aug. 10, 1840. D. Jan. 17, 1891.

John Page. Admiral Argentine Navy. Com. Pilcomao Exp'n. B. Nov. 29, 1840. D. 1890.

Th. Jeff. Page, Jr. Maj. C. S. A.

Fred. M. Page. Capt. U. S. A. Professor of University of Va. B. Apl. 15, 1852. D. Oct. 25, 1900.

Thomas Nelson Page. Mem. U. S. Ct. Survey. B. Aug. 26, 1881. D. Jan. 30, 1902.

John Page, of Oakland, B. Apl. 26, 1821. D. Oct. 30, 1901. Capt. and Maj. on Staff of Chief Artillery A. N. Va. C. S. A. Com. Atto. Han. Co., Va.

All these kept the faith.

This tablet is erected by the Circuit Court of Gloucester County, the home of the Virginia Pages."

———

"In Memoriam—Mordecai Cooke, of Mordecai's Mount, Gloucester Co. Married, 1648, Susannah, mother of Henry Peasley, the founder of the 'Gloucester Charity School.'

Mordecai Cooke, Justice, Sheriff and Burgess, 1696-1705.

Thomas Cooke, Surveyor of Gloucester and Middlesex Counties, 1702-1717.

Giles Cooke, Tobacco Agent and Burgess, 1714-1722.

Mordecai Cooke, House of Delegates, 1795.

Col. Mordecai Cooke, war of 1812. House of Delegates from Portsmouth, Va., 1815-1817. 1836-37 Sheriff of Norfolk Co. and Grand Master of Masons 1824-1826. Born in Gloucester Co., Va., Apr. 19, 1785. Died in Portsmouth, Va., April 29, 1845.

Giles Buckner Cooke, Mayor of Norfolk City.

John Samuel Cooke, Clerk of Courts 1870-1887.

Merritt Todd Cooke, member of Norfolk Light Artillery Blues in the War Between the States, and House of Delegates from Norfolk, 1891-1898, through whose generosity the Court has been enabled to erect this tablet."

———

"In Memoriam—Nathanael Bacon, the younger, General and Member of the Governor's Council. Born in Suffolk, England 1630-40. Died in this county in 1676. Originator of the so-called Rebellion, whose influence in the formation of the Spirit of Americanism is immeasurable, the Washington of his day, popular and patriotic, whose magnanimity strongly contrasts with Berkeley's malignity. A soldier, a statesman, a Saint, Gloucester who honors the noble dead, and cherishes the memory of kingly men, and in whose soil the body of Bacon is said to sleep, erects this monument to the great patriot, by the authority of the Circuit Court, through the generosity of friends."

———

"In Memoriam—John M. Gregory. Governor of Va. 1842. Judge of the Circuit Court 1860-1865. Born in Charles City Co., Va., July 8, 1804. Died in Williamsburg April 9, 1884. This tablet is erected by the Court through the generosity of Mrs. Matty Gregory Galbraith, his daughter, Spartanburg, S. C., and Mrs. Amanda Caskie Thomas, his granddaughter, New York City, N. Y."

[34]

"On Sept. 13, 1851, was born in this county Walter Reed, M. D., M. A., L. L. D., major and surgeon in the Army of the U. S., who, by demonstrating in Cuba the transmission by mosquitoes of yellow fever gave to man control of that scourge of our hemisphere and placed his name on the roll of the benefactors of humanity. Died at Washington, D. C., Nov. 23, 1902. This tablet was erected by the Court of Gloucester and a few of his friends Nov. 23, 1903."

———

"1917-1918—To the Honor of the men of Gloucester who on land and sea, in field, camp and air, gave themselves and their services to our Country. Erected in heartfelt appreciation by the women of Gloucester April 5, 1919."

———

DESCENDANTS WIDELY SCATTERED

While many persons moved from Gloucester to the new territories west of the Alleghanies in the period just after the Revolution, the exodus was hardly as great as from the upland counties. Hanover, King William, King and Queen, Caroline, Goochland and Louisa lost so many of their most enterprising young men and women that the loss was serious.

Historians have reiterated the belief that the impoverishment of the soil from tobacco-growing accelerated the emigration from these old counties, but this is hardly true. The facts are that the men and women who went from Virginia to Kentucky and the Northwest Territory were of a pioneering stock, passionately devoted to freedom and ownership of lands of their own. Their fathers before them, impelled by the same urge, had pushed back Virginia's frontiers from the tidal rivers. The opening of the territories west of the Alleghanies was to them the beckoning hand of

[35]

opportunity. The Virginians who settled in those regions were in no sense expatriates.

All along the westward route from the York River to the mountains have lived families whose origins were in Gloucester, and, after the passage of almost three hundred years, it is doubtful if there is a State in the Union in which there are not citizens who can trace their descent directly or indirectly to old plantations in Gloucester. The names are significant. Wherever, for instance, there is a Taliaferro, a Page, a Tabb, a Mann, a Burwell or a Throckmorton, it is probable that he had a grandfather in Gloucester. The Colonel Throckmorton who was the leading character in one of Irvin Cobb's delightful Kentucky stories could have come from nowhere else.

New Kent County

New Kent Courthouse

New Kent County

DESPITE the fact that New Kent is very old and a very important county, historical information about it is somewhat meager for two reasons. In the first place, the destruction of records has been pathetic. In the second place, the present New Kent County is only a fraction of what the County once was, for it originally embraced Hanover, King William, King and Queen and the counties which later were formed from them.

The beautiful old building which now is the courthouse of King William was once the courthouse of New Kent, which was formed from York in 1654. The boundaries were defined as follows:

"It is ordered that the upper part of York County shall be a distinct county called New Kent, from the west side of Scimino Creek to the heads of the Pamunkey and Mattaponie Rivers, and down to the head of the west side of Poropatanke Creek."

The Pamunkey River now forms its north border and the Chickahominy is its southern boundary. Contiguous to the earliest settlements, its family names are old, and they frequently recur in the newer counties.

There is a tradition that the name was suggested by Colonel William Claiborne and that it was called New Kent after Kent Island, in the upper waters of Chesapeake Bay, from which Claiborne was driven by Lord

Baltimore during the quarrel in the founding of Maryland. Some say it was named for the county of Kent in England simply because so many of the early settlers came from there.

Orapax was an Indian village in New Kent near the Hanover line which in his latter years was the principal seat of Powhatan. It is believed that the great chief died there. But Orapax was a significant spot because of still earlier history, when Captain John Smith was led there a captive in 1607.

It was here that the redoubtable Captain Smith not only saved his life by his wits but so impressed the Indians with his marvellous prowess that they regarded him as something of a demigod ever afterward.

It will be recalled that Captain Smith made a journey of exploration in the winter of 1607 up the Chickahominy and was captured in a swamp in the edge of what is now Hanover County and led before Opechancanough. This chieftain was at Orapax at the time. Captain Smith realized that he must use his ingenuity if he was to save his life, a lone white captive in the hands of several hundred savages.

So he presented Opechancanough a compass which immediately aroused the curiosity of the warriors. As best he could, Captain Smith explained by signs what it was for, while they marvelled that they could see the play of the needle but could not touch it because of the glass. Smith had drawn Indian blood before they effected his capture, and their lust for vengeance was keen. So despite the wonders of the compass, they bound him to a tree and a number of the warriors with drawn bowstrings were about to snuff out his life. But

Opechancanough decided that this was too valuable a captive to put to death, so he ordered a stay of execution and again held up the compass before the tribesmen. They unbound the white captive and took him to Orapax.

Again Smith's life was endangered by the father of one of the Indians Smith had wounded, but Smith pledged that if his life should be spared and they would let him go to Jamestown he would come back with a "wondrous water" which would save the wounded man's life. Opechancanough was too shrewd to let Smith go to Jamestown, but sent messengers who took to Jamestown a note from Smith in which he begged the settlers to fire cannon and impress the messengers with the wonders of the white men's weapons. The note warned that Jamestown was about to be attacked and also asked that certain things be delivered to the messengers to be brought back to Smith at Orapax.

In the meantime the Indians at Orapax regaled their captive with a fantastic entertainment, and so much bread was set before him that he thought they "would fat him to eat him." Opechancanough promised Smith "life, liberty, land and women" if he would tell him the best way to attack Jamestown. When the messengers returned the wounded man had died, but there was still more amazement among the Indians, who thought the little piece of paper Smith had sent to Jamestown could talk.

It was at Orapax that Opechancanough decided Smith was indeed an important captive and determined to parade him about among the tribes, with the result that Smith was carried from village to village as far remote as the Potomac River and finally was brought before Powhatan at Werowocomoco and miraculously saved by Pocahontas.

The county has played a part in several celebrated courtships. It was associated with the courtship of the Indian Princess Pocahontas by John Rolfe, and on its soil a little later, Sir Thomas Dale courted, by proxy, another of Powhatan's daughters without success. Finally it was the scene of the courtship and marriage of George Washington.

On the site of Eltham, seat of the distinguished Bassett family on the Pamunkey River, stood Matchot, apparently a thriving Indian village when first visited by the white settlers.

It will be recalled that Pocahontas, after the accidental discharge of a powder flask which sent Captain John Smith back to England sorely wounded in 1609, left her father's house and went to live with relatives on the Potomac River. Here the princess, virtually in exile from her people, was kidnaped by Captain Samuel Argall and brought to Jamestown, it being hoped by the settlers that they might purchase peace with the Indians with her freedom as the price.

In 1612 Sir Thomas Dale set out up the York River with the captive Pocahontas on board his ship and visited Powhatan at his village in Gloucester. When Powhatan refused to ransom his daughter, Dale and his followers burned Werowocomoco to the ground and proceeded up the river to Matchot, which stood on the south side of the Pamunkey where it unites with the Mattaponi. It was across the river from Pamaunkee, the village of Opechancanough, which was on the site of West Point.

Dale found several hundred Indians at Matchot, who demanded a truce until Powhatan could be heard from. This was granted and two of Powhatan's sons came on board to visit their sister, Pocahontas. Finding her well, contrary to what they had heard, they were gratified that she was being well treated and promised that they would try to persuade their father to make peace and forever be friends with the English.

It is not known exactly where Powhatan was at the time, but John Rolfe and another Englishman named Sparks were sent to treat with the Chief. Powhatan entertained them hospitably but would not admit them to his presence. They saw the wily Opechancanough, and he promised to use his influence with Powhatan in favor of peace, a promise which was not carried out. Dale returned to Jamestown, because of the approach of planting time, and intended to renew hostilities later.

It was during this time that John Rolfe and Pocahontas became engaged, and the match was gladly sanctioned by the authorities at Jamestown. Powhatan also seems to have been reconciled to the union, and he sent an uncle and two brothers of Pocahontas to the wedding, which took place with Christian ceremonies in Jamestown in April, 1613.

During the following year the village of Matchot again was visited by Englishmen, this time for the purpose of securing the hand of another of Powhatan's daughters in marriage. Ralph Hamor held a discourse with Powhatan at Matchot in 1614 and wrote an account of it. Despite the fact that Powhatan seemed reconciled over the marriage of Pocahontas to an Englishman, the Indian chieftain was deeply suspicious of the white settlers.

When Hamor informed him that Sir Thomas Dale had heard of the charms of Powhatan's younger daughter and desired that he send her to Jamestown because Dale wanted to marry her, Powhatan refused, declaring that he had promised the child, who was referred to as being twelve years old at the time, to another. Hamor quoted Dale as believing that there could be no better bond of peace and friendship than such a union.

The remains may still be seen of a remarkable old stone house on the bank of Ware Creek, a tributary of the York, and the dividing line between New Kent and James City Counties. It is one of the most curious relics of Virginia antiquity and many stories have been told of its origin.

Apparently it was never finished. It was about fifteen by eighteen feet and had a basement and one story above, with a wide doorway giving entrance to both apartments. There were narrow apertures in the walls. It stood on a high promontory, 100 feet above Ware Creek, which wound around its base. The spot is approached only by a long, circuitous defile, so narrow that two wagons could not pass abreast.

Perhaps the most plausible theory in regard to the origin of this curious old house was that it was built by Captain John Smith in 1609. In his own History of Virginia is the following passage:

"We built also a fort for a retreat neere a convenient river, upon a high commanding hill, very hard to be assaulted and easie to be defended, but ere it was finished this defect caused a stay. In searching our casked corne, we found it halfe rotten and the rest so consumed with so many thousands of rats that increased so fast, but their originall was from the ships, as we knew not how to keepe that little we had. This did drive us to our wits end, for there was nothing in the country but what nature afforded. . . . But this want of corne occasioned the end of all our works, it being work sufficient to provide victuall."

Moysonec was an Indian village on the Chickahominy about eight miles east of Providence Forge in 1607, and a few miles to the westward is the present home of the remnants of the once powerful Chickahominy tribe. Near Moysonec the colonists established Fort James in 1645.

It will be noted that many of the public officials prior to 1691, when King and Queen was cut off from New Kent, resided in localities which are now other counties.

Members of the Council from New Kent were William Claiborne, 1623; John Lightfoot, 1692; and William Bassett, of Eltham, 1702.

Members of the House of Burgesses were: 1654, Captain Robert Abrell; 1657-59, William Blacke; 1659-60, Col. Manwaring Hammond, Lieut.-Col. Robert Abrahall; 1663, Col. William Claiborne; 1666, Col. William Claiborne, Capt. William Berkley; 1685, Col. John West, Richard Littlepage; 1688, John West, Joseph Foster; 1693, Capt. John Lyddall, Capt. William Bassett; 1696-97, William Bassett, Gideon Macon; 1702, William Bassett, Joseph Foster; 1710, Nicholas Meriwether; 1714-22, Nicholas Meriwether, John Massie; 1735-40, William Macon; 1742-44, William Stanup (Stanhope); 1722-26 John Thornton, Thomas

Bassett (died), William Gray; 1745-47, William Gray; 1748-49, William Hockaday, William Massie; 1752-58, Richard Adams, James Power; 1758-60, Richard Adams, Lewis Webb; 1761-62, Richard Adams, Gill Armistead; 1762-65, Richard Adams, Burwell Bassett; 1766-69, Burwell Bassett, William Clayton; 1769, William Bassett, William Clayton; 1770-71, Burwell Bassett, William Clayton; 1772-75, Burwell Bassett, Bartholomew Dandridge.

All conventions of 1775: Burwell Bassett and Bartholomew Dandridge.

Convention of 1776: William Clayton and Bartholomew Dandridge.

The intimate connection between the land grants, the formation of new counties and the gradual movement in Colonial Virginia to the westward is illustrated by the fact that a number of men successively represented two or more counties in the House of Burgesses.

Nicholas Meriwether, who represented New Kent from 1714 to 1722, was one of the first Burgesses from Hanover. Later he became a large property-owner in Albemarle. Col. John West, who lived at the site of West Point, was a Burgess from New Kent from 1685 to 1688 and was one of the first Burgesses from King William. He probably represented King and Queen, although the records are destroyed, during the interim from 1691 to 1701 when King William was a part of King and Queen. Dr. Thomas Walker represented, successively, Hanover, Louisa and Albemarle.

The good chief Totopotomoi, of the Pamunkeys, held sway in New Kent and that part of New Kent which is now Hanover. In 1656, twenty years before

Bacon's Rebellion, six or seven hundred members of a tribe known as the Rechahecrans came down from the mountains and seated themselves not far from the falls of the James River. Colonel Edward Hill was put in command of a body of men and ordered to dislodge them. He was reinforced by Totopotomoi, with 100 warriors. Hill was disgracefully defeated and Totopotomoi, with most of his men, was slain. It is probable that Bloody Run, near Richmond, derived its name from this sanguinary battle, rather than from the battle fought here later by Bacon, when the power of the Indians was crushed.

No doubt Bacon and his adherents had clashes with the Indians in New Kent. Certain it is that the last chapter of Bacon's Rebellion was written on New Kent soil. About 300 men had rallied after Bacon's death under Drummond and Lawrence. William Drummond, staunch adherent of Bacon, was the first governor of North Carolina, having been appointed in 1664 by the Lords Proprietors of North Carolina as head of the "government of Albemarle." Governor Berkeley, himself, was one of the Proprietors.

Drummond was captured in a swamp in New Kent and, as he was an object of Sir William Berkeley's special hatred, he was courtmartialed and hanged without out a decent hearing, after having been subjected to peculiarly insulting treatment at the hands of Virginia's irascible old Colonial Governor.

In 1658 and 1670 Richmond Terrell received grants of land in New Kent, and he was the ancestor of the Terrells of Louisa and Hanover. In 1673 Philip Ludwell, Tobias Handford and Richard Whitehead renewed a grant of 20,000 acres in New Kent, on the south side of the Mattaponi, "due for the importation of 400 persons into the Colony."

Colonel William Claiborne, Jr., was appointed in 1676 to the command of a fort at Indiantown Landing.

St. Peter's Church is a relic of ancient times in New Kent. The parish may have been erected at the time the county was formed in 1654, and is known to have existed as a separate parish in 1656. Work on the church edifice began in 1701 and was near enough to completion in 1703 for services to be held in it. It cost 146,000 pounds of tobacco. The steeple was added twelve years later and in 1719 it was encircled by a wall. The belfry was added in 1722. It was the church where Martha Washington worshiped in her earlier years, and distinguished men of that region had worshiped there long before her time.

In the registers is recorded an order of 1742 for "Coll. William Macon, Major Joseph Foster, Coll. [Daniel Parke] Custis, and Major [John] Dandridge or any two of them to agree with Mr. Edward Russell towards Repairing the Spire & Erecting Dormant windows for the steeple."

The Rev. David Mossom, who officiated at the marriage of Washington, died in 1767, and there is a tablet to his memory in St. Peter's Church. In the autobiography of another divine of that period is a story about Parson Mossom which might be of interest here.

It seems that one day Parson Mossom had a quarrel with his clerk, and assailed him from the pulpit in his sermon. The sermon over, the clerk, nothing daunted, gave out from his desk a version of the 2nd Psalm, containing the lines,

> "With restless and ungovern'd rage,
> Why do the heathen storm?
> Why in such rash attempts engage,
> As they can ne'er perform?"

His revenge was as humorous as it was pointed.

There is also a tablet to the memory of William Chamberlayne, vestryman and for many years a warden of the parish, who died in 1736. It sets forth that the deceased was descended from an ancient and worthy family in the County of Hereford, and married Elizabeth, daughter of Richard Littlepage, of New Kent County.

Among scattered records of the county may be found references to John Lightfoot, colonel, Joseph Foster, lieutenant-colonel, and William Bassett, major, in 1699; George Keeling, who was sheriff in 1708; Captain Charles Crump, who commanded a company of New Kent militia in 1758; and Captain John Lacey, who was an officer in the New Kent militia in 1777.

Perhaps the most interesting private residence in New Kent in earlier days was The White House, for which the present home of the presidents in Washington was named. It was the home of Martha Custis, who, after the death of her husband, Daniel Parke Custis, became the wife of George Washington. She was the daughter of Major John Dandridge, brother of Col. William Dandridge, of Elsing Green.

Because of the narrative which is to follow, it might here be mentioned that Poplar Grove, on the Pamunkey nearby, was the home of the Chamberlaynes. In more recent years it came into possession of James Patterson, of Richmond, and a peculiarity of the place was that Mr. Patterson found on the property an enormous quantity of brick evidently baked in the Colonial period or imported, which either had not been used or had been part of another building. It is now the property of Frank V. Baldwin.

The following vivid account of the courtship of Washington is taken from Custis' Life of Mrs. Martha Washington, which was written early in the 19th Century:

"It was in 1758 that Washington, attired in a military undress, and attended by a body servant, tall and militaire as his chief, crossed the ferry called Williams' over the Pamunkey, a branch of the York river. On the boat touching the southern or New Kent side, the soldier's progress was arrested by one of those personages who give the beau ideal of the Virginia gentleman of the old regime the very soul of kindness and hospitality. It was in vain the soldier urged his business at Williamsburg, important communications to the governor, &c. Mr. Chamberlayne, on whose domain the militaire had just landed, would hear of no excuse. Col. Washington was a name and character so dear to all Virginians that his passing by one of the castles of Virginia without calling and partaking of the hospitalities of the host was entirely out of the question. The Colonel, however, did not surrender at discretion, but stoutly maintained his ground till Chamberlayne, bringing up his reserve in the intimation that he would introduce his friend to a young and charming widow, then beneath his roof, the soldier capitulated, on condition that he should dine—only dine—and then by pressing his charger and borrowing of the night, he would reach Williamsburg before his excellency could shake off his morning slumbers. Orders were accordingly issued to Bishop, the colonel's body servant and faithful follower who, together with the fine English charger, had been bequeathed by the dying Braddock to Major Washington on the famed and fated field of

Monongahela. Bishop, bred in the school of European discipline, raised his hand to his cap, as much as to say, 'Your orders shall be obeyed.'

"The colonel now proceeded to the mansion, and was introduced to various guests (for when was a Virginia domicile of the olden time without its guests?) and, above all, to the charming widow. Tradition relates that they were mutually pleased on this, their first interview—nor is it remarkable, they were of an age when impressions are strongest. The lady was fair to behold, of fascinating manners, and splendidly endowed with worldly benefits. The hero was fresh from his early fields, redolent of fame, and with a form on which 'every god did seem to set his seal, to give the world assurance of a man.'

"The morning passed pleasantly away, evening came, with Bishop, true to his orders and firm at his post, holding the favorite charger with one hand, while the other was waiting to offer the ready stirrup. The sun sank in the horizon, and yet the colonel appeared not. 'Twas strange, 'twas passing strange; surely he was not wont to be a single moment behind his appointments—for he was the most punctual of all men.

"Meantime, the host enjoyed the scene of the veteran at the gate, while the colonel was so agreeably employed in the parlor, and proclaiming that no visitor ever left his home at sunset, his military guest was, without much difficulty, persuaded to order Bishop to put up the horses for the night. The sun rode high in the heavens the ensuing day when the enamored soldier pressed with his spur his charger's side and speeded on his way to the seat of government, where, having dispatched his public business, he retraced his steps, and, at the White House, the engagement took place, with preparations for marriage.

"And much hath the biographer heard of that marriage from the grey-haired domestics who waited at the board where love made the feast and Washington the guest. And rare and high was the revelry at that palmy period of Virginia's festal age; for many were gathered at that marriage, of the good, the great, the gifted, and they, with joyous acclamations, hailed in Virginia's youthful hero a happy and prosperous bridegroom.

[49]

"The precise date of the marriage the biographer has been unable to discover, having in vain searched the records of the vestry of St. Peter's church, New Kent, of which the Rev. Mr. Mossom, a Cambridge scholar, was the rector and performed the ceremony."

The idea has been often advanced that the marriage took place at St. Peter's church, but it undoubtedly was performed at The White House. An artist of a few years later portrayed the wedding, and his conception was that the brilliant scene was enacted in a private residence, in which had been erected a temporary pulpit.

The estate was inherited by the great-granddaughter of Martha Washington, who was the wife of General Robert E. Lee. Mrs. Lee, a fugitive from Arlington, was there during the Peninsula Campaign of McClellan in the War Between the States. Having to flee once more, she took refuge at Marlbourne, the Ruffin home in Hanover. She placed a card on the White House when she left, asking that protection be given the home of Martha Washington. But her appeal went unheeded and the old mansion was burned. Mrs. Lee's son, General William H. F. Lee, lived on the estate for some years after the war, and it is now owned by Dr. George Bolling Lee.

Martha Washington spent her childhood at Chesnut Grove. Her father, Major John Dandridge, married Frances Jones, daughter of Orlando Jones, Burgess from New Kent, who married Martha Macon, daughter of Gideon Macon, all prominent figures in New Kent history.

The citizens of New Kent and of King William appear to have been particularly fun-loving, and in few sections of the country was there as much gayety in the years before the Revolution. Horse racing was the king of sports, and fox hunting, enjoyed by George Washington and George Mason, was also a great sport in New Kent. Gambling of various sorts was condoned. There was a popular race-course at Spring Hill, the plantation of Richard Graves.

The *Gazette* of May 23, 1775, carried a news item to the effect that "On Tuesday, 6th of this inst., was determined at New Kent Courthouse the great cock match between Gloucester and New Kent for ten pistoles a battle and 100 the main. There fell eighteen of the match of which New Kent won ten and Gloucester seven, and one drawn battle."

In still earlier days lotteries were frequent. In 1753 the *Gazette* advertised a lottery to raise money for "preserving the country against the French." There were 25,000 tickets at a pistole each. In 1768 Richard Graves announced a lottery to dispose of his estate in New Kent. Also, in the same year, William Byrd III, of Westover, in a neighboring county, advertised in the *Gazette* for disposing of his properties at Shockoe and Rocky Ridge, as Richmond and Manchester were then called, and in the same issue he advertised one "for raising the sum of £900 to make a road over the mountains to the Warm and Hot Springs in Augusta County"—one of the early transportation projects to the West.

In passing, it might be pointed out that the girls married very young in those days, and William Byrd II, in a playful reference in his writings to his daughter Evelyn, remarked that she seemed to be the only "ancient maid" in the community. She was then twenty. Martha Wayles, who married Thomas Jefferson, was left a widow when she was nineteen by her first husband, Bathurst Skelton.

Martha Washington was only seventeen at the time of her first marriage.

New Kent sent many sons into the Revolutionary army, but specific records of the services of many of them will never be found. Perhaps the most distinguished Revolutionary soldier from New Kent was Major Thomas Massie. Members of his family not only were prominent in the Colonial history of Virginia, but had much to do with the settlement of the Northwest Territory, notably Ohio.

Peter Massie, patented land in New Kent in 1698, and was surveyor of roads. He died in 1719. His younger son, Charles, was father of Nathaniel Massie, Sr., who moved about 1760 to Goochland County and was the father of General Nathaniel Massie and Major Henry Massie, both prominent in the settlement of Ohio.

An elder son of Peter Massie was Thomas Massie, who was a vestryman of St. Peters and member of the House of Burgesses from New Kent 1722 to 1726. His son, William Massie, was a Burgess in 1748-49. William Massie married a daughter of William Macon and was the father of Major Thomas Massie.

In 1775 Thomas Massie was captain of a large company in the clash with Lord Dunmore. He fought with Washington in the north, was with Washington in the celebrated Christmas crossing of the Delaware, and took part in the defeat of the Hessians at Trenton.

In 1778 he was promoted to the rank of major. On

the eve of Monmouth, it was Major Massie who personally carried the order from Washington for General Charles Lee to attack, which General Lee disobeyed, bringing a sharp rebuke from Washington and arrest. Major Massie took part in the victory at Monmouth Courthouse.

He was aide to General Nelson in the Winter of 1780-81 when Benedict Arnold invaded Virginia and destroyed the public stores and buildings at Richmond and the arsenal and foundry at Westham. Major Massie was at the siege of Yorktown, and, for his outstanding services in the Revolution received 5,333 acres of land in Ohio and Kentucky. Some of this land, in the Scioto Valley, is still owned by members of the family.

Major Thomas Massie was one of the wealthy men of his time. His home was near Bottom's Bridge, at a spot which is now called Savage's Farm. There still are to be seen a number of crumbling old tombstones on the place, the latest of which is that of Major Thomas Massie's father, who died in 1751.

There is a legend in the Massie family which was probably true. At any rate it throws some light on the habits and customs of the people of his era. Major Massie moved to Frederick County about 1780 and thence to that part of Amherst which is now Nelson County and built the palatial residence Level Green, where he died in 1834. The legend is that Major Massie decided to dispose of his home in New Kent and move elsewhere because his boys could not be prevented from racing their horses with the horses of the boys of neighboring planters and gambling on the results. Major Massie regarded it as hurtful to his sons and moved away for that reason. His wife was the daughter of Bowler Cocke, Jr., of Turkey Island.

Major Thomas Massie's son, Dr. Thomas Massie, educated abroad, settled in 1807 at Chillicothe, Ohio, where his father and his cousins, General Nathaniel Massie and Major Henry Massie, owned large landed interests, but he later returned to Nelson County.

Providence Forge is an interesting old house now in the little village bearing that name. The first known owner was the Rev. Charles Jeffrey Smith. He and William Holt, of Williamsburg, operated an iron foundry which was profitable for many years. Francis Jerdone bought Smith's interest. There is on record a deed of trust dated January 1, 1775, from William Holt and Mary, his wife, conveying to Sarah Jerdone, of Louisa County, all his "moiety in land held in company with the late Francis Jerdone, of Charles City and New Kent, on which are forge, grist mill and other improvements, together with ten slaves employed at the forge, two carters, two millers, two smiths, one collier, one woodcutter, one waterman, eight women and two boys."

Eltham, on the site of the Indian village Matchot and directly across the Pamunkey River from West Point, was the seat of the celebrated Bassett family. It was one of the largest and finest Colonial houses in Virginia, but was burned to the ground in 1875.

Captain William Bassett, the immigrant, had served in the Civil War in England and was in the English garrison at Tangier. He came to Virginia prior to 1665 and died in 1672. William Bassett II was a member of the Council in 1702 and married Joanna Burwell. John Fontaine, in his diary kept while accompanying Governor Spotswood on his journey over the Blue Ridge in 1716, says that the Governor was ferried across the river here on August 20 of that year, and on September 16, returning from the celebrated expedition, "we came to Mr. West's plantation, where Col. Bassett waited for the Governor with his pinnace, and other boats for his servants. We arrived at his house by five of the clock and were nobly entertained."

William Bassett III, who married Elizabeth Churchill, was a member of the House of Burgesses at the time of his death in 1744. His son, Burwell Bassett, who was born in 1734, was a Burgess for many years from New Kent and died in 1793. It was he who purchased Bassett Hall in Williamsburg as a town house, and entertained lavishly. He married Anna Maria Dandridge, daughter of Col. John Dandridge, of New Kent, and sister of Martha Washington.

Burwell Bassett II was a member of Congress, and John Bassett moved over into Hanover and built Clover Lea. Washington was a frequent visitor at Eltham and was there in November, 1781, at the deathbed of his stepson, John Parke Custis, a soldier of Yorktown.

For about forty years Eltham was in possession of the Lacy family and was the home of Judge Benjamin W. Lacy, a distinguished lawyer and member of the Virginia Supreme Court of Appeals. He lived in later life at Marl Spring. His son, Richmond T. Lacy, was commonwealth's attorney of the County. Ellsworth was another home of the Lacy family.

Hamstead was the Colonial home of the Webb family. George Webb was treasurer of Virginia during the Revolution and for some time afterward. The present house was built by Conrad Webb in 1820 and is perhaps the stateliest house in New Kent. In more recent years it was the home of Col. W. W. Gordon, of the 27th Virginia Infantry, Stonewall Brigade, a celebrated Virginia lawyer who was born in Essex and practised in Richmond. At Hamstead are many Webb tombstones of interest.

Mount Prospect, or Prospect Hill, was the home of Col. William Macon (1694-1773) who was a colonel of New Kent militia and member of the House of Burgesses from 1735 to 1740. It also was probably the home of Gideon Macon, secretary to Sir William Berkeley and Burgess in 1696-97. It was the residence of Col. William Hartwell Macon (1759-1843) an officer in the War of 1812.

Criss Cross, one of the oldest residences in the County, was the home of the Terrells. It is in the shape of a cross and there is a door with massive crosses carved upon it. The name by which it is called is, of course, a corruption of "Christ's Cross."

Cumberland, on the Pamunkey River a mile north of the Courthouse, was settled by the Littlepages about 1700, and here was one of two enormous encampments of Union soldiers in the Peninsula Campaign of 1862. The other was at the White House.

Chestnut Grove, also on the river, was the home of Major John Dandridge and his daughter Martha, the wife of Washington. From this home also came the wife of Burwell Bassett, of Eltham and Williamsburg.

It passed to Thomas Claiborne, and later to Robert Christian.

Foster's Castle, near Tunstall, was built about 1690 as a fort. It was later owned by the Bromleys, and is now a Gregory place.

Grove Hill was the home of William Lacy. Here Cornwallis tarried on his way to Yorktown in 1781.

Rockahock, on the Chickahominy, was owned by the Custis family prior to the Revolution.

Windsor Shades, one of the oldest of the plantations, was first the property of the Osbornes. It passed to Major Edmund Christian and then to Robert Christian.

Orapax, according to tradition, was settled by the Christians as early as 1624, and they doubtless made use of the lands cleared by the Indian villagers. Later the property passed to John P. Turner.

Dunreath Abbey, on the road from Diascund bridge to the Courthouse, was owned by Henry Vaiden.

Sunny Side, a very old settlement, was first owned by two Hill brothers. It was owned by a family named Geddes some years prior to the Revolution, and about 1800 it was owned by William B. Bailey.

Spring Hill was owned by Richard Graves, who had a racecourse there and also operated a tavern. It passed from his family to Thomas Sherman, in all probability in the lottery in 1768 in which Richard Graves advertised tickets for sale. The place later passed to James Bradley.

Orchard Grove was built about 1700, later buildings being erected in 1720. It was first owned by the Lacy family, and was sold to Thomas Vaiden.

Holmes Farm was an early seat of the Holmes

family. It was bought by Col. Watkins, of James City County and remained in the Watkins family for many years. At one time it was owned by St. George Colter.

Poplar Grove was the home of the Chamberlaynes. From this family came Byrd Chamberlayne, who was a lieutenant in the Virginia Navy of the Revolution and lost his life at sea together with his son, Otway Byrd Chamberlayne, sometime after February, 1799. They were referred to in some records as being from King William County.

Cedar Grove was another seat of the Christian family.

One of the oldest buildings in the county is the New Kent Tavern, across the road from the courthouse. Its walls could tell many stories, could they but talk. It is known that Washington frequently tarried there when in the county looking after the landed interests of his wealthy wife. The road itself was one of the earliest improved roads in the Colony.

Early in 1781 Lafayette crossed the County, being pursued by Cornwallis, and later in the same year the tables were turned and Lafayette and Wayne pursued Cornwallis to the eastward. On May 4, 1781, Lafayette camped near Bottom's Bridge, and on May 28 Cornwallis camped there. Cornwallis camped there again on June 21, while retiring before Lafayette and Wayne. He passed over the road by the Courthouse the following day. Lafayette was at Providence Forge in July and August, 1781.

Stores for the Virginia Navy of the Revolution were destroyed by the British at Diascund Bridge in July and August, 1781.

Just in the edge of New Kent was Camp Bottom's

Bridge, a large training establishment in 1814 for militia to repel threatened British invasion.

New Kent witnessed much military activity during the War Between the States, especially in the Peninsula Campaign of Gen. George B. McClellan in 1862. He made The White House his base of operations and the county was desolate at the close of the war.

There was a sharp engagement a short distance up the Pamunkey from West Point on May 7, 1862. Franklin's division of McClellan's army had crossed at Eltham Landing and threatened the wagon trains of the Confederates, who were retiring toward Richmond. Gustavus W. Smith commanded the Confederate force which drove Franklin back to the river. The Confederate army, retiring toward Richmond, passed through New Kent Courthouse a few days later, shortly followed by McClellan.

Much of General J. E. B. Stuart's famous ride around McClellan's army was on New Kent soil. The intrepid cavalry leader, on his way from Hanover Courthouse, rested several hours at Talleysville June 13, 1862, the next day crossed the Chickahominy at Soane's Bridge, near Providence Forge, and joined Lee's forces, having completely encircled the Union army.

In June 1864, the Second and Fifth Corps of Grant's army crossed the Chickahominy at Long Bridge, on the way to Petersburg, and the Sixth and Ninth Corps crossed at Soane's Bridge.

As is unfortunately true in many of the Virginia counties, the records of the military services of the men of New Kent are very meager. The following list of officers from New Kent who served in the War Between the States is undoubtedly incomplete, but those who are mentioned are known to have served:

Captains: Melvin Vaiden, Telemachus Taylor, Jones Christian and John C. Timberlake; lieutenants, George F. Brumley, William E. Clopton, O. M. Chandler, B. W .Lacy, R. G. Smith, Benjamin L. Farinholt, B. B. Jones and Miles C. Timberlake; and Dr. Leonard A. Slater was a distinguished surgeon.

COURTHOUSE IS MODERN

The courthouse of New Kent is quite new, having been built on the site of an earlier one in 1909. Apparently four buildings have served as courthouses for New Kent. In the early years, before the county was divided in 1691, court was held in the present courthouse of King William. There are references to the destruction during the war of a building where the present structure stands, and the third was demolished when the present building was erected.

As was the case with Hanover and Gloucester, the records were sent to Richmond for safekeeping during the War Between the States and were destroyed in the fire at the evacuation of Richmond.

There is only one portrait in the courtroom—a very striking oil painting of Martha Washington, bearing the following inscription: "Presented by her great-great-great-grandson, Dr. George Bolling Lee, May 7, 1929." The artist was Ellis M. Silvette.

On the court green is a granite shaft to the memory of the members of the military units organized in the county in the Sixties. These were the Pamunkey Rifles, the Barhamsville Grays and the New Kent Cavalry.

King William County

KING WILLIAM COURTHOUSE

King William County

THE story of King William county is largely the story of the noble homesteads and the men of note who lived there. If the English system had prevailed in Virginia, King William would undoubtedly have been the land of a number of great barons who not only held lordly possessions but were direct descendants of the English nobility. Thomas West, governor of the colony in 1610, while spoken of as the Third Lord Delaware, was in reality the tenth baron of that line, and thus the King William Wests trace their ancestry back to Alfred the Great and Robert the Bruce. The Wallers go back to the time of the Norman conquest, and the Taliaferros, Claibornes, Peytons, Ayletts, and Fontaines equally as far. There was an unusually large migration of Huguenots to this county.

The county officers in 1702 were as follows: Burgesses, John West and Nathaniel West; sheriff, John Waller; justices, Henry Fox, John Waller, John West, Henry Madison, William Claiborne, Richard Gossage, Daniel Miles, Martin Palmer, Roger Mallory, Thomas Carr, William Hay, George Dabney and Thomas Terry; escheater, Mathew Page; clerk, William Aylett; and surveyor, Harry Beverley.

The north and south boundaries are the Mattaponi and Pamunkey rivers, which join and form the York at the southeast extremity of the county. The region was of old known as Pamunkey Neck. King William county was formed from King and Queen in 1701. The early history of King William is so closely associated with that of several neighboring counties that their genesis might be here reviewed. When the Colony was divided into eight shires in 1634, Charles River was one of them. In 1643 its name was changed to York. The county of New Kent was formed from York in 1654, and in 1691 King and Queen, including what is now King and Queen, King William, and perhaps the whole of Caroline and part of Spotsylvania was formed. King William was, of course, named for the British king.

The county is rich in Indian lore. The land on which West Point now stands was the site of the village of the wily old savage chief Opechancanough, brother of Powhatan. It was here that the horrible massacre of 1622 was planned, and it was here that Opechancanough was captured after the massacre of 1644 when the power of the Pamunkies was finally broken. Opechancanough, aged and infirm and almost blind, led his warriors into battle borne on a litter. He was brutally murdered by his sentry at Jamestown after his capture.

Opechancanough has been generally regarded as the arch-fiend among the Virginia savages, but with the passage of almost three centuries since his barbarities have been feared, civilized man is beginning to view his career in a somewhat different light. If there was ever a chieftain in history who in his own person symbolized his race, that chieftain was Opechancanough.

Under the curious law of succession among the Indians whereby the kingship passed to a deceased ruler's brothers but never to the sons of male members of the family, Opechancanough came into power with the death of his brother, Powhatan. It is probable that had Opechancanough been in his brother's place when the first colonists came to Jamestown they would not have survived. Powhatan, largely because of the genius of Captain John Smith, temporized with the white men until they got a foothold. This Opechancanough would not have done.

While Powhatan resented the inroads of the English, Opechancanough did a lot about it. He saw clearly the impending fate of the Indians, and saw, too, that if the red men were to survive, the white men must be exterminated. To this end he devoted his life, bringing into play all the cunning and courage and savage statecraft at his command. If it be admitted that his diabolical cruelty was the heritage of his race and if it be condoned at this late date in analyzing his character, Opechancanough stands out as a heroic figure in early American history.

Believed to have been over a hundred years of age when he was the victim of a dastardly murder at Jamestown, he led his people until the end. Too feeble to stand, he was borne into battle upon a litter; his lids paralized, they must be propped open for him to see. Had he been captured by a redskin tribe and put to the severest torture they could have devised, Opechancanough would not have flinched. He fought for a lost cause, but with prophetic vision fought valiantly against the doom of his people which he foresaw.

The remnants of the Pamunkey tribe still live at Indian Town, on a reservation set aside for them by the Colonial government. They hunt and fish as of old across the river from White House, where Washington wooed and won the widow Martha Custis.

Piping Tree ferry across the Pamunkey derived its peculiar name from the fact that a council was here held and the pipe of peace was passed around, after which it was deposited in a hollow tree. When the whites disregarded their agreements they were reminded by the Indians of the "pipe in tree."

Nathaniel Bacon and his followers were often in the county and the remnant of his band surrendered at West Point. Benedict Arnold and Cornwallis committed many depredations here prior to the siege of Yorktown.

Many years ago an old cannon, said to have been left there by Cornwallis, was found partly buried in the ground at Lanesville. It was dug up and renovated and was fired with much patriotic enthusiasm when the King William citizens heard the news of Virginia's secession from the Union in 1861.

Remnants of the Mattaponi tribe of Indians also reside in the county and on the banks of Moncuir creek, just above Goodwin's Island, were found the remains of two Indian mounds. There was once an Indian village in the vicinity on the Pampatike estate.

Governor John West was a member of the King's Council for twenty-nine years, from 1630 to 1659, and Col. William Dandridge was a member in 1727.

Members of the House of Burgesses from King

William were: 1702, John West, Nathaniel West; 1710, John Waller; 1714, John Waller, Orlando Jones; 1718, Orlando Jones, Thomas Johnson; 1720-22, John Waller, Thomas Johnson; 1723, William Aylett, John Childs; 1726, William Aylett, Philip Whitehead; 1736, Cornelius Lyde, Leonard Claiborne; 1738-40, Leonard Claiborne, John Aylett; 1742, Thomas West, James Power; 1744-47, Bernard Moore, James Power; 1748-49, Bernard Moore, Francis West; 1752-55, Bernard Moore, John Martin; 1756-58, Bernard Moore; Francis West; 1758-60, Peter Robinson, Harry Gaines; 1761-65 Bernard Moore, Carter Braxton; 1765, Carter Braxton, Harry Gaines; 1766-67, Carter Braxton, Henry Gaines; 1768-69, Carter Braxton, Thomas Claiborne; 1769-71, Carter Braxton, Bernard Moore; 1772 Philip Whitehead (died), William Aylett, Augustine Moore; 1773-74, Augustine Moore, William Aylett; 1775, Carter Braxton, William Aylett.

Conventions of 1775: Carter Braxton and William Aylett.

Convention of 1776: William Aylett and Richard Squire Taylor.

The story of the first settlement of King William County is intimately associated with the point of land on which West Point now stands. It has been the site of three distinct villages. First, as the seat of Opechancanough, it was called "Pamunkee" by Captain John Smith. Then there was the village of Delaware Town which was obliterated as a town, a historian of 1845 stating that even as late as that year only one house and a few ruins remained of what had been Delaware Town.

Finally came West Point, and both English towns derived their names from the family of Thomas West, the third Lord de la Warre, who came to Jamestown as Governor in 1610, his arrival saving the starving Colonists, who were on the point of abandoning the Colony when his ships came into the Bay. The Wests established themselves at what is now West Point and remained until the Revolution.

Three brothers of this family came to Virginia and all were Governors of the Colony. Captain Francis West was Governor in 1627 but left no descendants.

Captain John West, the youngest of the three, was probably the first white settler in Pamunkey Neck. In 1633 he was granted an additional 2,000 acres of land because his son John was the first Christian born in that region. He was for almost three decades an influential member of the King's Council and was named as Governor of the Colony during the period when the settlers deposed Sir John Harvey and sent him back to England.

Col. John West (1633-1691), of West Point, mentioned above as the first white child born in Pamunkey Neck, was a member of the House of Burgesses, a colonel of militia, first sheriff of King and Queen County, was senior justice of the Colonial General Court and sat on the courts martial which tried the followers of Bacon. He married Ursula Croshaw, daughter of Major Joseph Croshaw, of York County.

Captain Nathaniel West, of West Point, who was born about 1655 and died in 1724, son of Col. John West, was a member of the House of Burgesses. He married the widow of Gideon Macon, of New Kent, and the only child of this union, Unity West, became the wife of Col. William Dandridge, of Elsing Green.

Delaware Town was laid out in 1706 by Harry Beverley, surveyor, and its first trustees were John Waller, Thomas Carr and Philip Whitehead, all King William men of prominence and members of the court.

Colonel William Claiborne defeated the Indians near the site of West Point in 1629. In 1644 he landed his army at Romancoke, just above the West properties on the Mattaponi, and here, in 1653, he obtained a grant of 5,000 acres and established the Romancoke estate.

Both the Wests and the Claibornes were Loyalists and aided Sir William Berkeley in his quarrels with Nathaniel Bacon.

There has been much discussion as to whether the brick in many of the Virginia colonial houses came from abroad. While native brick-making was early inaugurated, there is conclusive proof that some of the brick used in King William was made in England or Holland and brought over either as cargo or ballast. At Waterville, the Carr home near Sweet Hall, the remains of an old house were found and the bricks were dated 1600—seven years before the colony was founded. A kind of glazed brick of a peculiar color was frequently used for chimneys, mantels and fireplaces, and this unquestionably came from abroad.

Lafayette maneuvered to his advantage in King William County before throwing his troops into the siege of Yorktown. A few miles northward from West Point, in August, 1781, he encamped his militia, consisting of Campbell's, Stevens' and Lawson's brigades, and about four miles to the northwest he placed his light infantry, consisting of Mühlenberg's and Frebiger's commands. These troops had been ferried across the Pamunkey from New Castle, in Hanover. General Wayne was at Westover, and within six weeks the Yorktown campaign began.

So many Union prisoners were held in Richmond the latter part of 1863 that the Federal commanders Kilpatrick and Dahlgren determined to make a surprise attack on Richmond and liberate them, the former from the North and the latter from the South. Kilpatrick was repulsed after he and his cavalry had almost made their way into the city.

Dahlgren was misled by his guide, whom he promptly hung, and wandered into King William County, where his depredations were intolerable. The younger men of King and Queen, who had formed themselves into a home guard, attacked his command and captured most of his followers. Dahlgren, himself, was killed March 2, 1864, in King and Queen County. McClellan landed a large force at West Point during the Peninsula Campaign and had a base of supplies at White House, just across the river in New Kent.

While Carter Braxton, (1736-1797) one of Virginia's seven signers of the Declaration of Independence, was born at Newington, in King and Queen County, he spent most of his active years in King William. His father was George Braxton, a wealthy planter and member of the House of Burgesses, and his mother was Mary, a daughter of Robert "King" Carter. Carter Braxton is believed to have built the original Chericoke mansion in King William and is known to have remodeled Elsing Green in 1758.

When he was only twenty-five years of age he was sent to the House of Burgesses from King William and was a member in 1765 when Patrick Henry introduced his famous resolutions against the Stamp Act. His name appeared with those of Washington, Jefferson, Henry, Peyton Randolph and others who signed the resolutions of 1769 that the Virginia House of Burgesses had the sole right to tax the colonists. When Berkeley in 1769 dissolved the Burgesses, Carter Braxton was one of those who repaired to the Apollo room of Raleigh Tavern at Williamsburg and signed the non-importation agreement.

He served in the Revolutionary conventions of 1774, 1775 and 1776 and it was he who doubtless prevented bloodshed by adjusting the dispute between Patrick Henry and Dunmore over the gunpowder stolen from the powder-horn in 1775. He was a member of the Committee of Safety and on the death of Peyton Randolph was appointed to fill the vacancy in the Continental Congress, taking his seat in 1776. When he returned as a member of the first Virginia legislature under the new State constitution, he and Jefferson received a vote of thanks for their services in Congress. He supported Jefferson's Virginia bill for religious freedom in 1785 and in 1786 moved to Richmond, where he died eleven years later.

It is a notable fact that the early settlers on the south side of the Mattaponi in what is now King William were of a different stripe from those who settled on the north side in King and Queen. The former, in

the main, were loyal to the established church and were
in many cases lovers of luxury and high living. The
latter were more seriously inclined and King and
Queen County was something of a stronghold for the
early dissenters.

Many notables were wont to pass through King
William on their journeys to and from Williamsburg,
lingering long to enjoy the hospitalities of the King
William planters. An example of this was that Washington was making such a trip when he met Martha
Dandridge Custis just across the Pamunkey River in
New Kent at White House. Due to lack of bridges
and roads, King William was considerably isolated
until comparatively recent years. A man's home was
literally his castle. Here may be made brief references
to some of those homes and their early owners.

Chelsea is a noble Colonial place on the Mattaponi
about five miles above West Point and was built on a
large grant of land by Augustine Moore, who had
come over from Isle of Wight County and was a direct
descendant of Sir Thomas Moore, Lord High Chancellor in the reign of Henry VIII. He cleared so
much land that his neighbors spoke of him as "Old
Grub Moore." Governor Spotswood and his party
were entertained here overnight on their tramontane
journey, and tradition has it that it was on the lawn of
Chelsea that the idea for the organization of the
Knights of the Golden Horseshoe was perfected. The
party crossed the Mattaponi at Clifton the next day
and proceeded to the home of Robert Beverley, then
journeyed on to Germanna, in Orange County, the
point of rendezvous. Many years later, a bit of colored

glass was dug up at Chelsea, apparently the stopper of a small bottle, with a horseshoe stamped upon it.

There persists a belief in the family that ,Bernard Moore, son of Augustine Moore, was one of the members of Governor Spotswood's party, but Bernard Moore was probably too young at the time. He became an outstanding citizen of King William and married Anne Catherine, Governor Spotswood's eldest daughter. He inherited Chelsea and was for many years an influential member of the House of Burgesses. Ann Butler Moore, one of the daughters of Catherine Spotswood Moore, was the grandmother of General Robert E. Lee, and another daughter, Lucy, was the grandmother of Dr. John S. Lewis, father of the late Herbert I. Lewis, a distinguished West Point lawyer. Bernard Moore and Alexander Moore, of the Chelsea family, fought throughout the Revolution, the latter serving as an aide to Lafayette, who made his headquarters at Chelsea just before the siege of Yorktown. The old homestead is now owned by P. L. Reed, of Richmond.

Elsing Green, on the Pamunkey about five miles from Lester Manor, is one of the handsomest estates in the County. It was the ancient seat of the Dandridges and was founded by Captain William Dandridge, of the Royal Navy, who also bore the army title "colonel." He had a varied naval career, served with Oglethorpe in the attack on St. Augustine, and served with great distinction in the siege of Carthagena. In the Virginia Historical Society is his portrait and also his sword, presented to him by Lord High Admiral Vernon for bravery at Carthagena.* In 1717 he owned a dock and operated his own ships at Hampton. In 1727 he was sworn in as a member of the Council. He died in 1743. His wife was Unity West, only child of Captain Nathaniel West, grandson of Governor John West. Unity West Dandridge, according to her will dated 1753, owned 4,832 acres in Hanover, which land passed to her son, Captain Nathaniel West Dandridge, who held a commission in the Royal Navy, and in later life was a wealthy property-owner and member of the House of Burgesses from Hanover. Nathaniel West Dandridge married Dorothea Spotswood, younger daughter of the Governor. One of the daughters of this union, Dorothea, was the second wife of Patrick Henry, and another daughter married Archer Payne, of Goochland. Major John Dandridge (1700-1756) the father of Martha Washington, was a brother of William Dandridge of Elsing Green, and was clerk of New Kent in 1747.

The Dandridges, Claibornes and Brownes intermarried and Elsing Green was for many years owned by William Burnet Browne, born at Salem, Mass., who bought it from Carter Braxton about 1767. The place had been bought and remodeled by Carter Braxton in 1758. It remained in the Browne family until 1820 when it was sold to William Gregory, father of Judge

*The expedition against Carthagena (often spelled Cartagena) an ancient fortified Spanish town on the north coast of South America, was the first occasion when American troops were ever sent out of this continent. Admiral Vernon failed to take Carthagena in this campaign which lasted from 1740 to 1742 and the Spanish retaliated by sending a force against Georgia, defended by Oglethorpe. A large number of Virginians participated in the attack upon Carthagena. Alexander Spotswood, who had served as Governor of Virginia from 1710 to 1722, was made a major-general and was to command the Colonial forces, but he died at Annapolis in 1740 while organizing his troops, and Governor William Gooch went in his stead. Among other Virginians was Lawrence Washington (1718-1752) half-brother of George Washington, who was a captain under Gooch and was wounded. Lawrence Washington named Mount Vernon, the Washington estate on the Potomac, for Admiral Vernon.

Roger Gregory, and the place has remained in the Gregory family ever since. The sturdiness of the old homestead is illustrated by the fact that young Miss Mary ¡Browne once rode her pony up the stairway on one side of the hall and down the other, and that during the war when Federal troops occupied it, they quartered their horses in the stone-paved halls.

Burlington was a King William homestead of the Gwathmeys. Major Joseph Gwathmey, of the fourth generation, moved over from King and Queen and owned Burlington, Wakefield and Frenchtown. The Burlington house stands on the site of what was once an Indian village and the farm has a frontage of approximately five miles on the Mattaponi. The original grant was to the Burwells, who built there in 1702 and called the place Burwelton. The foundations of the original Burwell house can still be seen in the yard. A part of the present house which survived the ravages of fire was built by Owen Gwathmey in 1759. The Meadow was another old Gwathmey estate on the Mattaponi.

Aspen Grove, the home of Hardin Littlepage, one of the justices in 1799, remained in the Littlepage family for over 100 years. It descended to a son, Col. Hardin Littlepage, and later to Robert Christopher Hill, who married his daughter.

Auburn was the home of Wilson Coleman Pemberton; Broadneck, of the Pages and Croxtons; and Brooklyn was the home of the Hooper and Edwards families.

Chericoke, a beautiful old place on the Pamunkey River, was the home of Carter Braxton, signer of the

Declaration of Independence, who moved there early in life from King and Queen. It is believed that he built the house. He also owned the land on which West Point now stands, it having been sold two years after his death for $35,000.

Cherry Grove, not far from the courthouse, was built by Ambrose Edwards about the middle of the 18th Century on a grant of 4,000 acres. Clover Plain was built by Thomas Edwards about 1790. Cool Spring was the homestead of Col. Edmund Littlepage and he and his wife were buried there.

Enfield was the original home of the Waller family in King William on the banks of the Mattaponi, the land being a part of the original grant from Charles II to John Waller.

Fairfield was a part of the original grant to the Ayletts, and on it may be seen a number of interesting tombstones .

Forest Villa was part of a grant to Ambrose Edwards, who built the house for his son, Thomas Edwards.

Langborne, the old Langborne mansion, was rebuilt in 1845 by John Pemberton. On this place is the tomb of the immigrant, William Langborne (1723-1766).

Montville, near the town of Aylett, was part of a large grant to Captain John Aylett, whose grandson, Philip Aylett, married Martha Dandridge, aunt of Martha Washington. The present house was built in 1803.

There are some curious relics at this place. Among others there is a saber carried by one of the Ayletts in the War of 1812 until broken in hand-to-hand encounter with a British antagonist. A pair of duelling pistols preserved here have a strange history. In 1809 young Philip Aylett was provided by his father with a negro, two horses, five hundred dollars and a gold watch which had been presented to his mother by Patrick Henry. Young Aylett started for Tennessee to practice law. Being a high-spirited young man, he soon got rid of his money, the negro and his horses, and became involved in a quarrel with Colonel Sam Houston which resulted in a duel. They fired twice at thirty paces, but neither was seriously injured. They afterward became such good friends that Houston made him a present of the pistols. These pistols were tampered with and disfigured by Union soldiers during the War Between the States.

Mount Pleasant, lately the home of James Armistead Robins, is said to have been built by the Gregory family in 1734.

Zoar, at Aylett, has twice been burned, the massive chimneys being all that remain of the original house built by Robert Pollard, for forty years clerk of the County.

Romancoke, the original Claiborne homestead, is in ruins, but there remains the tomb of Thomas Claiborne, who died in 1683.

Pampatike, a valuable estate on the Pamunkey River, was conveyed prior to 1700 by the queen of the Pamunkey Indians to Mann Page. Later it came into the hands of Charles Carter, of Shirley, father of Ann Hill Carter, the mother of Gen. Robert E. Lee. Charles Carter devised it in his will, dated 1803, to his son, Robert Carter, and the property descended to Col.

Thomas H. Carter, one of the County's heroes in the War of the '60s. He commanded Carter's Battery, composed largely of residents of King William County, who were among the bravest soldiers of the Army of Northern Virginia.

The Piping Tree estate, on the Pamunkey, was an old Gregory plantation.

Rumford Academy was a celebrated school for boys prior to the War Between the States and in 1833 was the only public institution of learning in the County worthy of note.

Spring Bank was the seat of the Burkes.

Sweet Hall, on the Pamunkey River, was owned by William Claiborne, first secretary of the Colony. After giving the County of New Kent its name, Claiborne retired to Sweet Hall in later life and there died and was buried. It afterwards came into possession of the Ruffins, who resided there during the Revolution. It later passed to the Lipscombs.

Waterville was built by James Ruffin in 1794.

Huntington was the original seat of the Fox family in King William. Henry Fox owned this tract and other large grants prior to 1700. The adjoining place is still called Fox's and there is an old house on it. Henry Fox married Anne West, a greatniece of Lord Delaware. He was one of the justices and a member of the House of Burgesses. He died in 1714.

Bear Garden is over two hundred years old and was once Gen. Fitzhugh Lee's headquarters. He scratched his name on a pane of glass with his diamond ring and it may still be seen.

Cownes, on the Mattaponi, was the home of Major

B. B. Douglas, able lawyer, member of the Confederate Senate from 1861 to 1865 and member of Congress after the War Between the States.

Landsdowne, while not built by them, has been the home of four generations of Whites since 1818. Horace White, the first of the family who owned it, married Hannah Temple Gwathmey, widow of Temple Dabney, in 1819. In 1860 James Gwathmey remodeled the building. A diary in the White family tells of the raids of Sheridan and of Grant's encampment in the fields of Landsdowne. The war left the house in a devastated condition. Recently it came into possession of J. W. Dabney, a grandson of Horace White.

The home of the late C. P. Snead at Etna Mills has gateposts which were made from nine kegs of bullets picked up from the battlefields of Fredericksburg, the Wilderness and Chancellorsville, many of these bullets doubtless having passed through the bodies of contending soldiers.

Green Level, two and a half miles from the courthouse, was built by Austin Lipscomb in 1754. It is now owned by Gay Taliaferro Hill.

There seems to be no official roster of the King William soldiers who served in the War Between the States except the list of names on the handsome Confederate monument which stands on the court green. For some of the companies the names of the officers are listed as "officers" but their rank is not given. The following facts are chiseled on this monument:

Lee Rangers, Co. H, 9th Virginia, Major B. B. Douglas.

Officers: T. W. Haynes, F. Meredith, W. H. Mitchell, W. V. Croxton, J. L. Slaughter, H. Anderson, T. J. Christian, F. R. Burke, J. Pemberton.

Taylor Grays, Co. D, 53rd Virginia, Col. Wm. R. Aylett.

Mattaponi Guards, Co. H, 53rd Virginia, Capt. W. G. Pollard.

Carter's Battery, Col. Thomas H. Carter.

Officers: F. King, J. G. White, W. P. Carter, S. R. Waring, W. A. Davis, P. H. Fountaine, W. H. Robins, T. J. Bosher, W. E. Hart, B. A. Littlepage, P. Fountaine, R. S. Ryland, J. W. Burke, A. Atkins, W. A. Hawes, J. H. Henry, T. G. Jones, W. B. Newman, E. J. Cocke, G. T. Tebbs, A. F. Dabney, J. N. Eubank, R. Temple, L. D. Robinson, J. D. Edwards, R. C. Robinson.

PRETTY OLD COURTHOUSE

King William courthouse is one of the finest surviving examples of the arched form of architecture used in the design of a large number of Virginia colonial courthouses. The stately arches were probably patterned after those of the connecting passageway between the two wings of the Colonial Capitol at Williamsburg.

King William courthouse is one of the few remaining which are enclosed by brick walls, and a large part of the wall around the court green is the original. In the early days all of the court greens were thus enclosed, the supposition being that the walls were erected for protection against straying livestock.

The exact date of this building is not known, but it was certainly erected prior to 1675 and may have been built as early as 1670. In January, 1702, only a few months after the formation of King William as a county, Henry Fox, who was the owner of Fox's Ferry, conveyed by deed to the justices of the county "two acres of land on part of which the courthouse now stands."

This building served as the courthouse of the vast County of New Kent until King and Queen was formed in 1691. It was then used as the courthouse of the large County of King and Queen until 1701, when King William was formed from King and Queen. There is proof that the bricks were unloaded at Horse Landing, on the Mattaponi, and on the edge of the channel at that point there still may be seen a pile of rocks which are supposed to have been brought over by ships from England as ballast.

On January 17, 1885, a disastrous fire destroyed the clerk's office and almost all of the priceless records it contained. A few old deed books, badly scorched, were preserved.

25 PORTRAITS ON WALLS

There are twenty-five portraits on the walls of the courtroom of King William, memorials to men of distinction who have been associated with the county's history. These portraits are of the following persons:

HERBERT I. LEWIS, of West Point, who was commonwealth's attorney from 1887 to 1928 and was a distinguished lawyer and legislator.

MAJOR BEVERLY B. DOUGLAS, commander of the Lee Rangers, member of the Confederate Senate and congressman from Virginia after the war.

WILLIAM CLARK, deputy commissioner of the revenue.

COL. WILLIAM R. AYLETT, commander of the Taylor Grays in the War between the States, commonwealth's attorney for many years and a man who achieved much prominence as a lawyer.

CAPTAIN W. G. POLLARD, who commanded the Mattaponi Guards, Company H, 53rd Virginia Regiment.

MATT WINSTON, for many years clerk of the county.

E. S. POLLARD, commissioner of the revenue.

JOHN WILLIAM TAYLOR, for many years sheriff.

COL. THOMAS H. CARTER, commander of Carter's Battery. He lived at Pampatike and conducted a prominent boys' school there.

THOMAS P. BAGBY, of King and Queen, who often appeared as an attorney in the court of King William.

CAPTAIN WILLIAM HAYNES, a gallant Confederate officer who lost a leg in the war.

BUSHROD DABNEY, one of the old time commonwealth's attorneys.

PATRICK HENRY AYLETT, another of the distinguished members of this old King William family.

PHILIP GIBSON was a large real estate owner and a respected citizen.

DR. JOHN LEWIS was a beloved physician and also served in the legislature.

CAMM GARRETT was for many years a teacher at Rumford Academy, and was president of the old court.

PHILIP AYLETT, another of the Ayletts of Montville, was a lawyer of ability.

A. T. MOOKLAR, a large land-owner, was chairman of the board of supervisors over a long period.

ROBERT POLLARD, one of the five members of the family of that name who served as clerks of the county.

JUDGE JOHN D. FOSTER was county judge in the reconstruction period.

JUDGE OWEN OVERTON GWATHMEY was county judge for many years until the county judicial system was abolished in 1904.

JUDGE J. M. JEFFRIES was from King and Queen and was circuit judge of the circuit embracing King William.

JUDGE ROGER GREGORY (1833-1920) of Elsing Green, was a jurist and lawyer of much distinction.

ROBERT POLLARD, JR., who wrote his name Ro. and was commonly called Robin, was clerk from 1818 to 1842.

THOMAS H. EDWARDS was a well-known lawyer.

CLERKS UNUSUAL MEN

In view of the fact that King William enjoyed the unique experience of being served by five members of one family as clerks over a period of seventy-three years, it may not be amiss here to pay tribute to the high-minded men who have served in this office throughout the State in the years gone by. They have, with very few exceptions, been men of intelligence, with unerring fidelity to their duties.

It is remarkable that in so many Virginia counties

[81]

the clerkship has been handed down from father to son, and in a vast majority of cases this has been advantageous. As a rule the sons served as deputies for their fathers and when the older clerks died, their sons were fully equipped to carry on the work. The clerks have occupied positions of unusual influence. Not only have they kept the precious old records, but they have acted as advisers to the citizens in all sorts of matters. The average citizen coming to the county-seat to transact legal business would have been bewildered without the advice and aid of the clerk.

While the clerkship is, of course, a political office, few of the clerks in Virginia's past have ever "taken the stump" in their campaigns, but the competent clerk has been hard to overthrow, for during his tenure of office he has come into contact with so many voters in a pleasant way and has accorded them so many favors that they have not liked to vote against him. In a large majority of cases the clerks have been men of unfailing courtesy.

In addition to the peculiar fact that King William was served by five Pollard clerks, it is remarkable that there seems to have been a tradition in the Pollard family that their sons must serve their counties as clerks and there were other Pollards who served for generations in King and Queen and Hanover counties. Pollard has been a good name in these three counties from early days.

The succession of Pollard clerks in King William was as follows:

> Robert Pollard 1797-1818
> Robert Pollard, Jr. 1818-1842

Robert Byrd Pollard........1842-1852
James Otway Pollard........1852-1865
Wm. Dandridge Pollard.....1867-1872

It will be noted that there was a gap of two years in the succession, from 1865 to 1867. This interregnum occurred in many counties for those were the years of reconstruction. Hardly an old clerk could take the oath of allegiance and swear that he had not taken part in the war. Men who could take the oath were elected as clerks, the old clerks serving as deputies, but carrying on the work just as if they were clerks in fact.

In King and Queen two members of the Pollard family served as clerks for seventy-six years. Robert Pollard served from (about) 1800 to 1835, and Robert Pollard, Jr., was clerk from 1835 to 1876.

Over in Hanover two members of the family served as clerks of the old county courts for eighty-nine years. William Pollard, Sr., was clerk from 1740 to 1781. William Pollard, Jr., known as "Billy Particular," the nickname implying much, was clerk of Hanover from 1781 to 1829. Then there were two Pollards, Thomas and W. T. H., who served for seventeen years as clerks of the circuit court. John R. Taylor was elected to the clerkship in 1870, and the office is now held by his son, Clarence W. Taylor.

Four generations of Millers have been serving as clerks in Goochland for over a hundred years, since 1791.

Four members of the Lee family served in Essex for sixty-nine years successively from 1745 to 1814.

[83]

Three generations of Woodsons served in Cumberland for exactly 100 years, from 1781 to 1881.

In Louisa Jesse J. Porter first entered the clerk's office in 1854 and was serving as clerk at the time of his death in 1912. Two of his sons carried on the succession. James died while in office and was succeeded by Philip B. Porter, the incumbent, a fine typification of the old time Virginia clerk. Thus the records of Louisa County have been in the keeping of the Porter family continuously for eighty-one years.

Hanover County

HANOVER COURTHOUSE

Hanover County

HANOVER COUNTY from earliest times has been prominent in the history of the State and Nation because of the stirring events which have occurred on its soil and through the influence of the great men the County has produced. Few counties suffered more from the horrible ravages of war than did Hanover in the War Between the States. Its lands were laid waste during the Revolution, and even in the very beginning of the Virginia Colony Hanover was a battleground.

It was on the Chickahominy not far from the New Kent line that Captain John Smith, on December 16, 1607, was captured by Opechancanough and his warriors, and thence paraded for weeks throughout eastern Virginia as far north as the Indian villages along the Potomac. Finally Captain Smith was taken before the great King Powhatan at Werowocomoco, in Gloucester, where his life was miraculously saved by Pocahontas.

The County was formed from New Kent in 1720, and New Kent had been formed in 1654 from York, which formerly had been known as Charles River, one of the original Shires dating back to 1634. Hanover was named for the ruling family in Great Britain.

Hanover supplied many brave militiamen who aided in keeping the Indians in subjection. When Braddock was defeated in 1755 there were a number of men from Hanover who played a distinguished part in saving the remnants of Braddock's defeated army. Shortly afterward the celebrated minister, the Rev. Samuel Davies, preached a notable sermon in which he urged the young men of Captain Samuel Overton's company to be of good courage. It is recorded that, as a result of this address, a larger number of young men volunteered than were needed. Captain Overton and his company were under the command of Andrew Lewis in the Sandy Creek expedition in 1756 and undoubtedly saw much active service in the West in the French and Indian War from 1756 to 1763. In all the wars subsequently fought by the American people, Hanover men played a prominent part.

In the early years there were two flourishing ports in Hanover on the Pamunkey River. One was Hanover Town, once known as Page's Warehouse, and Newcastle, the former some fifteen miles above the present bridge on the Tappahannock Highway, and the latter a short distance below it. Both are now abandoned. As late as 1830 Newcastle was an important shipping point for tobacco, and in the debates which preceded the removal of the capital of Virginia from Williamsburg to Richmond, Hanover Town came within a few votes of being made the capital of the State.

When Hanover was formed, the people were just beginning to get away from the navigable streams. A hundred years after Jamestown was settled, there were few homes which did not have their private wharves. Gradually the younger generations married, built homes for themselves further back into the uplands, and chopped down the forests. These were hardy people—especially the women—and their courage and determination have never been overestimated.

With the increase in population came musters of the militia, church attendance, court days and other gatherings. Horse racing, racing balls, fox hunting, cockfighting, drinking and card playing were common diversions among the wealthier planters. An article in the *Virginia Gazette* of October, 1737, gives an insight into the pastimes of the people at large:

"We have advice from Hanover County that on St. Andrew's Day there are to be horse races and several other diversions for the entertainment of ladies and gentlemen at the old field near Capt. Brickerton's, in that county, the substance of which is as follows—viz.: It is proposed that 20 horses or mares do run around a three miles' course for a prize of £5.

"That a hat of the value of 20 shillings be cudgelled for, and that after the first challenge made, the drums are to beat every quarter of an hour for three challenges around the ring, and none to play with their left hand.

"That a violin be played for by 20 fiddlers, no persons to have the liberty to play unless he bring a fiddle with him. After the prize is won they are all to play together, and each a different tune, and to be treated by the company.

"That 12 boys 12 years of age do run 112 yards for a hat of the cost of 12 shillings.

"That a flag be flying on said day 30 feet high.

"That a handsome entertainment be provided for the subscribers and their wives, and such of them as are not so happy as to have wives may treat any other lady.

"That drums, trumpets and hautboys be provided to play at said entertainment.

"That after dinner the Royal health, His Honor, the Governor, &c are to be drunk.

[87]

"That a quire of ballads be sung for by a number of songsters, all of them to have liquor sufficient to clear their windpipes.

"That a pair of shoe buckles be wrestled for by a number of brisk young men.

"That a pair of handsome shoes be danced for.

"That a pair of handsome silk stockings, of one pistole value, be given to the handsomest young country maid that appears on the field; with many other whimsical and comical diversions too numerous to mention."

It was at Newcastle, on May 2, 1775, that Patrick Henry assembled the Hanover volunteers and marched to Williamsburg to force Lord Dunmore to return or pay for the powder which he had stolen from the powder-horn and conveyed to his ship in the river. And it was Ensign Parke Goodall, of Hanover, who with sixteen men, browbeat Dunmore into paying for the ammunition.

References to Hanover County in the memoirs of the Marquis de Chastellux, a French officer attached to the Continental army in the Revolution, are so charmingly written that they are here quoted in part:

"As you approach Newcastle, the country becomes more gay. This little capital of a small district contains twenty-five or thirty houses, some of which are pretty enough. We continued our journey to Hanover Courthouse. We arrived before sunset, and alighted at a tolerably handsome inn. [The old part of the present tavern at that point.] A very large saloon and a covered portico are destined to receive the company who assemble every three months at the courthouse, either on private or public affairs. . . . The county of Hanover, as well as that of New Kent, had still reason to remember the passage of the English. Mr. Tilghman, our landlord, though he lamented his misfortune in having lodged and boarded Lord Cornwallis and his retinue, without his lordship's having made the least recompense, could not yet help laughing at the fright which the unexpected arrival of Tarleton spread amongst a considerable number of gentlemen, who had come to hear the news, and were assembled in the courthouse. A negro on horseback came full gallop to let them know that Tarleton was not above three miles off. The resolution of retreating was soon taken; but the alarm was so sudden, and the confusion so great, that everyone mounted the first horse he could find, so that few of these curious gentlemen returned upon their own horses. The English, who came from Westover, had passed the Chickahominy at Bottom's Bridge and directed their march towards the South Anna, which Lafayette had put between them and himself.

"The next morning the Marquis left the courthouse and arrived about noon at Offley, near the North Anna river, the seat of the then ex-Governor Nelson, where he passed two or three days in the enjoyment of the hospitalities of the family."

Chastellux eulogizes the patriotism and zeal of the Governor, whose acquaintance he made later at the siege of Yorktown, and compliments the beauty, artlessness and music of the young ladies, describing them as "pretty nymphs, more timid and wild than those of Diana." The Marquis then goes on to describe the venerable ex-secretary Nelson, the father of Governor Nelson, whose elegant house, being occupied by Lord Cornwallis during the siege of Yorktown, was fired upon by the Americans.

As it was in Hanover, so it was in all of the older Virginia counties, and it may not be amiss here to point out the important fact that the Virginians of old insisted upon proper education for their sons. It is amazing how many great educators and scholars have gone from Virginia counties in which there were no public schools and in which the facilities for acquiring learning had to be provided through the zeal of the

[89]

individuals. As a background for the education of the younger generations were the fine private libraries accumulated in the homes of the vast majority of the men of means, and their passionate devotion to literature. They engaged private tutors for their children who gave sound instruction. William and Mary was the only available college until 1825 when the University of Virginia opened. After receiving adequate preparation and much intellectual inspiration at home, the boys were sent off to private schools and academies, of which there were many in Hanover.

In 1778 Washington-Henry Academy was established not far from what is now Atlee Station, and has since been converted into a modern high school with a department devoted to agriculture. Also, prior to the War Between the States, there was the Meadow Farm Academy, at the residence of William B. Sydnor, and at Ellington, north of Hanover Junction, was the Fox School, taught by the Rev. Thomas H. Fox. Near Humanity Ford, on Little River about two miles east of Hewlett, was Humanity Hall, taught by the Rev. Peter Nelson, a Baptist minister.

At Edgewood, the home of Dr. Carter Berkeley, was a noted boys' school, and to this school went Col. William Nelson, of Oakland, the Berkeleys, of Airwell, and Judge William W. Crump, the distinguished Richmond jurist. Many years later, Thomas Nelson Page attended a school at the same place taught by Charles L. C. Minor and his brother, Berkeley Minor. Taylor's Creek, the home of Charles Morris, was a notable school to which came the scholarly Judge Beverley T. Crump and his brother Edward, Charles

E. Bolling, distinguished engineer and public servant of Richmond, and Judge Page Morris, of Indianapolis.

At Mont Air, home of the Nelsons, was a school taught by Miss Jenny Nelson, who afterwards taught in Wellesley College and at Chatham. Among her pupils were Alfred Byrd, of New York, Nelson Noland and Frank Noland, Rear Admiral Hilary P. Jones, William Overton Winston, of Minneapolis, and Lewis D. Aylett, of Richmond. The Aaron Hall Free School, in the upper end of the county, was established by the will of Aaron Hall and, except during the war of the 60s, has been actively run since 1844. Its endowment in recent years was increased by Thomas Nelson Page and Marcellus T. Eddleton.

Pinecote was endowed by Thomas Nelson Page as the Florence L. Page Visiting Nurse Association. Edward G. Gwathmey, a gallant artilleryman, severely wounded at Hamilton's Crossing during the battle of Fredericksburg, and a Master of Arts of the University of Virginia, conducted a private school to which went many eminent men, at Bear Island, the old Gwathmey estate on Little River. There were other private schools and many notable private tutors, as for instance Miss Louisa Webb, an English lady, who tutored at Beaverdam, home of the Fontaines, Woodland, home of the Winstons, and Hickory Hill, home of the Wickhams.

Within a mile of Fork Church, in the angle of the Chesapeake and Ohio and the Richmond, Fredericksburg and Potomac railroads, was Hanover Academy. This noted boys' school was established by Col. Lewis Minor Coleman, afterwards professor of Latin at the

University of Virginia. It was continued after the war, in which he was killed, by another distinguished artillery officer, Col. Hilary P. Jones. It is now the home of a man who is perhaps Hanover's most celebrated living citizen, Admiral Hilary P. Jones.

The most outstanding institution of learning in the county is Randolph-Macon College at Ashland, the oldest Methodist college in the United States. It was chartered February 3, 1830 and operated in Mecklenburg County until the new plant opened at Ashland October 1, 1868. It was named for John Randolph of Roanoke and Nathaniel Macon, of North Carolina. Strange as it may seem, neither of these men was a professed Christian and neither showed any especial interest in the school.

It was the alma mater of the great naval constructor, Admiral David Taylor; James M. Page and Thomas Walker Page, of the faculty of the University of Virginia; Secretary of the Navy Claude A. Swanson; Walter Hines Page, the noted publisher and ambassador to England, and a large number of other notable men.

Traces of what was once a famous racetrack were visible until twenty years ago near Hanover Junction, now Doswell. At Bullfield, as the place was called, were the celebrated stables of three generations of Doswells. Major Thomas W. Doswell was perhaps the most widely-known of these pioneer breeders and importers of fast horses. Planet, the most famous thoroughbred of his time, stood at the head of a long list of noted horses at Bullfield, including Nina, Fanny Washington, King Bolt, Abdel-Kadir, Eolus, Algerine,

Morello and a great gelding called Bushwhacker, all of which names are familiar in the history of the American turf.

To the stables at Bullfield may be traced the ancestry of many of the celebrated horses of modern times, including My Own, Wise Counsellor, Ladkin, Sarazen and the great French horse Epinard. The most noted trainer in his time in America was a colored man known far and wide as Old Phil, who trained the Doswell horses.

Members of the House of Burgesses from Hanover were: 1722, Nicholas Meriwether, John Syme; 1723-26, Nicholas Meriwether, Richard Harris; 1736-40, William Meriwether, Robert Harris; 1742, Robert Harris, John Chiswell; 1744-49, William Meriwether, John Chiswell; 1752-55, John Chiswell, Henry Robinson; 1756, John Syme, Henry Robinson; 1757-64, Nathaniel West Dandridge, John Syme; 1764-65, James Littlepage, John Syme; 1766-68, Samuel Meredith, John Syme; 1769-71, William Macon, Jr., Patrick Henry, Jr.; 1772, Patrick Henry, Jr., John Smith; 1773-75, Patrick Henry, Jr., John Syme.

Conventions of 1775: March, Patrick Henry, Jr., John Syme; July, Patrick Henry, Jr., John Syme (Garland Anderson, alternate); December, John Syme, Samuel Meredith.

Convention of 1776: Patrick Henry and John Syme.

In Colonial times large acreages were owned by Nicholas Meriwether, one of the first Burgesses, and he also in 1727 was granted 13,762 acres in what became Albemarle County, the tract including the site of Castle Hill. Col. John Chiswell also owned a large tract in

Albemarle. The original Overton grant in Hanover extended along the south side of Little River from its junction with the North Anna westward into Louisa County. Other large tracts in Hanover were owned by the Winstons, Pages, Symes, Littlepages, Merediths and others, and Unity West Dandridge, only child and heir of Nathaniel West, in her will dated 1753, conveyed 4,832 acres in Hanover, the land passing to her son, Nathaniel West Dandridge, husband of Dorothea Spotswood.

After the Revolution the largest land-owner in the county was General Thomas Nelson, who owned Bullfield, which later passed to the Doswells, Offley, containing more than 11,000 acres, and other large tracts. For the payment of debts incurred in behalf of the government 8,000 acres were conveyed to Robert Saunders, R. Andrews and D. Jameson.

Among other large property-owners might be mentioned Nelson Berkeley, Thomas Anderson, George Brackenridge, Charles Crenshaw, William Dandridge, Peter Johnson, James Winston, Charles Carter, William Macon, John Austin, the Burnleys, the Tinsleys (John and Cornelius), Geddes and William O. Winston, William Pollard, Benjamin Fowler, Joseph Shelton, Benjamin Oliver, Nathan Bowe, Holderby Dixon, Col. W. Miles Cary and Col. Nathaniel West Dandridge. Carter Braxton owned a tract of land in Hanover.

Several militia companies were accredited to Hanover in the Revolutionary period by subsequent military historians. There was Captain John Winston's company. Captain Thomas Nelson commanded a troop of cavalry, of which George Nicholas was first lieutenant and Hugh Nelson second lieutenant. This company marched to Philadelphia where they received the thanks of Congress and were discharged in 1778. Captain John Price's company fought with General Greene in the South. Captain Thomas Doswell's company was at Sandy Point in 1780. Then there were Captain John Harris' company, of which Ralph Thomas was first lieutenant, Thomas Jones second lieutenant, and William Jarman cornet; Captain Edward Bullock's company, and Captain Nicholas Hammer's company. The last two joined Lafayette in 1781, as did Captain Frank Coleman's and Captain John Thompson's companies.

Hanover County saw much action during the Revolution, especially in the Spring of 1781 when the entire army of Cornwallis was on Hanover soil. It was from Hanover that Cornwallis sent Colonel Banastre Tarleton to surprise Governor Jefferson and the legislature at Charlottesville, which raid undoubtedly would have been successful had it not been for the famous ride of Jack Jouett, described in the chapter on Louisa. Lafayette's masterly retreat from the superior numbers of Cornwallis' army was made across Hanover, and it was here that the British commander gave it up as a bad job, Lafayette going on to the Rapidan, where he was joined by "Mad" Anthony Wayne.

Hanover County has basked in the glory of having produced Patrick Henry and Henry Clay. Along with the many other notable citizens of Hanover County there was one who preceded Henry and Clay chronologically and was perhaps as great in his field. That

[95]

man was the Rev. Samuel Davies (1723-1762) often referred to as "the father of the Presbyterian church in Virginia." Although Davies richly deserved that title, he was not the first minister of that faith. The first Presbyterian minister in America was the Rev. Francis Mackemie, who came over from Ireland about 1690 and established the "first regular presbytery that was organized in the new world" in Accomac County, on the Eastern Shore of Virginia. He died in 1708.

The Rev. Samuel Davies came to Hanover from Delaware just after his ordination in 1747 and revealed himself as a fervent patriot and a speaker of remarkable eloquence, which faculty he employed no less effectually in recruiting troops for the French and Indian wars than in fighting the devil and in leading the dissenters against the rules and regulations of the established church. Patrick Henry heard him frequently, from his eleventh to his twenty-second year, and it is believed that it was from "Parson" Davies that Henry received the inspiration for the development of his own matchless oratory.

In 1753 Mr. Davies and Gilbert Tennent were commissioned to go to Great Britain to raise money for the College of New Jersey, at Princeton, which had been in sore need of funds since its inception in 1747. They met with remarkable success, raising over £3,000 for the college. Davies was the fourth president of what is now Princeton University.

During his stay in the old country, Mr. Davies received many invitations to preach, and his fame as a pulpit orator became widespread. An incident occurred while he was in England which is revelatory of the character of the man.

King George II, hearing of Davies' eloquence, decided that he would go to hear this preacher from the wilds of America. The King had not listened long before he became amazed at the powers of this pulpit orator. With the rudeness which more or less characterized all of the Georges, the King made audible exclamations of surprise and commented in praise of passages from Mr. Davies' sermon in tones that could be heard half way across the auditorium.

Mr. Davies, observing that the King was diverting attention from his sermon, paused. Looking his Majesty full in the face, he gave him the following rebuke, in emphatic tones: "When the lion roareth, let the beasts of the forest tremble; and when the Lord speaketh, let the kings of the earth keep silence!" The King shrunk back in his seat and remained quiet during the remainder of the discourse. His Majesty was not offended. The next day he sent for Mr. Davies and gave him fifty guineas for his college.

Mr. Davies used to declare that every discourse of his which he thought worthy of the name of a sermon cost four days of hard study in the preparation. Often, when pressed to speak extemporaneously, he declined, with the following statement: "It is a dreadful thing to talk nonsense in the name of the Lord."

The career of Patrick Henry has been so fully described by the historians and his biographers that there is no need of here sketching his life. But the "Parsons' Cause," one of the most celebrated cases at law ever tried in America, was so intimately associated with

Hanover County that it may be briefly described. It was tried in the building pictured at the beginning of this chapter, and when Patrick Henry was importuned by the people to take their case, he was at the tavern which still stands just across the road, then run by his father-in-law, John Shelton. He was probably chopping wood, tending bar or doing other chores about the house. Until this time, Henry, a raw country specimen then twenty-seven, had been adjudged a failure in life.

It was in this case that Patrick Henry's amazing oratory first burst forth, and he leaped from obscurity to undying fame. The quarrel was between the clergy and the people. The clergy had rebelled against acts of the Burgesses which specified that they, along with other public officials, should be paid in tobacco at a fixed price, whereas tobacco had trebled in value. The case had been tried and the clergy had won. The acts of the Burgesses which applied had been declared void by the King. Nothing remained undetermined but the amount the clergymen could recover. The "Parsons' Cause" was a test case, watched with interest all over Virginia, in which the Rev. James Maury sought to obtain the difference in his salary at the rate fixed by legislation and at the market price of tobacco. John Lewis, attorney for the people, retired from the case. They called upon Henry.

The case was tried in Hanover Courthouse at the Fall term of 1763—thirteen years before the Declaration of Independence—and Henry defied the King in his speech, which has been referred to by many as the "opening gun of the Revolution." Patrick Henry's father, John Henry, was the presiding justice, and twenty prominent clergymen ranged themselves behind his chair smugly awaiting the slaughter. The place was packed. The Rev. Patrick Henry, the young orator's uncle, drove up in his buggy before the trial, and the younger Patrick Henry went out to him and asked him not to attend, for the clergyman's feelings might be hurt at what would be said. So the clergyman drove off and was not present when his nephew made his great speech.

The scene has been so graphically described by William Wirt, in his book published eighteen years after Henry's death, that it will not be amiss to quote his words:

"The array before Mr. Henry's eyes was now most fearful. On the bench sat more than twenty clergymen, the most learned men in the colony, and the most capable, as well as the severest critics before whom it was possible for him to have made his debut. The courthouse was crowded with an overwhelming multitude and surrounded with an immense and anxious throng, who, not finding room to enter, were endeavoring to listen without, in the deepest attention. But there was something still more awfully disconcerting than all this; for in the chair of the presiding magistrate sat no other person than his own father. Mr. [Peter] Lyons opened the case very briefly . . .; he then concluded with a highly-wrought eulogium on the benevolence of the clergy.

"And now came on the first trial of Patrick Henry's strength. No one had ever heard him speak, and curiosity was on tiptoe. He rose very awkwardly and faltered much in his exordium. The people hung their heads at so unpromising a commencement; the clergy were observed to exchange sly looks with each other; and his father is described as having almost sunk with confusion from his seat. But these feelings were of short duration, and soon gave place to others of a very different character. For now were those wonderful faculties which he possessed for the first time developed; and now was first witnessed that mysterious and almost supernatural transformation of appearance which the fire of his own eloquence never failed to work in him. For as his mind rolled along and began to glow from its own action, all the *exuviæ* of the clown seemed to shed themselves spontaneously. His attitude by degrees became erect and lofty.

"The spirit of his genius awakened all his features. His countenance shone with a nobleness and grandeur which it had never before exhibited. There was a lightning in his eyes which seemed to rivet the spectator. His action became graceful, bold and commanding; and in the tones of his voice, but more especially in his emphasis, there was a peculiar charm, a magic, of which anyone who ever heard him will speak as soon as he is named, but of which no one can give any adequate description. They can only say that it struck upon the ear and upon the heart in a manner which language can not tell. Add to all these his wonder-working fancy, and the peculiar phraseology in which he clothed its images; for he painted to the heart with a force that almost petrified it. In the language of those who heard him on this occasion, he made their blood run cold and their hair to rise on end.

"It will not be difficult for any one who ever heard this most extraordinary man to believe the whole account of this transaction which is given by his surviving hearers; and from their account, the courthouse of Hanover county must have exhibited, on this occasion, a scene as picturesque as has been ever witnessed in real life. They say that the people, whose countenances had fallen as he arose, had heard but a few sentences before they began to look up; then to look at each other with surprise, as if doubting the evidence of their own senses; then, attracted by some strong gesture, struck by some majestic attitude, fascinated by the spell of his eye, the charm of his emphasis, and the varied and commanding expression of his countenance, they could look away no more.

"In less than twenty minutes they might be seen in every part of the house, on every bench, in every window, stooping forward from their stands in death-like silence; their features fixed in amazement and awe, all their senses listening and riveted upon the speaker, as if to catch the last strain of some heavenly visitant. The mockery of the clergy was soon turned into alarm, their triumph into confusion and despair, and at one burst of his rapid and overwhelming invective, they fled from the bench in precipitation and terror. As for the father, such was his surprise, such his amazement, such his rapture, that forgetting where he was and the character which he was filling, tears of ecstasy streamed down his cheeks, without the power or inclination to repress them.

"The jury seem to have been so completely bewildered . . . that they had scarcely left the bar when they returned with a verdict of one penny damages. A motion was made for a new trial, but the court, too, had now lost the equipoise of their judgment, and overruled the motion by unanimous vote. The verdict and judgment overruling the motion were followed by redoubled acclamation from within and without the house. The people, who had with difficulty kept their hands off their champion from the moment of closing his harangue, no sooner saw the fate of the cause finally sealed than they siezed him at the bar, and, in spite of his own exertions and the continued cry of 'order!' from the sheriffs and the court, they bore him out of the courthouse, and, raising him upon their shoulders, carried him about the yard in a kind of electioneering triumph."

Patrick Henry was a son of John Henry and Sarah Winston, the widow Syme. He was born at Studley in 1736 and died at his Red Hill estate in Charlotte County in 1799. His was an illustrious career. He was first governor of the State of Virginia and served again as governor later. The esteem in which he was held may be illustrated in a negative way by a recital of the honors he declined.

He declined a seat in Congress, and when the Philadelphia constitutional convention met in that city in 1787 he refused to serve, feeling that the new federal constitution restricted the rights of the States. After its adoption and Washington was made President, Henry became reconciled. From 1794 until his death he declined the following honors in succession: United States Senator; Secretary of State in Washington's cabinet; Chief Justice of the United States; Governor of Virginia, offered him for the third time; and envoy to France.

Henry Clay (1777-1852) was born at Slash Cottage, or Clay Spring, a few miles southeast of the present town of Ashland, which was named for Clay's beautiful estate in Kentucky. On the southern outskirts of Ashland was Lankford's mill, where Clay, as a boy, was often seen astride a bag of corn on a horse or mule. He was often referred to as "the mill-boy of the slashes," but he became the leading citizen of America in his period. In 1797 he was admitted to the Richmond bar, but the following year moved to Lexington, Kentucky.

He served for many years in the United States Senate, his first appointment to an unexpired term when he was only twenty-nine years of age, contrary to the constitutional provision. He was Secretary of State in John Quincy Adams' cabinet. He was perhaps the most powerful advocate of the War of 1812 and at its conclusion was sent abroad to serve as one of the peace commissioners and signed the Treaty of Ghent. He was spoken of as "the great pacificator."

The 74th was the Hanover militia regiment in the War of 1812, commanded by Col. William Trueheart. Captains of companies were Nathaniel Bowe, Thomas Jones, Bentley Brown, William Hundley, Joseph F. Price, Charles Thompson, Jr., and Hudson M. Wingfield. The Fourth regiment had a troop of cavalry commanded by Captain James Underwood.

There were four companies of infantry and three of artillery in the War Between the States. The Patrick Henry Rifles, the Ashland Grays and the Hanover Grays later combined as Company G of the famous 15th Virginia Regiment, under Captain Williams C. Wickham, who was wounded, promoted to colonel and then brigadier-general. Another captain, William B. Newton, was killed, and its last captain, D. J. Timberlake, was twice wounded.

The Morris Artillery was first captained by Lewis Minor Coleman, promoted to lieutenant-colonel, who was mortally wounded at Fredericksburg, afterward by R. C. M. Page, of Albemarle, and Charles R. Montgomery.

The Hanover Artillery was under Captain William Nelson, promoted to colonel, and Captain G. W. Nelson, captured while on the staff of the chief of artillery. The Ashland Artillery was under Captain Pichegru Woolfolk. The names of Hanover's soldiers are inscribed on a handsome Confederate monument which stands on the court green.

The officers, above the rank of lieutenant, named on this monument, are as follows:

Brigadier-General Williams C. Wickham (wounded), Colonel D. C. Harrison (killed), Colonel G. W. Richardson, Colonel H. W. Wingfield, Colonel L. M. Coleman (killed), Lieut.-Colonel H. P. Jones, Lieut.-Colonel W. Nelson (wounded), Lieut.-Colonel W. B. Newton (killed), Lieut.-Colonel C. St. G. Noland, Lieut.-Colonel H. St. George Tucker (died in service), Major R. T. Ellett, Major J. B. Fontaine (killed), Major P. Fontaine (wounded), Major J. Page, Major

P. Sutton (wounded), Major L. F. Terrell (died in service), and Captains C. W. Dabney, T. S. Garnett, J. C. Govers (wounded), J. P. Harrison (died), C. R. Montgomery, G. W. Nelson, G. B. Swift, W. C. Talley, D. A. Timberlake (wounded), J. D. Waid, P. B. Winston and P. Woolfolk.

Both Colonel Lewis Minor Coleman and Colonel Hilary P. Jones were artillery officers of exceptional distinction.

Hanover's soil was literally drenched in blood in the War of the 60s. The famous Seven Days Battles of the McClellan campaign in 1862 were fought back and forth in Hanover and Henrico, the fiercest engagements in Hanover being Mechanicsville and Gaines' Mill, where Stonewall Jackson, after his remarkable Valley Campaign, joined in the conflict and McClellan's army was defeated.

Again, in 1864, Grant's march on Richmond was halted on Hanover soil in the Battle of Cold Harbor. Besides these great campaigns there were disastrous raids in the county by Kilpatrick, Stoneman and Sheridan. Early in the war Colonel John S. Mosby (then a private) was captured at Beaverdam, but was exchanged, and Lee's stores at that point were burned by Sheridan in 1864.

A large part of Stuart's famous ride around McClellan's army, its right flank extending almost to Hanover Courthouse, was in Hanover, and it was in Hanover that Captain William Latane, of Essex, was killed. His brother, Lieutenant John Latane, took the body to Summer Hill, the Page and Newton homestead, while a detachment of Federal troops stood by to place him under arrest as soon as his grim mission was over. The ladies and servants of Summer Hill tenderly laid the remains of Captain Latane to rest and the scene was re-enacted and portrayed by the eminent artist, W. D. Washington. Engravings of this famous picture, "The Burial of Latane," hang in many Virginia homes today.

Many were the clashes and many were the visitations of the armies of both North and South in Hanover, all of which are fully recorded in more formal histories.

COURTHOUSE IS HISTORIC

The courthouse was built in 1735, and there have been few alterations since its erection. It is one of the finest examples of the "arched form" of architecture, so popular with the builders of the early Colonial public structures. In comparatively recent years the authorities put concrete facings within the arches to preserve them, but the ladies of Hanover have prevailed upon the supervisors to have these removed.

The first clerk's office of which there is definite knowledge was at Buckeye, the home of William Pollard, who served as clerk from 1740 to 1781. It was about eight miles east of the courthouse. The road from Enon Church to Studley, which passes Buckeye, is still spoken of as the "old clerk's office road." This first of a long line of Pollard clerks took his books home with him each night. The present clerk's office was built sometime between 1780 and 1800.

Just across the road from the court green is Hanover Tavern, built about 1723. It formerly faced the other way. After the courthouse had been built and when a new road was constructed, foundations of a number of houses were found, indicating there was something of a settlement. The old road ran to the west of the tavern, and it is supposed that the courthouse was built on its present site because the tavern was there. This tavern was one of a string of prominent public houses along the old stage road from Richmond through Bowling Green to Fredericksburg. A large part of this old tavern is the original structure.

For many years there has been a plausible tradition that it was at this tavern that Col. John Chiswell killed Robert Routledge, an event which was a juicy piece of news in 1766, with considerable scandal attaching. Inasmuch as Col. Chiswell was a prominent citizen of Hanover and represented Hanover in the House of Burgesses for many years before he went to Williamsburg to live, it was not unnatural that it should have been conjectured, a century and a half later, that the event occurred at Hanover Tavern.

But the *Virginia Gazette* of July 3, 1766, printed a news story to the effect that "Col. John Chiswell killed Robert Routledge, a merchant of Prince Edward County, in Ben Mosby's tavern at Cumberland Courthouse." Col. Chiswell called Routledge a "refugee rebel, and a Presbyterian fellow." Chiswell was a man of great prominence, living in Williamsburg at the time, and a little later the *Gazette* printed a profuse apology for having reported the event in such a way as to have intimated that it was a murder rather than a duel.

At any event, Chiswell was arrested for murder, the

members of the court were censured for admitting him to bail, and while he was at liberty on bond died before coming to trial, the *Gazette of* October 17, 1766, reporting his death as follows: "On Wednesday last (15th) about 2 P. M. Col. John Chiswell died in Williamsburg after a short illness. The causes of his death, by the judgment of his physicians on oath, were nervous fits owing to a constant uneasiness in mind."

PORTRAITS ARE INTERESTING

On the walls of the courtroom are fifteen portraits and one tablet. Behind the judge's bench there are portraits of that great triumvirate, the Rev. Samuel Davies; Patrick Henry, bearing the simple inscription, "Give me Liberty or give me Death"; and Henry Clay.

The lives of the first three have been fully recorded by historians and biographers. Brief memoranda in regard to the careers of the others are as follows:

DR. HENRY ROSE CARTER (1852-1925), the great sanitarian and epidemiologist, was born at Clifton, in the edge of Caroline County. He took a civil engineering degree at the University of Virginia in 1873 and taught mathematics there for three years. He changed the direction of his career and was graduated from the University of Maryland in medicine in 1879 and entered the Marine Hospital Service. He early became a student of yellow fever and was the principal contributor in the eradication of that dread disease. He acted as special adviser to the Cuban and Peruvian governments and organized the quarantine system of the Panama Canal Zone. He rendered invaluable service in combatting malaria in the Southern States and was made assistant surgeon-general in 1915. At the instance of the International Health Board, he was well on the way to completion of his History of Yellow Fever when he died.

JUDGE SAMUEL CORNELIUS REDD was born at Jericho Mill on the North Anna River, in the edge of Caroline County, and in early childhood moved with his parents to Hybla, on the Little River in Hanover. He was a son of Samuel Redd and Cornelia McLaughlin Redd. He was a jurist of much ability and was noted for his incorruptible personal character. He served as judge of Hanover County for thirty-four years, until the county judicial system was abolished in 1904.

BRIGADIER-GENERAL WILLIAMS CARTER WICKHAM, regarded as one of the most stubborn fighters in the cavalry of the Confederacy, was born at Hickory Hill, now the home of his son, Henry T. Wickham. General Wickham participated in many daring exploits in the war which are fully recorded in formal history. After the war he returned to the practice of law and was influential in the State legislature. He was the first president of the Chesapeake and Ohio Railroad.

RICHARD HENRY CARDWELL entered the Confederate army at the age of sixteen. He was born in Rockingham County, N. C., in 1845 and moved to Hanover in 1869. He farmed and read law. In 1874 he started the practice of law. He was elected to the House of Delegates in 1881, serving until 1895. During eight of those years he was speaker. He was a member of the State debt commission which in 1892 settled the public debt of Virginia, and was chairman of the joint commission from the legislatures of Virginia and Maryland to settle the controversy over the boundary line between these two States. In 1894 he took his seat as a member of the Supreme Court of Appeals, serving with distinction until his retirement. He lived to be eighty-four.

JOHN ROBERT TAYLOR, a son of William G. and Eliza Marshall Taylor, of Taylorsville, served as clerk from 1865 to 1904 when the judicial system was changed. His son, Clarence W. Taylor, has served as clerk since 1907.

GEORGE PITMAN HAW (1838-1930) was a son of John and Mary Austin Watt Haw, and was born at Oak Grove, near Studley. He volunteered six days after the ordinance of secession in Company I, 15th Virginia Infantry and was later commissioned first lieutenant in the company of Captain James D. Waid. He was serving as captain at Sharpsburg in a fierce encounter in which only three of his company escaped unscathed when he was struck by a minnie ball in his left arm, which had to be amputated. He suffered untold agonies when his hospital unit fell into the hands of the Union troops, until he was found by a cousin in the Federal army, Captain O'Connor. He was later exchanged. He worked with his father in the manufacture of "Pecker" sawmills, a type all but forgotten now, and made money enough to send himself to Washington and Lee, receiving his law degree in 1867. He was commowealth's Attorney of Hanover County for over forty years and was a vigorous prosecutor. His office was in Richmond, and he appeared in many celebrated cases. He was particularly gifted as an orator.

THOMAS WHITE SYDNOR (1837-1901) of the old Sydnor family in Hanover was a first lieutenant of cavalry in the War Between the States.

JOHN ENOCH MASON (1854-1910) was born at Edge Hill, Albemarle County, and his mother was a great-granddaughter of Thomas Jefferson. He was admitted to the bar in 1878 and practiced in King George County. He served with distinction in both houses of the legislature and in 1898 was elevated to the bench. As judge of the circuit of which Hanover is a part, he was regarded as a jurist of much ability.

THOMAS NELSON PAGE (1853-1922) was one of the most widely-known and most beloved of all of Hanover's noted sons. He was born at Oakland and was a son of Major John Page and Elizabeth Burwell Nelson. Both his father and his mother were grandchildren of General Thomas Nelson, signer of the Declaration of Independence, governor of Virginia, and commander of the Virginia forces at the siege of Yorktown. Thomas Nelson Page studied at what was then Washington College, at Lexington, and took his law degree at the University of Virginia. He practiced in Richmond until 1903, when he gave up the law for a literary career. His first story, "Marse Chan," published in a Northern magazine, brought him immediate recognition. Through his many short stories and novels, filled with sentiment, he became the foremost interpreter of *ante-bellum* Virginia. In 1913 he was appointed Ambassador to Italy by President Woodrow Wilson and proved himself a diplomat of much ability in a trying period. His last notable literary work was his "Life of Dante."

HILL CARTER was recognized as one of the foremost lawyers of his time. He was born at Clifton, on the North Anna River in the edge of Caroline County. He was a son of Henry Rose and Emma Coleman Carter. He was commonwealth's attorney of Hanover at one time and was an influential member of the constitutional convention of 1901-2. He was noted for his joviality and his never-failing humor, had an immense practice, and was a formidable adversary in court.

ADMIRAL HILARY P. JONES, was born at Hanover Academy, in the upper end of the county, and was a son of the distinguished Confederate artillery officer, Colonel Hilary P. Jones. Admiral Jones, commanding the entire forces of the United States Navy, is perhaps the most distinguished of Hanover's living sons.

The single tablet on the wall of the courtroom at Hanover is to the memory of WILLIAM BROCKEN-BROUGH NEWTON. He was a captain, but was acting colonel when he was killed at Kelly's Ford while leading a desperate charge October 11, 1863.

RECORDS ARE DESTROYED

The county court records prior to 1865 were all destroyed in the evacuation of Richmond, with the exception of two books. They were regarded as so valuable that they were sent to the State Office Building for safe-keeping. Ironically, they would be safe if they had been left in the clerk's office at Hanover.

Six books of circuit court records from 1809 to 1860 were preserved. All the other will books, deed books and marriage bonds were destroyed.

A few excerpts from the two old record books may be of interest:

In 1733—Peter Marks was permitted to keep an ordinary at Hanover.

In 1734—Nicholas Meriwether conveyed to John Aylett, of King William County, 623 acres in St. Martin's Parish.

In 1735—Nicholas Meriwether conveyed to John Henry, of St. Paul's Parish, 1,110 acres, and Isaac Winston and John Henry qualified as administrators of Edward Willis, deceased.

Between 1784 and 1791 many lots in Hanover Town were conveyed from Mann Page, executor of Mann Page, deceased, of Spotsylvania County.

In 1785—John Hatley Norton conveyed to Richard Morris, of Louisa, 881 acres in the upper end of Hanover on Taylor's Creek, adjoining General Nelson, William Morris and others.

In 1790—William Pollard, Jr., of Hanover, named William Meriwether, of Louisa, his attorney in a suit for lands in Kentucky.

PRODUCED MANY NOTED MEN

So many men of note have gone from Hanover that it is difficult to accord them even casual mention in a work of such limited scope. It was nothing uncommon in the early years of the Colony for men of means to own properties in several counties, and in many cases men were born in one county but reared in another. As an instance of this, the two celebrated Carter brothers, Dr. Henry Rose Carter and Hill Carter, were born in Caroline, but the former was reared in Hanover and the latter spent his entire life in Hanover.

A few more noted men of Hanover, in addition to those already mentioned, may be referred to.

Colonel James Littlepage was born in Hanover in 1714 and died between 1765 and 1769. When Louisa was formed from Hanover in 1742, Littlepage was Louisa's first clerk, serving through a deputy. He was a member of the House of Burgesses from Hanover, and one of Patrick Henry's first efforts as a member was to appear for Nathaniel West Dandridge, who contested Littlepage's seat. Patrick Henry lost and Littlepage was seated. Among other properties of Littlepage sold in 1766 were 4,000 acres known as South Wales.

His son, General Lewis Littlepage (1762-1802) was one of the most colorful figures Hanover has produced. When John Jay was appointed Ambassador to Spain in 1779, Littlepage, then seventeen years of age, was to be a member of Jay's official household. He tarried in France and did not go to Spain until a little later. Littlepage, in the French service, participated in the campaigns against Mahon and Gibraltar. In the successful siege of Port Mahon, Littlepage was aide to the Duc de Crillon and was wounded. His ship was sunk in the unsuccessful siege of Gibraltar in 1782, and he was highly praised by the French king for his gallantry in that action. He became an intimate of Jefferson, Lafayette, Henry, John Paul Jones, Kosciusko and many of the other celebrated men of that period.

He became chamberlain of the King of Poland and saw much active service in the Polish army as a major-general, and also served on many delicate diplomatic missions to other courts of Europe, especially Russia. While on leave from Poland in Virginia he was entrusted by Governor Henry with money to pay the debt of Virginia for the Houdon statue of Washington which now stands in the State Capitol. Jay caused Littlepage's arrest for debts contracted abroad while Littlepage's affairs were in a tangle during the American Revolution, but he was released and the famous sculptor received his money.

His principal heir and executor was his half-brother Waller Holladay, of Louisa County.

Nathaniel West Dandridge was a Burgess for Hanover from 1758 to 1764, when he was defeated by Col. James Littlepage. Dandridge contested the election and was represented by Patrick Henry, whose second wife was his daughter. In this case, Henry made the second great speech of his career, but lost and Littlepage was seated. Nathaniel West Dandridge was a son of Col. William Dandridge, of Elsing Green, King William County, who married Unity West, granddaughter of Governor John West. Unity West Dandridge owned 4,832 acres in Hanover in 1753, and Nathaniel West Dandridge already had received 700 acres in Hanover at the death of his father in 1743. Nathaniel West Dandridge was born at Elsing Green in 1729 and died in Hanover in 1786. He was twice married. His first wife was Dorothea, the daughter of Governor Alexander Spotswood, and from this union came the second wife of Patrick Henry and the wife of Archer Payne, of Goochland. His second wife was Jane Pollard, daughter of Joseph Pollard, this second marriage taking place in 1779.

Dolly Payne Madison, the wife of President James Madison, lived at Scotchtown. She was a daughter of John Payne, who married Mary Coles and moved to North Carolina, later moving back to Virginia and acquiring Scotchtown. Dolly Madison was the widow Todd and had one son when Madison married her.

Burkwell Starke, of Hanover, was the first student to matriculate at the University of Virginia for the opening session 1825-26.

Judge Peter Lyons, while he was born in Ireland, came to Virginia about 1750 and was intimately associated with Hanover. He owned Studley and died there in 1809. He was attorney for the Rev. James Maury in the Parsons' Cause. In 1779 he was made member of the general court and thereby became an *ex-officio* judge of the first supreme court of appeals. In 1789 he was appointed a member of the new court of appeals, consisting of five judges, and became the second president of the court.

Richard Morris, of Taylor's Creek, represented his district in the famous convention of 1829-30, where his eloquence gave him rank with the other great men of that convention.

His son, Charles Morris, was born at Taylor's Creek in 1826. For many years he was commonwealth's attorney. In 1859 he was made professor of law at William and Mary, serving until the war. He held the rank of major and after the war opened a school in Hanover. He went to the University of Georgia as professor of English and in 1876 resigned to accept the chair of Greek at Randolph-Macon College.

Judge Richard Henderson (1734-1785) was born in Hanover. In 1762 he moved to North Carolina and in 1769 became a member of the superior court of that State. While thus serving he was assailed in his courtroom and forced from the bench by a mob enraged at the taxes enforced by Governor Tryon. He was one of five who ran the western boundary line between Virginia and North Carolina. He owned immense properties west of the Alleghanies. Resigning his seat on the bench after the Declaration of Independence, he headed the Transylvania Land Company, which had bought half of what is now the State of Kentucky from the Cherokee Indians, and tried to form an independent State. Henderson's company acquired the land between the Cumberland River, Cumberland Mountains and the Kentucky River, for which the Indians were paid £10,000. Henderson's plan for a new political division was defeated largely through the statesmanship of George Rogers Clark, who insisted upon the recognition of Kentucky as a Virginia county. Henderson was the employer of Daniel Boone. One of his sons, Archibald, was sent to Congress, and another, Leonard, became chief justice of North Carolina.

John Kilby, of Hanover, was a gunner under John Paul Jones, on the *Bon Homme Richard,* and John

Paul Jones, himself, spent about two years in Hanover near Turkey Creek, the home of Nathaniel West Dandridge, prior to the Revolution. Dorothea Spotswood Dandridge, who later became the second wife of Patrick Henry, is alleged to have been the object of the affections of the intrepid naval officer.

Samuel Meredith, brother-in-law of Patrick Henry, commanded a detachment from Hanover in Henry's march against Lord Dunmore.

Judge Spencer Roane (1762-1822) was born in Essex, a son of Col. William Roane and Elizabeth Ball Roane. He bought beautiful Spring Garden in Hanover from Meriwether Jones and lived there for many years. He later owned the home in Richmond at the northeast corner of Ninth and Leigh streets. His portraits hang in the Supreme Court and in the courtroom of King and Queen. Judge Roane studied law under Chancellor Wythe at William and Mary. He served in the House of Delegates and in 1794 was made a judge of the supreme court and was a staunch friend of Jefferson. He married Anne Henry, daughter of Patrick Henry in 1787.

William B. Giles, governor of Virginia and United States Senator, 1804 to 1815, and John Pryor, of the noted Southside family of that name, are believed to have moved to Amelia County from Hanover. Governor Giles' name has been so intimately associated with Amelia County that some of his biographers have assumed that he was born there.

John Carter Littlepage, son of Captain James Littlepage and brother of Gen. Lewis Littlepage, was a member of the Virginia convention of 1788 and was attorney-general of Virginia in 1792.

John Page of Page Brook (1760-1838) was born at Broad Neck, Hanover County, and shortly after the Revolution moved to Clarke County and built Page Brook. He was a son of Robert Page, and married a daughter of William Byrd III.

Thomas Sumter (1734-1832) for whom Fort Sumter was named, was born at French Hay, on the Tappahannock highway just north of the Chickahominy river. He served in the French and Indian Wars and was present at Braddock's defeat in 1755. He later moved to South Carolina. After the fall of Charleston in 1780 he escaped to North Carolina and took the field as a brigadier-general, serving with much distinction in a number of important battles. His vigilance and bravery earned him the sobriquet "gamecock." He died at South Mount, S. C.

Edmund Ruffin (1794-1865) who fired the first shot on Fort Sumter, while born in Prince George County, lived at Marlbourne in Hanover. He was buried at this place near the Tappahannock highway. He wrote extensively on agriculture and founded the *Farmers' Register* in 1833, serving as its editor for ten years. He was agricultural surveyor for South Carolina in 1842 and in 1843 became secretary of the State Board of Agriculture of Virginia. He was buried in Hanover wrapped in the folds of the Stars and Bars. An oil painting of him hangs in the reading room of the State Library.

William Overton Winston (1747-1815) eldest son of John and Alice Bickerton Winston, was a captain in the Hanover Militia 1779-1782, was referred to as major in 1785, and was sheriff of Hanover 1786-88. He was born at Woodberry.

Philip Bickerton Winston (1786-1853) son of William Overton Winston, was for many years clerk of the County. He lived first at Blenheim and later at Signal Hill, where he died. He married Sarah Madison Pendleton, of Louisa.

William Overton Winston (1812-1862) son of Philip Bickerton Winston, lived at Courtland and was clerk. He was a colonel of the Home Guards in Hanover in April, 1861.

Captain John Winston, a younger brother of the first William Overton Winston mentioned above, was a gallant officer in the Revolution and is referred to as being from both Hanover and Louisa. The indications are that he lived in Louisa, as did still another brother, Captain James Winston. Three sons of John and Alice Bickerton Winston, of Hanover, were captains in the Revolution.

Dr. George Hutcheson Denny, president of the University of Alabama and one of the most distinguished educators of the South, was born in the lower end of Hanover in 1870, son of a Presbyterian minister. He was an M. A. of Hampden-Sydney and a Ph. D. of the University of Virginia. He was president of Hampden-Sydney and of Washington and Lee University, going to Alabama to head the State university in 1912.

Henry Taylor Wickham, son of Gen. Williams C. Wickham, was born at Hickory Hill in 1849 and has had a long, distinguished career. He was a student at what is now Washington and Lee University when General Robert E. Lee was there after the war. For over sixty years he served the law department of the Chesapeake and Ohio Railway, becoming vice-president and general counsel of the road. First going to the House of Delegates as a "debt payer," he was elected to the State Senate in 1888 and for nearly fifty years has been an outstanding member of that body.

Mention should be made of another living Hanover man of note, Rosewell Page, brother of Thomas Nelson Page. Rosewell Page, present owner of the old Nelson and Page estate, Oakland, for many years practiced law in Richmond and served in the legislature. He was second auditor of Virginia until that office was abolished and is an author of note.

Francis Johnson Duke was born in the County in 1842 and spent practically all of his life in the service of the Richmond, Fredericksburg and Potomac Railroad and became its treasurer. He was in the telegraph service of the Confederacy and was taken prisoner and confined at Point Lookout, where he remained until the close of the war.

MANY OLD HOMESTEADS

There were dozens of old homesteads in Hanover where were nurtured the ancestors of countless men and women of worth of today. Studley was where Patrick Henry was born, and Scotchtown was where he lived after his return from Louisa and prior to his removal to Charlotte County. Scotchtown also was the home of Dorothea Payne, who became the wife of

President James Madison. Clay Spring was the birthplace of Henry Clay. Taylor's Creek was the home of Richard Morris. Hickory Hill was and is the home of the Wickhams. Oakland, built by the Nelsons, was the home of Thomas Nelson Page, and North River was the home of Dr. Henry Rose Carter.

Rural Plains, erected in 1670, the oldest home in the county, was built by the Sheltons, who still own it. It was here that Patrick Henry wooed and won his first wife, and in that house today are the swords of officers who fought in every war in which the American people have engaged, from the French and Indian Wars to the War Between the States.

Among the many old places and their early owners were Clover Lea, Bassett and Haw; Airwell, Berkeley and Noland; Beaverdam, Fontaine; Bear Island, Gwathmey; Dewberry, Cooke, White and Dixon; Courtland, Winston; Dundee, Price and Haw; Sligo, Redd; South Wales, Littlepage, Carter and Winston; Totomoi, Tinsley; Turkey Creek, Dandridge; Belmont, Taylor; Blenheim, Winston; Broad Neck, Page and Carter, now the Virginia Manual Training School; Buckeye, Pollard; Cabin Hill, Carter; Taylor's Creek, Morris; Bullfield, Nelson and Doswell; Canterbury, Meredith; Broom Field, Berkeley; Chantilly, Coleman; Hybla, Anderson and Redd; Janeway, Cooke and Hunter; Ingleside, Braxton; Laurel Spring, Trueheart and Ellerson; Hanover Academy, Coleman and Jones, home of Admiral Hilary P. Jones; Montpelier, Morris and Jones; Summer Hill, Page and Newton (where Latane was buried); Hanover Town, Page; Noel, Landram; Verdon, Anderson; Newcastle,

Braxton and Broaddus; Prospect Hill, Cardwell;
Plain Dealing, Thomas and Parkinson; Cedar Grove,
Newman; Cedar Hill, Garnett; Churchland and
Clazemont, Morris; Scotchtown, Henry, Cary and
Dandridge; Signal Hill, Winston; Taylorsville, Tay-
lor; Clay Spring, where Henry Clay was born; Rural
Plains, Shelton; and Studley, where Patrick Henry
was born, its early owners being in turn Syme, Henry
and Lyons.

King and Queen County

KING AND QUEEN COURTHOUSE

King and Queen County

F IT be inaccurate to refer to King and Queen County as the cradle of religious liberty in Virginia it can nevertheless be said that the County constituted a large part of the nursery. While many stirring events occurred on its soil and many eminent men were nurtured within its boundaries, perhaps the most significant thing about the history of the County has been the piety of its citizens and their influence in matters religious.

King and Queen County was formed in 1691 from New Kent and was named for King William and Queen Mary of England. The act of the General Assembly creating the County set forth that "Whereas sundry and divers inconveniences attend the inhabitants of New Kent County and all others who have occasion to prosecute suites there, by reason of the difficulty in passing the river," it was enacted that New Kent be divided into two distinct counties, so that Pomunkey River shall divide the same, and so down York River to the extent of the county, and the part which is now on the south side of the Yorke and Pamunkey Rivers be called New Kent, and that on the north side with Pomunkey Neck be called and known by the name of King and Queen County."

Despite the inconvenience of crossing the river, those living in what is now King and Queen continued using the old courthouse of King William until that county was cut off from King and Queen by act of 1701. The original county embraced King William, Caroline and a large part of Spotsylvania. It is probable that there was hardly a white person in King and Queen prior to 1644, for in 1648 a "Grand Assembly" repealed an act which had made it a felony to go north of the York River and settle. The Charles River (York) had obviously been the dividing line in a treaty with the Indians, and it will be recalled that it was in 1644 that Opechancanough was captured and the power of the Indians was broken after their uprising in that year.

At Piscataway the northern forces of Nathaniel Bacon assembled and an engagement was fought with forces of Governor Berkeley July 10, 1676. A number of men were killed and wounded and several houses were burned. The Rebels passed on to the Pamunkey and were there joined by their leader, Bacon.

Of half a dozen colonial meetinghouses of the Church of England, not one of them is now in use by the Episcopal church, and the intoned words of the Book of Common Prayer have given way to rousing revivals. While the persecutions of the dissenters in all parts of Virginia were mild as compared to those of some other localities, dissenting preachers were often imprisoned, fined or made to give bond for preaching their doctrines without permission. There is a record that in 1772 James Greenwood and John Lovall, who were Baptists, conducted a meeting, probably under a tree—near where Bruington church now stands, and each was arrested and imprisoned for sixteen days.

The unpopularity of the Church of England was particularly pronounced in the two or three decades immediately preceding the Revolution. It was associated with royal authority. People did not like to be required to attend worship. More particularly, they rebelled against paying taxes for the support of a church not of their choosing. Patrick Henry's victory in the "Parsons' Cause" at Hanover in 1763 was a severe blow to the Church of England.

Passage of the Bill of Rights in 1776 also hurt the Episcopal cause immensely, and then came the long but persistent fight for Jefferson's bill for complete religious freedom, the measure seriously affecting all church buildings and the glebes, which the dissenting denominations contended they had helped pay for. So it was not until 1802 that the General Assembly passed an act for the sale of the glebes, the proceeds going largely to charity. Many of the stately old churches then stood idle for years, most of them which had not gone to decay finally coming into possession of other denominations than the Protestant Episcopal.

A notable example of the transition from the colonial to the modern in church affairs lies in the story of Mattapony church. There is no documentary evidence as to when the original building was erected, but there are tombstones in the churchyard dated as early as 1708. In colonial times it was known as Brick Church, or the Lower Church of St. Stephen's Parish. The tomb of George Braxton, father of the signer of the Declaration of Independence, is here.

The building was little used after the Revolution and finally was entirely deserted and remained so for fifty years. In 1824 the Baptists began using it and twelve years later it became their property by a grant from the Governor of Virginia. The Baptists changed its name to Mattapony church, and thus they spelled it. The Rev. William Todd was its first Baptist pastor and continued his ministry for twenty-seven years. He was among many notable Baptist ministers who were identified with King and Queen County. The Rev. Robert Semple and the Rev. Andrew Broaddus were others. The massive font of the ancient church is now in use at Fork church in Hanover.

Perhaps the oldest institution of learning in the County was the school established in 1763 on the river about ten miles above Dunkirk by Donald Robertson, a Scotchman. James Madison came over from the Northern Neck and attended this school and later in his career said: "All that I have been in life I owe largely to that man." It is also probable that George Rogers Clark was one of his pupils, for Clark spent his boyhood in that vicinity, and the schoolmaster married Clark's aunt.

In 1839 another Scotchman, Oliver White, established an academy at Fleetwood, six miles above Bruington church. About the same year Col. John Pollard and John Bagby opened a school at Stevensville, with Major James G. White as headmaster. At Bruington Capt. Thomas Haynes opened an academy of which Judge J. H. C. Jones was principal. At Newtown a school was conducted about 1850 by Lewis Kidd, later by Spencer Coleman, and the female seminary conducted at Locust Cottage by the Southgates was famous. Aberdeen Academy was operated by Col. J. C. Council.

The Mattaponi river was a great avenue of traffic in the early years and there was much social intercourse between the old families on the King and Queen side and the residents in the colonial mansions across on the King William side. There were prominent public tobacco warehouses at Todds, at Mantapike, and at Shepherd's as early as 1730, and Dunkirk was once a center of much trade. Many vessels have sailed out of the Mattaponi river bound for England.

It is unfortunate that so little is known of the early history of King and Queen, but all of the records of the County were destroyed by fire in 1864. Records of the early members of the committee of safety, members of the Burgesses and other officials are preserved, but sources of information about intimate details of the colonial history of the County are fragmentary.

The following men were sworn in as members of the King's Council in the years set opposite their names: Richard Johnson, 1696; Richard Corbin of Laneville, 1750; William Robinson, 1751; and Gawin Corbin in 1775.

Members of the House of Burgesses who represented King and Queen were: 1692-93, Captain William Leigh, Captain John Lane; 1696-97, William Leigh, Joshua Storey, who was made sheriff; 1700, William Leigh; 1702, William Leigh, James Taylor; 1703, William Leigh; 1704, William Bird; 1706, Robert Beverley; 1711, John Holloway; 1714, John Holloway, William Bird; 1718, John Baylor, George Braxton;

1720-26, Richard Johnson, George Braxton; and 1727, George Braxton.

In 1736 John Robinson was sent to the House of Burgesses and remained continuously until 1766, when he died in office. Serving with him during this thirty-year period were: 1736-40, Gawin Corbin; 1742-49, George Braxton; 1752-58, Philip Johnson; 1758-61, George Braxton; 1762-65, John Pendleton; 1765, George Brooke.

From 1766 to 1768 the Burgesses were George Brooke and Richard Tunstall; 1769-71 William Lyne, John Tayloe Corbin; 1772-74, George Brooke, John Tayloe Corbin; and in 1775, George Brooke and George Lyne.

In all three of the conventions of 1775 the representatives were George Brooke and George Lyne, and in the convention of 1776 they were George Brooke and William Lyne.

It is known that General John Young, quartermaster-general under Washington, lived near Walkerton and died a bachelor. Col. Richard Corbin, of Laneville, was a man of great wealth and influence. There is a tradition in the county that he was a Royalist and hid many of the colonial archives in a cellar at Laneville, and it is recited that he was probably the man whom Patrick Henry sought with a company of soldiers as treasurer when Henry finally made Lord Dunmore pay for the powder stolen from the powder horn.

George Braxton was an outstanding citizen and was a member of the House of Burgesses for many years before his son, Carter Braxton, came into prominence.

Dr. Thomas Walker, who was born in King and Queen in 1715, and moved to Albemarle, was one of the first to traverse the mountains into Kentucky and was present at Braddock's defeat in 1755.

Colonel George Brooke was for many years a member of the Burgesses. He was a member of the Committee of Safety, of the Virginia conventions of 1775-6, and was a colonel in the Revolutionary army. Robert Brooke, his uncle, was a Knight of the Golden Horseshoe. Col. William Campbell was a captain in the Revolution and raised a quota of King and Queen men who joined the First Virginia Regiment. After the war he was commissioned major in the regular army and assigned to command the arsenal at Harper's Ferry. Thomas R. Dew, the elder, served for a short time in the Revolution and was a captain in the War of 1812.

Robert Beverley, Knight of the Golden Horseshoe, who was a son of Major Robert Beverley, of Middlesex, was clerk of the council in 1697 and clerk of King and Queen County from 1699 to 1702. For a number of years he was a member of the House of Burgesses as the representative of Jamestown, and was a Burgess from King and Queen in 1706. He was presiding justice in King and Queen in 1718. Robert Beverley married Ursula, a daughter of William Byrd, of Westover, and was the author of an excellent history of Virginia.

Judge Thomas Todd, born in the County, served in the Revolution and was a graduate of Liberty Hall, now Washington and Lee University. He went to Kentucky in 1784 and practiced law at Danville. He held many judicial honors in Kentucky and became a member of the United States Supreme Court in 1807. He died at Frankfort in 1826.

Among the presiding justices from 1830 to 1860 were John Lumpkin, Alexander' Fleet, Thomas Haynes, John R. Bagby, Samuel Tunstall, Robert Courtney, Robert Bland, Robert Spencer and John Pollard. As was the case prior to the Revolution, the justices for many years thereafter occupied positions of great dignity and responsibility.

John Robinson had the unique record of serving in the House of Burgesses for thirty consecutive years, from 1736 to 1766. Twenty-eight of those years he served as speaker and he was treasurer of the Colony.

The career of Carter Braxton is sketched in the chapter on King William, for it was there that he lived during most of his career.

Names of officers from the County in the War of 1812 are preserved as follows: 4th Regiment, Virginia Militia, Col. Elliot Muse; Captain John Bagby; first lieutenant, John Gill; second lieutenant, George Hill; third lieutenant, Whit Campbell.

9th Regiment, Colonel William Boyd, Surgeons John Hoskins and M. G. Fauntleroy.

9th Regiment, Artillery, Colonel William Boyd; captain, T. C. Holmes; lieutenants, A. R. Harwood and James Gresham.

Names of county judges prior to the War Between the States are available as follows: 1831, William Browne; 1835, A. P. Upshur; November, 1835, John B. Christian; 1852, John Tayloe Lomax; 1857, Richard H. Coleman.

Nathaniel Bacon was often in the county during Bacon's Rebellion in 1676, and the British raided the county during the Revolution. Hillsboro, the Hill homestead, suffered from their depredations.

Due largely to the fact that the rivers intervened between King and Queen and Richmond, the county escaped major engagements in the War Between the States, but there were a number of raids which were disastrous. The county was hard hit by the loss and maiming of a large number of its young men, but these casualties occurred in the main away from home. King and Queen soldiers played conspicuous parts at Seven Pines and at Petersburg and took part in practically all of the battles of the Army of Northern Virginia.

The home guard of King and Queen had plenty of *esprit de corps* and took part in some thrilling adventures. The first sally into the county by the Federals was a small affair, but worth recording. Major J. R. Bagby, home on leave, had come into the River Road near Mantua Ferry. There a Mathews citizen named Holder Hudgins, with a wagon load of provisions on the way to Richmond, was halted by a squad of Union cavalry. The major remonstrated against the arrest of private citizens. Without disclosing the fact that he was a Confederate officer, he passed on but paused to await developments. Two Union soldiers approached at a rapid rate and, refusing to halt, the major fired, killing one of them, and the rest of the squad was captured by the home guard.

A squad of Union cavalry came up from Gloucester Point on July 8, 1862, and camped at King and Queen

Courthouse. Their object was to break up boats and prevent crossing the river on the road to Richmond. The story of an encounter next day at Walkerton is recorded in the diary of Dr. B. H. Walker.

The following is from Dr. Walker's diary:

"So soon as we learned that the Yankees were coming up the road towards Walkerton, Major Bagby and I arranged a plan to capture them. I was to go the Ridge Road by Butler's Tavern, gather all the men I could, and make for Walkerton. When I reached that village I found several of the home guard and others, including Mordecai Cook, a youth, eight in all. In half an hour a Yankee lieutenant with five men rode up, inquired for the ferryboat; but the ferryboat had been hastily taken down the river. Presently the lieutenant walked into the store. My gun was lying on the counter. He and I scuffled over the gun. William Turner shot him with a pistol, but he ran out into the yard and Alfred Gwathmey shot him with buckshot. A fusillade began between us and the remaining four men. One man was shot from his horse and another from behind a tree by Mordecai and killed. The rest were scattered. I then agreed to go up to Richmond and post the authorities about conditions in our county. Colonel Goode at White House was ordered by General Lee, through myself, to send soldiers to our aid. Before he could do so, the enemy had retired to Gloucester Point."

Kilpatrick, commanding a body of cavalry, came into the county May 5, 1863, and camped in a field at Stevensville. He sent word to Mrs. John N. Gresham at Locust Cottage, nearby, that he and his aides would take tea with her. She prepared for them, and the company sat down. As she poured the tea, she remarked:

"Did I ever think it would come to this, that I should pour tea for Yankee soldiers, come to waste and destroy!"

Kilpatrick, not at all disconcerted, replied:

"Never mind, madam, we have only come to seek and to save that which was lost."

The cavalrymen were courteous and did no special damage except that a number of horses were taken, and next morning they left. Stragglers, however, not under the eyes of their officers, were very offensive. Old citizens, notably Samuel P. Ryland and James Robert Fleet, were unhorsed, robbed and beaten.

Perhaps the most stirring event in which the King and Queen home guards participated was the slaying of Colonel Ulric Dahlgren and the capture of his force, which had wandered into the county through Hanover and King William, crossing the river at Aylett. After an unsuccessful raid upon Richmond, they were trying to make their way to Gloucester Point. This occurred on the night of March 2, 1864, at what is still known as "Dahlgren's Corner," on the River Road about half-way between Walkerton and the Courthouse.

The home guards mustered, and as soon as it was learned that Dahlgren had crossed the river they attacked his rear not far from Bruington. A detachment of the home guard under Captain Edward Campbell Fox, who was at home on leave, moved ahead and stationed themselves at the junction of the road from Stevensville and the River Road. This force was small, composed of old men and boys, and soldiers home on furlough or on recruiting duty. Dr. Bernard H. Walker, who played a conspicuous part, was at home on leave.

The home guards waited, and it was not until midnight that the Union troops arrived. Seeing that his path was blocked, Dahlgren demanded surrender and fired his pistol. The reply was a volley from the home guards, and Dahlgren fell, pierced by five bullets. His forces retreated into the fields and marshes and were located by Christopher B. Fleet and A. C. Acree. All surrendered except the officers, who were captured afterward by Captain R. H. Bagby, who commanded the home guards of King and Queen.

A grave was dug for Colonel Dahlgren and he was about to be lowered into it when word came to send the body to Richmond. It was buried in Oakwood cemetery, thence it was removed through the agency of Miss Van Lew, the noted Union spy in Richmond, and buried at Laurel. After the surrender it again was dug up and returned to his father, Admiral John Adolph Dahlgren, of the U. S. Navy.

Dahlgren's death was soon avenged, for on March 10th, Kilpatrick, at the head of a large cavalry force, came to King and Queen Courthouse from Gloucester Point. Under the direction of Colonel Spears, of the 11th Regiment, Pennsylvania, the courthouse, clerk's office, hotel and practically all other buildings in the village were burned to the ground.

Part of Burnside's corps passed through the upper part of the county in May, 1864, and later General Phillip Sheridan, returning from the Battle of Trevilians, Louisa County, camped at the Courthouse, but shortly left and joined General Grant on the Chickahominy. The depredations of Sheridan's men were unbearable. They burned Walkerton Mill and otherwise inflicted much damage. Sheridan encamped again later at Farmington.

King and Queen sent an unusual number of valiant

sons into the maelstrom of the War Between the States
and the rosters of the numerous companies are carefully preserved. Officers are recorded as follows:

The 26th Virginia Regiment was commanded by
Colonel Powell Page; lieutenant-colonel, J. C. Council; majors, Joseph Garrett and N. B. Street.

Company C, 26th Virginia (Wise's Brigade) : Captain, N. B. Street; first lieutenant, James R. Houser;
second lieutenants, John W. Hundley and James R.
Hart.

Company G, 26th Virginia: Captain, R. H. Spencer, captured at Petersburg in '64; first lieutenant, R.
B. Roy, captured at Hatcher's Run in '65; second
lieutenant, M. B. Davis, wounded and captured at
Petersburg in '64 and killed at Hatcher's Run; third
lieutenant, A. P. Bird (wounded and died at home.)

Company H, 26th Virginia: Captain, R. A. Sutton;
first lieutenant, J. D. Taylor; second lieutenant, W. C.
Gayle; third lieutenant, G. P. Lively.

Company I, 26th Virginia: Captain, J. W. Smith;
first lieutenant, S. P. Latane; second lieutenant, A. C.
Walker; third lieutenant, A. F. Fleet.

The 34th Virginia Regiment was commanded by
Colonel T. F. Goode. Its lieutenant-colonel was ——
Harrison, and J. R. Bagby was its major.

Company K, 34th Virginia: Captain, A. F. Bagby,
wounded on retreat from Petersburg; first lieutenant,
J. Ryland, wounded June 17, 1864, at Petersburg, captured October 28, 1864; second lieutenant, William T.
Haynes, discharged in 1865 to join Mosby; third lieutenant, B. H. Walker, killed December 18, 1864.

Company E, 5th Virginia Cavalry, had the following officers: Captains: Marius P. Todd, Campbell Fox, Richard Hoard, William C. Nunn; lieutenants, W. C. Nunn, W. S. Dicks, William Hoskins, William P. Bohanan and Robert B. Hart.

Bagby's Company, 4th Artillery, serving as heavy artillery, was a part of the command of Colonel C. A. Crump, under Major-General John B. Magruder, at one time. This company, under the command of Captain John R. Bagby (afterward major) saw valiant service at Seven Pines. It was first known as the King and Queen Artillery and was organized in May 1861 with John R. Bagby as captain; Josiah Ryland, Jr., first lieutenant; A. F. Bagby, second lieutenant; and Josiah Ryland, Sr., third lieutenant.

There is not a mile of railroad in the county and until very recent years the people of King and Queen were isolated by poor roads and the lack of bridges across the rivers. They have preserved their ancient piety and clung to the customs of their forefathers. There is hardly a county in Virginia where the life of *ante-bellum* days is to a greater degree typified, and it would be hard to find a section anywhere in which hospitality is more open-handed.

Court Buildings Burned

The courthouse of King and Queen, pictured in the accompanying illustration, was built after the War Between the States. On March 10, 1864, both the courthouse and clerk's office were burned to the ground by Union troops. Every single county record was destroyed, with the exception of four land books. However, copies of the land books of all counties were sent to Richmond and are carefully preserved.

Apparently the courthouse has always occupied the same plot of ground on which the present building stands, for at a very early date one acre of land for a courthouse was conveyed to the county by Edmund Tunstall. From the formation of the county until 1701 the present courthouse of King William was used.

While the county records were destroyed, a number of old papers were found at Newington which have proven of much value.

FIFTY-FOUR PORTRAITS ON WALLS

On the walls of the courtroom of King and Queen hang fifty-four portraits, and there are two tablets. Brief mention of the subjects of these memorials may be made as follows:

JUDGE J. H. C. JONES, of Bruington, was a prominent lawyer and was judge of the county court. He was the father of Judge Claggett B. Jones. He was president of the Baptist General Association of Virginia.

JUDGE J. M. JEFFRIES lived at Cumnor and was a circuit court judge.

JUDGE J. D. FOSTER was county judge after the war.

MAJOR NAPOLEON B. STREET was from a large family living on both sides of the Piankatank in King and Queen and Essex. His father, Walker Street, lived about six miles below Carlton's Store. Major Street was a gallant officer in the Confederate army and was for many years a respected supervisor of the county.

MAJOR J. R. BAGBY (1826-1890) a son of John Bagby, was a colonel of militia prior to the War of the 60s and at the outbreak of the conflict raised a company known as the King and Queen Artillery, which saw valiant service. He was made major in 1862 and played a conspicuous part in the battle of Seven Pines, where he had a horse killed under him. He was wounded near Petersburg in 1865 and was for many months incapacitated as a result of that wound.

DR. ROBERT BAYLOR SEMPLE (1769-1831) was the first pastor of the Bruington congregation, and one of the most celebrated of the early Baptist ministers of Virginia, serving from 1791, when they built their first house of worship, until his death. He was buried in the churchyard. He received Doctor of Divinity degrees from Brown University and from William and Mary College.

REV. WILLIAM TODD was a member of the prominent Todd family of Toddsbury in Gloucester. The first of the Todds in King and Queen, William, owned large properties near Dunkirk overlooking the Mattaponi river. The Rev. William Todd was the first Baptist pastor of Mattapony church, which in colonial times was the lower church of St. Stephen's Parish, being taken over by the Baptists in 1824. He was its pastor for twenty-seven years and also preached at Bruington.

JOHN ROBINSON, known as "Speaker Robinson," was for twenty-eight years speaker of the House of Burgesses and was treasurer of the colony. He lived at Pleasant Hill, although he was born at Hewick in Middlesex County.

CARTER BRAXTON, sketched in the chapter on King William.

COL. JOHN POLLARD (1803-1877) was a lieutenant-colonel of Virginia militia, prominent lawyer, and commissioner of the revenue.

COL. SMITH ACREE was a prominent merchant of Walkerton.

COL. ALEXANDER DUDLEY might be called the father of the Richmond and York River railroad, for he conceived the idea, sold the stock, built the road and served as its first president.

COL. ROBERT BLAND was born in 1800, a son of Captain Robert Bland, who served in the War of 1812. He was a colonel of militia, presiding justice of the court and was an extensive farmer.

COL. RODERICK BLAND was a large landowner in the county.

CAPT. ROBERT COURTNEY was a soldier of the War of 1812 and was for many years one of the justices.

THOMAS GARNETT was the progenitor of the Garnett family in King and Queen.

DR. JOHN MUSCOE GARNETT, a beloved physician, lived at Lanefield.

JUDGE T. R. B. WRIGHT, of Essex, was circuit judge.

JUDGE THOMAS RUFFIN was born at Newington in 1787. He studied at Princeton and first practised law in Petersburg, where he was associated with Winfield Scott, the future general. He moved to Rockingham County, N. C., and opened a law office in 1808. He became speaker of the North Carolina house and had a large law clientele. In 1825 he was appointed a judge of the Superior Court; in 1829 he was elected a judge of the Supreme Court, and in 1833 arose to the position of Chief Justice. He died in 1870 and was buried at Hillsboro, N. C.

JUDGE SPENCER ROANE is sketched in the chapter on Hanover.

WILLIAM H. ROANE was a son of Chief Justice Spencer Roane and his mother was Anna, the daughter of Patrick Henry. William H. Roane served his State in the U. S. Senate.

J. R. F. VAUGHAN was treasurer of the County for thirty years.

CAPT. ARCHIBALD ROANE HARWOOD, of Newington, was born in 1786 and served in the War of 1812 as a captain of militia. Later he served in both the House of Delegates and the Virginia Senate. He was nominated for Congress but was defeated by a small majority in 1837 by R. M. T. Hunter. He died in 1837.

WALTER GRESHAM, generally known as Watt Gresham, was a well-known citizen of the County.

DR. RICHARD H. COX was a noted physician at Centreville, later moving to West Point. He represented the County in the legislature and was a member of the Virginia Convention of 1861.

DR. WILLIAM HOSKINS was a surgeon in the Confederate Army.

BENJAMIN F. DEW, son of Professor Thomas R. Dew, was a graduate of William and Mary and a prominent lawyer, farmer and teacher. He was the father of Judge John G. Dew.

[140]

DR. JOHN N. GRESHAM was a member of the old Gresham family who lived near Upper King and Queen Church.

THOMAS GRESHAM, another member of the same family, was a lawyer of distinction in Essex.

THOMAS RODERICK DEW (1802-1846), college president and author, was one of King and Queen's most distinguished sons. He was a son of Thomas R. Dew, a large land and slave owner in the county, who served for a short time in the Revolution and was a captain in the War of 1812. Professor Dew was graduated from William and Mary in 1820, after which he continued his studies abroad. In 1826 he accepted the chair of History and Political Law at William and Mary College and had much to do with the establishment of history as a major course in American colleges. In 1836 he became president of William and Mary College, serving until his death. He died in Paris, France.

REV. ANDREW BROADDUS, a celebrated Baptist divine, was pastor of Upper King and Queen church for forty years, and it was during his ministry, in 1860, that the well-constructed brick place of worship was erected.

DR. ROBERT RYLAND, a noted minister and educator of the County, was a son of Josiah Ryland, for sixty-five years a deacon in Bruington church, and Catherine Peachy. He was born in 1805 and lived to be ninety-three. For thirty-four years he was president of leading Baptist institutions of learning, first of the Virginia Baptist Seminary and then of Richmond College, which later developed into the University of Richmond. The early growth of Richmond College was largely attributed to his able administration.

DR. SAMUEL GRIFFIN FAUNTLEROY, JR., was a decandant of one of three Fauntleroy brothers who owned a large part of the Northern Neck in the early days. They were Huguenots and had to leave France because of persecution. One of them, Samuel Griffin, settled in King and Queen, at Farmers' Mount.

SAMUEL TUNSTALL was one of the justices.

JAMES PARKE CORBIN was from the wealthy family of that name whose colonial seat was Laneville. James Parke Corbin, a prominent citizen of the county, was the last owner of Laneville before it passed into the hands of the Blands.

COL. ROBERT SPENCER was one of the justices.

ALEXANDER FLEET was a justice and Virginia legislator. He was descended from a proud old King and Queen County family, the first of the name, William, having been a member of the House of Burgesses in 1652. This family claims direct descent from Charlemagne and from several of the English kings after William I.

WILLIAM BOULWARE, who was born about a mile above Newton, served as U. S. Minister to Naples during the administration of President James K. Polk.

CAPT. EDWARD CAMPBELL FOX commanded Company E, 5th Virginia Cavalry. He was in command at Dahlgren's Corner and was killed in the battle of Yellow Tavern.

JAMES SOUTHGATE lived at Locust Cottage, where the Southgates conducted a noted school.

COL. WILLIAM B. DAVIS was a prominent citizen of the county who lived at Millers.

ROBERT HUTCHINSON represented his county in the legislature.

DAVID P. WRIGHT was one of the justices.

JUDGE JOHN G. DEW, able jurist and life-long resident of King and Queen, was a graduate of the University of Virginia and was of the old family in the upper end of the county who owned large acreage in the early years. He was a grandson of Thomas R. Dew, regarded as a man of great wealth, and was a nephew of Professor Thomas R. Dew, the younger, who was president of William and Mary College. He was county judge for sixteen years and Second Auditor of Virginia.

SPOTSWOOD WILFRED CORBIN, a useful citizen, was of the Corbin family who settled in the parish of Stratton Major about 1650.

HENRY R. POLLARD was one of the most highly respected men King and Queen has produced in more recent years. A lawyer of outstanding ability and a man of delightful manners and high Christian character, "Speaker" Pollard, as he was often called, was city attorney of Richmond over a long period of years.

CAPT. R. H. SPENCER commanded Company G, 26th Virginia Infantry, and rendered valiant service in the war. He was captured at Petersburg in 1864. After the war he proved to be a man of unusually keen intellect, was highly respected and was a supervisor.

WILLIAM LYNE WILSON was a grandson of William Lyne III, was Postmaster General in the cabinet of Cleveland and president of Washington and Lee University.

JUDGE JAMES WILLIAM FLEET was for many years commonwealth's attorney and county judge.

HENRY CORBIN, of Stratton, was the immigrant of that family and died in 1680.

C. W. PORTER was a man of wide personal popularity and served as county treasurer for many years.

ROBERT POLLARD served as clerk for thirty-five years.

ROBERT POLLARD, JR., was clerk for forty-one years.

In addition to all these portraits, there are two tablets of unusual interest. The first of these is a marble slab bearing the following inscription.

Christopher Harwood, died 1774.

His son, Capt. William Harwood (1734-1773) married Priscilla Pendleton.

His son, Major Christopher Harwood (1786-1837) married Martha Fauntleroy, of Holly Hill. War of 1812. Senate of Virginia.

His sons, Samuel Fauntleroy Harwood, of Newington, born 1817, married Betty Brockenbrough. Senate of Virginia. Vestryman. Major Thomas M. Harwood, of Newington, born 1827, died at Gonzales, Texas, 1900. Married Cornelia Brown. Willis' Battalion, Waul's Texas Legion, C. S. A. Special judge Supreme Court of Texas 1886. Regent University of Texas 1882-1895. Ruling Elder 1877-1900.

* * *

Just back of the judge's seat is a handsome bronze tablet bearing this inscription:

James Taylor, of England. Emigrant, lawyer, public officer. Lived in St. Stephen's Parish, King and Queen County, Va. Died

April 30, 1698. First wife Frances ——, died April 22, 1680. Second wife, Mary Gregory, of Essex County. Married August 12, 1682.

From him were descended President James Madison, President Zachary Taylor, Col. James Taylor, Knight of the Golden Horseshoe, Judge Edmund Pendleton, John Penn, signer of the Declaration of Independence, John Taylor, of Caroline, General James Taylor of Kentucky, Admiral David Taylor, Admiral Hugh Rodman, Admiral Robert M. Berry, and other distinguished churchmen, soldiers, sailors and officials in each generation who assisted in the formation and perpetuation of the colonies and this nation.

This tablet given by Jaquelin P. Taylor, seventh in descent, June 1933.

OLD HOMES NUMEROUS

Among the many old homes in King and Queen and the families who founded them, some of these may be referred to.

The Mount, formerly called Todd's, was the early home of the Todd family near Dunkirk. Members of the family had moved over from Toddsbury, in Gloucester. One of the Todds married a Fauntleroy, and the place passed into the hands of that family.

Chatham Hill, a short distance below the bridge at Ayletts, was the home of Joseph Temple.

Beudley, a beautiful old place on the Mattaponi, was supposed to have been built by Captain Mariott, a Scotchman, at a very early date. In more recent years it was the residence of Bishop Latane. It is now in possession of Rutherfoord Fleet.

Canterbury, also on the Mattaponi, was the home of Owen Gwathmey, who built the residence in 1736, the original wall facing the river being a part of the present house. Members of the family still own the home and part of the original land. Owen Gwathmey, who was of the third generation in Virginia, married Hannah Temple, and also owned large acreage on the Mattaponi in the upper end of King William.

White Hall was the colonial seat of the Garlicks, later passing to the Govans.

There were three old Walker places, two of which are still in the family, being among the few in Virginia still held by the families to whom the original 17th Century grants were made.

Locust Grove, formerly called Rye Field, Mt. Elba and Hay Battle all were Walker homes. The first of the name in Virginia was Col. Thomas Walker and his grant extended for ten miles along the Mattaponi. He founded Walkerton and was the father of Dr. Thomas Walker, of Albemarle, owner of Castle Hill.

In this vicinity also was the home of the Tunstalls.

Hillsboro was built by Col. Humphrey Hill about 1722. It was the scene of a raid by the British in the Revolution. Later it was owned by the Temples and Henleys.

Rickahoc was the seat of the Smith family many years ago and Francis Smith, of that family, at one time represented the district in Congress.

Mantua was a famous hunting place for those who were fond of marsh shooting. It is a matter of doubt as to who originally built it, but it was at one time the property of Carter Braxton and at a later date came into possession of his son, Carter M. Braxton.

Hockley Neck was for many years owned by William Gregory.

Mantapike, on the Mattaponi, was the home of the Brooke family for many generations.

Newington, adjoining Mantapike, was established in the early years of the county by the Lumpkin family, of whom very little is known. At Mattapony church there is a marble tablet to the memory of Col. Jacob Lumpkin, stating that he died in 1708. He was a supporter of Berkeley in Bacon's Rebellion. Newington came into possession early in the 18th Century of George Braxton, and was afterward owned by the Roanes. Newington was where Carter Braxton, signer of the Declaration of Independence, was born in 1736. His parents, George and Mary Carter Braxton, are buried at Mattapony church.

Melrose was occupied by the Rowe family and they may or may not have built it. After the War Between the States it was bought by Jacob Turner, who dismantled it.

Pleasant Hill was built by the Robinson family and was the home of John Robinson, for many years Speaker of the House of Burgesses and treasurer of the Colony.

Laneville, one of the most historic places in the county, was the original home of the Corbins, who built it many years before the Revolution and lived there for many generations. On the estate stood the parish church of Stratton Major parish, and while it went to decay many years ago, the registers are still preserved.

Locust Cottage, about one mile east of Stevensville, was the location of the Southgate female school.

Clark's, a place about half-way between Stevensville and Cumnor, was the home of John Clark and his wife, Ann Rogers, the parents of George Rogers Clark, defender of Kentucky and conqueror of the Northwest, and of his younger brother William. George Rogers Clark's parents moved to Albemarle about the time of his birth, where they remained for seven years, thence moving to the lower part of Caroline.

Bell Air was an old Pollard home from which came Henry R. and John Pollard, D. D. The latter, who married Virginia Bagby, was the father of John Garland Pollard, who also was born in King and Queen. John Garland Pollard has been a member of the constitutional convention of 1901-2, a writer of wide reputation on legal subjects, Attorney General of Virginia and Governor.

Norwood was one of the Ryland homes, and here was born Dr. Charles H. Ryland, for many years treasurer and librarian of Richmond College. Ingleside was another Ryland home.

A large number of families from King and Queen migrated to Kentucky and other States west of the mountains during and immediately after the Revolution. Almost the entire family connection of John Clark and his wife Ann Rogers followed their son George Rogers Clark to the West after he had played so large a part in making the western country safe for habitation.

Essex County

ESSEX COURTHOUSE

Essex County

WHILE Essex is many miles from Jamestown, with many rivers intervening, it is remarkable how closely the County was associated with the first colonists. Undoubtedly Captain John Smith was the first Englishman ever to tread the soil of what is now Essex County. While in captivity in the winter of 1607-8, he was paraded for seven weeks to the Indian villages as far north as the Potomac. He, himself, expressed the wish, on his first voyage of exploration in Chesapeake Bay later in 1608, to visit his acquaintances among the Rappahannocks. He almost lost his life from the poison of a stingray at the mouth of the Rappahannock river and his visit had to be deferred until later in the summer of that year. The place is still called Stingray Point.

On his second voyage of exploration in that summer, Captain Smith, with about a dozen companions in an open boat, came up the Rappahannock which he in his description of the voyage called "the river of Rapahanock, by many called Toppahanock." It was at or near the site of Tappahannock that the Englishmen saw a few Indians on the shore who made signs of friendship and motioned to Smith to steer his boat into what is now called Hoskins Creek. Smith, however, would not be beguiled into an ambush, and, as was his usual custom in dealing with the savages, demanded an exchange of hostages. This was effected and Anas Todkill went ashore, while an Indian came aboard.

Todkill soon saw that there was treachery afoot, for there were several hundred Indians concealed among the trees. He shouted to his companions, and at that moment the Indian hostage jumped overboard but was killed in the water by one of the Englishmen. Todkill dropped to the ground and was protected by the fire from the boat while hundreds of arrows sped above him. The Indians withdrew in fear of the white men's firearms and Todkill was rescued, and the canoes of the Rappahannocks were seized and carried away. Proceeding further up the river, the white men again were attacked, but the arrows of the Indians did little damage, since Captain Smith had protected the deck of his open boat with a rude shield of interwoven rushes and reeds.

On the journey up the Rappahannock the white men had made friends with the Moraughtacunds, a tribe to the eastward with whom the Rappahannocks were at war, due to the fact that the chief of the latter tribe had stolen three of the Moraughtacund women. On the way back down the river Captain Smith made peace with the Rappahannocks and one of the stipulations was that the three women should be returned. Peace was sealed between the two tribes when Smith, acting the role of a Solomon, gave one of the women to the chief of the Rappahannocks, one to the chief of the

Moraughtacunds, and the third to an Indian named Mosco, whose services to the white men in the expedition had been of much value.

This Indian called Mosco deserves mention here, for some day some student of Indian lore may be able to trace his ancestry. Certain it is that he was one of the most remarkable specimens encountered among the Virginia Indians. He was first seen by the white men on the Potomac, and joined them later on the voyage up the Rappahannock. The strange thing about him, in addition to his kindness to the English, was the fact that he had a bristling beard—something unheard-of among the aborigines. This led the Englishmen to believe that his father must have been French, and, indeed, this bearded warrior may have made his way down from the fringes of the French settlements in Canada, or he may have had a grandfather in the crew of Giovanni Verrazano, who brought a French ship along the coast from North Carolina to New England in 1524.

One of the earliest of the colonists was buried on Essex soil, for on Smith's journey in 1608, Richard Featherstone, Gent., died of a fever and was buried by the river and a volley fired. Historians generally agree that the Indian village on the river within two miles above Tappahannock was the village of "Appamatuck." It will be remembered that at the grand gathering at the village of Powhatan in Gloucester, when Captain Smith was to be slain and was miraculously saved by Pocahontas, food was first set before the captive and the "Queene of Appamatuck" brought water for him to wash his hands, while another queen brought feathers with which he might dry them.

Essex County is a part of what was the ancient and now extinct county of Rappahannock, which included both Essex and Richmond. It seems strange that Rappahannock County should have endured as a political subdivision as long as it did—1656 to 1691—with the broad waters of the Rappahannock cutting it in half. It took the name of Essex County, England. The act of April, 1691, which created Essex County is here quoted in full:

"An Act for Dividing Rappahannock County.

"Whereas sundry inconveniences attend the inhabitants of Rappahannock County and all others who have occasion to prosecute law suits there, by reason of the difficulty in passing the river—

"Be it enacted by their Majesty's Lieut Gov., Councell and Burgesses of this present Gen. Assembly and the authority thereof, and it is hereby enacted, that the aforesaid county of Rappahannock be divided into two distinct counties, soe that Rappahannock River divide the same; and that part which is now on the North side thereof be called and known by the name of Richmond County, and that part which is now on the South side thereof be called and known by the name of Essex County.

"Be it enacted by the authority aforesaid, and it is here enacted, that the Court of the said county of Richmond be constantly held by the justices thereof on the first Wednesday of the month in such manner as by the laws of this country is provided and shall be by their commission directed.

"And the Court for the said county of Essex be constantly held by the justices on the tenth day of the month in such manner as by the laws of this country is provided and shall be by their commission directed.

"Be it enacted by the authority aforesaid, and it is hereby enacted: That whereas the Town land lying at Hobbe's Hole [Tappahannock] on the South side of the said County was purchased by the entire

County as now it is, the charge thereof being equally defrayed by the whole number of tytheables of said county; that the moyety of the tobacco arising from the sales thereof to the several takersup of the aforesaid lands be paid unto the inhabitants of the North side thereof, upon the taking up of the said land at the town aforesaid, and that the records belonging to the County Courts of Rappahannock before this division be kept in Essex County, that belonging wholly to their Majesties and the other to the Proprietors of the Northern Neck."

From the fragmentary records which have come down to the present, it is obvious that the men of Essex played a conspicuous part in Bacon's Rebellion of 1676. There was a complaint to Williamsburg that in January of that year sixty plantations in Essex were destroyed within seventeen days. It is impossible to say how many Essex citizens were with Bacon's northern force in Essex in the summer of 1676, nor can it be told how long Bacon's men were in the county. But they marched south from Essex and on July 10 fought a battle with the forces of Governor Berkeley at Piscataway. There were a number of casualties and some houses were burned, after which the Rebels passed on to the Pamunkey and were there joined by Nathaniel Bacon.

There were a number of cases in Essex in which participants in Bacon's Rebellion were required to come into court with halters about their necks and appeal, on bended knee, for forgiveness for having taken part in the rebellion. Thomas Goodrich and Benjamin Goodrich were among those subjected to this indignity, as were John Bagwell and William Potts.

One of the acts of the Burgesses of 1677 indicates that even the Rappahannock justices were not entirely in sympathy with Governor Berkeley's methods of punishing the erstwhile rebels, for it recites that "whereas Thomas Gordon and John Bagwell were adjudged to appear at Rappahannock County Court with halters about their necks, appeared with small tape instead—which was accepted—the Assembly take it as a contempt upon them and order their clerk to enquire into it."

The Rappahannock Indians were a stubborn race and bitterly contested the encroachments of the white men along both sides of their river. As early as 1654 the settlers of the Northern Neck complained to the Burgesses of "divers injuries and insolencies by the Rappahannock Indians" and danger of open war. Whereupon a troop was raised and, under the command of Major John Carter, was ordered to march to the Indian towns and demand satisfaction. In the clerk's office of Richmond county at Warsaw there are records of trials of Indians for massacres up to 1703, nearly a hundred years after the Jamestown settlement.

The original courthouse of Rappahannock county was at Caret, and Hobbe's Hole, referred to in the act for the formation of the county, was laid out in 1680. The purchase of fifty acres of land was ordered for the purpose, for which was paid 10,000 pounds of tobacco, and various privileges were granted to settlers in the new town. The origin of its peculiar name is more or less shrouded in myth, some having advanced the theory that in the elastic spelling of the period the name was Hobbe's Hold, that is to say the land "holden" by Hobbe. But no one seems to know anything about this man Hobbe. In 1682 a port was established here by law and called New Plymouth. The name of the town was changed to Tappahannock in 1808.

The earliest justices of the county of Essex were Captain John Caslett, Captain William Mosely, Robert Broky, John Taliafero, Thomas Edmundson, Francis Taliafero, Captain John Battaill, Bernard Gaines, James Boughan, Francis Gouldman and Richard Covington. The first clerk was William Colson.

With the formation of the county in 1692, it was divided into two parishes of the Established Church, St. Anne's and South Farnham, North Farnham parish being across the river in Richmond. The two churches were Upper and Lower Piscataway, and the Rev. Lewis Latané, a Huguenot who took charge in 1700, was the first minister of South Farnham Parish.

Vauter's was the church of upper St. Anne's parish and survived the other colonial churches of Essex. The northern half of the structure was built about 1719, and the southern wing in 1731. There is still preserved a communion set presented by Queen Anne. Sixty years later a curious thing happened, in the light of the modern attitude toward lotteries, raffles and other forms of gambling. On May 14, 1792, St. Anne's Parish conducted a lottery for the purpose of repairing the church. There were 1,118 prizes, first prize being $1,000, and 3,332 tickets were offered for sale at $2 each.

As was true of all the river counties in eastern Virginia, the export of tobacco played an important part in the development of Essex. Public warehouses for the inspection of tobacco were established in 1730 at

Tappahannock, upon John Griffon's land; at Bowler's Ferry, upon Adam's land; and at Laytons. Twelve years later a warehouse was established on Piscataway creek and another on Occupacia creek.

There are many quaint old records in the clerk's office at Tappahannock, some of them dating as early as 1656. Two of these so reflect the attitude of the people of Essex toward the crownheads of the mother country that it might be well to reproduce them here. Following is one of them:

"It having pleased Almighty God to bless his Royal Majesty with the birth of a son, and his subjects with a Prince of Wales, and forasmuch as His Excellency hath set apart the 16th of this instant of January for solemnizing the same, in the end therefore that it may be done with all the expressions of joy this community is capable of, this court have ordered that Captain George Taylor do provide and bring to the North Side Court House for this county as much rum or other strong liquor with sugar proportionable as shall amount to six thousand five hundred pounds of tobacco. To be distributed amongst the troops of horse, of foot and other persons that shall be present at the said solemnitie, and that the said sum shall be allowed him at the next laying of the levy."

A later record, written in 1691, is illustrative of the unswerving loyalty of the Virginians to the Stuart line in England even after they had been deposed in 1688 and William of Orange and his wife, Mary, ruled the kingdom. This record is truly remarkable:

"Whereas, It is manifestly made to appear before this court by sufficient evidence that Roger Loveless of this county, on the 11th day of July now past, did drink a health to King James and cuss his present Majesty, King William, and use some other irreverend expressions toward his said Majesty, this court have therefore ordered that the sheriff of this county or his deputy do forthwith take into safe custody the body of the said Roger Loveless and give him twenty lashes upon his bare back, well layed on, and that he remain in Goal until he give bonds with sufficient securitie for his future good abarance."

Appointed to the King's Council were John Robinson, of Piscataway, in 1720; and William Beverley, of Blandfield, in 1750.

Members of the House of Burgesses from Essex were:

1692-93, Captain John Battaile, Captain Edward Thomas; 1693 (Oct.) John Catlett, Thomas Edmondson; 1695-96, William Moseley, John Catlett; 1696-7, John Battaile, Thomas Edmondson; 1698, James Boughan; 1699, John Taliaferro, James Boughan; 1700-02, Thomas Edmondson, John Catlett; 1703-05, Richard Covington, James Boughan; 1706, Francis Gouldman, Francis Meriwether; 1710, James Boughan, John Hawkins; 1711, John Hawkins; 1712, Francis Meriwether, Francis Gouldman; 1714, John Hawkins, Francis Gouldman; 1718, John Hawkins, William Daingerfield; 1720-22, John Hawkins, Richard Covington; 1723-27, Robert Jones, William Daingerfield; 1734-40, Thomas Waring, Salvator Muscoe; 1742-47, William Beverley, James Garnett; 1748-49, William Beverley, William Daingerfield; 1752-53, Francis Smith, Thomas Waring; 1754-58, Francis Smith, William Dangerfield; 1758-60, John Upshaw, Francis Waring; 1761-65, John Upshaw, John Lee; 1765-68, John Lee, Francis Waring; 1769, Francis Waring, William Roane; 1769-74, William Roane, James Edmondson; 1775, James Edmondson, Meriwether Smith.

All conventions of 1775 and 1776 James Edmondson and Meriwether Smith.

Tappahannock gradually increased in importance under a free town government conducted by eight elected citizens called "benchers", who, in turn, named one from their own number to be "director." The town was made a port of entry and the walls of the custom house, built about 1680, one of the first in Virginia, are still standing. These walls, a yard thick, are the foundations of the attractive Latané house of today.

In 1702 there were two ferries across the Rappahannock, one at what is now Tappahannock, and the other at what is now Bowler's Wharf. Settlements increased rapidly and by 1748 there were twenty public ferries. There was an act of 1744 to prevent the citizens of Tappahannock from raising hogs at large in the town, and another in 1769 prohibiting the use of wooden chimneys. In that year provision was made for laying out a town at Layton's to be called Beaufort.

It is not known how many Essex men were present at Braddock's defeat in 1755, nor how many joined the ranks of Colonel George Washington's regiment of 1,600 troops in 1756, which played such a large part in the French and Indian Wars. There is a record indicating that Captain Forest Upshaw was an officer from Essex.

There were evidences of much indignation in Essex in that troubled period leading up to the Revolution. While the people, with an inborn love for the mother country hated to think that a mother could thus treat her child, they subscribed fully to Patrick Henry's resolutions against the Stamp Act in 1765 and his *pro-nunciamento* that the sole right of taxation rested with the colonists. There was an important meeting of the freeholders and other inhabitants of Essex on Saturday, July 4, 1774, and resolutions adopted at that meeting clearly reflect the feelings of the Essex people.

While this is a historic document of much significance, quotation of only a few paragraphs will indicate the trend of thought in Essex at that time. It was resolved:

"That the Legislature of this Colony, for the purpose of internal taxation, is distinct from that of Great Britain, founded upon the principles of the British constitution and equal in all respects to the purposes of legislation and taxation within this Colony."

"That the people of this Colony in particular and of America in general have a clear and absolute right to dispose of their property by their own consent expressed by themselves, or by their representatives in Assembly; and any attempt to tax or take their money from them in any other manner and all other acts tending to enforce submission to them is an exertion of power contrary to natural justice, subversive to the English constitution, destructive of our charters, and oppressive."

"That the town of Boston, in our sister Colony of Massachusetts Bay, is now suffering in the common cause of North America for the just opposition to such acts, and it is indispensably necessary that all the colonies should unite firmly in defense of our common rights."

"That it is the opinion of this meeting that an agreement to stop all exports to and all imports from Great Britain and the West Indies, firmly entered into and religiously complied with, will at all times prove a safe and infallible means of securing us against the evils of any unconstitutional and tyrannical acts of Parliament, and may be adopted upon the principles of self-preservation—the great law of nature."

"That the inhabitants of this county will firmly join with the other counties of this Colony and the other colonies on this continent, or a majority of them, to stop all exports to and imports from Great Britain and the West Indies and all other parts of the world except the colonies of North America . . ."

"That the spirited conduct of the town of Boston hath been serviceable to the cause of freedom (all other methods having failed), and that no reparation ought to be made to the East India Company or other assistants for any injury they have sustained, unless it be the express condition on which all our grievances shall be removed.

"That a subscription be set on foot for raising provisions for the poor of Boston, who now suffer by the blockading up of their port, and that Robert Beverly, John Lee and Muscoe Garnett, in St. Anne's Parish, and Archibald Ritchie and John Upshaw, in the upper part of South Farnham Parish, and Meriwether Smith and James Edmondson, in the lower part thereof, take in subscriptions for that purpose, who are to consign what may be raised to some proper person to be distributed; and the before-mentioned gentlemen are empowered to charter a vessel and send it to Boston."

Thus it will be seen that as far as Essex county was concerned the struggle which ultimately resulted in American independence had gotten well under way in the summer of 1774, and in December of that year the freeholders elected their Committee of Safety. John Upshaw was unanimously elected chairman, and William Young, clerk. The following were members: William Roane, James Edmondson, John Upshaw, Thomas Boulware, John Lee, Meriwether Smith, Thomas Roane, Robert Beverly, Muscoe Garnett, William Young, John Henshaw, William Smith, Augustine Moore, John Beal, Henry Garnett, Robert Reynolds, John Brockenbrough, Thomas Sthreshly, Thomas Waring and Archibald Ritchie.

It is a noteworthy fact that Colonel William Dangerfield, of Essex, commanded the Seventh Continental Regiment in the Revolution, and Colonel John Dangerfield was in command of the Essex troops in the War of 1812.

The War of 1812 was very real to the people of Essex, for it was brought to their very doors. Admiral Cockburn, of the British Navy, came up the Rappahannock in 1813, pillaging the country and stealing slaves. A severe engagement was fought in the river above Urbanna. Cockburn proceeded up the river and shelled Tappahannock on December 1, 1814. The old courthouse was partially destroyed by the British, but was shortly thereafter restored, and is now a part of a church edifice in one corner of the courthouse square.

Essex was a county of large estates and the increase in population up to the time of the War Between the States was comparatively slow. The county was greatly isolated until very recent years, the river remaining the principal avenue of transport. Finally the Tappahannock Highway was built and the Downing bridge across the Rappahannock was erected. Even to this day the people retain, to a very marked degree, the manners and customs of the olden times.

While Essex sent many of her sons into the War Between the States, there was comparatively little actual fighting on Essex soil. The depredations of detachments from the Federal gunboats in the Rappahannock river were very severe. Many of the old manor houses were despoiled and the Federal Government sent an especial expedition which resulted in the capture of R. M. T. Hunter.

As a matter of record the names of the officers from Essex, taken from the handsome Confederate monument at Tappahannock, are here given:

Brigadier General Richard B. Garnett and Brigadier General Robert S. Garnett; with the 55th Virginia Regiment, Col. Francis Mallory, Col. William S. Christian, Lieutenant-Colonel Evan Rice, Major William N. Ward, Major Thomas M. Burke, Major Andrew J. Saunders and Major Charles N. Lawson; Colonel William W. Gordon, 27th Virginia Regiment, and Lieutenant-Colonel Meriwether Lewis, 9th Virginia Cavalry.

Company A, 55th Virginia: Captain, William J. Davis; lieutenants, John Haile, R. L. Pendleton, Thomas Dobyns, John T. Boughan, T. R. B. Wright and Robert Rouzie.

Company D, 55th Virginia: captains, G. G. Roy, Austin Brockenbrough, L. D. Roane and P. C. Waring; lieutenants, William Kemp Garnett, William J. Duff and C. C. Roy.

Company F, 55th Virginia: captains, William A. Wright, Robert G. Haile and Albert Rennolds; lieutenants, A. R. Micou, John R. Mann, John H. Tupman, H. W. Daingerfield and Edgar J. Saunders.

Company G, 55th Virginia: captains, George W. Street and William A. Street; lieutenants, Leonard Henley, Logan Fleet, John W. Street, George A. Bohannon and Richard Sadlet.

Company K, 55th Virginia: captains, William Latane Brooke and James A. Haynes; lieutenants, William H. Haynes, William A. Elliott and Robert B. Whitlocke.

Company F, 9th Virginia Cavalry: captains, Richard S. Cauthorn, William Latane and William A. Oliver; lieutenants, John H. Wilson, William L.

Waring, Aubrey H. Jones, Waring Lewis and John Latane.

In other commands: captains, Edward R. Baird, A. W. Broaddus, A. F. Bagby, Thomas Croxton, Z. S. Farland, A. S. Garnett, John M. Garnett, J. A. Muse, B. H. Robinson, P. A. Sandy and B. L. Sale; lieutenants, W. Harvey Bray, R. L. Dobyns, Theodore S. Garnett, James Hunter, James D. Hunter, John M. Owen, Robert Roy and R. L. Williams.

Surgeons were David S. Garnett, Henry Gresham, Henry R. Noel, A. R. Rouzie and W. D. Sale.

COURTHOUSE AT TAPPAHANNOCK

The present courthouse of Essex County at Tappahannock was erected in 1848, its stately white columns showing the Jeffersonian influence upon the architecture of the Early Republic.

The first courthouse and clerk's office of the former Rappahannock County stood near Caret and were used from 1665 to 1693.

The first courthouse at Tappahannock was built in 1728 and a part of it is still standing, forming a part of the church edifice which stands in one corner of the courthouse square. This building was partially destroyed by the British of Admiral Cockburn's fleet in the War of 1812, but was restored and used as the courthouse until the new building was erected.

The picturesque clerk's office at Tappahannock, now used as the home of the Essex Woman's Club, was built at an indeterminate date prior to 1750, and the debtors' jail, which also stands on the courthouse square, is very old.

Both the exterior and interior of the present courthouse were restored and beautified in comparatively recent years through the generosity of the late Alfred I. DuPont, who married Miss Jessie Ball, of Lancaster County.

There is a tradition that there was still another courthouse for Essex County, used between 1693 and the completion of the former brick building in Tappahannock erected in 1728. It is believed that this early courthouse stood near the site of Piscataway Church, but authoritative sources of information about it are lacking.

COURTROOM HALL OF FAME

The courtroom at Tappahonnock is verily a hall of fame for Essex County. From its walls look down the likenesses of nearly three score men of note from Essex. In addition to these, there are twelve tablets and two prints of historic pictures in which scenes Essex men played a part.

Following are the men whose portraits hang upon the courthouse wall:

Judge T. R. B. Wright, of Tappahannock, judge of the Twelfth Judicial Circuit. To him must be attributed a large part in the movement which spread throughout the older counties of the State which has resulted in making county shrines of the courtrooms. Judge Wright was much interested in securing portraits of the distinguished sons of the counties of his circuit and hanging them in the courtrooms, and many other counties have taken up the idea with results that are historically important.

R. M. T. Hunter, perhaps the most noted of all the sons of Essex, was a distinguished member of the United States Senate and was Secretary of State in the cabinet of President Jefferson Davis of the Confederacy.

John Lee, clerk of the courts from 1745 to 1761.

Judge Thomas Evans Blakey was Commonwealth's Attorney, State Senator and judge of the County Court.

Judge Thomas Croxton was a member of Congress and county judge.

Judge Edward Macon Ware was Commonwealth's Attorney, commissioner in chancery and chairman of the local board in the World War.

Judge Henry W. Daingerfield was County Judge, collector of the port and member of the Legislature.

Col. Richard Rouzie was a justice of the old county court.

James Roy Micou was clerk of the county for fifty-seven years.

Meriwether Smith was a member of Congress from 1778 to 1782.

John P. Lee was clerk from 1793 to 1814.

Harrison Southworth was clerk and member of the Legislature.

Larkin Hundley was president of the old county court.

Lieutenant John Latane, gallant cavalry officer, was wounded and captured in 1864 and died that year in Lincoln Hospital.

James M. Garnett was a member of Congress.

General Robert S. Garnett was a gallant Confederate officer and also was a member of Congress.

Alexander Baylor was a member of the old county court.

Richard Baylor was a member of the county court and of the Legislature.

Judge Spencer Roane, a noted Virginia jurist sketched more fully in the chapter on Hanover, was a member of the Supreme Court of Appeals.

Thomas Ritchie, generally known as "Father" Ritchie, was editor of the *Richmond Enquirer* and a powerful figure in both State and National political thought.

Judge William Brockenbrough served as judge of the Circuit Court and was then sent to the Supreme Court of Appeals.

Lewis Henry Garnett was Commonwealth's Attorney.

Warner Lewis was a justice of the county court.

Thomas W. Lewis also was one of the justices.

Henry W. Latane, Sr., was a justice of the county court and member of the Legislature.

Judge Muscoe Garnett was judge of the county court and was a member of the Constitutional Convention of 1901-2.

Judge A. B. Evans presided over the Circuit Court.

Governor George William Smith, while serving as Governor of Virginia, lost his life in the burning of the Richmond theater December 26, 1811. This portrait was presented to the County by M. Gertrude von Stremyng Kriete.

M. R. H. Garnett was a member of Congress.

Edmund F. Noel was a member of the county court and of the Legislature.

Judge William Browne was judge of the Circuit Court. This portrait was donated by his daughter, Mrs. Virginia L. Bayless, of Evanston, Ill.

Judge John Critcher was judge of the Circuit Court and member of Congress.

William Baynham Matthews was clerk from 1814 to 1830.

Dr. A. P. Montague became president of Furman University, South Carolina.

Rufus S. Rennolds was Commonwealth's Attorney.

H. Clay Tompkins became Attorney General of Alabama.

Col. George Wright was Commonwealth's Attorney.

Judge Eustace Conway was judge of the Circuit Court.

Judge Selden S. Wright was a distinguished jurist first in Mississippi and then in California.

Judge John Tayloe Lomax was judge of the Circuit Court and professor of law at the University of Virginia.

James M. Matthews was reporter of the Supreme Court of Appeals, lawyer and author.

Judge John B. Christian was a jurist of distinction.

Judge Richard Parker was president of the court in the period prior to the War of 1812. He was born in 1729 and died in 1814.

Judge John Thompson Jones, born in Essex October

11, 1813, became a judge in the State of Arkansas. This portrait was donated by Mr. and Mrs. Paul Jones, of New York.

Captain A. W. Broaddus, an officer in the Confederate army, was also a member of the county court.

Meriwether Lewis was a lieutenant-colonel in the Confederate army and a member of the Virginia Senate.

Captain L. D. Roane, C. S. A.

Captain Austin Brockenbrough, C. S. A.

Captain William A. Wright, of the Essex Sharpshooters, C. S. A., was killed in the battle of Frazier's Farm.

Ensign Richard Edward Wright, C. S. A., was killed in the Petersburg campaign.

Evan Rice was a lieutenant-colonel in the army of the Confederacy.

Captain William A. Oliver, C. S. A.

Major Thomas M. Burke was an officer in the Confederate army.

Captain Robert G. Haile, Jr., C. S. A.

Captain William Latane Brooke, C. S. A.

Charles C. Roy, lieutenant, C. S. A.

Captain William A. Street, C. S. A.

Captain George W. Street, C. S. A.

One of the prints on the walls of the courtroom is the famous picture, "The Burial of Latane." The painting, by W. D. Washington, was made after the event, the artist being struck with the pathos of the scene, which was enacted at Summer Hill, the Page and Newton home in Hanover County. It was on Stuart's famous ride around McClellan's army that Captain William Latane, of Essex County, was killed. His younger brother, Lieutenant John Latane, conveyed the body to Summer Hill, but while en route was intercepted by a detachment of Union soldiers who told him that as soon as he discharged his grim trust they must take him captive. There being no clergyman available and no white men on the place, Captain Latane was buried by the ladies and faithful slaves.

The other historic picture on the wall of the courtroom is a print of the headquarters of General Zachary Taylor (of Orange County) at Walnut Springs, near Monterey, Mexico, just after the battle of Buena Vista. Shown in the group is General Robert S. Garnett, of Essex, then a major in the United States Army in the Mexican War.

There are twelve tablets, their inscriptions bearing so much accurate data of interest to their descendants that they are quoted here in full:

In Memoriam: Muscoe Garnett of Ben Lomond. Born March 17, 1808. Died October 5, 1880. Virginia Convention 1849-50; House of Delegates; judge of the County Court; and seven Confederate sons.

Lewis H. Garnett. Co. F, 9th Va. Cavalry, C. S. A. Commonwealth's attorney. Born in Hopkinsville, Ky., Dec. 28, 1827. Died in Essex Co., Va., Sept. 20, 1895.

George William Garnett. Treasury department, C. S. A. Prisoner of war in Forts LaFayette and Delaware. Born at Dunbars, King and Queen County, Va., August 31, 1829. Died in Essex Co., Va., June 18, 1903.

Muscoe Garnett, Jr. Co. F., 9th Va. Cavalry, C. S. A. Born at

Farmers Retreat, King and Queen County, Va., Jan. 1, 1832. A prominent and honored county official.

David S. Garnett, M. D. Surgeon on Don Pedro Railroad, South America. Surgeon C. S. Army. Born at Ashland, Essex Co., Va., October 3, 1834. Died at Ben Lomond October 3, 1862.

Booker Garnett. 2nd Richmond Howitzers. House of Delegates. Born at Stock Hill, Essex Co., Va., Dec. 4, 1837.

William Kemp Garnett. Lieutenant Co. D, 55th Va. Regiment, C. S. A. Born in Middlesex Co., Va., June 25, 1839. Killed at Cold Harbor June 27, 1862.

F. B. Garnett. Sergeant Co. F, 9th Va. Cavalry, C. S. A. Born at Ben Lomond April 2, 1843. Died in Richmond, Va., from camp fever July 6, 1862.

The two last, sons of Hon. Muscoe Garnett and Sarah A. Garnett.

Donated through Essex Circuit Court by his family.

———

Bartholomew Hoskins. Patented land where Tappahannock now stands in 1645. House of Burgesses 1654.

John and Samuel Hoskins. Patented land in St. Stephen's Parish in 1738.

Captain John Hoskins. Seventh Division Va. Militia in 1780-81.

Lieutenant Robert Hoskins. First Virginia Regiment, Continental Line, Revolutionary War, 1777-1780. Was at Valley Forge, Monmouth Court House, Middle Brook and Stony Point.

William Hoskins. Born in King and Queen County, Va. Moved to Garrard County, Kentucky, in 1801.

Ensign George Hoskins. Ninth Va. Militia. 1812-1814.

John Hoskins, M. D. Surgeon 9th Va. Militia U. S. service 1812-14.

John Thomas Hoskins. Commissioned captain in 9th Regiment, 14th Brigade, 4th Division Va. Militia May 4, 1839. Justice. Va. Legislature for Essex Co. 1874-75. Collector of Port of Tappahannock.

William Hoskins, M. D. Va. Legislature for King and Queen County 1874-75. Surgeon 57th Va. Infantry. Assistant surgeon 26th Regiment C. S. A.

John R. B. Hoskins, M. D. Co. C, 26th Va. Infantry C. S. A.

Col. William A. Hoskins. Twelfth Kentucky Volunteers, infantry, U. S. Army 1861-65.

Thomas Taliaferro Hoskins. Co. F, 9th Va. Cavalry. Killed at Manassas Oct. 19, 1863.

Richard Lewis Hoskins. Va. Reserves, C. S. A. 1863-65.

Captain Robert G. Haile, Sr. Sixth Va. Regiment, War of 1812. Inspector of tobacco 1816-1832. School commissioner 1845. Died May 12, 1863.

Captain Robert G. Haile, Jr. Co. F, 55th Va. Regiment, C. S. A. Mortally wounded at Gaines' Mill. Died July 26, 1862.

Lieutenant John Haile. Co. F, 55th Va. Regiment C. S. A. Justice County Court. Died Aug. 15, 1893.

William J. Haile, M. D. Acting surgeon C. S. A. Died July 9, 1899.

Austin Meredith Trible, son of John Trible and Hannah Meredith. Born at Johnville, Essex County, Va., Mch. 12, 1818. Died in Lynchburg, Va., Oct. 12, 1872. Bachelor of law William and Mary College, class of 1838-39. Member Va. Senate 1847-50. Moved to Lynchburg, Va., and elected to Congress of the Confederate States, but failed to take his seat because of fall of Confederacy.

Presented by his daughter, Julia Trible Huger.

John Rennolds. Emigrant 1740.

Sthreshley Rennolds. Captain in Revolutionary War. Presidential elector. Sheriff, old court.

William D. Rennolds. Captain Va. Militia.

Albert Rennolds. Captain in Texas Revolution on staff of General Houston.

Henry S. Rennolds, M. D. Surgeon U. S. Navy.

Robert B. Rennolds, M. D. Noted surgeon and physician.

Albert Rennolds, C. S. A. Captain Co. F, 55th Va. Regiment. Surveyor and educator.

C. S. A. William Latane, M. D. Captain Co. F, 9th Va. Cavalry. Born Jan. 16, 1833. Fell in battle June 13, 1862.

Lewis Latane. Served in Home Guard. Born May 10, 1838. Died Oct. 15, 1864.

John Latane. Lieutenant Co. F, 9th Va. Cavalry. Born May 10, 1838. Wounded and captured May 18, 1864. Died in Lincoln Hospital June 1864.

Sons of Henry Waring and Suzanne Latane of "The Meadow."

———

Thomas Waring. Emigrant 1680.

Col. Frank Waring of Goldberry. Burgess 1765. Died 1771.

Henry Waring. Lieutenant 7th Va. Regiment.

Thomas Gouldman Waring and William Waring. War of Revolution.

William L. Waring. Captain 111th Va. Regiment 1814.

———

Richard Brooke Garnett. Brigadier General C. S. Army, son of Col. William Garnett and Anne Maria Brooke. Born at Rose Hill, Essex Co., Va., 1819. Killed at Gettysburg, Pa., July 3, 1863, while in command of one of the brigades of Pickett's Division in the famous charge on Cemetery Ridge. Tablet erected by his niece, Mrs. John B. Purcell.   ———

Robert Brooke. Gentleman Justice of ye old Court 1692-1706.

Robert Brooke, Jr. Clerk of ye old Court 1700 and Horse-shoe Knight. [Here is shown a horseshoe, bearing Spotswood's motto: *Sic Juvat Transcendere Montes.* 1716.]

Judge Francis T. Brooke. Supreme Court of Appeals 1811-1851.

William Hill Brooke. Gentleman Justice.

———

Thomas Gresham. Ensign 9th Va. Regiment, War of 1812. Commonwealth's attorney 1813-1835. Born April 5, 1774. Died July 5, 1838.

Henry Gresham, M.D. Graduate of medical universities of Philadelphia and Paris. Superintendent of schools 1872-1883. President Board of Supervisors. Surgeon C. S. Army. Born August 27, 1833. Died August 23, 1883.

William B. Matthews. Clerk of Essex County 1814-1830. Born June 1787. Died October 1830.

———

This tablet is erected in recognition of the public spirit and generosity of Alfred I. Du Pont, who made possible the remodeling of this building. Erected 1848. Restored 1926.

MANY NOTABLE ESTATES

There were many fine old estates in Essex, some of which should receive brief mention here. In most cases these places were owned by original settlers of Essex who had come by the river. In some instances homes of later date were erected by descendants of old families of the Mattaponi and Pamunkey country who came overland to Essex.

Brooke Bank was one of the most conspicuous of the earlier homesteads. A corner-stone indicates that it was erected in 1731. Christopher Brooke was named as one of the Council in England under the second charter issued by King James in 1609 to the colonists in Virginia. William Brooke, first of the name in Virginia, settled in Essex. His son, Robert Brooke, born in 1652, was one of the justices, and Robert Brooke II was clerk and one of the Knights of the Golden Horseshoe who accompanied Governor Spotswood over the mountains in 1716. Richard Brooke, son of the second Robert Brooke, married Elizabeth Taliaferro.

Still another Robert Brooke was Governor of Virginia and married a niece of Governor Spotswood. Francis T. Brooke was a justice of the Supreme Court of Appeals of Virginia. Colonel John Brooke was the designer of the ironclad Virginia *Merrimac* and was

[173]

the inventor of the Brooke gun. He was a member of the faculty of the Virginia Military Institute for many years.

The Brooke Bank property was an original grant. Its wharf was a direct shipping point to England prior to the Revolution, and during the War Between the States it was shelled by Federal gunboats. The place was often visited by Roger Brooke Taney, celebrated Chief Justice of the United States, who was from the Maryland branch of the Brooke family.

Blandfield was another of the magnificent old estates which maintained its own landing on the Rappahannock. There were 3,450 acres, and it has been perennially the home of the Beverleys. It was on this property that the first courthouse of Essex stood.

William Beverley, the first owner of the estate, was clerk from 1710 to 1740, and named the place for his wife, who had been Elizabeth Bland. This first of the Beverleys in Essex was a son of Robert Beverley, of Beverley Hall, King and Queen County, Knight of the Golden Horseshoe and historian of his State. Robert Beverley, the historian, married Ursula Byrd, of Westover.

In 1736 Governor Sir William Gooch granted William Beverley, of Essex, Sir John Randolph, of Williamsburg, Richard Randolph, of Henrico, and John Robinson, of King and Queen, 118,491 acres in what is now Augusta County. The following day the other grantees released their interest in the patent to Beverley, and the property was called Beverley Manor. This grant of land had much to do with the early settlement of the regions west of the Blue Ridge.

William Beverley, the Essex clerk, had a son named Robert who was educated in England and married Jane Tayloe, of Mt. Airy. It was he who built the Blandfield manor house in 1760. There are twenty-four rooms, all large and with high ceilings. On a window-pane of a bed-room on the second floor is scratched with a diamond the following bit of a young girl's philosophy: "Contentment alone is true happiness, Anna Munford Beverley, Jan. 20, 1790."

One of the most unwarlike pieces of vandalism perpetrated by any detachment of Union troops during the War of the 60s was at Blandfield. Soldiers from gunboats in the river raided the estate, drinking up the wine and destroying everything they could not carry away. Eighteen wagon-loads of furniture, most of it imported, and *all the family portraits* were taken away.

Fonthill was the home of Robert Mercer Taliaferro Hunter, perhaps the most distinguished of all the sons of Essex. The family had formerly resided at Hunter's Hill and the Fonthill house was built by him soon after his graduation from the University of Virginia. An especial expedition against Fonthill was sent in 1863. The mill was burned by troops from gunboats in the river, and all the horses and cattle were taken from the place.

R. M. T. Hunter's first public service was as a member of the Virginia Legislature. He was sent to Congress in 1837, serving until 1847, when he was elected to the Senate, in which body he was the contemporary of Calhoun, Clay and Webster. In 1853 he declined a portfolio in the cabinet of President Franklin Pierce, and was prominently mentioned as a presidential candidate in 1860. When the war broke out he served as Secretary of State in the Confederate cabinet, then served in the Confederate Senate. His latter years were spent as treasurer of Virginia.

In May 1865 he was placed under arrest by the Federal government and imprisoned at Fort Pulaski with James A. Seddon, the last Confederate Secretary of War, and other leading Confederates. His release was obtained through his wife, who made a personal appeal to the President after the war.

Otterburn, another old place of rare charm, was the home of Phillip Stephen Hunter.

Elmwood for more than 200 years has been the ancestral home of the Garnetts of Essex. There is a tombstone here, bearing the following inscription:

"Robert Mercer Taliaferro Hunter. Born April 21, 1809, died July 18, 1887. To his native State he devoted the culture of his life, and his highest attainments were for the service of his country."

Kinlock, not far from the Caroline County line, was one of the handsomest homes in the county and was built by one of the younger generation of the celebrated Baylor family of Caroline. The Kinlock manor house was erected in 1849 by Richard Baylor. From an observatory on the roof can be seen five counties—King George, Westmoreland, Richmond, Caroline and Essex. Kinlock was the scene of many fox hunts and much gayety in ante-bellum days.

Edenetta, another beautiful home, was the residence of Harry Latane Baylor.

The Brockenbrough house at Tappahannock, noted

for the open-handed hospitality there dispensed, was the home of generations of Brockenbroughs.

The Rectory, while the present building is the third in the history of Colonial St. Anne's Parish, is on hallowed ground which has been trod by many distinguished men in the last century and a half.

Epping Forest was the home of Captain Edward R. Baird, for many years prior to his death the only survivor of General Pickett's staff.

Vauter's Church, the church of upper St. Anne's Parish, was completed in 1731, and is an interesting landmark in Essex. It would probably have gone the way of the two historic churches of South Farnham Parish—Upper and Lower Piscataway—and wrecked for the building material had it not been for Mrs. Muscoe Garnett, of Elmwood. Finding that vandals were carrying away paving-stones from the aisles, she threatened prosecution. The ground on which she based her authority was the claim that the church stood on her land.

The old Ritchie home at Tappahannock, the oldest residence in the town, is also one of the most picturesque. It was the home of the Ritchies of Colonial times, and was built by Archibald Ritchie prior to 1767. The Henley home is perhaps equally as old.

Ben Lomond was the residence of Judge Muscoe Garnett, and Hundley Hall was the home of Deane Hundley. Hill and Dale was the home of Prof. William C. Garnett, educator and historian.

The Micou place was at Paul's Cross Roads.

Pigeon Mill, at Tappahannock, was the home of the Roanes.

The home of Judge T. R. B. Wright, at Tappahannock, was converted into the prominent St. Margaret's Episcopal School for Girls.

The Meadow was a Latane home.

Bathurst was the home of Meriwether Smith, Burgess and Revolutionary leader, who married Lady Bathurst, of England. It is one of the lovely old places which is still standing.

Caroline County

CAROLINE COURTHOUSE

Caroline County

WHILE Westmoreland County, birthplace of Washington and the Lees, has often been spoken of as "The Athens of America," Caroline also has been in the forefront in nurturing men who have wrought mightily in shaping the destiny of the Commonwealth and the Nation. From Caroline came Edmund Pendleton, John Penn, signer of the Declaration of Independence for North Carolina, General William Woodford, John Taylor, Col. George Armistead, Col. George Baylor, Col. John Baylor, and General William Clark, of the Lewis and Clark expedition, and it was here that General George Rogers Clark spent the formative years of his youth.

The County was formed in 1727 from Essex, King and Queen and King William, and was named for Queen Caroline, wife of George II. It is a large county, stretching from the North Anna on the southwest to the Rappahannock on its northeast border, and is in direct line between Richmond and Washington. Its western boundary at the time of its formation was more or less indeterminate, as was the case with most of the early counties. Settlers came in perhaps earlier by way of the Rappahannock than over land from the York River country.

Caroline was traversed for its entire length, from north to south, by one of the oldest stage roads in

Virginia, and later (1836) the Richmond, Fredericksburg and Potomac, one of the oldest railroads in the country, afforded a new means of transportation. Over the stage route passed John Penn, on his way from the Province of North Carolina to Philadelphia; Edmund Pendleton, General William Woodford, George Washington, Lafayette and a host of other distinguished men. Lafayette marched south over this route to the defense of Richmond and camped at Bowling Green April 27, 1781.

As late as 1836 the stage line was regularly operated by Jourdan Woolfolk, of Caroline, but however slow and uncomfortable may have been the early steam trains the stage line was shortly abandoned. There were five taverns on the stage route in colonial times and later, and they were community centers of importance in their day. Not only did the passengers on the stages stop at them for refreshment or to spend the night, but they were resorts for the social element of the surrounding country. Especially on Saturday afternoons the people assembled to engage in scientific, literary or political discussion, or to indulge in horse racing, wrestling, target practice, shooting-matches and other amusements. Usually the militia mustered near these old public-houses, and here they frequently held their barbecues.

The first one approached by the traveler coming from the north was Tod's Tavern, afterward Villboro, about six miles from the Spotsylvania line. The next was New Hope Tavern, on the site now occupied by the hotel at Bowling Green. Ten miles south of Bowling Green stood Union Tavern, at the junction of the stage route with the Penola road. Four miles further south was White Chimneys. Five miles from Page's bridge, on the Pamunkey, the southern boundary of the county, was Needwood Tavern, perhaps the best tavern on the road through Caroline.

Port Royal was one of the principal shipping points on the Rappahannock river in colonial times, and its importance as an outlet for the tobacco crop was recognized throughout that section. It was named for Thomas Roy's warehouse. Established in 1744 by the House of Burgesses, it conducted an extensive tobacco trade with England. Just across the river in King George County was Port Conway, near where James Madison was born. There is now a fine concrete highway bridge across the river.

Port Royal, while much of its former glory has departed, boasts the oldest charter in the possession of any Masonic Lodge in the United States, and the Grand Lodge of Virginia in 1785 ranked it as the first lodge in Virginia, although this latter claim may have been due Royal Exchange Lodge, in the borough of Norfolk.

Port Royal's lodge was Kilwinning Crosse and was chartered December 1, 1755, at the annual meeting of the Grand Lodge of Scotland at Edinburgh. The charter bears the signature of the Right Honorable and Most Worshipful Sholto Charles Lord Aberdour, Grand Master, as well as those of many other leading Scottish Masons. The lodge building was raided by Federal soldiers during the war and many articles were stolen, but the lodge still has many of its jewels and regalia sent over from Scotland with the charter. Two books of the secretaries' records from 1754 to 1859 were found in Philadelphia twenty-five years ago and were bought for $250 and returned to the lodge.

Another lot of the properties of the lodge at Port Royal which had been taken during the war was found in 1887 in the possession of the lodge at Easton, Mass., and returned to Kilwinning Crosse Lodge with much courtesy and the exchange of fraternal and personal intercourse between members of the two lodges.

Little is known of the Indian history in Caroline, but on the Rappahannock were two of the principal towns of the Portobago tribe, which in 1669 had about sixty bowmen and hunters.

Peumansend creek, just below Port Royal, derived its peculiar name from that of a pirate named Peuman, who frequently made inroads into the Rappahannock country by way of the river, robbing the colonists and the boats that plied the stream. Finally a party of men arose in arms determined to capture the marauder. They sighted him on the river and pursued him upstream so closely that he turned off into this creek in an effort to escape. He was overtaken when his boat could go no further and was slain. Hence the creek was called Peuman's End.

Governor Spotswood and his Knights of the Golden Horseshoe in 1716 stopped at Windsor, the Woodford estate about ten miles below Fredericksburg on the Rappahannock, and tarried there again on their return from the mountains. At the Hoomes home, formerly known as Bowling Green, now called the Old Mansion, Washington is said to have stopped after his victory at

Yorktown and given a large party on the lawn in honor of Lafayette.

In connection with the naming of Bowling Green may be cited a fact which indicates how hard it always has been to legislate morals into the Virginia people. Especially has it been hard to curb their gaming proclivities. There was a period in which the game of "nine pins" was very popular both in Virginia and in England. In the belief that the game was injurious to the morals of the settlers, the House of Burgesses passed an act making it illegal. So the devotees of the sport simply added one more pin, and the game of "ten pins" did not come within the wording of the prohibitive act.

A few miles to the westward from Port Royal stood Old Mount Church, the colonial place of worship for St. Mary's parish. No one knows how early in the pre-Revolutionary period it was erected. In 1808 the church had come into disuse and was appropriated by the State for school purposes. Rappahannock Academy, at this site, was one of the most noted schools in Virginia.

Members of the House of Burgesses from Caroline were Henry Armistead, 1727-1735; Robert Fleming and Johnathan Gibson, 1736-1737; Johnathan Gibson and John Martin, 1738-1741; Lunsford Lomax and John Baylor, 1742-1751; and from 1752 to 1776 Edmund Pendleton served continuously, with the following colleagues: 1752-1755, Lunsford Lomax; 1756-1765, John Baylor; 1766-1768, Walker Taliaferro; 1769, Francis Coleman; 1770-1773, Walker Taliaferro; and from 1774 to 1776, James Taylor.

Caroline promptly named its Committee of Safety

on November 10, 1774, consisting of twenty of the leading citizens. Edmund Pendleton was its chairman until he was appointed chairman of the Committee of Safety for the entire Colony, and was succeeded by Col. James Taylor.

A number of Caroline men took part in the French and Indian Wars, among them William Woodford who so distinguished himself that he was made colonel of one of the three Virginia regiments assembled at Williamsburg in 1775. Patrick Henry and Hugh Mercer were colonels of the other two. Lord Dunmore fled from Williamsburg to Norfolk on board a British warship and began to terrorize the citizens along the coast. The Virginia Committee of Safety sent Col. Woodford, in October, 1775, and his regiment, in which John Marshall was a lieutenant, together with the Culpeper Minute Men to Norfolk to the relief of the people.

Lord Dunmore sought to establish himself in Norfolk and stationed a detachment of troops at Great Bridge. Here a sharp engagement occurred between Col. Woodford's regiment and the British. The British were repelled with heavy losses and Dunmore had to evacuate the city and seek safety on a warship in Chesapeake Bay. This was one of the major engagements prior to the actual outbreak of the Revolution. Not many months elapsed before Dunmore was attacked at Gwynn's Island by General Andrew Lewis and driven from the Colony.

Caroline in colonial times was noted for the hospitality of its citizens and the ancient manor-houses were the scenes of many gayeties. Nevertheless, there was much of the same strain of piety which marked the people of King and Queen and there was vigorous protest in Caroline against the Established Church.

Near the northern entrance to the town of Bowling Green there is a stone monument with a bronze tablet bearing the following inscription:

"1771-1922. This tablet is placed here in the year 1922 by the churches of the Hermon Baptist Association to commemorate the heroism of Bartholomew Chewning, John Young, Lewis Craig, Edward Herndon, John Burrus and James Goodrich, who, by the order of the court 151 years ago, were imprisoned in the Caroline County jail, near this spot, on the charge of 'teaching and preaching the Gospel without having Episcopal ordination or a license from the General Court'."

The ground on which Bowling Green now stands has an interesting history, especially to lovers of the race horse. At the race course on this property were frequently held the races of the American Jockey Association. Race meets of the Virginia Jockey Club were held there regularly as early as 1790, and there were important races at Bowling Green long before that. It was here that the fine horses of Col. John Hoomes, of Bowling Green, Col. John Tayloe, of Mt. Airy, Richmond County, Col. John Baylor, of Newmarket, and probably those of the Doswells, of Bullfield, Hanover County, would match their speed.

Col. John Baylor, who died in 1772, was one of the most noted of all importers of blooded horses in Colonial times. His stud included nearly a hundred horses at the time of his death and among many other fine horses he imported was "Fearnaught," one of the most famous stallions in American turf history. Fearnaught cost Col. Baylor one thousand guineas and was

[185]

brought over from England in 1764. In 1799 John Tayloe, of Mt. Airy, advertised "Stirling," a famous horse brought from England by John Hoomes, of Bowling Green.

Fearnaught, whose offspring included Apollo and Regulus, two of the most famous horses of their time, was responsible for a revolutionary change in American racing. Hitherto racing had been confined to short dashes, and speed was emphasized rather than stamina. Fearnaught and his progeny, with the characteristic bottom of the English thoroughbred, popularized the longer flat races in America.

Names of the men who represented Caroline in the various conventions may be here mentioned. Edmund Pendleton was one of the county's representatives in the conventions of 1774, two of the three conventions in 1775, in 1776 and 1778 and was president of the last three. James Taylor served in the conventions of 1774, March 1775, July 1775, December 1775, in 1776 and 1788. William Woodford was a member in July 1775.

In the convention of 1829-30 the Caroline district sent John Roane, William P. Taylor, Richard Morris and James M. Garnett. In 1850-51 the district sent Francis W. Scott, Corbin Braxton, Eustace Conway, Beverly B. Douglas and Edward W. Morris. In the Secession convention of 1861 Edmund T. Morris was the member. In the Reconstruction convention of 1867-68 the district sent John L. Marye, Jr., Frederick S. C. Hunter and John J. Gravatt. W. L. Cobb represented Caroline in the convention of 1901-2.

Caroline sent large numbers of men into the Revolution as, indeed, the county did in all of the nation's wars. The roll is too long for reproduction here. There is a long list of men also who qualified as officers of militia during the Revolutionary period. Those above the rank of lieutenant were Colonel Thomas Lowry; Lieutenant-Colonels James Upshur and Anthony Thornton, Jr.; Majors Richard Buckner and Philip Johnson, and Captains Philip Buckner, William Buckner, Samuel Coleman, William Durritt, —— Fletcher, Robert Graham, George Guy, John Jones, John Long, George Madison, John Marshall, Anthony New, Roger Quarles, Joseph Richeson, William Streshly, Peyton Sterns, James Sutton, Samuel Temple, John Thilman, Francis Tompkins and Robert Tompkins.

While many of the militia organizations in the War of 1812 in the various counties saw no active service, such was not the case in Caroline, where the soldiers were frequently called out to repel the British, who made their way up the Rappahannock, made incursions into Caroline, destroyed private property and carried off Negroes.

There were eight militia units in the county, as follows: Captain Armistead Hoomes' company, first under Major William Armistead, afterward under Col. John H. Cocke—first lieutenant, John Battaile, second lieutenant, Richard Hoomes; Major John T. Woodford's squadron of dragoons—adjutant, Armistead Hoomes, surgeon, James Henderson; Capt. William F. Gray's company—lieutenants, C. L. Johnson, Benjamin Clark, Claiborne Wiglesworth and Peter Lucas; Capt. Robert Hill's company—lieutenant, William C. Latane, ensign, Johnson Munday; Capt.

Thomas D. Pitt's company—lieutenant, William Gray.

Captain Smith P. Bankhead, 1st Virginia Volunteers, was called into service in 1846 in the Mexican War. His first lieutenant was Robert F. Coleman.

Not only did Caroline's sons play a distinguished part in shaping the political structure of this country, but they played a conspicuous part in extending its physical boundaries and in making the United States the empire that it is today. The two Clarks—George Rogers and his younger brother William Clark—were in the forefront among American pioneers. George Rogers Clark, defender of Kentucky, hero of Vincennes and conqueror of the Northwest, was born in Albemarle, but moved to Caroline when a small boy. His career is sketched in the chapter on Albemarle.

General William Clark, of the Lewis and Clark Expedition, was born in the southwestern part of Caroline in 1770, his father, John Clark III having inherited the large estate of his uncle, John Clark II, and moved back to tidewater after a residence of seven years in Albemarle. William was the ninth of ten children. He was still a youth when his parents moved to Kentucky, where George Rogers Clark had gone as a territorial surveyor.

Shortly after reaching Kentucky, William Clark enlisted under his brother, who had been made a general, and took part in the Wabash expedition. Soon afterward William Clark joined Col. John Hardin's ill-fated expedition against the Indians north of the Ohio. He took a prominent part in the Indian campaigns under Generals Scott and Wilkinson. He took part in many daring exploits as a lieutenant under

General Wayne, and his last service with the Western Army was as a bearer of a message from General Wayne to the Spanish authorities at New Madrid protesting against the erection of a fort at Chicasaw Bluffs.

In 1803 William Clark received a letter from his old friend and comrade-at-arms in Wayne's army, Captain Meriwether Lewis, of Albemarle, inviting Clark to go with him through the Spanish territories to the Pacific ocean. Congress, in accordance with the wishes of President Jefferson, who had long dreamed of exploring the Far West, made an appropriation for the expedition, and permits were obtained from both French and Spanish officials for the journey to be made, the enterprise having been announced as "a literary pursuit."

The expedition set out in the spring of 1804 and the entire summer and fall were spent in the long voyage up the Missouri river. The winter of 1804 was spent in log huts among the Indians not far from the spot where Bismarck, North Dakota, now stands. In April 1805 they set out for the headwaters of the Jefferson fork of the Missouri and made their way over the Bitter Root mountains and descended the Columbia river, reaching the Pacific in November. After many hardships and an absence of over two years, they made their way back to St. Louis.

Both Lewis and Clark were almost immediately called to high office. Lewis was made governor of the territory of Louisiana, and Clark was made Superintendent of Indian Affairs in the territory and brigadier-general of the territorial militia. Lewis was killed in a tavern in Tennessee while on his way to the east to publish the journals of the expedition. Shortly after his death the name of a part of the Louisiana territory was changed to Missouri and General Clark was appointed by President Madison as the first governor of the territory, in which office he remained until the State was admitted to the Union in 1821.

President Monroe named General Clark as Federal Superintendent of Indian Affairs, an office newly created, and here he remained until his death in 1838.

Edmund Pendleton has often been referred to as "Caroline's most distinguished son." Certain it is that his works had much to do with the shaping of the destiny of the State and Nation. Jefferson said of him: "Taking it all in all he was the ablest man in debate I have ever met." He was particularly distinguished as a statesman, presiding officer and jurist.

Edmund Pendleton was a son of Henry Pendleton and grandson of Philip Pendleton, who immigrated to Caroline County from Lancashire in 1676. He was born in 1721. While in his fourteenth year he was apprenticed to Benjamin Robinson, first clerk of the Caroline County Court, read law and was admitted to practice in 1741. From that time forward honors and responsibilities came to him rapidly.

For twenty-four years he represented his county in the House of Burgesses; was a justice of the peace; County Lieutenant in 1774; and was a delegate to the first Continental Congress. He was president of the Committee of Safety in 1775 and as such had virtual control of the military and naval operations of Virginia. He was speaker of the first Virginia House of Delegates under the new Constitution and for fifteen years was head of the Virginia judiciary. He, together with Jefferson and George Wythe, revised the Virginia laws, when independence was declared, and in 1789 Washington appointed him as judge of the United States District Court of Virginia. Until his death in 1803, at the age of eighty-two, he was leader of the Federalist party in Virginia.

Another service of Edmund Pendleton was his influence upon his nephew, John Taylor, another eminent Caroline man. John Taylor, born at Mill Hill in 1754, was orphaned when ten years of age and was adopted by his uncle, Edmund Pendleton. He was privately tutored in the Pendleton home, became a graduate of William and Mary, then read law in Edmund Pendleton's office at Bowling Green.

Throughout Taylor's career he was a Virginian first and an American second, saw eye to eye with Patrick Henry, and was apprehensive of too much power in the hands of a central government. His political career began in 1766 when, with Patrick Henry and Richard Henry Lee, a winning fight was waged to break the power of a long-established and well-entrenched dynasty in Virginia. When a very young man he enlisted in Col. Henry's 1st Virginia Regiment and participated in the defeat of Lord Dunmore at Great Bridge, near Norfolk, under the command of Col. William Woodford. Shortly after that battle, Taylor was made a major.

Along with Patrick Henry and Richard Henry Lee, Taylor sincerely believed, in the early stages of the Revolution, that Washington was unfit for the command of the Continental Army. Taylor became so dissatisfied with the conduct of military affairs that he resigned his commission and returned to Caroline, there to plunge into Virginia politics. He was sent to the Legislature.

Taylor's attitude toward General Washington obviously changed later, and while Lafayette was in Virginia watching Cornwallis, who was then in North Carolina, Taylor organized a force of volunteers and joined Lafayette with the rank of lieutenant-colonel. He was ordered to Gloucester, where the British were playing havoc by their depredations, and was stationed there in the Yorktown campaign. After the war Taylor's law practice in Caroline was lucrative, and he established himself at Hazelwood, a handsome estate on the Rappahannock near Port Royal, and devoted himself to agriculture.

John Taylor, in the early years of the Republic, played a conspicuous part in crystallizing the Virginia idea of States' Rights. Along with Patrick Henry, he strenuously opposed the Federal Constitution when it was ratified by Virginia largely through the influence of Washington in the memorable convention of 1788. It will be noted that his views were entirely at variance with those of Edmund Pendleton, his father by adoption, who presided in that convention and was an ardent Federalist.

In the first United States senatorial campaign in Virginia, Taylor threw his influence to William Grayson and Richard Henry Lee, who were overwhelmingly victorious on a States' Rights platform. When Lee resigned, because of feeble health, Taylor was appointed by the Governor to serve out the unexpired term. For the ensuing term he was regularly elected, but he declined the honor. In 1794 he was invited by two New England Senators, King and Ellsworth, to a conference to consider a quiet and peaceable dissolution of the Union, the East from the South. But Taylor counselled against it, and urged that the Union be given further trial. This procedure was recorded in his own hand-writing and has been published.

Taylor had a facile pen and as a pamphleteer and contributor to newspapers and periodicals wielded a wide influence. He was again appointed to the Senate in 1803 and as a member of that body was a strong supporter of Jefferson in the Louisiana Purchase. In the early years of the Republic he was a staunch and able supporter of the party led by Jefferson, Madison and Monroe. Later he declined to support Madison, because of Madison's "tendency toward federalism," but was an able supporter of Monroe and did much toward paving the way for Monroe's later political successes.

John Taylor was probably the staunchest advocate of States' Rights Virginia has produced. The idea was almost a religion with him. He criticized Marshall's "nationalistic opinions" from the bench, and later berated the "nationalistic teachings" of Clay, Calhoun and John Quincy Adams in politics. But when General Andrew Jackson loomed as a political figure, Taylor said he would support either Calhoun or Adams, as the "lesser of two evils."

Taylor was active in public life for the remainder of his seventy years and was a member of the United

States Senate when he died at Hazelwood in 1824. A county in West Virginia was named for him.

John Penn, signer of the Declaration of Independence, was another who came under the influence of Caroline's great citizen, Edmund Pendleton. Penn also lived a part of his youth in the household of Pendleton, and, as did John Taylor, "read" law in Pendleton's office at Bowling Green. When he was thirty-three years of age he moved to Granville County, North Carolina, and attained almost immediate prominence because of his ability.

John Penn was born near Port Royal in 1741 and lived all of his early life in Caroline. A year after he became a citizen of North Carolina he was sent by the people of Granville County to represent them in the Provincial Congress which met in Hillsborough in August 1775. His eloquence and zeal won him immediate favor, and he was named on many important committees, among others a group to prepare a civil constitution for the Province.

The Provincial Congress further honored him by electing him to succeed Richard Caswell as a delegate to the Continental Congress in Philadelphia. He was an ardent patriot. He was in North Carolina and the Provincial Congress was in session when a committee of this body framed a resolution, which the congress adopted, authorizing North Carolina's delegates in the Continental Congress to join other delegates in declaring independence from Great Britain. Thus North Carolina under Penn's leadership, has been accredited as the first of the colonies in declaring for a complete separation from the mother country.

When Cornwallis defeated Gates at Camden and shortly thereafter made his way into the western part of North Carolina, Penn was invested with almost unlimited power for the peoples' defense, and when the British were defeated at King's Mountain, they retired to the South.

Penn was successively re-elected to Congress in 1777, 1778 and 1779, and the General Assembly of North Carolina unanimously directed the Speaker of the House to transmit to Penn a resolution of thanks for his many great and important services as a delegate to Congress.

He received many honors from his State in his later years and became the progenitor of a prominent family in Virginia and North Carolina. He died in 1788 in Granville County and was there buried. In 1894 his remains were reinterred on Guilford battle grounds, a few miles from Greensboro, and there is a monument there to Penn and North Carolina's other two signers of the Declaration of Independence.

General William Woodford was a picturesque figure in Caroline's history, although he died in British captivity at the height of his career in the fall of 1780. He it was who commanded the colonial forces and defeated Lord Dunmore and his British troops at the battle of Great Bridge. He was born at Windsor, on the Rappahannock, in 1734.

Early in 1776 he was given the rank of general and commanded the First Virginia Brigade, which played a conspicuous part in the battle of Brandywine. The Seventh Regiment, of his brigade, was literally cut to pieces in that action, and General Woodford was severely wounded.

In 1778 Woodford served as a brigadier-general in Lafayette's division and rendered valiant service. In the siege of Charleston General Woodford was made a prisoner of war and was taken on board a British ship to New York harbor, where he died November 13, 1780. He was buried in Trinity church yard in New York City.

There were several members of the celebrated Baylor family who distinguished themselves, all descended from John Baylor I, who owned property in Virginia as early as 1650. His sons, John and Robert, came to Virginia toward the close of the 17th Century and were shortly afterward followed by their father. John Baylor II in 1696 married Lucy Todd, of Gloucester, and represented that county in the House of Burgesses. He later moved to King and Queen and was a Burgess from that county. He was a man of wealth, a "factor" as well as a planter, employing his own ships for transoceanic trade, and his principal warehouses were at a place called "Baylor", on the Mattaponi, between Walkerton and King and Queen Courthouse.

His son, the third John Baylor, born at Walkerton and educated in England, was granted a large tract of land on which he built the fine old mansion Newmarket. His plantation was established the year before that part of Caroline was cut off from King and Queen. He was a colonel of Caroline militia and a Burgess from 1742 to 1765. He was also County Lieutenant for Orange where he had been granted a vast tract of land and where he spent his summers. He was the great turfman and importer of fine horses, his stable containing a hundred thoroughbreds at the time of his death in 1772. He was an intimate of Washington. Just after his marriage, Washington sent an order to England for a pair of shoes to be made "on Colonel Baylor's last—but a little larger than his—and to have high heels."

General George Baylor, one of Caroline's most illustrious sons, was a son of John Baylor III and was born at Newmarket in 1752. He also was educated in England. He was a member of the Caroline Committee of Safety and entered the Continental army at the outbreak of the Revolution. As a lieutenant-colonel, he was aide-de-camp to General Washington from August, 1775, to January, 1777. When he brought news of the victory over the Hessians to Congress, that body voted that a horse, properly caparisoned, be presented to him.

In 1777 George Baylor was colonel of the Third Continental Dragoons, and in September of that year his command was surprised in a midnight attack by the British near Tappan, N. Y. Sixty-seven were killed and the rest captured. Col. Baylor received a bayonet-thrust through the lungs from which he never fully recovered, although he returned to active service and commanded the First Continental Dragoons until the end of the war. He was commissioned Brevet Brigadier-General in 1783, but pulmonary trouble developed from his wound at Tappan and he sought relief in the West Indies. He died in Barbadoes in 1783 and was buried there.

Major Walker Baylor, younger brother of George

Baylor, was another valiant soldier of the Revolution, but he was disabled at Germantown when a bullet shattered his foot. Walker Baylor was the progenitor of the Baylor families of Kentucky and Texas.

Colonel George Armistead also was born at New-market. His father, John Armistead, inherited large properties in Caroline from Henry Armistead, first Burgess from Caroline, and married Lucy Baylor, sister of George and Walker Baylor. Col. John Armistead's date of birth was April 10, 1780, and he was one of seven children. All six boys of the family served in the War of 1812.

George Armistead became county lieutenant for Caroline in 1799 and a first lieutenant in the American army in 1800. He was promoted to a captaincy in 1806 and was made major of the Third Artillery in 1813. He distinguished himself at the capture of Fort George, Canada, in that year and became celebrated for his bravery and resourcefulness. His outstanding achievement was as commander of the force at Fort McHenry, Baltimore, in 1814, when he successfully defended the city from the British. For his gallant defense of the city he was brevetted Lieutenant-Colonel and was acclaimed as the "Hero of Fort McHenry."

It was during this engagement that Francis Scott Key was inspired to write "The Star Spangled Banner." The flag which flew over Fort McHenry, and which Key saw, was presented to Colonel Armistead by the government and remained in the family until recent years, when it was presented to the National Museum in Washington, where it is displayed under glass.

Few counties of any State sent more men into the

gray ranks of the Confederacy than did Caroline. There were no fewer than eleven units from the county. Officers of the various commands were as follows:

Company G, 13th Regiment, Virginia Infantry: captains, Thomas B. Coghill, resigned early in '62 because of ill health, S. E. Swann, served unexpired term, and G. Allensworth, who was elevated to the captaincy in '62; lieutenants, W. J. Hancock, Genette Anderson (mortally wounded in '62) and W. A. Gatewood.

Company H, "Sparta Grays," 13th Virginia Infantry: Milton Gouldin, captain; Julian Broaddus, 1st lieutenant, William M. Kelly, 2nd lieutenant, and Richard F. Broaddus, 3rd lieutenant. Preston Broaddus was made a lieutenant later.

Company E, "Caroline Grays," 13th Virginia Infantry: R. O. Peatross, captain, promoted to major in '63 and wounded at Drewry's Bluff and at Five Forks; John W. Scott, made captain; lieutenants, Philip Samuel (wounded at Drewry's Bluff), William E. Norment (died in '62), Lewis A. George (mortally wounded in '65.)

Company B, "Caroline Light Dragoons", 9th Virginia Cavalry: captains, S. A. Swann, promoted, and John Ware; lieutenants, Cecil Baker, James Boulware, Charles Wright and E. C. Moncure.

Company F, "Bowling Green Guards," 30th Virginia Infantry: captains, Jacob Currance, W. D. Quesenberry, John M. Hudgin and G. Allensworth; lieutenants, J. L. Burruss and John H. James.

Caroline Light Artillery: captain, Thomas R. Thornton; lieutenants, J. D. Powers, Wilson Dickinson, Thomas F. Lewis, Robert C. Thornton and James S. Bowie.

Company F, 24th Virginia Cavalry: captain, L. W. Allen; lieutenants, Thomas B. Anderson, J. E. Broaddus and H. B. Catlett.

Company E, 47th Virginia Volunteers: captain, Robert W. Eubank; lieutenants, John W. Rollins, Charles P. Powers and Stephen B. Rollins.

Company K, 47th Virginia Volunteers: captain, John P. Ware; lieutenants, James R. Dickinson, Joseph T. Terrell and Thomas C. Chandler.

Company G, 47th Virginia Volunteers: captain, Luther Wright; lieutenants, Clarence L. Woolfolk, Andrew M. Frayser and George W. Marshall.

Company H, 47th Virginia Volunteers: captain, Thomas R. Dew; lieutenants, Eugene G. DeJarnette and Joseph F. DeJarnette.

This list of officers is not necessarily complete. Throughout the war mortality among commissioned officers was as heavy as among privates, and when an officer was killed or incapacitated, another was named in his place. The same applies in other Virginia counties. The officers herein named were known to have served.

Opposing armies in the War Between the States were frequently on Caroline soil, and it was at Moss Neck, the hospitable home of the Corbins, that General "Stonewall" Jackson encamped for the winter of 1862-63, his last, and it was on Caroline soil that the great Confederate leader died. Colonel James Parke Corbin insisted upon Jackson's making the mansion his headquarters, but Jackson declined on the grounds that he was unwilling to enjoy such comforts when his men were poorly clad and in tents. So Jackson camped with his men until a serious cold contracted during the severe winter caused Dr. Hunter McGuire to insist upon his moving into an office which stood on the place.

It is familiar to all how General Jackson, in the battle of Chancellorsville, rode forward with a small detachment to reconnoiter and was shot by mistake by his own men. He was wounded by a bullet in the palm of the right hand, another through his left wrist and a third through his left arm half-way between elbow and shoulder, shattering the bone and severing an artery. In a field hospital Dr. McGuire amputated the left arm near the shoulder, and it is horrible to contemplate the suffering of the great commander, in a day when the use of anæsthetics was practically unknown.

General Jackson was brought to Guinea Station, in Caroline, and in a building on the ancient Thornton estate, Fairfield, then owned by Thomas Coleman Chandler, the great commander died on March 9, 1863.

Perhaps the most exciting incident which ever occurred in the Port Royal neighborhood, old in story, was the slaying of the assassin, John Wilkes Booth, which took place on the farm of Richard H. Garrett, a few miles distant from the town. It was on April 14, 1865, that Booth executed his dastardly conspiracy and shot President Abraham Lincoln in the Ford theater in Washington. Ten days later, he and his accomplice, Herold, made their way to Port Conway and were ferried across the Rappahannock river to Port Royal.

Booth was not a Southern man, and his exclamation,

"Sic semper tyrannis!" as he leaped from a box to the stage after firing the fatal shot, fracturing his own leg as he did so, carried no implication that the crazed actor's conspiracy had been hatched up by any other than himself.

Despite conflicting reports in regard to the motives of John Wilkes Booth, Caroline citizens are unanimous in their belief in the story handed down to them by their fathers. In this story it is alleged that the true motive for the assassination was to avenge the death of Captain John Y. Beall, Booth's close friend, whom Booth thought had been unjustly executed.

In the Fall of 1864, Captain Beall, a Virginian, undertook a hazardous enterprise on Lake Erie and was captured and sentenced to die as a pirate. Booth interested himself in Beall's behalf and procured documents to prove that Beall was a commissioned officer in the Confederate Navy and should be treated as a prisoner of war. Booth felt that the hanging of Captain Beall at Governor's Island should have been prevented by Lincoln and Secretary Seward and immediately organized a conspiracy for the assassination of both Lincoln and Seward. It will be remembered that Seward was dangerously stabbed on the night of Lincoln's assassination.

Booth and Herold made their way to the home of R. H. Garrett, where Booth, posing as a wounded Confederate soldier, was left, Herold going on to Bowling Green. The next day Herold came back to the Garrett place and later in the day a troop of Federal cavalry passed in search of Lincoln's assassin.

This aroused Mr. Garrett's suspicion, and he urged the departure of his questionable guests, who then sought refuge in the woods nearby. After nightfall the assassins returned and pleaded so earnestly for shelter that Jack Garrett, a son of the house, told them they might sleep in a tobacco barn.

On April 26, Booth's whereabouts having been ferreted out, the Union cavalrymen returned to the Garrett place. They were told that the two suspicious characters were in the barn, and the building was surrounded. On Booth's refusal to surrender, fire was applied to the building. Herold surrendered, and Booth was shot as he attempted to make his escape. The wounded assassin died on the porch of the Garrett home. Four of the conspirators were hanged, three others were sentenced to life imprisonment and another was given a shorter term. It was the most dastardly conspiracy in the history of America.

Since Reconstruction days Caroline, although desperately impoverished by the war, has prospered greatly and has sent forth many more men who have been valuable citizens of the State and Nation. Perhaps the most outstanding industry in the county since the war has been the manufacture of excelsior, introduced by William P. Lyon, of Woodford. Captain H. H. George established a thriving lumber business prior to the war, which since has been conducted by himself and members of the family, and the sumac plant at Milford, established by Thomas Haight and later bought by William Pettus Miller, of Kentucky, is said to be the largest plant of its kind in the United States.

BOWLING GREEN COUNTY SEAT

The erection of the present Courthouse of Caroline was started in 1801 and was finished in 1807 by the executors of George Hoomes. So far as is known, there was only one other courthouse building prior to the one now in use, and it stood about two miles northeast of Bowling Green.

The present building stands in practically the geographic center of the county on land which was once a part of the Bowling Green estate of the Hoomes family. The manor house, still standing on the southern outskirt of the town, is now called the Old Mansion, and on the property were the race course, the Bowling Green and New Hope Tavern. Not only did the county acquire the land from Col. John Waller Hoomes, but took the original name of his estate for the county seat.

Judges who have served on the circuit bench since the judiciary system of 1819 was established were John Taylor Lomax, Richard H. Coleman, John Critcher, J. M. Chapman, W. S. Barton, J. E. Mason, R. H. L. Chichester and Frederick W. Coleman, the incumbent.

Five portraits hang on the courtroom wall, four of them of distinguished citizens of Caroline. They were placed there in memory of

> George Washington
> Judge Edmund Pendleton
> John Taylor
> Gen. William Woodford
> A. B. Chandler, Sr.

The last named was a prominent Caroline lawyer and commonwealth's attorney for many years.

MANY MEN OF MARK

In addition to the distinguished men of early years whose lives have been briefly sketched, Caroline has produced many others who have attained prominence in various fields. Among them may be mentioned:

Governor James Hoge Tyler, born at Blenheim, the Tyler estate in Caroline in 1846, was of the ancient Tyler family claiming descent from Wat Tyler, who led the Wat Tyler rebellion in England in the reign of Richard II. James Hoge Tyler was elected Lieutenant-Governor of Virginia in 1889 and was elected Governor in 1897.

General Jo Lane Stern, prominent Richmond lawyer and military and social leader, was born at Ruther Glen. Enlisting as a private in Company C, 1st Virginia Regiment, in 1871, he arose by successive stages to the rank of adjutant-general of Virginia.

Lewis Melville George Baker, native of Caroline, founded the Baker-Himel school in Knoxville, Tenn., and afterwards became one of the city's leading lawyers.

James B. Wood, a son of Col. Fleming Wood, was born near St. Margaret's church and was at one time a deputy under Sheriff T. D. Coghill. He later moved to Richmond, where he became active in the city government.

Nicholas Ware, United States Senator from Georgia, was born in Caroline.

[205]

Francis Johnson, member of the 16th, 17th and 18th Congresses from Kentucky, was a native of Caroline. His home in Kentucky was Bowling Green, named for the Virginia county seat.

Anthony Thornton, of Ormesby, settled in Illinois, and after holding other positions of trust, was a member of the 39th Congress.

Judge Richard Hawes moved to Kentucky when he was fifteen years of age. He represented his State in Congress and was installed as Provisional Governor in 1862. Afterward he was made county judge of Bourbon County.

Dr. J. A. C. Chandler, noted Virginia educator, was born near Guinea Station. His entire career was devoted to teaching and educational administrative work. He was a professor at a college in Baltimore when called back to his native State in 1900 to become an instructor in the Richmond Woman's College. He was then professor at Richmond College and in 1909 was made superintendent of the Richmond public school system. The growth and increase in influence of the ancient College of William and Mary under his guidance as president were phenomenal. For many years until his recent death Dr. Chandler was an acknowledged leader in every educational movement in Virginia. He was active in the preservation of the history of his State and himself wrote a number of outstanding books.

A. B. Chandler, Jr., of Bowling Green, was another influential educator from Caroline. He studied law and practised for a while in Georgia with his brother,

John W. Chandler. Teaching appealing to him more than the law, he returned to Virginia, first as a teacher in Richmond, and then as professor of Latin at the Fredericksburg State Teachers' College when it was established. In 1919 he became president of that college and rendered notable service. He, also, has written a number of valuable books.

Charles Pichegru Williamson was born at Holly Hill, the home of his maternal grandfather, Pichegru Woolfolk. His father, Gabriel Galt Williamson, was a commander in the navy and was detailed to Cuba in command of the *Fulton*. His ship was wrecked in a tropical hurricane in 1859, and he died a month later of yellow fever in Florida. At the time of his death, Commander Williamson's family was living in the Wythe house in Williamsburg, but at the outbreak of the war they moved back to Holly Hill. Charles Pichegru Williamson was educated for the Disciples ministry and became president of Madison Female Institute, in Richmond, Ky. He attained wide prominence as editor of religious publications of his denomination in the South.

John Vaughan Kean, although a son of Dr. Andrew Kean, of Goochland, spent most of his productive years in Caroline. Having married Caroline Hill, of Caroline, he established the school at Olney. One of his sons, Robert Garlick Hill Kean, became a distinguished lawyer of Lynchburg, and was chief of the bureau of war of the Confederacy, under his cousin, Col. George W. Randolph.

Frederick William Coleman exerted a wide and

beneficent influence as master of Concord Academy. He was born there and, after taking a Master of Arts degree at the University of Virginia, in 1835 joined his brother, Atwell Coleman, in the conduct of the school. His brother shortly afterwards moved to Alabama, and Frederick W. Coleman conducted this famous old school for fifteen years.

His nephew, Lewis Minor Coleman, came from Hanover to Concord in 1846 as assistant master, and in 1849, Frederick W. Coleman decided to close the school, giving as one of his main reasons the fact that he wished to further the interests of his nephew in conducting Hanover Academy, in Hanover. A brief sketch of Lewis Minor Coleman, who became a professor at the University of Virginia and later a gallant colonel of artillery, losing his life in the battle of Fredericksburg, is to be found in the chapter on Hanover. Judge Charles Woolfolk Coleman became judge of the Fifth Circuit, including Norfolk County.

Another Caroline educator was Samuel Schooler, who, after graduation from the University of Virginia and service as assistant to Lewis Minor Coleman at Hanover Academy, established Edge Hill Academy in Caroline. It was closed at the outbreak of the war and he became a captain of artillery assigned to the Richmond Arsenal, where he served most of the war. In collaboration with Col. W. L. Broun, Captain Schooler worked out a system of civil service for the Confederacy from which was taken and applied the first Civil Service in the nation. He died in 1873 and was buried at Locust Grove, near Guinea. He was a poet of distinction and often contributed to the *Southern Literary Messenger*.

Colonel Archibald Samuel was a distinguished Caroline citizen who was an adjutant in the War of 1812 and represented his county in the House of Delegates. His home was Bath, nine miles north of Bowling Green, and many of his descendants reside in Tennessee.

L. Hazelwood Kemp, sheriff and afterward county treasurer of Henrico for many years, was born at Greenwood, in Caroline.

John Bernard Lightfoot, who founded the prominent tobacco firm which bore his name in Richmond, was born at Port Royal.

Caroline has produced an unusual number of outstanding ministers of the Gospel.

First should be mentioned the Reverend Jonathan Boucher, who came from England and was one of the early leaders of St. Mary's parish. He was an intimate friend of George Washington, but finally quit the Colony in 1775 and returned to England, so staunch a Loyalist was he.

The Broaddus family contributed seven members to the Baptist ministry, the first three of them, the Andrews, I, II, and III, having attained great prominence. The others, most of whom lived and wrought away from the county of their nativity, were Mordecai, W., M. E., Julian and Luther Broaddus.

Among other noted ministers from Caroline were H. T. Anderson, E. H. Rowe, Henry Wise Tribble, Henry G. Segar, Spilsby Woolfolk, Thomas Conduit, John Shackleford, Theodrick Noel, Jeremiah Chandler, Rufus Chandler, Littlebury W. Allen, Warren G. Roane, Elliott Estes, William and William A. Baynham, both M. D.s who also preached, Charles A. Lewis, James D..Coleman, Andrew Tribble, Robert Hunter Beazley, M. E. Shaddock, Richard Baynham Garrett, Robert Walker Cole, George M. Donahoe, Robert T. Daniel, Simeon U. Grimsley, John Young, John Herndon Wright, Andrew V. Borkey, William Oswald Beazley, Roland J. Beazley, and James H. Marshall.

Judge Eustace Conway Moncure practised law at Bowling Green, was commonwealth's attorney and county judge, and was a Confederate scout. He is buried at Bowling Green.

Topping Castle, on the North Anna in Caroline, has sent forth at least three sons who deserve more than passing mention. John Minor married Sarah, the daughter of Thomas Carr and Mary Dabney Carr, and from his father-in-law he received Topping Castle as a gift. He was one of the justices and prominent in his county.

His son, Major John Minor, was one of the most successful men of affairs of his day. He never aspired to public office but was a planter on an extensive scale. In addition to looking after his own broad acres, he supervised the affairs of General Thomas Nelson in Hanover from time to time when the General was away. Major Minor took part in the siege of Yorktown. Among his children was Diana, the mother of Matthew Fontaine Maury. A son, Lancelot Minor, was the father of John B. Minor, the celebrated teacher of law at the University of Virginia, and of Lancelot

Minor, Jr. and Lucian Minor, of Louisa. Another son was Dr. Charles Minor, an eminent physician of Charlottesville.

The most distinguished of Major Minor's sons was General John Minor III, who as a mere boy was with his father at the fall of Yorktown. When the War of 1812 broke out, he was made a general and stationed in and around Norfolk. At the close of the war he engaged in the practice of law at Fredericksburg, until his death, using Topping Castle as his summer home. He took a fancy to a lad who appeared as a witness in a famous trial at Culpeper and took him to Fredericksburg to be educated. The boy was Benjamin Botts, who became a celebrated lawyer and counsel for Aaron Burr in his trial for high treason. Botts named his eldest son for his benefactor.

General Minor, as a member of the House of Delegates in 1790, was an ardent advocate of measures looking to the emancipation of the slaves. He was a warm friend of President Monroe. While making a speech at a dinner in Richmond in honor of members of the Electoral College he was stricken with apoplexy and died.

It is impossible to make reference in a work of this scope to all of the men of note from Caroline, but from all of the following old families of the county have come men of distinction: Athey, Anderson, Armistead, Baylor, Blanton, Boutwell, Boulware, Bowie, Broaddus, Burke, Campbell, Chandler, Chapman, Carter, Coghill, Coleman, Corbin, Dew, DeJarnette, Dickinson, Dorsey, Garrett, George, Glassel, Gravatt, Hawes, Hurt, Martin, Minor, Motley, Peatross, Pratt, Redd,

Ricks, Scott, Smith, Sutton, Taliaferro, Taylor, Thomas, Thornton, Terrell, Waller, Washington, Woolfolk and Wyatt.

Major T. D. Coghill, a gallant Confederate officer, was sheriff of the county for many years.

E. R. Coghill, one of the most popular men in Caroline in his time, was clerk, and was succeeded by his son, E. S. Coghill.

R. L. Beale, although born in Westmoreland, practised law at Bowling Green and was a distinguished member of the bar.

William T. Chandler was also a lawyer of note.

Major R. O. Peatross went into the War of the 60s as captain of the Caroline Grays, was promoted and twice wounded. He was also an able lawyer.

Captain J. M. Hudgin, of the Bowling Green Guards, was an attorney of distinction.

Reuben Chapman was Governor of Alabama in 1847.

Judge Thomas N. Welch was county judge just after the war.

Colonel Samuel A. Swann, a brave Confederate officer, served his county for many years as treasurer and was superintendent of the State penitentiary.

Thomas W. Valentine, clerk of the circuit court from 1870 to 1892, together with his son, who is now in the clerk's office, have served ever since the circuit court was established.

Dr. Richard A. Patterson was born in Caroline, a son of Thomas Patterson, of King William. Dr. Patterson became a prominent practicing physician in Richmond. His friends liked his tobacco so well that Dr. Patterson established a small tobacco factory in

Richmond which developed into the celebrated R. A. Patterson Tobacco Company, original makers of Lucky Strikes. Dr. Patterson was a surgeon in the 56th Virginia Infantry, C. S. A.

ESTATES ARE MANY

Among the many fine old estates in Caroline, with the names of their founders, may be mentioned: Aspen Hill, Campbell; Auburn, Moncure; Airy Hill, Broaddus; Bath, Samuel; Belleville, Miller; Blenheim, Tyler; Brandywine, Boutwell; Burton Hall, Chandler; Berry Grove, Lewis; Camden, Pratt; Clay Hill, Martin; Cedar Creek, Lightfoot; Chestnut Valley, Dickinson; Cedar Vale, Redd; Clifton, Wyatt; Edgewood, Wyatt; Ellerslie, Moncure; Edge Hill, Schooler; Elson Green, Chandler; Eldorado, Coleman; Fairford, George; Fairfield, Chandler; Gaymont, Bernard; Green Fall, Wright; Greenwood, Seay; Hayfield, Taylor; Hampton, DeJarnette; Hazelwood, Taylor; Holly Hill, Woolfolk; Hillford, Motley; Ingleside, Chandler; Idlewild, Chandler; Jack's Hill, Smith; Landora, Anderson; Locust Hill, Catlett; Lake Farm, Buckner; Mill Hill, Taylor; Moon's Mount, Dickinson; Moss Neck, Corbin; Mulberry Place, Woolfolk; Maple Swamp, Tompkins; Marl Hill, Coleman; Marengo, Martin; Milwood, Lewis; Melrose, Quesenberry; Mt. Gideon, Hill; Mt. Zephyr, White; Midway, Taylor; Newmarket, Baylor; Nyland, Chandler; North Wales, Carter; Normandy, Boutwell; North Garden, Thornton; Ormesby, Thornton; Old Mansion, Hoomes; Oakley, Goodwin; Oak Ridge, Hoomes;

Port Tobago, Corbin; Providence, Anderson; Poplar Grove, Campbell; Palestine, Wright; Row's Hill, Row; Rosedale, George; Springfield, Minor; Shepherd's Hill, Woolfolk; Spring Hill, Buckner; Spring Grove, DeJarnette; Santee, Gordon; Sunnyside, Buckner; Thornhill, Hurt; Topping Castle, Minor; Thornberry, George; The Neck, Buckner; The Hill, Bowie; The Grove, Wortham; Vernon, Thomas; Windsor, Woodford; Woodlawn, Coleman; Woodpecker, Washington; Walden's Towers, Walden; Walnut Hill, Waller; White Plains, Pendleton; Waverly, Lightfoot; and Yew Spring, Corbin.

Goochland County

GOOCHLAND COURTHOUSE

Goochland County

GOOCHLAND COUNTY was once the land of the powerful Monacan Indians, the foes of King Powhatan. In fact, for many years after the first settlers arrived at Jamestown, the land which is now Goochland was rich in Indian history. The Iroquois Trail, over which the fierce northern tribes made their way to their hunting grounds and their wars further south, passed through Goochland. The ancient trail, which led south through the foothills east of the Blue Ridge Mountains, has long since been obliterated, but it is known that it passed near Goochland Courthouse, and it was near this point that the warriors crossed James River.

The first Englishmen to visit the soil of Goochland paid that visit in 1608. Captain Christopher Newport had come back from England with specific orders that he must explore the Monacan country above the falls and seek a passage to the South Sea. For the purpose he brought over with him a boat in five pieces, in order that it might be carried above the falls and rapids and then launched. He and his party went forty miles above the falls, but nothing was heard of the South Sea.

The earliest colonists found that the Indians had some vague knowledge of the Great Lakes, and the theory was that if the headwaters of the eastern Virginia rivers could be found, explorers could descend other rivers flowing westward and thus reach the South Sea. This notion prevailed for a good many years and the Jamestown colonists were often embarrassed by imperative orders from England to find the South Sea. At a much later date, efforts were made to join the rivers flowing east with those flowing west.

The Monocans, as far back as 1607, played a part in the history of the Colony which may have been more important than is generally supposed, for they were involved in the release from captivity of Captain John Smith in that year. The original Colony could not have survived without his services. It will be recalled that Captain Smith was captured by the Indians in the Fall of that year, paraded around among the tribes for weeks, and finally brought before King Powhatan at Werowocomoco and was there saved from the clubs of Powhatan's executioners by Powhatan's little daughter Pocahontas. Two days later, in a mysterious ceremonial, Powhatan adopted Smith into the tribe, promising him land and wives. Smith was then sent, with an escort of Indians, back to Jamestown, a free man.

The main reason for the Indian chief's giving freedom to Captain Smith, whose prowess was greatly admired by the tribes, was that Powhatan assumed that Smith would help in subduing the fierce Monocans, who lived above the falls of James river. So far as is known, they were the only tribe in Virginia east of the mountains which had not been brought under subjection by Powhatan. They continued to hold their tribal independence for sixty years longer. While they lived also on the south side of the James, it should be borne in mind that in the early years Goochland County included the lands on both sides of the river and what are now Cumberland and Powhatan Counties were once a part of Goochland.

Goochland was formed from Henrico in 1727 and was the first division of that original shire. Cumberland, on the south side of James River, was formed from Goochland in 1748, and in 1777 Powhatan was cut off from Cumberland. Goochland was named for Sir William Gooch, the Colony's chief executive from 1727 to 1749.

The Monacan Indians thwarted more than one effort on the part of the white settlers at Jamestown to establish homes at the falls of the James, where Richmond now stands. Fort Charles was established there by act of the Assembly of 1644-45. The Assembly finally granted William Byrd I certain privileges if he would settle fifty armed men in the vicinity of the falls as a protection against the Indians. Byrd, who was the father of William Byrd II, founder of Richmond, received large grants of land and Fort Charles was restored and maintained for many years thereafter.

The final overthrow of the Monacans also is intimately associated with the ground on which Richmond now stands, for it was there that they were defeated in a fierce battle by Nathaniel Bacon in 1676. The Monacans had been joined by the Rechahecrans from the mountains, and other fierce tribes. The menace of these Indians above the falls of the James was in reality the beginning of Bacon's Rebellion, for it was against them that Bacon mustered an army and marched without a commission from the governor, Sir William Berkeley. Apparently the Monacans left the country after the year 1676. The name survives in the village of Manakin, and it will be seen that their abandoned village was occupied by the Huguenots a little later.

In 1672 the Five Nations of New York had completely overthrown the Susquehannocks, who retreated southward, pursued by the Algonquins and Senecas. These hostile tribes first menaced Virginia in the north, and they were opposed in the Northern Neck, along the Potomac and Rappahannock by militia commanded by two distinguished grandfathers. One was Colonel George Mason, grandfather of the author of the Virginia Bill of Rights and co-author of the Virginia Constitution, and the other was Colonel John Washington, grandfather of The Father of his Country.

Nathaniel Bacon (1648-1676) lived at what is now Curles Neck and also owned an estate further up the river on the outskirts of what is now Richmond, the name Bacon Quarter Branch still surviving.

In May, 1676, word came to Bacon that the Indians had attacked the upper estate and killed his overseer and one of his servants. A crowd of armed planters assembled and offered to march against the Indians under Bacon. He made a stirring speech to them and they started their march. Meantime Bacon dispatched a courier to Governor Beverley to ask for a commission. Bacon had not gone far before a proclamation from the governor overtook him, ordering the party to disperse.

They continued on their way despite the proclamation and defeated the Indians at the falls. Later in the same year Bacon returned at the head of an army and drove the Red Men away from the white frontier.

While a majority of the French Protestants, called

Huguenots, who came to Virginia in 1700, settled on the south side of the river in that part of Henrico Shire which is now Powhatan County, it later was a part of Goochland, and many of the Huguenots settled north of the river in what still is Goochland County. So it is not improper here to give a brief account of that very remarkable and important migration to the New World.

The religious persecutions and civil wars of France have no place in this story, but one or two events are relevant. It was in 1572 that Charles IX, under the influence of his mother, Catherine de Medici, plotted the horrible St. Bartholomew's Day Massacre, in which thousands of Protestants were murdered in the three days of carnage. Religious wars broke out afresh and continued relentlessly until 1598, when Henry IV issued the Edict of Nantes, which gave reasonable religious freedom to the Protestants.

Comparative peace reigned for ninety years, but already thousands of the very best people of France had left the country. On October 22, 1685, Louis IX not only revoked the Edict of Nantes but prohibited emigration. But in spite of this, approximately 100,-000 families escaped from France, many of them going to the British Isles.

In 1698, Colonel William Byrd was largely responsible for a special invitation for a large number of the Huguenots in England to come to Virginia. When they arrived, he also was responsible for the fact than instead of their settling elsewhere (near the North Carolina line or in Norfolk County) they were sent some twenty miles above the falls of the James, and the heart of the new colony was Manakintowne, on the south side of the river, the French utilizing the village and cleared lands abandoned by the Monacans.

Governor Francis Nicholson, in his report to the London Board of Trade dated August 12, 1700, stated that the first of the Huguenots, led by the Marquis de la Muce and Monsieur de Sailly, arrived July 23, 1700 (new style). They were met at the falls of the James by Colonel Byrd and were hospitably treated until they could make homes for themselves up the river. The first party consisted of 207 persons. The second ship, in September, brought 169 more. From the third and fourth ships, the last landing at New York, some of the French made their way to the Manakintowne settlement.

A full roster of the first settlers is preserved and there are too many names to be reproduced here, but some of them in their Anglicized forms, are so prominent and so familiar in America today that a few may be mentioned. There were the Marquis Olivier de la Muce, Ch. de Sailly (Sallee), Pierre Chastain, Pierre du Loy, Isaac Chabanas (Cabaniss), Jean Parmentier, Adam Prevost, Pierre Ferrier, Isaac Arnaud, Jean Tardieu, Pierre Gaury and many others. These were among the first 207 who came over in the ship *Mary and Ann*. Among other names associated with the Manakintowne settlement were DuVal, Cottrell, de Guilliaume (Gilliam), Michaux, Flournoy, St. Clair, Trevillian, Forloynes, Marye, Bondurant, Latane, Maupin, Boisseau, and Lanier.

By an act of the Assembly in December, 1700, King William Parish was set aside as their parish and the parishioners were exempted from all taxes, except parish taxes, for seven years. In 1714 there were only 291 persons, according to the parish record; in 1728, 130 titheables, the number of individuals unknown. They had scattered to other parts of Virginia and to other Colonies.

The Virginia government gave them a tract of land on both sides of the river which consisted of 10,033 acres when surveyed by the Henrico surveyor, and the object was to give each family 133 acres. A plot of Manakintowne still survives. It was intended that the French should build an industrial community there, but this proved impractical and the French spread themselves to the farms.

A large number of them settled on the north side of the river in a section which they knew as Dover. The word has survived to this day in Dover Mills, Dover Mines, Bendover, Little Dover and Dover, the Seddon homestead. It was here that the Dover Baptist Association was formed many years later. Sabot Island was so named because it was shaped like a shoe.

If there were any English settlers in what are now Goochland and Powhatan Counties when the French arrived, they were few. These industrious and pious Huguenots were not only valuable in developing the lands of wealthy grantees living further down the river, but they formed a bulwark against the Indians. Be that as it may, it seems that Nathaniel Bacon effectually crushed the Indians and there is no record of any clashes between the Red Men and the Huguenots.

The French had not been long at Manakintowne

before dissentions arose as to who should govern them. Furthermore there was a misunderstanding as to their status under the Virginia government. The Huguenots apparently regarded themselves as a separate unit of government and called themselves the "French Colony." In the minutes of a meeting of the Virginia Council July 15, 1702, it is recorded that the Governor proclaimed that "the refugees should not use the title of colony, and that all future petitions should be presented to his Excellency in the English tongue." This was the largest unified settlement of the French Protestants in America, but the colony soon disintegrated and, according to the contemporary historian Robert Beverley, within two years there were only about 250 settlers left. The others had spread far and wide. The same historian says that there had been between 700 and 800 persons.

Framed on the wall of the clerk's office at Goochland is a remarkable old document. It is the original of the commission to the first justices, dated 1728 and signed by Governor William Gooch. Those named are Thomas Randolph, John Flemming, William Mayo, John Woodson, Daniel Stonar, R. Sallee (illegible), Tarleton Fleming, Allen Coward and Edward Scott. There also is an original bond signed by Peter Jefferson, father of the Author of the Declaration of Independence, and Arthur Hopkins.

The deed and will books run back to the beginning of the county and are very valuable. One record, often quoted as indicative of the carefree lives and fondness for high-living of the early Virginians, may be here quoted:

"William Randolph for and in consideration of Henry Wetherburn's biggest bowl of Arrack punch to him delivered at and before the sealing and delivery of these presents, the receipt whereof the said William Randolph doth hereby acknowledge, hath granted &c unto the said Peter Jefferson and to his heirs and assigns one certain tract or parcell of land 400 acres on the north side of the Northanna in the Parish of St. James, 18 May 1736."

Peter Jefferson was the father of the Author of the Declaration of Independence, and this transaction is an evidence of the friendship which existed between himself and his wife's cousin, William Randolph of Tuckahoe. They had acquired adjoining grants in what is now Albemarle and Jefferson wanted a more suitable piece of land for the erection of his dwelling. This tract was the one on which he built the Shadwell mansion. The Henry Wetherburn mentioned in the deed was keeper of Raleigh Tavern in Williamsburg.

It was between the years 1740 and 1750 that coal was discovered in the county, and it was successfully mined for many years thereafter. This is said to have been the first coal mining operation in America, and the product was shipped as far north as Philadelphia. The mines were worked successfully until the Chesapeake & Ohio Railroad was built and started bringing in cheaply mined coal from the mountains. The Dover mines, as they were called, were last operated in 1870 by General Charles P. Stone, formerly of the United States Army and on the staff of the Khedive of Egypt.

Here may be given the names of the men who served Goochland County in the House of Burgesses:

1727-28, Richard Randolph, John Bolling; 1732, John Fleming, Dudley Digges; 1736, Edward Scott, James Holman; 1738-40, James Holman, Isham Randolph; 1742, William Randolph, Benjamin Cocke; 1745, Benjamin Cocke, George Carrington; 1746, Benjamin Cocke; 1747, Benjamin Cocke, George Carrington; 1748-49, George Carrington, Archibald Cary; 1752-57, John Payne, John Smith; 1758-59, John Payne, Reuben Skelton; 1760, John Payne, John Smith; 1761-65, John Payne, Josias Payne; 1766-68, John Payne, John Bolling; 1769, John Woodson, Josias Payne, Jr., 1769-75, John Woodson and Thomas Mann Randolph.

Conventions of 1775 and 1776: John Woodson and Thomas Mann Randolph.

Not a great deal of accurate information is available about Goochland in the period leading up to the Revolution, except that a number of fine gentlemen had come into the county and made their fortunes. Many splendid manor houses had been built, where hospitality was extended with free hand.

Perhaps the most interesting of these was Tuckahoe, the ancient seat of the Randolphs, which still is a show place. Some say that it was built by William Randolph, of Turkey Island, for his son Thomas Randolph in 1690. Others hold to the belief that it was erected about 1710 by Thomas Randolph, after his marriage to Judith Churchill. The estate passed to William Randolph, who was born at Tuckahoe in 1712. He married Mary Page, of Rosewell, Gloucester County. The place then descended to Thomas Mann Randolph, who married Ann Cary, of Amthill, and they had thirteen children, two of whom may be here mentioned: Thomas Mann Randolph II was governor in 1819 and married Thomas Jefferson's daughter, Martha Wayles;

Mary Randolph married William Keith and was the grandmother of Chief Justice John Marshall.

The small window-panes at Tuckahoe have a number of names scratched upon them during the Revolutionary period with diamonds, notably the name of Colonel Ball, 1st Virginia Regiment, Continental Line. The one-room schoolhouse which still stands is believed to be where Thomas Jefferson received his earliest schooling from the tutor of the young Randolphs. Be that as it may, in the plaster of the wall still may be seen the name of the author of the Declaration of Independence in a scrawling, boyish hand.

The historic old Tuckahoe Mansion early in the 19th Century passed to Hezekiah Wight, then to the Allens, and later to Jefferson Coolidge, of Boston.

Another son of William Randolph, of Turkey Island, settled in Goochland. He lived at Dungeness, and his name was Isham Randolph. He married Jane Rogers, and it was his daughter Jane who married Peter Jefferson and was the mother of Thomas Jefferson. Among many other offices held by Peter Jefferson, he was Sheriff of Goochland at one time, but he lived at Shadwell, now in Albemarle, and it was there that Thomas Jefferson was born, the year before Albemarle County was formed from Goochland.

Here may be mentioned a peculiar thing in connection with the formation of Albemarle, which took place in 1744. While the records in the clerk's office at Charlottesville are complete, there are no records of deeds between the years 1752 and 1758. But there are deeds recorded both in Goochland and in Louisa in that period conveying lands which now are in Albemarle. The boundary lines of Albemarle appear to have been clear, but the county seat in that period was at Scottsville. One logical solution of this unusual circumstance is that citizens were so far from the Albemarle county seat that they had their legal papers recorded elsewhere for the sake of convenience. Some of these deeds were re-recorded in later years in Albemarle.

When, in 1775, committees of safety were organized in the various counties, who were to have virtual control of preparations for impending war, Goochland acted promptly, and the following distinguished citizens were named: John Woodson, Thomas Underwood, John Hopkins, William Holman, Robert Lewis, Colonel Randolph, Matthew Vaughan, Joseph Woodson, Joseph Watkins, Tarleton Fleming, John Payne, Nathaniel Massie, Reuben Ford, John Ware, Thomas Fleming, Matthew Woodson, Stephen Sampson, Elisha Leek, William Royster, William Roberts and Robert Coleman.

Goochland citizens saw many British soldiers in the last year of the Revolution, for in June 1781 the entire army of Cornwallis was within the county's boundaries, with possible exception of Tarleton's cavalry, away at the time on their raid to Charlottesville in an attempt to capture Governor Jefferson and the legislature. It was from Goochland Courthouse that Cornwallis detached Colonel Simcoe and sent him up the river to Point of Fork to destroy the miltary stores which Baron von Steuben was defending. Simcoe tricked von Steuben into believing that he was being attacked by the entire British army, and the Continental officer had to retire, leaving the stores to be destroyed. This was on June 4, 1781.

From June 7 to June 15, 1781, Cornwallis made his headquarters at Elk Hill, once owned by Thomas Jefferson. He then turned eastward leaving the place pillaged and carrying off the slaves. A beautiful spot overlooking the river has been called Cornwallis' Point ever since. Cornwallis, who had been pursuing the wily Lafayette and finally gave up the pursuit in Hanover County, now became the pursued. Lafayette pushed on to the Rapidan river and was joined by General Anthony Wayne. He turned south over the old trail which is still known as the Marquis' Road, through Orange, Louisa and Fluvanna, and from that time until the Battle of Yorktown Lafayette almost continuously harassed the rear and flanks of Cornwallis' force.

As is unfortunately true of many Virginia counties, the rosters of officers and soldiers Goochland sent to the Revolution are difficult to find. It may be of interest to note, however, that in 1771 Stephen Sampson was commissioned a captain and John Guerrant a lieutenant by Governor William Nelson. In February, 1781, the following Goochland men were commissioned: Edward Redford, first lieutenant; Nathaniel Raine, second lieutenant; John Guerrant, Jr., ensign; Richard Allen, second lieutenant; John Bott, ensign; Tandy Holman, lieutenant; Robert Bradshaw, ensign; Thomas Miller, lieutenant, and Thomas Harding, ensign. A roster of a large number of the officers is to be found elsewhere in this volume.

Goochland contributed largely to the Revolutionary

[227]

cause, and one of her Revolutionary soldiers was an important figure in the ultimate settlement of Kentucky and Ohio. That man was General Nathaniel Massie. His kinsman, Major Thomas Massie, of New Kent County, received grants of land in the Scioto Valley, near what is now Chillicothe, Ohio, as a mark of appreciation for his services in the Revolution. General Massie was followed by his younger brother, Major Henry Massie, who founded Portsmouth, Ohio, in 1803. They were sons of Nathaniel Massie, Sr., member of the committee of safety for Goochland, who had moved to the county from New Kent about 1760 and married Elizabeth Watkins.

General Massie, who was born in 1763 and died in 1813, served with the Goochland militia and was probably present at the siege of Yorktown, although only seventeen. At twenty, in the year 1783, he set out for Kentucky, where his father had been granted lands. As was true of a number of great men of that period, he was a surveyor and became an expert woodsman. In 1791 he established a village which later became Manchester, and it was one of the four earliest settlements in what is now Ohio.

He laid off the town of Chillicothe and it is recorded that in 1796 a hundred families, mostly from Virginia and Kentucky, took part in the drawing for lots. Massie was the first Major General of the 2nd Division, Ohio Militia, when Ohio was admitted as a State, serving until 1810. He held many high offices, including the presidency of the Senate.

It is impossible to say how many families from

Goochland followed General Massie to Kentucky and Ohio. Kentucky was admitted as a State in 1792, with approximately 100,000 people—the Federal census of 1790 gave Kentucky 73,677. It was estimated that perhaps two-thirds of the white people in Kentucky at that time had come from Virginia, and it is certain that a majority of the Virginians in Kentucky were from the counties treated in this book.

Just a little later two other brothers from Goochland played a conspicuous part in the founding of Missouri. They were Frederick and Edward Bates. They were sons of Thomas F. Bates and Caroline Matilda Woodson Bates, and were born at Belmont. Frederick Bates moved to Missouri in 1813 and was governor of Missouri from 1824 to 1826.

Edward Bates (1793-1869) immediately after his discharge from service in the War of 1812, went to Missouri at the age of twenty. He became Missouri's first attorney general and was sent to Congress in 1826. He was named by President Fillmore as Secretary of War, but declined to serve. Edward Bates was a contender for the Republican nomination for the Presidency when Lincoln was named as the standard-bearer and elected. He served as Attorney General under Lincoln.

The remarkable fact was true that Goochland County furnished a son for the cabinet of each of the opposing governments during the War Between the States, Edward Bates in the cabinet of Lincoln, and James A. Seddon in the Confederate cabinet of Jefferson Davis.

Two other members of the Bates family in Goochland became prominent. James Bates served as a member of Congress from Arkansas, and Thomas Fleming Bates was a member of the Virginia Convention of 1829.

William Miller was sheriff of the county in 1751, after serving as one of the justices in 1747.

Payne was a prominent name in Goochland County. The will of George Payne, sheriff of the County, of the Parish of St. James, Goochland, dated December 3, 1744, mentions his wife, Mary Woodson, and his sons, Josias, George and John.

Colonel John Payne (1713-1784) perhaps the most illustrious of the name, was a Burgess from Goochland from 1752 to 1768 and was lieutenant-colonel of militia. In his will, which bequeathed a large estate, he left his residence White Hall to his son, John Payne, Jr., and he left Newmarket to his son Archer, who married the daughter of Nathaniel West Dandridge, of Hanover, and his wife, Dorothea Spotswood, daughter of the Governor. The Paynes were closely related, through marriages and by blood to the Spotswoods, to Martha Washington and to Dolly Payne Madison.

Josias Payne, brother of Col. John Payne, was in the House of Burgesses from 1761 to 1765, and Josias Payne, Jr., was a Burgess in 1769. Captain Tarleton Payne, Captain Thomas Payne and Ensign Joseph Payne were officers in the Revolution. In the old Payne burying ground near Goochland Courthouse is the gravestone of Colonel Matthew Mountjoy Payne—"born in Goochland 1787, served forty years in the U. S. Army, wounded at Palo Alto. Died 1862, aged

75." There are also the gravestones of George Payne (1743-1831) and his wife Betty McCarthy Morton. Josias Payne, Jr., in 1784 moved to Tennessee and married his second wife, Mary Barnett, at Nash's Lick, now Nashville. His first wife was a daughter of Tarleton Fleming, of Goochland County.

James Pleasants, who was U. S. Senator and Governor of Virginia, (1822-25) was born at Contention and was an illustrious son of Goochland. He was a son of James Pleasants, Sr., of Contention, who was a son of Jonathan Pleasants and Anne Randolph, of Dungeness. He lived at Pleasant Green, and an unmarked grave there is believed to be his tomb.

Strange to say, the name Tarleton in Goochland originated with the family in England of Colonel Banastre Tarleton, the British cavalry officer whose name struck terror because of his depredations in Goochland and many another Virginia county. He encountered his own coat-of-arms in Goochland, as will be shown.

Rock Castle, overlooking the James, is one of the very old places in Goochland. The plantation, early in the 18th Century, became the property of Tarleton Fleming, who married Mary Randolph, of Tuckahoe. When Col. Tarleton raided Rock Castle during the Revolution he angrily cut down and bore away the Tarleton coat-of-arms from the paneling of the parlor. The property passed to Thomas Mann Fleming, son of Tarleton Fleming, and at his death was bought by Col. David Bullock, a prominent Richmond lawyer. It then passed to Governor John Rutherfoord and became the residence of his son, John Coles Rutherfoord. In the War Between the States the place again was invaded by the enemy, who sacked it and would have burned it had it not been for the entreaties of the colored servants. Rock Castle later passed to Dr. George Ben Johnston, the distinguished Richmond surgeon, who married a daughter of John Coles Rutherfoord.

Another famous homestead on James River was Bolling Hall, built by Col. William Bolling, who moved over from Cobbs, in Chesterfield County. He was a militia officer in the War of 1812 and a man of wealth and prominence. He was a direct descendant of the Indian Princess Pocahontas, whose granddaughter married the immigrant Robert Bolling.

Bolling Island was left by Col. William Bolling to his son, Thomas Bolling, who built the manorhouse. Later it was owned by A. Y. Stokes, of Richmond. Charles E. Bolling, city engineer of Richmond and for many years a valuable servant of the city, was born at Bolling Island.

Among the officers of the militia companies from Goochland in the War of 1812, taken from the payrolls of the 8th Regiment, 4th Brigade, commanded by Brigadier General John H. Cocke, were: Captain Abram Buford, Lieutenants John Poindexter and Leonard Sheffield, and Ensigns Thomas Poindexter and William Bates; Captain Robert L. Coleman, Lieutenants William Hall and James P. Garland, Ensigns John Myers and Charles Wingfield; and Captain Triplett T. Estes, Lieutenants Wilson C. Nicholas and

Robert B. Sthreshley, and Ensigns David Rhodes and George W. Marshall.

From Goochland came Joseph R. Underwood, United States Senator from Kentucky and colleague of Henry Clay. Thus at one time Kentucky's two representatives in the Senate were from adjoining counties in Virginia—Underwood from Goochland, and Clay from Hanover. Joseph R. Underwood was the grandfather of Oscar W. Underwood, the distinguished Senator from Alabama.

Joseph Rogers Underwood, whose mother was a first cousin of General George Rogers Clark, was born in 1791 on Licking Hole Creek about two miles north of the James in Goochland. He was a son of John Underwood, who served in the Virginia Legislature, and a grandson of Thomas Underwood, who was a member of the committee of safety and in the Legislature almost continuously from 1777 to 1790.

Joseph R. Underwood was given by his parents to his uncle, Edmund Rogers in 1803, who took him to Kentucky and educated him. Joseph R. Underwood lived first at Glasgow and then at Bowling Green and held many high offices, including a seat on the Court of Appeals, membership in Congress for a number of terms and finally membership in the Senate, to which office he was elected in 1847. He was a lieutenant in the War of 1812 and was severely wounded in Dudley's defeat in 1813.

Senator Joseph R. Underwood left a remarkable diary which is an intensely human document and throws much light upon the life and customs of his time. Many intimate references are made to Henry Clay, John C. Calhoun, John Quincy Adams, John J. Crittenden, Daniel Webster and others. His description of his journey to Kentucky when he left the home of his mother's relatives in Caroline County in the Spring of 1803, a boy of twelve years, contrasts strikingly with the modes of transportation of today. The "Aristocracy of the Covered Wagon" of the Far West has its counterpart in the regions between the Alleghanies and the Mississippi, for hundreds of families from Virginia moved with all their possessions into the new country in very much the same way as did Senator Underwood. His diary is here quoted in part:

"My uncle had made all suitable preparations for the journey, and we left with a wagon and team, a riding horse and some half-a-dozen negro slaves. We passed through Fredericksburgh, which was the first town I ever saw, thence to Winchester, and to Brownsville on the Monongahela. At this place my uncle purchased a boat in which to float down the river to Louisville. Before we reached Brownsville, we fell in with a widow woman by the name of Lane and her family, emigrating West. She also purchased a boat in which to descend with her family. The two boats were lashed together and descended in company to Louisville.

"As it would take a little time to load the boats and fit them for the journey, and as it was thought best not to put the horses on board until the boats reached Wheeling, I was sent across to that point with the horses and two negro boys. . . . My uncle arrived all safely; the horses were put on the boats and, all on board, the voyage was resumed down the river. These boats were such as traders used in freighting tobacco and other articles from the rivers of Kentucky to New Orleans. They had roof sufficient to keep us dry and comfortable in rainy weather. The voyage was tedious and monotonous. I recollect the mouth of the Big Kanawha being pointed out to me. Cincinnati was then not as large as Bowling Green now is, and there was lying in the Ohio river above Louisville the first sloop or vessel to navigate the ocean that ever was built upon the Ohio river.

"I was put on shore about six miles above Louisville on the left bank of the river, with directions how ,to find the residence of Major William Croghan, after which my uncle passed on with the boats to Louisville. I found Major Croghan at home and introduced myself as the relative of his wife and children. The family received me with open arms; the Major ordered his horse and went directly to meet my uncle in Louisville. I remained some days at the Major's, when my uncle having made arrangements to resume the journey with the wagon, I was sent for, went to Louisville, then a mere village, and we again commenced with the journey with wagon and team to my uncle's residence on the south fork of Little Barren river, near the present town of Edmonton, where we arrived towards the last of April or first of May, 1803.

"After crossing Green River we had no roads in traveling through what was then called ,the Barrens, where the country was destitute of timber, and my uncle steered through the prairies until we reached the stock country near McKinney's Station. Near this station Mc-Kinney, the proprietor, was killed by ,the Indians, and it is believed that he was the last man killed by a hostile Indian in the State of Kentucky. From this station we wound our way through the woods to my uncle's residence about four miles, where I found a new hewed log house, and four or five acres of cleared land, and my new home ,in a new and wild country."

Goochland was intimately associated with one of the most picturesque transportation systems in American history, for its entire southern boundary was traversed by the James River and Kanawha Canal. The canal boats, drawn by horses or mules, have often been pictured in song and story. They plied between Richmond and Lynchburg, with many stopping places in Goochland. A trip on one of these bateaux was usually in the nature of a lark, the ladies and gentlemen from the manor-houses pursuing their leisurely travels in friendly intercourse.

The dream of the leaders in the latter part of the 18th Century was to connect the tidewater of the James with the Ohio River and establish intercourse with the rapidly growing settlements in the Ohio Valley. As early as 1784 the Virginia Legislature granted papers of incorporation to the James River Company, for the primary purpose of improving navigation in the James. In 1785 George Washington became the first president of the company.

When Washington was hardly more than a boy he was engaged in surveying the millions of acres of Lord Fairfax, and it was during these early years of surveying that he conceived the idea of establishing transportation to the West.

The connection of Washington with the James River Company and the Midland Trail, which was surveyed under Washington's direction by General Andrew Lewis, is the basis for the fact that Washington was the founder of the original predecessor company of the present Chesapeake and Ohio Railroad. Later the towpath of the James River canal and the Midland trail became roadbeds of the modern railroad.

In 1820, the James River Company was made trustee for the State of Virginia to carry on the work which had been projected thirty-five years before. In March, 1832, the James River and Kanawha Company was incorporated, the objective being to make the James navigable from Richmond to Dunlop's Creek, in Albemarle County, and to make the Great Kanawha navigable from the Great Falls to the Ohio, and the two terminals were to be connected by a turnpike.

Only four years later the Louisa Railroad was built, its roadbed now being a part of the main line of the Chesapeake and Ohio, and other short lines were projected. The enthusiasm over canals for transportation gradually faded and finally all of the properties, canals and highways, of the James River Company passed to the Richmond and Alleghany Railroad and its properties passed in turn to the Chesapeake and Ohio. More in regard to the early history of this great railroad system will be found in the chapters in this volume on Louisa and Albemarle Counties, and in a separate chapter on transportation to the West.

The last old packet boat on the canal was the Marshall, on which the body of General Stonewall Jackson was carried from Richmond to its last resting place at Lexington.

Sabot Hill, overlooking the river, was erected in 1855 by James A. Seddon, afterward Secretary of War of the Confederacy.

Dover, nearby, was built by Arthur Morson.

Howard's Neck was built by Edward Cunningham in 1825. It was purchased in 1842 by John B. Hobson, who married Martha Bland Selden, of Westover. The place passed to Saunders Hobson.

Bendover is a beautiful old Goochland home which became the residence of the late William T. Reed, Richmond tobacconist and philanthropist.

Robert P. Letcher, of Goochland, was Governor of Kentucky 1840-44.

William Leake, the first of his name in America,

emigrated in 1685 and settled in Goochland. From him came a long line of descendants, many of them attaining prominence.

Captain Walter D. Leake commanded the Goochland Artillery in the War Between the States and after the war practiced law in Goochland. His son, Judge Andrew Kean Leake, was a lieutenant in the Army of Northern Virginia. He was a lawyer and became county judge. Judge William Josiah Leake, born in Goochland in 1843, became judge of the Virginia court of chancery in Richmond. He served four years in the army.

Captain Charles Woodson commanded a company in the Revolution.

Goochland sent many brave sons to the army of the Confederacy, many of whom never returned.

Almost the entire county was laid waste in 1864 by Colonel Ulric Dahlgren, who passed through the county on his bold but unsuccessful raid on Richmond early in 1864. Dahlgren and Kilpatrick planned a surprise attack on the city, the former attacking from the south, while the latter was to storm the fortifications to the north. Kilpatrick was beaten back, and Dahlgren's plans miscarried, as will be shown.

Dahlgren's force of cavalry left Stevensburg, in Culpeper County, February 28, 1864, and moved toward the James River. After tearing up the railroad at Fredericks Hall, in Louisa, he entered Goochland County about eight miles east of Goochland Courthouse, destroying mills and barns on his march. On

March 1 the Union cavalrymen raided Sabot Hill, home of James A. Seddon, Secretary of War of the Confederacy, burned the barn and pillaged the place.

On the same day, Dahlgren turned eastward and attempted to cross James River and strike Richmond from the south. A negro guided him to a ford, but the river was high and could not be crossed. Dahlgren, thinking that his guide had deceived him, hung the negro to a tree in the edge of Henrico County.

Thwarted in his effort to cross the river, Dahlgren fought an action with Confederates defending the city on the same evening, but was repulsed. He then tried to make his way around the north of the city, wandered through Hanover and King William Counties, and finally was slain in King and Queen. There also was a cavalry fight at Goochland March 11, 1865.

COURTHOUSE IS THE THIRD

The stately courthouse of Goochland, erected in 1826, was the third, and stands on land which once belonged to Col. Benjamin Anderson. The second courthouse was built about 1760 on this site, and the first was built in 1727 on part of what is now the property of the Women's State Farm.

The deed and will books in the clerk's office run back to 1727.

There are no portraits on the walls of the courtroom, but there is one bronze tablet bearing the following inscription:

"In remembrance of those who gave their lives and as a tribute in honor of those from Goochland County who served in the armed forces of the United States during the World War. Erected by citizens of the county."

It would be a fine thing if a movement should be started which would result in the collection of portraits of some of Goochland's many illustrious sons. Surely there must be a picture in existence of Tarleton Woodson, who was a Captain of the 10th Virginia Regiment in 1776, a Major in the 2nd Canadian Regiment in 1777, and was taken prisoner by the British on Staten Island August 22, 1777.

Many men named in this book—and they are not all—richly deserve memorials of some sort in the county of their birth.

Louisa County

LOUISA COURTHOUSE

Louisa County

IN telling the story of Louisa County its roads must be taken into consideration. Over them thundered the troops, both friend and foe, of the Revolution and of the War Between the States. Still earlier, Continental soldiers passed through Louisa on the way to their clashes with the Indians in the West and with the French and their Indian allies in the French and Indian War. Lying between Richmond and Charlottesville, and almost in the geographical center of the State, Louisa has been on the passageway between east and west.

The Three Chopt Road, along its southern border, is the oldest of these highways. The Louisa road, which traverses the County from end to end, was one of the most important stage routes in the State. The Old Mountain Road, which wound through the County to the westward along a now indeterminate route, was a great thoroughfare in early times. It is easy to visualize the carriages of Jefferson, Madison, Monroe and their predecessors floundering over the rocks and through the mud of the Old Mountain road on their journeys to and from Williamsburg, perhaps pausing at Yanceyville for refreshment. Yanceyville was quite a village in the early days and was strongly urged for the county-seat. Also, as will be shown, the first east and west railroad in Virginia was laid through Louisa.

Another road, perhaps less important but no less interesting, cut across the western part of the County and still is called "The Marquis' Road." In 1781 the Marquis de Lafayette fell back to Raccoon Ford, on the Rapidan, hoping there to be joined by General Anthony Wayne, who was on his way from Leesburg. Hearing of Wayne's approach, Lafayette turned southward and was overtaken by Wayne in Orange County. A forced march to the south was decided upon, to intervene between Cornwallis, who was then in Goochland, and military stores in Albemarle. It was over this road (which he partially built) that Lafayette crossed Louisa County from Brock's Bridge, on the North Anna, to the Fluvanna line. He encamped on June 12, 1781, at Boswell's Tavern, which is still standing.

Louisa was formed from Hanover in 1742 and was named for Queen Louise, of Denmark, daughter of George II. Its records, with the exception of one old order book, are practically complete and contain much that is of interest. In 1761 a portion of Louisa was cut off and added to Albemarle, which had been formed from Goochland in 1744. The original boundaries of both Albemarle and Louisa were somewhat vague, but apparently Louisa embraced most of the territory east of the Rivanna and extending to the Blue Ridge. The Walkers, Lewises, Meriwethers and others held large grants of land in that part of Louisa, and their land transactions were recorded at Louisa.

There was much romance in the first hundred or more years of the Virginia Colony, but, unfortunately, a majority of the stories of these romances have long since been forgotten. When Charles I was beheaded in 1649, hundreds of adherents of the Stuart family fled to Virginia as a refuge. Men came to Virginia for other reasons, and doubtless there were many cases in which sweethearts were left on the other side. In those days of fragile sailing ships the Atlantic Ocean was a serious obstacle in cases in which it divided lovers.

There is one case on record in which an English girl refused to be baffled by it. She followed her sweetheart to Virginia, married him and became the ancestress of one of the fine old American families.

In the early 1700s there was a man living in what is now Louisa County named John Poindexter. He was a man of large property, and when the county was formed in 1742 he was one of the first justices. He was a captain of militia, then in existence to keep down the Indians. From the various duties entrusted to him, he seems to have been a highly respected citizen. He died in 1753.

This John Poindexter had a grandson, also named John, who became clerk of Louisa County and served from 1790 to 1820. In the latter years of the life of this grandson, he became a Baptist and while he was serving as clerk preached from time to time at a church in the Roundabout neighborhood of Louisa County. Because of his activities as a pioneer Baptist preacher, his life was sketched in a publication called "Virginia Baptist Ministers," and that publication is authority for the story here told about his grandfather.

The elder John Poindexter, then a young man, was a French Protestant. Because of persecutions by the

Catholics in France, he fled to England, and there he fell in love with an English girl.

His father was a man of wealth and position. As there was considerable disparity in the station of this girl and young Poindexter, the father objected to the match. So strenuously did he object that he determined to send his son to Virginia and thus break it up. Accordingly his father gave John Poindexter a large grant of land, money and his passage to Virginia.

But this stout-hearted girl was not to be outdone. She loved her man and knew that he loved her, and she determined that the Atlantic Ocean should not keep them apart.

From the earliest days of the colony there was a system under which a person in England who lacked money for the passage over could indent himself as a servant for a period of years and thus make his way to Virginia.

That is what John Poindexter's girl did. She indented herself as a servant for four years and came to Virginia. Whether there had been any communication between them—probably not—is not known. But when she landed in Virginia John Poindexter was on hand to obtain one of the indented servant-girls of whose arrival he had heard.

He paid the charges, married her and took her to his plantation in Louisa. A few of their descendants still live in and around Louisa County. One of them was a Governor of Mississippi. Others have scattered far and wide, and it is a respected name in many States of the Union.

Mining operations have been in progress in Louisa

since earliest times, and even now men not infrequently spend a day "panning" the sands of Gold Mine creek, finding sufficient free gold to pay them for their labors. In the early 1800s gold was diligently mined in a rock formation near that creek. The workings were shallow. There were at least two well-organized mines—Walton's and Tinder's, from which last $20,000 was taken, $10,000 of which was found within the first six days of operation. In fact, there is a well-supported belief that at one time all the native gold in this country for the minting of coin came from Louisa and some adjoining counties.

At one time there was a thriving quarry five miles northeast of Louisa Courthouse for the production of whetstones, and at a much later date mining on a large scale for iron pyrites was carried on not far from what is now the town of Mineral. Enormous sums were invested in these properties, but the mines are practically all shut down now because of the fact that cheaper processes than the old have been found for making the acids which were formerly made from Louisa pyrites.

Until the year 1800, or shortly thereafter, there was a prominent health resort in Louisa. In a remarkably fertile area in the western part of the county now spoken of as "The Green Springs Neighborhood," there is a spring of mineral waters which in olden times was known far and wide as the Green Spring. At this spring were a number of substantial buildings for the accommodation of guests, and the patronage of the place seems to have been large. The final reference to it which is available is one in which it is stated that

Colonel Morris died, some of the buildings burned, and the project was abandoned.

This Green Springs Neighborhood is still a remarkable area. In the form of a more or less regular circle five or six miles in diameter, the land in the old days was owned by only four or five wealthy planters. Formerly the land seemed particularly adapted to the growing of wheat. So much wheat was supplied the Southern armies that during the war this comparatively small territory was often spoken of as "The Granary of the Confederacy."

When the Louisa railroad was being organized, it was decided that the planters of the Green Springs would be offered stock. These old gentlemen conferred and agreed that yes, a railroad would probably be a good thing and they would take stock, provided, however, that the tracks would not be laid within five miles of their property. That is the reason why the roadbed of the Chesapeake and Ohio is almost in the arc of a circle from Louisa to Gordonsville.

Louisa furnished many officers and men both for the Revolution and for the French and Indian wars of 1756-1763. Many went from Louisa to the War of 1812, and an unusually large number to the army of General Lee.

Such things do not appear in court records, but during the Revolution a man named Holland, presumably from Louisa, and another patriot, captured two Tories who had attached themselves to the British forces as marauders and hanged them in Louisa near the Goochland line. Twenty or thirty of the Louisa citizens witnessed the hangings and connived at them.

In 1781, Washington sent the young Marquis de Lafayette to Virginia. In addition to his other duties he was to watch Cornwallis. In this period, shortly before Cornwallis was surrounded at Yorktown, Lafayette with his forces spent much time in and around Louisa. There are frequent references in the Louisa records to recompense to Louisa citizens for goods impressed for the public good both by Lafayette and Wayne.

Members of the House of Burgesses from Louisa were: 1742, Abraham Venable, Charles Barrett; 1744-46, Charles Barrett, Robert Lewis; 1747, Charles Barrett; 1748-49, Charles Barrett, Abraham Venable; 1752-53, Abraham Venable, Thomas Walker; 1754-55, Abraham Venable, Robert Anderson; 1756-58, Robert Anderson, Charles Barrett; 1758-59, Thomas Johnson, Thomas Walker; 1760, Thomas Johnson, Charles Smith; 1761-64, Thomas Johnson, William Johnson; 1765, Thomas Johnson, Patrick Henry; 1765-68, Patrick Henry, Richard Anderson; 1769-72, Richard Anderson, Thomas Johnson; 1773-74, Richard Anderson, Dabney Carr (died), Thomas Johnson; 1775, Thomas Johnson, Thomas Walker.

Conventions of 1775: Thomas Johnson and Thomas Walker.

Convention of 1776: Thomas Johnson and George Meriwether.

By far the most remarkable single act of heroism with which the County has been associated was Jack Jouett's ride.

Richmond had fallen and Governor Jefferson had gone to Monticello, and the Legislature was in session at Charlottesville. It is not known just what Jack Jouett was doing at Cuckoo Tavern, but he was probably having a drink with friends. It was on the night of June 3, 1781. The intrepid British cavalry officer, Col. Banastre Tarleton, had already been laying waste the country to the east of Cuckoo, and there were rumors from the lower end of the County that Tarleton might make a dash for Charlottesville to surprise Governor Jefferson and the legislature.

That is exactly what Tarleton attempted to do—over the old Louisa Road. Jack Jouett heard the hoof-beats of a body of cavalry approaching Cuckoo Tavern and knew what it meant. He dashed out of the tavern, mounted his horse and galloped away for Charlottesville. For thirty-eight miles that all-night ride continued, but he arrived in time to warn Mr. Jefferson and members of the legislature. The legislature then met in Staunton and voted Jack Jouett "an elegant sword and pair of pistols." The distance from Cuckoo to Charlottesville by modern highway is thirty-eight miles, and Jack Jouett could not have cut much from that distance. His route was probably longer.

No poet has described the ride of Jack Jouett as Longfellow has so beautifully portrayed the ride of Paul Revere. But historians throughout the nation have acclaimed Jack Jouett's remarkable exploit.

Tarleton stopped at Castle Hill, the home of Dr. Thomas Walker in Albemarle, to capture members of the legislature visiting there, and tarried briefly for breakfast. Had he not done so, Jack Jouett's ride might have been in vain. As it was, Governor Jefferson escaped and all the members of the legislature got away but seven who were captured by the British.

Patrick Henry moved from Hanover to Louisa in 1764 and in the session of 1765 was sent to the House of Burgesses, the first legislative office he ever held. He was re-elected from Louisa for the following term. He lived at a place called "Roundabout," being not far from the old Johnson and Fox estate, Roundabout Castle. The remains of the house in which Henry lived stood until a few years ago.

Henry had hardly taken his seat in the House of Burgesses before he introduced his celebrated resolutions condemning the Stamp Act, which are generally conceded to have been the first formal opposition to the Stamp Act and the scheme of taxing America by the British Parliament. It was in advocacy of these resolutions, written on a blank leaf of an old law book, that Henry made his famous oration: "Cæsar had his Brutus, etc." Patrick Henry fortunately preserved this old page of a lawbook which had been blank, but on which such momentous words were written by him. Later in life he wrote an endorsement upon it and among his papers there was found, after his decease, one sealed and thus marked:

"Enclosed are the resolutions of the Virginia Assembly in 1765, concerning the Stamp Act. Let my executors open this paper."

On the back of the paper containing the resolutions was the following endorsement:

"The within passed the House of Burgesses in May, 1765. They formed the first opposition to the Stamp Act and the scheme of taxing the American people by the British parliament. All the colonies, either through fear, or the want of opportunity to form an opposition, or from influence of some kind or other, had remained silent. I had been for the first time elected a burgess a few days before, was young, inexperienced, unacquainted with the forms of the house and the members who composed it. Finding the men of weight averse to opposition, and the commencement of the tax at hand, and that no person was likely to step forth, I determined to venture; and alone, unaided and unassisted, on the blank leaf of an old law-book wrote the within. Upon offering them to the house, violent debates ensued. Many threats were uttered, and much abuse cast on me by the parties for submission. After a long and warm contest, the resolutions passed by a very small majority, perhaps one or two only. The alarm spread throughout America with astonishing quickness, and the ministerial party were overwhelmed. The great point of resistance to British taxation was universally established in the colonies. This brought on the war, which finally separated the two countries and gave independence to ours. Whether this will prove a blessing or a curse will depend upon the use our people make of the blessings which a gracious God hath bestowed on us. If they are wise, they will be great and happy. If they are of a contrary character, they will be miserable. Righteousness alone can exalt them as a nation. Reader, whoever thou art, remember this; and in thy sphere, practice virtue thyself, and encourage it in others. P. Henry."

If, in a sense, Patrick Henry's glory was "borrowed" from Hanover, where he was born, Louisa has a claim in its own right to undying fame in connection with the events which led up to the Revolution. It came about through one of Louisa's own native sons, Dabney Carr, brilliant orator and lawyer, and indefatigable patriot. Unfortunately he was cut off in the very prime of life at the age of 30 and shortly after the fulfillment of the events which are to be related.

All students of pre-Revolutionary history are familiar with the importance of that powerful engine of resistance, the Committee of Correspondence between the legislatures of the several colonies. The Virginia

House of Burgesses was credited with the honor of furnishing the member who introduced the measure on March 12, 1773. That member was Dabney Carr, and he was appointed on the standing committee of correspondence and inquiry.

William Wirt says in this connection: "In supporting these resolutions, Mr. Carr made his debut, and a noble one it is said to have been. This gentleman, by profession a lawyer, had recently commenced his practice at the same bar with Patrick Henry; and although he had not yet reached the meridian of life, he was considered by far the most formidable rival in forensic eloquence that Mr. Henry had ever yet had to encounter. . ."

Unfortunately, within two months after Mr. Carr took so notable a stand in the House of Burgesses he was stricken. He was the husband of Jefferson's sister Martha. In the clerk's office at Louisa is a record dated September 13, 1773, showing that on that day appeared Thomas Jefferson, as the executor of Dabney Carr. Carr's Bridge over Elk Creek was named for him.

Dabney Carr's father was John Carr, who lived at Bear Castle, on the North Anna river about 18 miles northeast of Louisa, and he owned land on both sides of the river. Dabney Carr's remains are in the burying ground at Monticello.

In the early years it was the general belief of citizens all over the country that canals and inland waterways would solve the transportation problems of the country. The state issued bonds for the construction of canals.

During that period, mainly through the enterprise

of Louisa men, the Louisa Railroad was incorporated February 18, 1836, and its tracks were laid from Gordonsville, on the west, through Louisa county to a junction with the Fredericksburg and Richmond railroad in Hanover. This little railroad was important. Not only was it one of the pioneer steam railroads in America, but it was the basis on which the great Chesapeake and Ohio system was founded. In 1848 provision was made for its "extension to the dock in Richmond." In 1850 an act was passed changing its name to the Virginia Central. Then came the Covington and Ohio railroad, to a point on the Ohio river, and the Blue Ridge railroad, from Mechum's river to Waynesboro. Intimately associated with the severe engineering difficulties of building these first disconnected roads through the mountains was the name of Col. Claudius Crozet, for whom the town was named.

The first two presidents of the old Louisa Railroad were Louisa men. First, Frederick Overton Harris, for whom the town of Frederick Hall was named, served until 1841, when Charles Y. Kimbrough was made president, serving until his death in 1845. Then came Edmund Fontaine, who served until 1865. Charles Thompson, a Louisa man, was one of the early directors, and John Garrett was another Louisa man among the founders. The first presidents were paid $1,500 annually, but later their salaries were cut to $1,000.

The Virginia Central was practically dismantled during the war, and at its close in 1865 the organization of what is now the Chesapeake and Ohio was begun. It was completed in 1873, and General Williams C.

Wickham, of Hickory Hill, Hanover County, was its first president. The story of early transportation to the West is so interesting that a separate chapter in this book is devoted to it.

In this connection it may be pointed out that the road which is now the Richmond, Fredericksburg and Potomac, in the old days popularly called the Fredericksburg and Richmond Railroad, ante-dated the Louisa Railroad very slightly. It operated the Louisa Railroad at one period. It was chartered in 1834 and the first steam train that ever pulled out of Richmond was on February 13, 1836. It ran only twenty miles to the South Anna River. In 1837 the line was completed through to Fredericksburg. Passengers and freight were there discharged and conveyed by stage to Aquia creek where boats were available for points further north. The first president was John A. Lancaster.

It may also be worthy of note that one of the early tobacco factories of America was operated near Buckner, in Louisa County, by Frederick Harris and members of the Goodwin family. They made pipe tobacco. Nathaniel Harris married a Goodwin.

Troops of both sides were frequently on Louisa soil during the War Between the States. Colonel Ulrich Dahlgren, in his famous although unsuccessful raid on Richmond in 1864, left Stevensburg, in Culpeper County, February 28, and tore up the Virginia Central Railroad near Frederick Hall. He then crossed the County into Goochland. The Federal General Stoneman raided Louisa Courthouse May 2, 1863, and destroyed the railroad at that point. On the eve of the Battle of Trevilians, General Fitzhugh Lee camped near the county-seat June 10, 1864. General Wade Hampton, on the same day, camped in the Green Springs neighborhood.

On June 11 and 12, 1864, was fought the Battle of Trevilians, in which there were more men engaged than in other cavalry engagement of the war. General Wade Hampton and General Philip Sheridan were the opposing commanders. It was a bloody conflict and there are many soldiers killed in that battle now buried in the cemetery just west of Trevilians, while still others lie in the cemetery at Louisa.

On June 11, General George A. Custer (the Indian fighter) moving westward, got between Fitzhugh Lee and Hampton's main force, capturing the Confederate wagons. Lee recaptured the wagons, but retired to join Hampton. There was fierce fighting.

On June 12, Sheridan's cavalry, coming from Trevilians Station, attacked Hampton's cavalry, who had taken a position across the road. A bloody engagement followed, and the Union cavalry was driven back. That night Sheridan withdrew to the eastward.

PRODUCED DISTINGUISHED SONS

Many men have gone from Louisa County who rendered notable service to their State and Nation.

James Overton was a gallant soldier from Louisa in the French and Indian War and was one of the band of Virginians who saved the remnants of Braddock's defeated army in 1755.

Colonel Thomas Overton, son of James Overton, was a captain of cavalry in the Continental line and also served in the War of 1812 on the staff of General Andrew Jackson.

John Overton (1766-1833) another son of James Overton, moved to Tennessee where he practiced law and was elevated to the bench. He was a prominent figure in politics and was a law partner of Andrew Jackson. He was a second in one of General Jackson's celebrated duels. Overton, regarded as the wealthiest citizen of Tennessee in his time, in partnership with Jackson in 1794 purchased the land and in 1819 they together founded the town of Memphis.

Another John Overton, nephew of James Overton, was a captain in the Revolutionary army and afterward represented Louisa in the State legislature.

Captain James Winston (1753-1826) was for many years one of the justices and lived at Malvern. He commanded a company in the Revolution and was with General Greene in the South. He was the grandson of William and Barbara Overton Winston, and the son of John and Alice Bickerton Winston. He married Sarah Marks.

Captain John Winston (1757-1800) a brother of Captain James Winston, received a warrant in 1783 of 4,000 acres for services as a captain in the Revolution. He married a daughter of Thomas Johnson, of Louisa.

Captain Anthony Winston is recorded as having served in the Revolution from Louisa, but available records conflict as to whether he was the Anthony Winston, of Buckingham County, who moved after the Revolution to Tennessee and thence to Madison County, Alabama, and was the grandfather of John Anthony

Winston, Governor of Alabama 1853-57, and also the grandfather of John Pettus, Governor of Mississippi.

Captain Anthony Winston, of Buckingham, was a Revolutionary soldier, sheriff of Buckingham, a Burgess from that County in 1775 and also was a member of the first of the three conventions of 1775. He was the foster-father of the celebrated Revolutionary giant, Peter Francisco. Some of Peter Francisco's descendants intermarried with Louisa families and settled in Louisa, where the name is still familiar.

Peter Francisco was one of the most picturesque figures in the Revolution. As a child of five or six years, he was left by a ship-captain at City Point in the year 1765. No one knows whence he came, but his clothing and the silver buckles on his shoes indicated that he was of a substantial family—probably in Portugal—and had been kidnapped. Anthony Winston, of Buckingham, took him home with him and cared for him.

Francisco grew to be a man of enormous size and strength. He was said to have been six feet six inches in height, and to have weighed 260 pounds. He volunteered for service in the army when very young and was noted for a number of single-handed exploits. On the battlefield of Guilford Courthouse there is a monument marking the spot where he killed eleven men in a fierce onslaught. Because of his great strength and valor, he was apparently something of a free-lance, and many remarkable exhibits of his courage and strength are recorded. The spot in Nottoway County is marked where in July, 1781, he defeated, singlehanded, nine of Tarleton's British dragoons.

[256]

Early in the war he complained that the regulation swords were not big enough for him, and one was specially made for him at Washington's direction over five feet from hilt to point. A massive sword given him by Col. Mayo is in the Virginia State Library. After the war he served for many years as door-keeper of the House of Delegates. He died in 1836.

Joseph Winston, a first cousin of Captains James and John Winston, was born in Louisa June 17, 1746, and died in North Carolina in 1815. At the age of seventeen he joined a company of rangers under Captain Phelps which on September 30, 1763, was drawn into an ambuscade by the Indians. Young Winston's horse was shot under him and he was twice wounded, finally escaping from the field in a miraculous manner. He was at Braddock's defeat in 1755 and in 1769 moved to North Carolina and settled in Forsythe County. He was a member of the Hillsboro convention in 1775 and served against the Cherokees in 1776 as a major. He commanded the right wing at King's Mountain and for his distinguished service on that day was voted an elegant sword by the North Carolina legislature. He was a member of Congress 1793-95 and 1803-07. The county seat of Forsyth County (now Winston-Salem) was named for him.

Captain Francis Campbell was another gallant officer of the Revolutionary army who lived in Louisa.

Dabney Carr, Jr., a son of the celebrated Louisa patriot hitherto mentioned, was a familiar figure in Louisa although he was born in Albemarle. He was a lawyer of marked ability and finally was honored with membership of the Supreme Court of Appeals of Virginia.

Chapman Johnson, born in Louisa, was another distinguished lawyer. He practiced for most of his career at Staunton and often appeared before the Supreme Court. He was a grandson of Thomas Johnson, who married Ann, the daughter of Nicholas Meriwether of Albemarle, and Thomas Johnson was the colleague from Louisa of Patrick Henry in the House of Burgesses.

Shelton F. Leake, who was a familiar figure at the Louisa Court, became a member of the Federal Congress and was Lieutenant-Governor of Virginia.

William Overton Callis (1756-1814) while serving as a lieutenant in the Revolutionary army, was desperately wounded at the Battle of Monmouth. When he recovered he went back into active service and was an aide to General Nelson, with the rank of major, at the siege of Yorktown. He represented Louisa in the convention of 1788 which ratified the Federal constitution. He for many years represented Louisa in the Legislature and voted for the Virginia resolution of 1798. He was elector for president and vice-president and voted for General George Washington for his second term. He was born near Urbanna, but lived at Cuckoo and died there.

Arthur Pendleton Bagby, born in Louisa in 1794, studied law and moved to Alabama to practice. In 1820 he was sent to the Alabama legislature and became speaker of that body. In 1837 he was elected Governor of Alabama, and in 1841 was sent to the

United States Senate. In 1848 he was appointed Ambassador to Russia.

George Poindexter (1779-1853) was another who was born in Louisa and moved from Virginia to another State to make a distinguished name for himself. He studied law and went to Mississippi to practice. He became Attorney General of that State and took part in efforts to bring Aaron Burr to trial. He was a member of the Mississippi territorial legislature and was sent to Congress. He afterward became a Federal judge and was aide to General Andrew Jackson at the Battle of New Orleans. After holding many high offices, including membership in both houses of Congress, he became Governor of Mississippi and while holding this office sponsored Mississippi's first code.

It is surprising how many great educators have gone from Louisa, when the facilities for obtaining education were in many cases limited.

One of the most notable men who ever went from Louisa was a teacher, John B. Minor, who for many years was the only law professor at the University of Virginia. He was a member of the law faculty for approximately fifty years, and hundreds of young men who afterward became prominent members of the legal profession throughout the Nation learned their law from him and were privileged to come under his benign influence. Law-books of which he was the author became famous throughout the land and are in use by the lawyers of today.

Herbert H. Harris was professor of Greek for many years at Richmond College, now the University of Richmond.

Dr. Robert Lewis Dabney, whose career is sketched further on in this chapter was one of the most distinguished of all the teachers and leaders of the Southern Presbyterian church.

Dr. James Morris Page, born at Sylvania in the Green Springs, a son of Thomas Walker and Nancy Watson (Morris) Page, was for more than thirty years a leader of the faculty of the University of Virginia and was dean for thirty years.

Dr. Charles W. Kent was professor of English at the University of Virginia, and Dr. Hunter Pendleton was of the faculty of the Virginia Military Institute.

Dr. John William Jones was a distinguished son of Louisa County who served as Chaplain of the 13th Virginia Infantry and was on the staff of General Robert E. Lee. He was known throughout the Confederate army as the "Fighting Parson" and was a celebrated minister after the war. His "Personal Reminiscences of General Robert E. Lee" is regarded as one of the most interesting books which has been written about the great Confederate leader. He also was author of a notable work called "Christ in the Camp."

Dr. William S. Fowler represented Louisa in the legislature. He was too old for service afield in the War Between the States, but was a voluntary aide to Governor Letcher and was assigned to General Pickett's brigade with the rank of colonel of cavalry.

David Richardson was an eminent mathematician and astronomer and an almanac which he published was famous throughout Virginia and the Carolinas.

Lucian Minor, a brother of John B. Minor, the

great law teacher, was a gentleman of studious habits who was born in the County and spent his latter years not far from the county seat. He studied law and was of the faculty of the College of William and Mary. He was a frequent contributor to the *Southern Literary Messenger* when Edgar Allan Poe edited that publication.

Lancelot Minor, Jr., another brother of the same family, became a prominent citizen of Amherst. He was a man of scholarly attainments and exerted a wide personal influence.

David Johnson, of Louisa, was Governor of South Carolina from 1846 to 1848.

Col. G. A. Goodman went into the Confederate army as a lieutenant of the Gordonsville Grays, later becoming colonel of the 13th Virginia Regiment.

William F. Gordon attained much acclaim as the author of his poem on secession, which was widely published and admired.

Captain Frank V. Winston was not only one of the ablest lawyers Louisa County has produced, but he was an outstanding Christian character who exerted a wide influence upon his fellow-citizens. He was a lieutenant of the militia company known as the Louisa Blues prior to the outbreak of the War Between the States and shortly after the beginning of hostilities was made captain of that company, serving with much distinction in the Army of Northern Virginia. He was sent to the legislature in the Fall of 1863.

Five of his brothers, all born at Malvern, on the South Anna river, may here be mentioned.

John Hastings Winston, eldest son of John Hastings Winston Sr., who was a son of Captain James Winston, became a distinguished educator. In his early life he founded Westwood Military Academy, in Campbell County near Lynchburg, then taught at New London Academy, and finally moved to Bristol and founded the school which is now King College.

James E. Winston, a young man of much promise, left the University of Virginia to join the army and was a sergeant in the Louisa Blues, commanded by his older brother, Captain Frank V. Winston. James E. Winston was killed at his brother's side in a charge near Chantilly, September 1, 1862.

Thomas S. Winston in early life moved to Louisiana, where he became a prominent sugar-planter.

William A. Winston, who inherited the home place, Malvern, which was the second of the old Winston places in Louisa (Riverside was the first) lived his life in farming the broad acres of his ancestors. He was influential in his community, reared a large family of men and women who attained prominence, and represented a fine type of the "old Virginia gentleman." Passionately fond of the chase, in his early youth he originated what is now the third oldest pack of foxhounds in America. He was a lieutenant of cavalry in the War Between the States and was wounded in the hand.

Joseph Barbee Winston, youngest of the brothers, for some years operated a private school at Louisa, then moved to Waynesboro where he established a private school for girls which was widely patronized.

Dabney A. "Tap" Trice deserves mention here because of his exceptional valor as a member of the Louisa company in the War Between the States. His commanding officer, Captain Frank V. Winston, used to say of him that Tap Trice was utterly impervious to fear and that often he apparently went out of his way to put himself in the most dangerous positions. He was seven times wounded and lost an eye. On June 22, 1862, he was so desperately wounded that when the hospital corps made their rounds the medical officer remarked: "There is no use in trying to do anything for that man. He is going to die." Tap Trice struggled to a sitting position and declared with emphasis, "I'll be damned if I am!" So they took him to the rear and he was back in ranks before many weeks had elapsed to receive several more wounds.

The man whose reputation has gone further afield, perhaps, than that of any other Louisa citizen still lives on his farm in the Green Springs neighborhood. That man is Admiral David Watson Taylor, in his prime recognized as the foremost naval constructor in the world. Perhaps the greatest chief of naval construction the United States Navy ever had, Admiral Taylor not only was consulted by many foreign governments but honored by them with decorations and other marks of appreciation of his skill in building great men-of-war. He was born at West End in 1864, a son of Henry and Mary Minor Watson Taylor, and now resides at Grassdale.

R. Lindsay Gordon, Jr., still lives on his farm near Louisa. For more than fifty years he practiced his profession at the Louisa bar. He was a member of the Constitutional Convention of 1901-2 and for more than twenty years represented his county in the legislature. A lawyer of the "old school," Mr. Gordon has been known for his rugged individuality, his eloquence and his high integrity.

Among other living sons of Louisa should be mentioned James Overton Winston and Thomas S. Winston, sons of William A. Winston, of Malvern. Through their energy, sound judgment and integrity they attained a position of leadership among American contractors. They built the dams for the great waterworks systems of New York, Boston, Providence and other large cities, in addition to other gigantic construction projects, and never failed to give employment to their neighbors in Louisa when practicable.

David Meriwether, of Louisa, was Governor of New Mexico Territory 1853-57.

COURTHOUSE IS NEW

The present courthouse, pictured in the accompanying illustration, was erected on the site of the old in 1904. The former courthouse was erected in 1818, and prior to that time there had been two other courthouses. The door stone of the 1818 courthouse, worn almost through by passing feet throughout the long years, lies on the court green now and is an interesting relic.

The first courthouse was built in 1742 on lands of Mathew Jouett and at his expense on Beaver creek, near what has been known in more recent years as the old Talley place, almost a mile from the present site of the courthouse. The lands of Mathew Jouett, probably the grandfather of Jack Jouett, who, however, was born in Albemarle, were extensive and reached from

Cuckoo almost to the southern corporate limits of what is now the Town of Louisa. Beaver Creek was the old name for the little stream just south of Louisa generally known as the Tanyard branch. This first courthouse was built of logs and not until two years later were glass windows put in.

This first courthouse was occupied until 1757 when a new one—a frame structure—was erected at the expense of the county. It stood on land of Thomas Johnson close to the site of the present building, "on the ground of Bonivita's store." Bonivita's store was a candy shop on the northwest corner of the courthouse square, a piece of property the county has never owned.

Joseph Bickley qualified as the first sheriff of Louisa and he built a log jail on his place, which was more than five miles from the courthouse. In 1745 the court ordered that a jail be built at the courthouse to save the expense of transporting prisoners such a distance. Accordingly, a log jail was erected at the courthouse which cost the county 1,632½ pounds of tobacco.

One of the first orders of the court was for the erection of a whipping-post and stocks. All criminal offenses in those days were punished by death, branding, whipping or fine, but not imprisonment. Imprisonment for debt was of frequent occurrence until 1850. The county levy was paid in tobacco assessed on the titheables as a poll tax. There was no property tax.

The first clerk of the county was James Littlepage, a prominent citizen of Hanover and member of the House of Burgesses. Littlepage served Louisa through his deputy. Thomas Perkins, who kept the county records at his own home. Later (1790-1820) John

[265]

Poindexter was clerk and the records were kept in a little brick building which stood until recently on the Winston Hall property, a few miles south of Louisa.

The first session of court held in Louisa as a separate county was on December 13, 1742. The following justices of the peace appeared and qualified: Robert Lewis, Robert Harris, Christopher Clark, John Carr, Ambrose Smith, Joseph Bickley, Abraham Venable, Joseph Fox, Charles Barrett, Thomas Johnson, John Poindexter, Thomas Merriwether and Joseph Shelton. William Wallace was King's attorney.

In the earliest records of the county it is apparent that the militia was well-organized, and there were frequent attacks from the Indians. In the county was a regiment of four companies, two of infantry and two of cavalry. Robert Lewis was colonel, Richard Johnson, lieutenant-colonel, and James Littlepage, major. John Poindexter and Nicholas Meriwether were captains of cavalry, and Abraham Venable and Ambrose Joshua Smith, captains of infantry. Men frequently carried their guns with them to church. Members of this early militia organization saw valiant service in the French and Indian wars.

Portraits Are Numerous

In connection with the portraits which hang on the walls of the court room it may be said that

James Lindsay Gordon, who was born in 1813 and died in 1879, was Commonwealth's Attorney of Louisa for 39 years and was regarded as an able prosecutor. He was particularly known for his scholarly attainments and his appreciation of poetry.

[266]

Judge Edward H. Lane was one of the old County judges whose ability as a jurist was recognized. He was judge of Louisa County from 1870 to 1880.

Judge Daniel Grimsley, while residing in Culpeper, was circuit judge of the circuit including Louisa and was much respected and beloved in Louisa.

Judge Frederick Wilmer Sims, while of a recent period, was one of Louisa's most distinguished citizens. He was born July 23, 1862, a son of Dr. F. H. Sims, who died in the County in 1883. His mother was M. L. Kimbrough, a daughter of Captain Charles Y. Kimbrough. Judge Sims was admitted to the bar in 1885 and enjoyed a wide practice in Louisa and adjoining counties. In 1890 he was elected County Judge, in which capacity he served until 1904 when the old county judicial system was abolished. He returned to active practice and enjoyed a large clientele. He served in the State Senate and was patron and advocate of a number of highly salutary legislative measures. In 1917 he was elected by the Legislature to serve as a member of the Virginia Supreme Court of Appeals. In 1924 he became president of the court and was serving in that capacity at the time of his death in 1925.

Jesse J. Porter was identified with the clerk's office over a period of fifty-eight years, from which the war years, of course, should be deducted. He first entered the clerk's office as a deputy in 1854 and was serving as clerk of the county at the time of his death in 1912. He was born in the county August 26, 1936, a son of James D. Porter and Catherine Harris Porter. In May, 1861, he enlisted as a corporal in Company D, 13th Virginia Infantry (the Louisa Blues) and soon rose to a lieutenancy. He was regarded as an unusually gallant soldier. He was wounded in the Battle of the Wilderness. Returning to his command, he was captured at Winchester, September 19, 1864, and held prisoner at Fort Delaware until June 1865.

John Hunter held the office of clerk from 1820 to 1852.

Col. William O. Harris was County Judge from 1837 to the time of his death in 1861. Although not of military age, he volunteered his services in the War of 1812 and was honorably discharged at its close. He was Colonel of the 40th Regiment of Virginia Militia. For many years Col. Harris was an influential member of the Legislature.

Dr. William Meredith was a beloved physician of the County.

Gen. Clayton G. Coleman was born in 1807 and died in 1872. He at one time headed the Louisa militia.

Matthew Anderson Hope was born in 1823 and died in 1882. He was one of the Justices and was regarded as the most powerful man, physically, in the County in his time.

Andrew J. Richardson was for many years a commissioner of the revenue.

J. C. Cammack was clerk immediately after the War Between the States.

Col. William B. Pettit resided in Fluvanna but had such a wide law practice at the court of Louisa that his portrait was hung in the courtroom. He was a member of the Constitutional Convention of 1901-2 and was regarded as a lawyer of ability.

Judge Egbert R. Watson resided in Albemarle, a

prominent lawyer in his day, and often appeared in cases at Louisa Courthouse.

Dr. Robert Lewis Dabney was born on the South Anna river March 5, 1820, and lived until January 3, 1897. He started his adult career as a minister and was the pastor of Tinkling Spring church, in Augusta. In 1853 he was called to the faculty of the Union Theological Seminary, where he remained until 1861. He was on the staff of General T. J. Jackson and after the war returned to the Seminary, where he remained until 1883. From 1883 to 1894 he was on the faculty of the University of Texas. Not the least of the contributions of his useful life was his "Life and Campaigns of Lieutenant-General T. J. (Stonewall) Jackson," written out of the fullness of his own personal associations with the great Confederate leader.

RECORDS ARE QUAINT

Following are a few excerpts from the old record books of Louisa County:

August 14, 1772.—Award was made to a plaintiff of twenty gallons of good rum.

———

William Phillips, Gent., came into court and complained that William Pettit, with evil disposition with intention to render him scandalous and despicable as a magistrate of this county, half said to the said Phillips that the said Phillips was a fool, an ass and a villain, and the said Phillips, being in court, waived his privilege of a further day for trial and submitted to a trial immediately, and the court, having heard the evidence, are of the opinion that he is not guilty, therefore it is ordered that he be discharged.

———

June, 1773.—His Majesty's Justices considered the case of a negro woman accused of administering poisonous medicines to two

[269]

of her neighbors. She was found guilty and was ordered to be burned in the left hand, then released from prison.

At a court held May 12, 1766, Patrick Henry and Robert Armistead took the oath as vestrymen.

(A majority of the references to Patrick Henry are as Patrick Henry, Jr.).

December 13, 1773.—David Thompson, being committed by a mittimus under the hand of William Phillips, Gentleman, he having been served with a warrant under the hand of a magistrate and carried before the said Phillips for having taught and preached the Gospel under the denomination of a Baptist without having a license for so doing, on hearing the matter it is the opinion of the court that the said Thompson be discharged.

There is a record in 1769 that Richard Anderson, Gent., was appointed a Major for the county by a commission from His Excellency Norborne Berkeley, Baron de Bottetourt, his Majesty's Lieutenant Governor.

There are a number of records in which citizens are recompensed for goods impressed by the Marquis de Lafayette and General Wayne.

July 11, 1743.—Charcoal, a negro belonging to Joseph Anthony, is adjudged fourteen years old.

In 1814 and 1815, there are a number of cases in which the court recommends militia officers: William Crawford, cornet; John Fleeman, 1st lieutenant; John H. Thompson, 2nd lieutenant; Pleasant Hackett, captain; James Michie, major; John Poindexter, lieutenant; William Barret, major; Isham Woodson, ensign; William A. Bibb, ensign; Thomas Jones, lieutenant; Lewis Shirley, cornet; William Jackson, Jr., captain; John Beadle, captain; Charles Dabney, ensign; Ralph S. Sandridge, major; Ralph Dickenson, lieutenant; William Toler, ensign; John Wood, captain; Matthew Michie, lieutenant; William Perkins, ensign; and Lewis Thistler, cornet.

At a court held for Louisa County on Monday the XIII day of June in the XII year of the Reign of our Sovereign Lord George the 2nd, by the Grace of God of Great Britain, France and Ireland king, defender of the faith, etc., Ann. Dom. 1743 before his Majesty's Justices of the Peace for the county, to-wit: Robert Davis, Abraham Venable, Charles Barret, John Poindexter and Ambrose Joshua Smith.

Whereas at a court held for this county on Monday the 11th of April last the Reverend Richard Hartswell, being then drunk, came into court and then and there in the presence of the Justices of the said court then sitting prophanely swore one Oath, therefore it is considered and accordingly ordered that the said Richard pay to the Church Wardens of the Parish of Fredericksville, wherein the offenses were committed, the sum of ten shillings or one hundred pounds of tobacco, that is to say five shillings or fifty pounds of tobacco for being drunk and five shillings or fifty pounds of tobacco for prophanely swearing each, for which execution may issue.

Six companies of infantry went from Louisa at the beginning of the War Between the States, and their rosters are recorded.

The Louisa Blues, Company D, 13th Virginia Regiment, Early's Brigade, Stonewall Jackson's Corps, was organized April 17, 1861. Its first captain was Henry W. Murray, who retired April 23, 1862. He was succeeded by Frank V. Winston, who had been serving as first lieutenant. When the Louisa Blues were re-organized in 1863, Frank V. Winston was captain; John W. Hibbs, first lieutenant; and Jesse J. Porter, second lieutenant.

The Frederick Hall Grays, Company G, 23rd Regiment, mustered at Richmond about May 1, 1861. Its officers were as follows: C. G. Coleman, captain, resigned in 1861. W. F. Coleman, captain, resigned 1862 and became adjutant. R. A. Trice, resigned 1862. Sam D. Rice, captain, killed at Kernstown, August 1864. W. B. Pendleton, first lieutenant, lost a leg at Cedar Mountain. W. A. Trice, first lieutenant, resigned 1862. T. O. Moss served as first lieutenant from 1862 to the end of the war. He was wounded in October, 1863. Joseph Sandidge, A. B. Cooke and J. T. Shelton were lieutenants, and James Nelson was made chaplain in 1862.

The Louisa Rifles, made up largely of men from the vicinity of Thompson's Cross Roads, were mustered into service May 15, 1861. Officers were as follows: Andrew J. Richardson was captain from the company's organization to November 23, 1863, when he was succeeded by Benjamin F. Walton, who had been lieutenant; lieutenants, John Zachary Harris, John Overton Harris, who died July 23, 1861, O. C. Sims, who was wounded in 1864, William A. Winston, wounded in the hand, Peyton J. Rawlings, and James E. Farrar, who had been serving as sergeant.

The Louisa Grays, composed largely of men from the upper end of the County, were mustered in June 30, 1861, as Company D, 23rd Virginia Infantry, commanded by Col. William B. Taliaferro. Officers were: William J. Sergeant and Hiram B. Saunders, who had served as lieutenant and was captured May 12, 1864; lieutenants, William J. Watson and William M. Long.

The Louisa Holliday Guard was mustered in July 9, 1861, as Company C, 56th Virginia Regiment. Officers were captain, Timoleon Smith; lieutenants, George W. May, Charles S. Jones and Robert S. Ellis.

The Louisa Nelson Grays were organized and mustered into service in the yard of Fork Meetinghouse July 25, 1861, becoming Company F, 56th Virginia Infantry. It was commanded by Captain John Richardson. Lieutenants were R. N. Thomas, W. H. Talley, William G. Walton, Thomas W. Cosby and Richmond Terrell.

MANY HOMES STILL STAND

There have been many old homes in Louisa from which men have gone forth to enrich the citizenship of this Nation. Most of them are still standing; some of them have been destroyed. Among these, along with the family names with which they have been identified, may be mentioned: Riverside and Malvern, Winston; Minor's Folly, where Professor John B. Minor and the other Minors were born (Diana Minor, the mother of Commodore Matthew Fontaine Maury, was buried here, although her body was removed in comparatively recent years); Woodberry was the old Kimbrough homestead near Yanceyville. Then there were Roundabout Castle, Johnson and Fox; Roundabout Plantation, where Patrick Henry lived while in Louisa;

Dunlora, Garland and Waddey; Cuckoo House, Pendleton; Bear Castle, Carr; Attonce, Bullock and Kean; Hartland, Hart; North Bend, Bullock; Ben Ghoil, Winston; Corduroy, Vest; Ingleside, Gooch; Kalona, Kent; Oakland, May; Westland, West; West End and Ionia, Watson; Grassdale, the Morris family, and present home of Admiral David Taylor; Bracketts, Brackett and Watson, now the property of Carl H. Nolting, where the annual meeting of the Virginia Foxhunters' Association is held; Prospect Hill, Overton; Sylvania, Morris; and Hawkwood, Morris.

Orange County

ORANGE COURTHOUSE

Orange County

AN imaginary line from which the Blue Ridge Mountains could be seen in the distance marked the western boundary of Anglo-Saxon civilization for more than a hundred years after the planting of the Jamestown Colony in 1607. West of this line there were few if any white pioneers until the early years of the 18th Century.

There were two good reasons for this. The rivers emptying into Chesapeake Bay afforded transportation and their valleys were fertile. The second and perhaps as potent a reason for the slow migration to the westward was the knowledge that between this imaginary line in sight of the mountains and the mountains themselves, the fierce northern Indians made periodical invasions to the southward in quest of game and the scalps of their southern redskin foes.

The Indians, perhaps in larger numbers, followed the trails down the Valley, but there were plenty of Indian activities east of the Blue Ridge. There was hardly a white man in what later became Orange County until Governor Alexander Spotswood established his little German colony at Germanna in 1714. The story of the Indians of this section prior to the coming of the white men is largely theoretical, but it is known that the Manahoacs lived here and, together with the Monocans, of the upper James River valley, were hostile to the eastern Virginia Indians. It is probable that it was the power of the confederation of Powhatan which shunted the northern invaders to the westward and away from the tidal basins of the eastern Virginia rivers. The Iroquois Trail is known to have crossed James River near Goochland Courthouse.

A remarkable Indian burial mound was found on the right bank of the Rapidan in Orange, near the Greene County line, but little is known of its history. Bones of more than 200 Indians were found when excavations were made, and these bodies appeared to have been dumped in unceremoniously at different periods. While it is the general belief that this mound was the burial place for the local tribes, it is a peculiar circumstance that no relics were found with the bones except a rough mortar, two arrowheads and a few fragments of pottery. Whether there was a connection between these skeletons and the inroads of the northern warriors is a matter of conjecture.

Orange County was formed from Spotsylvania in 1734 and was named for the Prince of Orange, who in that year married Princess Anne, daughter of George II. He was a successor of King William of Orange, who died in 1701. In 1730 an act provided for the division of St. George's parish, and bounds of the new St. Mark's parish were roughly defined. Four years later it was enacted by the Burgesses that Spotsylvania should be divided and the county of Orange formed.

The act under which Orange County was formed is quoted in part as follows: "That . . . the said County of Spotsylvania be divided by the dividing line between the parish of St. George and the parish of St. Mark; and that that part of the said county which is now the parish of St. George remain and be called and known by the name of Spotsylvania county; and all that territory of land adjoining to and above the said line, bounded southerly by the line of Hanover county [now the Louisa line], northerly by the grant of the Lord Fairfax, and westerly by the *utmost limits of Virginia,* be thenceforth erected into one distinct county, to be called and known by the name of the county of Orange."

The western boundaries of the "frontier" counties of Virginia in a number of cases were very vague, but the contention of its citizens that Orange was at one time the largest county ever formed is justifiable. Vast grants of land were made to citizens of eastern Virginia as far west as the Mississippi river and at the time Orange was formed its western area included practically all of the territory west of the Blue Ridge and east of the Mississippi. An old map is in existence of Augusta County, formed from Orange in 1738, which shows the Great Lakes on its boundaries. Thus Orange retained its empire in area for a period of four years.

The story of the formative years of Orange County is so intimately associated with that of Governor Spotswood that mention should here be made of his career as Governor of Virginia. Born at Tangier in 1676, of noble Scottish ancestry, he entered the army and was wounded at the battle of Blenheim. He arose to the rank of lieutenant-colonel and in 1710 was sent to

Virginia as lieutenant-governor, under the nominal governor, the Earl of Orkney.

Spotswood was one of the most energetic and efficient of all the royal governors of Virginia. He rebuilt the College of William and Mary and took measures for the conversion and education of Indian children. He was first to cross the Blue Ridge mountains and he dealt vigorously with the enemies of the Colony. He fitted out the expedition, under the command of Captain Maynard, who killed the notorious pirate, Edward Teach, known as "Blackbeard", and captured his crew. He served as governor until 1722, then continued to live in Virginia; was appointed deputy postmaster for the colonies; was commissioned major-general in 1740 and was collecting forces for the expedition against Carthagena when he died.

In 1714, twenty years before Orange became a separate county and seven years before Spotsylvania was formed, Governor Spotswood brought over twelve German families, forty-two persons in all, and placed them at Germanna, in what is now the northeastern part of Orange. It then was a part of Essex. These Germans, skilled artizans, were from Westphalia and were imported for the specific purpose of working Governor Spotswood's iron mines at Germanna. How he found that there was iron ore at this point is not known. Spotswood built a residence at Germanna and lived there later in life.

Thus these staunch Germans may be regarded as the "first settlers" of Orange County. Two other German groups were brought over in 1717 and 1719. Many of them, by 1726 had acquired lands of their own and moved over into nearby counties. If there were any white settlements in what is now Orange at the time the Germans settled at Germanna in 1714, they were very few. Germanna was the county seat of Spotsylvania for a time, but it is now deserted.

Colonel William Byrd II, of Westover, in his interesting account of his visit to Germanna in 1732, describes "Colonel Spotswood's enchanted castle on one side of the street, and a baker's dozen of ruinous tenements on the other, where so many German families had dwelt some years ago; but are now removed ten miles higher in the fork of the Rappahannock, to land of their own."

William Byrd's description of his arrival at the Spotswood mansion and the familiar incident of the shattered mirror gives such an intimate glimpse of home life on the Orange frontier that it will bear repetition here:

"Here I arrived about three o'clock, and found only Mrs. Spotswood at home, who receiving her old acquaintance with many a gracious smile, I was carried into a room elegantly set off with pier glasses, the largest of which came soon after to an odd misfortune. Amongst other favorite animals that cheered this lady's solitude, a brace of tame deer ran familiarly about the house, and one of them came to stare at me as a stranger. But unluckily spying his own figure in the glass, he made a spring over the tea table that stood under it and shattered the glass to pieces, and falling back upon the tea table, made a terrible fracas among the china. This exploit was so sudden, and accompanied with such a noise, that it surprised me and perfectly frightened Mrs. Spotswood. But it was worth all the damage to show the moderation and good humor with which she bore the disaster."

According to Governor Spotswood's own words, he

was not only the first in Virginia, but the first in America to erect a regular iron furnace. In 1732 a mine was being worked thirteen miles below Germanna, and the finished product from his furnaces was carted fifteen miles to the river.

Germanna was also the final point of departure for Governor Spotswood and his "Knights of the Golden Horseshoe" on their memorable expedition in 1716 over the Blue Ridge. It was then that the beautiful Valley of Virginia was discovered, and the first deliberate step was taken in the ultimate extension of the Anglo-Saxon domains to the Pacific ocean.

The Governor and John Fontaine started from Williamsburg and made their way through King William, King and Queen, Caroline and Spotsylvania, being joined by gentlemen all along the route. The Governor left his carriage at the Beverley home in King and Queen and took to his horse. At Germanna they were joined by others, including two small companies of rangers and four Meherrin Indians. Germanna was the point of departure for the expedition, which may properly be called the first step in the conquest of the West. The journey of the Knights of the Golden Horseshoe is more particularly described in a separate chapter in this book.

Among the gentlemen who made the trip were Governor Spotswood, John Fontaine, Robert Beverley, the historian, William Robertson, James Taylor, Robert Brooke, George Mason, Captain Jeremiah Clouder and Austin Smith, who had to abandon the expedition the second day after leaving Germanna because of illness. The names of a number of gentlemen of the cavalcade are unknown.

There were about fifty in the party, gentlemen, servants and guides and, as one journalist of the expedition puts it, they had "an abundance of provisions and an extraordinary variety of liquors." Another historian has suggested that but for the frequent manifestations of loyalty in drinking the healths of the royal family and themselves, a better idea could have been formed of the exact route followed. Suffice it to say that it was a merry party. The horses were shod at Germanna for protection of their hoofs against the rocks of the mountains, and the Governor on their return presented each of the gentlemen of the expedition a small horseshoe of gold, with gems for the nailheads.

Members of the House of Burgesses from Orange were: 1736-38, Robert Green, William Beverley; 1740, Robert Green made sheriff; 1742, Henry Downs, expelled; 1747, George Taylor; 1748-49, George Taylor, John Spotswood; 1752-58, George Taylor, Benjamin Cave; 1758-59, George Taylor, William Taliaferro; 1760, Benjamin Cave, James Taylor; 1761-65, James Taylor, James Walker; 1765-68, James Walker, Zachariah Burnley; 1769-71, James Walker, Thomas Barbour; 1772-73, Zachariah Burnley, Thomas Barbour; 1774, Thomas Barbour; 1775, Thomas Barbour and James Taylor.

Conventions of 1775: Thomas Barbour and James Taylor.

Conventions of 1776: James Madison and William Moore.

After the Revolution, the convention which ratified

the Federal Constitution in 1788 found Orange represented by James Madison and James Gordon. In 1829-30 the delegates were James Madison and Philip Pendleton Barbour; in 1850-51, John Woolfolk; in 1867-8, Frederick W. Poor; and in 1901-2, A. C. Walter.

It is a pity that the story of the conquest of the western fringes of the Virginia Colony from the Indians is so fragmentary, for this was accomplished largely by citizens of Orange and other counties just east of the mountains, and especially by the men of Augusta, that vast county which was the very spearhead in the advance of white civilization to the westward. It will be remembered that the French claimed the Ohio. They incited the Indians to massacre and pillage the Virginians, established forts,and even planted lead plates in the banks of the Ohio River claiming all that territory for France. One of these is preserved in the museum of the Virginia Historical Society.

The French contented themselves principally in inciting the Indians to massacre and battling against the English and especially during the era of the great chief Cornstalk there was much bloodshed, open warfare continuing until the treaty in 1763, concluding the French and Indian War. Among a number of names of men from Orange who fought the Indians have been found those of Ambrose Powell, ancestor of General A. P. Hill; James Cowherd; William Bullock; William Rogers; Henry Shackleford; James Riddle; Col. William Russell, at one time sheriff of Orange, and sent in 1753 as a commissioner to the Indians to the region where Pittsburgh now stands; Francis Cowherd, who was at the Battle of Point Pleasant; Hancock Taylor, uncle of President Zachary Taylor, killed by the Indians in Kentucky in 1774. Colby Chew, who served against the Shawnees in 1756, was an ensign in Washington's command in 1757, was wounded near Fort Duquesne in 1758 and fell into the river and was drowned; and his brother, Larkin Chew, was wounded in 1754 and was a lieutenant in the 2nd Virginia Regiment.

As was true of perhaps all of the Piedmont counties of Virginia, Orange in the early years maintained a well-organized militia to keep the Indians in subjection. A large number of names of officers in these militia companies, from 1735 to the close of the French and Indian Wars, are preserved. Zachary Taylor, for whom the future president was named, for instance, was a lieutenant in 1768 and a captain in 1774. Likewise, there is a carefully-preserved list of a large number of officers from Orange who served in the Revolution.

The freeholders of Orange in 1774 elected the following to the Committee of Safety: James Madison, Sr., James Taylor, William Bell, Thomas Barbour, Zachariah Burnley, Rowland Thomas, William Moore, Johnny Scott, James Walker, William Pannill, Francis Moore, James Madison, Jr., Lawrence Taliaferro, Thomas Bell and Vivian Daniel. The committee elected James Madison, Sr., as chairman and Francis Taylor as clerk.

Large numbers of Orange men were with the Culpeper Minute Men when Lord Dunmore's forces were defeated at Great Bridge, near Norfolk, by the Colonial force under command of Colonel William Woodford, of Caroline, in December, 1775. This was a bloody engagement in which Dunmore, who had sought to establish himself at Norfolk, was driven on shipboard, and has been rightly called the first battle of the Revolution on Virginia soil.

In 1781, Lafayette, in his masterly retreat before Cornwallis, made his way through Hanover and Spotsylvania, crossing the Rapidan probably at Germanna Ford, intending to meet General Anthony Wayne with his force proceeding south from Leesburg at Raccoon Ford. Learning that Wayne was approaching and could overtake him, the young marquis turned his retreat into an offensive and recrossed the river into Orange. Over what is still known as the Marquis' Road in Orange and Louisa Counties, crossing the North Anna at Brock's Bridge, the Continental troops marched south to intervene between the British and stores in Albemarle. They then turned eastward over the old Three Chopt Road to Richmond.

While President James Madison (1751-1836) was not born in Orange, but at Port Conway, in King George County, his Madison forebears were from Orange and all of his active career was identified with Orange. His mother was Nelly Conway, of King George. He died in 1836 and is buried at his beautiful Orange estate, Montpelier.

Madison, who was fourth President of the United States and "Father of the Constitution," was recognized as one of the greatest of all American statesmen. First mention of him as a public figure was as a member of the Orange Committee of Safety in January, 1775, of which his father was chairman. In 1776 he was sent to the Virginia convention and went to the Continental Congress in 1779.

In the Virginia General Assembly of 1784 he fought against general assessments for the support of the Episcopal church, and introduced Jefferson's bill for religious freedom in Virginia, fighting strenuously for that measure until it was passed in 1785. In 1787 he drew up a plan of government, which became the "Virginia Plan" and was the basis of the deliberations which resulted in the favorable vote on the Federal Constitution September 17, 1787. Madison rendered remarkable service in maneuvering for the adoption of the Constitution. He kept the rest of the Virginia delegation in line, his colleagues, George Mason and Edmund Randolph, opposing it.

Again in 1788 Madison played a highly important part in the final adoption of America's present form of constitutional government. Eight States had ratified when it came up for ratification by Virginia in the State convention of 1788, and it was conceded that New York would not have ratified had not Virginia done so, and the whole new system of government would have fallen through. Here Madison met with powerful opposition from Patrick Henry, George Mason, James Monroe, Benjamin Harrison, William Grayson and John Tyler. Madison championed the Constitution with consummate skill and it was largely through his efforts that Virginia ratified it.

Fear of aggrandizement by a centralized Federal government was strong in Virginia at that time and, as a result of his activities in behalf of the Constitution Madison was defeated for the Senate, but he won a seat in the House of Representatives over James Monroe in 1789.

Madison was Jefferson's Secretary of State and played a large part, through his coöperation with Jefferson, in the Louisiana Purchase. It was Jefferson's wish that Madison should succeed him, and it was so decreed by the electorate. He was President during the War of 1812.

Following his retirement from the presidency, he lived at Montpelier until his death, taking no part in public life except that he served in the Virginia convention of 1829-30 and was a dominating influence in that convention despite the fact that he was nearing fourscore years of age.

His wife was Dorothea Payne, the widow Todd, who, as Dolly Madison, acquired a wide reputation in her own right.*

He was an able writer, and both in speech and with his pen, he was convincing. Chief Justice John Marshall said of him: "If I were called upon to say who of all the men I have known had the greatest power to convince, I should, perhaps, say Mr. Madison, while Mr. Henry had, without doubt, the greatest power to persuade."

A remarkable educational movement was identified with Orange, and deserves mention here. In 1749 William Monroe obtained his right to take up fifty

---

*There has been so much discussion as to how Mrs. Madison signed her name that the matter may be here cleared up. Through the courtesy of Mr. J. W. Browning, clerk of Orange County, the author examined a number of papers signed by her. In her early married life she signed her name "Dolley Madison", and in almost every case she spelled it with an "e". Later, she signed a number of deeds 'D. P. Madison.' Later in life she seems to have adhered strictly to the signature "Dolly Madison", dropping the "e" in Dolly.

acres of land, after having been imported as an indentured person. In his will twenty years later, he left his whole extensive estate, after the death of his wife, to the cause of education. His property was sold and the funds invested, until in 1811 the Orange Humane Society was incorporated. The Monroe bequest, along with the money from the sale of the glebe lands of the Episcopal church, was administed by a group of the most respected men of the county and many poor children were educated. The fund was swept away in the maelstrom of the War Between the States, but throughout a long period of years poor children profited through the generosity of William Monroe, the first philanthropist of that region, who, himself, was probably illiterate.

A remarkable character in Orange history was the Reverend Samuel Waddell, "the blind preacher," who came to Orange in 1786 from the Northern Neck. The disintegration of the Established church and the trend toward liberalism in matters of doctrine in that period was strikingly illustrated in the fact that he, although a Presbyterian, was brought to Orange by vestry of the Episcopal parish, there being no Episcopal clergymen in the county, and he not only preached but administered the Lord's Supper. His little church was a half-mile northeast of Gordonsville.

The Blind Preacher also conducted a small school nearby to which went Meriwether Lewis and Governor James Barbour. He preached for a time in Augusta. Little is known of this devout minister except that he must have been gifted with outstanding eloquence and exerted a wide influence. He was immortalized by

William Wirt, who attended a service at his church two years before the minister died in 1805, and wrote a classic description of the scene.

Few facts are known about the participation of Orange soldiers in the War of 1812, but it is an unusual coincidence that at the time of that conflict two Orange citizens, President James Madison and Governor James Barbour, held the highest executive positions in Nation and State. It was often referred to by the unenthusiastic as "Madison's War." One company is known to have been called from Orange into active service in 1813, known as Captain Smith's Company of the 2nd Virginia Regiment. Captain Smith's lieutenants were Hay Taliaferro and George W. Spotswood. There also was a company of "mounted riflemen" commanded by Captain William Stevens, and this company was stationed at Hampton in 1814.

The military service of General Zachary Taylor, twelfth President of the United States, dated back prior to the War of 1812. He was born in Orange in 1784, a son of Lieutenant-Colonel Richard Taylor, Revolutionary officer and one of the first settlers of Louisville, Ky. Zachary Taylor was taken to Louisville in his boyhood where he grew up on a farm, with little formal education.

In 1808 he was given the lieutenancy in the regular army made vacant by the death of his older brother, and in 1810 was made a captain. In 1812, with a feeble force, he defended Fort Harrison, on the Wabash, against a large force of Indians led by Tecumseh. He was promoted to major for gallantry and did valiant service during the War of 1812 in fighting the Indians on the western frontiers who were allied with the British.

He served as a colonel in the Black Hawk war and in 1836 defeated the Seminoles at Okechobee, for which service he was made a brigadier-general and put in command of the forces in Florida. General Taylor emerged as the chief hero of the Mexican War.

In 1846, with a comparatively small force, he defeated General Arista at Palo Alto and drove him across the Rio Grande. After a ten-day siege, during which time there was terrific fighting against heavy odds, he reduced the city of Monterey. His most conspicuous military achievement was at Buena Vista, where, with a force only one-fourth as large, he defeated an army of 21,000 led by the Mexican President, Santa Anna.

Fresh from his military triumphs, this son of Orange was nominated for the presidency over Henry Clay, Daniel Webster and General Winfield Scott, and easily won in the election. He died while in office. In 1848 the Virginia General Assembly voted him a sword with the inscription: "Presented by Virginia to her distinguished son, Major-General Zachary Taylor, for his gallantry and conduct at Palo Alto, Resaca de la Palma, Monterey and Buena Vista." He also was presented with the silken sash on which the body of General Braddock was borne from the field of his disaster in 1755.

As was true of many of the Virginia counties, there was strong sentiment in Orange in 1860 and early in 1861 against dismemberment of the Union, and Orange citizens struggled doggedly to avert war. But Lincoln's proclamation and the attempted reinforcement of Fort Sumter convinced them that war was inevitable, and Orange entered wholeheartedly into the prosecution of the war from its very beginning. Jeremiah Morton, the Orange delegate to the Secession Convention of 1861, was a secessionist.

Troops of the opposing armies were frequently on Orange soil during the war. There were cavalry skirmishes at Rapidan, Locust Grove, Morton's Ford, New Hope Church, Orange, Liberty Mills, Zoar, Germanna, on the pike northwest of Gordonsville, and at Toddsberth, the two most important battles being Mine Run, in 1863, and part of the great battle of the Wilderness in 1864. The Rapidan was General Lee's line of defense for many months and his army spent the winter of 1863-64 in Orange. His own headquarters were about a mile and a half east of the courthouse, leaving in May, 1864, to commence the Wilderness campaign.

On November 28, 1863, General Meade, advancing south from the Rapidan, found General Lee in an entrenched position at Mine Run, about thirteen miles east of the courthouse. Fighting continued for two days, but Meade decided that Lee's lines were too strong and retired across the Rapidan. Nearby was Robinson's Tavern, where Meade wished to concentrate his forces for the Mine Run campaign, but his plan was abandoned. At the same place, Ewell, moving east from Orange in the later Wilderness campaign, camped May 4, 1864.

Ewell's corps constituted the left wing of Lee's army in the battle of the Wilderness and engaged in a fierce conflict in the northeastern section of Orange with

Warren's corps of Grant's army on May 5, 1864. The battle raged back and forth until Ewell drove Warren back, then followed up his success by pursuing and attacking the Federals the next day. Meanwhile Lee's right wing engaged Grant's forces a few miles to the south.

The story of the suffering, the starvation and the fortitude of the Orange people during the war would be a tragic chapter, which, however, can not be related here. One or two outstanding instances may be related. Colonel James Magruder, of Frascati, had five sons of military age when the war broke out. Three of his sons were killed in battle, one was disabled, dying from his wound after the war, the fifth was seven times wounded and a son-in-law was killed. Lancelot Burrus, at one time sheriff, had six sons, all taking part in the war. Five of them were in the battle of Gaines' Mill and three of them were killed and the other two wounded in a single day. The sixth and youngest son also was wounded elsewhere. And Larkin Willis, of the northeastern part of the county, had ten sons in the Confederate army at one time.

Perhaps the most distinguished soldier in the War of the 60s identified with Orange County was General James Lawson Kemper, who also served as Governor of Virginia. While he was born in Madison, he spent the later years of his life at Walnut Hills, near Orange Courthouse. Having been commissioned a captain in 1847, he joined General Taylor's forces in Mexico. He then served for ten years in the House of Delegates, a part of the time as speaker.

He was colonel of the 7th Virginia Infantry in 1861,

was made brigadier-general in 1862 and was desperately wounded and left on the field in Pickett's charge at Gettysburg. In 1864 he was in command of the reserve forces around Richmond with the rank of major-general. He was elected Governor of Virginia in 1873 and after the expiration of his term practiced law in Orange and adjacent counties.

The roster of the Montpelier Guards, organized in 1857, is preserved. When John Brown's raid occurred two years later, this troop was sent to Charles Town, where John Brown was imprisoned, and the company was John Brown's military escort to the scaffold.

The rosters of the Orange officers and men in the war are incomplete, but such of the officers as are known to have served are here given:

Montpelier Guard, Company A, 13th Virginia Infantry: captains, Lewis B. Williams (promoted to colonel and killed in Pickett's charge at Gettysburg), B. F. Nalle, Champe G. Cooke (killed) and George Cullen; lieutenants, Isaac T. Graham, Charles C. Moore, Wilson S. Newman (killed) Thomas T. Wilroy (killed), M. S. Stringfellow and H. C. Coleman.

Gordonsville Greys, Company C, 13th Virginia Infantry: captain, William C. Scott, subsequently, G. A. Goodman, P. P. Barbour and Benjamin F. Baker; lieutenants, G. A. Goodman, E. F. Cowherd and C. H. Richards.

The Barboursville Guard was organized about 1859, with the following officers: captain, W. S. Parran; lieutenants, Andrew Jackson Eheart, A. J. White and Joseph T. Wood. At a reorganization in 1862, A. J.

Eheart was captain; C. L. Graves, Conway Newman and R. C. Macon, lieutenants. Captain Parran became a surgeon and was killed at Sharpsburg while helping to man a field piece. Captain Eheart was killed at Spotsylvania Courthouse in 1864. C. L. Graves was made captain in 1864, but had to retire, disabled, and Conway Newman became captain in 1865.

Company C, 7th Virginia Infantry, was first commanded by Captain John C. Porter, of Culpeper, the other officers also coming from that county. Later, J. W. Almond, of Orange was captain, and his lieutenants were N. T. Bartley and Jeremiah Pannill.

Peyton's Battery, later known as Fry's Battery, in Cutshaw's Battalion: captain, Thomas J. Peyton; lieutenants, C. W. Fry, John Moore and Robert Cannon. Later, C. W. Fry became captain, with Mercer Slaughter as a lieutenant.

Orange Rangers, Company I, 6th Virginia Cavalry: captains, G. J. Browning, subsequently, John Row, William J. Morton, and John W. Woolfolk; lieutenants, William H. Walker, John A. Roberts and John S. Sale, subsequently, C. B. Brown and J. T. Mann, both killed at Brandy Station, William Willis, J. H. White, James Roach and Samuel Andrews.

PRESENT COURTHOUSE IS RECENT

The courthouse at Orange shown in the accompanying illustration was built in 1852, being the third which has stood at the present county-seat.

William Robertson's house, on Black Walnut Run, was designated as the first place for holding court and the first session of the court was held there January 21, 1734. The first building owned by the county was finished within four years and stood near Somerville's Ford. In 1738 notice was given that at the next term a certain Peter Russell must keep the building clean and "provide candles and small beer for the justices."

After Culpeper was cut off from Orange in 1748, the courthouse being near the very edge of the county, it was decreed that Orange should be the county-seat and it was ordered that court should convene at the house of Timothy Crosthwait and that two acres of land should be acquired from him on which to build a courthouse.

The first building erected at Orange was finished in 1752. It was sold in 1804 and a building was erected which is still standing and was converted into stores when the county sold it in 1852 and the present building was put up. The location of the courthouse was spoken of in the records as the "Old Tavern" lot.

The first clerk of the county was Henry Willis, a prominent citizen of Fredericksburg, who took the oath in 1734 and served through a deputy. He it was whom Col. William Byrd visited in 1732 and referred to as "the top man of Fredericksburg."

Eleven Portraits Are Hung

On the walls of the courtroom at Orange are eleven portraits, a tablet and an interesting display in connection with an ambulance given by citizens of Orange and which saw much service in the World War.

The following distinguished men are portrayed:

Zachary Taylor (1784-1850)

Philip P. Barbour
Alexander Spotswood
James Madison
James Madison's death mask
James Barbour
Lewis B. Williams (1802-1880)
Gen. William Fitzhugh Gordon (1787-1858)
General Robert E. Lee
Garrett Scott (1808-1885)
Robert Collins, one of the Justices.

A marble tablet to the memory of William Monroe, bears the following inscription: "In memory of William Monroe, philanthropist and benefactor of the poor children of Orange."

A photograph of the ambulance donated by Orange citizens in 1917, together with a brass plate from the ambulance and some interesting correspondence in connection with it are displayed framed. The brass plate, found after the Armistice in a dugout by a soldier and brought back to Orange, bears the following words: "Rapid Ann River. Given by the people of Orange, Va., and their friends. Captain C. F. Rowland, realizing the interest of the Orange people in this ambulance which saw constant service on the battlefronts, sent a photograph of it taken abroad during the war."

RECORDS WELL PRESERVED

The records of Orange County are excellently preserved and contain much that is of interest. The wills of James Madison and his wife are here recorded. There is a long list of persons who in order to be able to come to Virginia imported themselves, or were imported, as servants, who afterward came into court and proved their importations in order to obtain their "head rights" to land. Practically all were from Great Britain, with the exception of the Germans brought over by Spotswood.

Some the punishments for crime were odd, and some were very severe, there being one record of the burning of a criminal, a slave, for poisoning her master.

In 1737, Peter, a slave of John Riddle, was convicted of murdering his master and hanged. It is recorded that after this order was carried out, the sheriff cut off his head and put it on a pole near the courthouse to deter others from doing the like.

In 1740 a man who had enlisted in his Majesty's service and deserted, was ordered to be sold to the highest bidder as a servant for a period of five years.

The lash was freely administered for various and sundry crimes. Many were fined in tobacco for habitual absence from church, the law providing that in the event that these fines were not paid, the recalcitrants should receive "ten lashes on the bare back." But there is no record of whippings for this particular offense.

In 1745 a negro slave of Peter Montague, was convicted of poisoning her master, and the verdict was as follows: "Therefore it is considered by the Court that the said Eve be drawn upon a hurdle to the place of execution and there to be burnt." The hurdle was a sort of sledge used for hauling prisoners to execution.

A female vagrant, for "profainly swearing four oaths before the Court and failing to pay the fine," received ten lashes and was ordered to leave the county. A slave was convicted for notoriously running away and lying out so his master could not reclaim him in 1776. So it was "ordered that the sheriff take him to the pillory and nail his ears to the same, and there to stand half an hour and then to have his right ear cut off."

A unique item is recorded in 1753: "On the motion of Daniel McClayland, who in a fight lately had a piece of his left ear bit off, it is by the court ordered to be recorded." Thus was the citizen relieved of the stigma of having had his ear cropped for crime.

There are records showing that the following distinguished men appeared from time to time in the Orange court as counsel or plaintiffs in lawsuits: Augustine and Lawrence Washington, George Wythe, Edmund Pendleton and Chief Justice John Marshall.

HOMESTEADS ARE NUMEROUS

There have been many old homes in Orange from which have gone many men of note, and there are a number of handsome places built in this fertile region in more recent times. Among the old mansions may be mentioned:

Barboursville, which at present is one of the most picturesque ruins in Virginia. It was gutted by fire on Christmas Day, 1884, the walls, now covered with ivy, remaining intact. On the grounds are perhaps the largest number of great boxwoods to be found at any residence in the State. This house, the home of the distinguished Barbour family, was built by Governor James Barbour in 1822, and Thomas Jefferson helped in its planning. It was one of the few houses in Virginia whose white-columned portico was approached

[297]

by means of a ramp, rather than steps. The remains of the sodded incline by which the mansion was entered is still visible. The original home nearby, much older than the building which was burned, still stands.

Burlington, about a mile east of Barboursville, was built by James Barbour Newman. The property was owned in Colonial times by the Burnleys, and members of that family were buried there. Zachariah Burnley was a Burgess and afterward an officer in the Revolution. It was at Burlington that John Randolph of Roanoke lived while attending school conducted by Walker Maury either at or near the place.

Campbellton, also near Barboursville, was the home of Captain William Campbell, of the Revolution and subsequently a major in the United States army. General Winfield Scott often visited the place.

Clifton, one of the oldest frame houses erected in the county, was built about 1729 by John Scott, whose son was a member of the Committee of Safety and a captain in the Revolution. There is a tombstone on this property, near Madison Run, said to be the oldest in the county, to the memory of Jane, wife of John Scott, "born 1699, died 1731."

Cameron Lodge, near Gordonsville, built by Col. Alexander Cameron, is one of the handsomest places in the county.

Frascati, near Somerset, was built prior to 1830 by Judge Philip Barbour Pendleton, using many of the same workmen who had completed the University of Virginia. Here also are the white columns of the Early Republic form of architecture introduced by Jefferson. It was owned for some years prior to the war by Col. James Magruder, and more recently by A. D. Irving, Jr. Until comparatively recent years there was a serpentine wall on the place similar to those at the University.

Hawfield, about half way between Orange and Raccoon Ford, was built prior to 1790. It was bought in 1847 by Jonathan Graves for his daughter, Fanny Elizabeth, who married William G. Crenshaw. It was enlarged in 1881 and is on an estate of more than 3,000 acres.

Locust Lawn, on the Marquis' Road, was a tavern during the Revolution.

Mayhurst, near the courthouse, was embraced in the vast Baylor grant to the Baylors of Caroline, and the mountain nearby is still known as Baylor's Mountain. The first residence was the Howard home, Col. John Willis purchasing the farm in 1859 and erecting the handsome Mayhurst residence. Later it became the home of William G. Crenshaw, Jr. General A. P. Hill's headquarters were here in the winter of 1863-64.

Montebello, near Gordonsville, is reputed to have been the place of birth of Zachary Taylor. There is a well-founded tradition that Col. Richard Taylor, the future President's father, started the emigration of his family to Kentucky in wagons and stopped at Montebello, and that Zachary Taylor was born there. It is an old Johnson estate.

Montpelier, one of the handsomest places in this part of Virginia, stands a few miles to the westward from the courthouse on a tract of 4,675 acres patented by Ambrose Madison and Thomas Chew in 1723. It was the home of the Madisons, and part of the present mansion was erected about 1760, being greatly enlarged and beautified in 1809. Few homes anywhere are placed amid more beautiful surroundings. In more recent years it was acquired by William du Pont, and it is now the property of Mrs. Randolph Scott. In its stables are many of the finest horses in America. A splendid racecourse has been laid out on the property.

Mount Sharon is the ancestral home of the Taliaferros, the land having been granted to them by the Crown. It commands magnificent views of the mountains.

Oakhill, two miles northeast of Gordonsville, was the home of Captain Francis Cowherd, of Indian warfare and Revolutionary fame, who distinguished himself particularly at Point Pleasant.

Pleasant View, not far from the Spotsylvania line, was the residence of Jonathan Graves about 1830, and also the home of Captain R. Perrin Graves, passing in more recent years to W. G. Crenshaw, Jr., a descendant.

Rocklands stands on what was once the property of Edmund Henshaw, and was acquired by Richard Barton Haxall, later passing to Thomas Atkinson. The old house was burned in 1905, the present handsome structure standing on the old site. It is near Gordonsville.

Rose Hill, near Rapidan, was the home of Col. Lawrence Taliaferro, who commanded the original Culpeper Minute Men. The present mansion was erected by Lewis Crenshaw and later enlarged.

Soldier's Rest, near Raccoon Ford, was originally built by Charles Bruce, who later became a captain in the Revolution, and was afterward the residence of his son-in-law, James Williams, a captain in the Revolution and major-general in the War of 1812. It passed to Dr. George Morton, who married General Williams' daughter, and later became the property of Judge James W. Morton. The residence was burned in 1857.

Somerset, near the railroad station named for it, is another of the homes commanding magnificent views. It was erected in 1803 by Thomas Macon, who married a sister of President James Madison. It became the seat of the Goss family.

Woodley, near Madison Run, was originally built by Captain Ambrose Madison, of the Revolution, brother of President Madison. Wings were added by Captain Madison's daughter, Mrs. Nelly Willis, the place later passing to W. W. Sanford.

Wood Park, near Rapidan, was built by Baldwin Taliaferro, son of Col. Lawrence Taliaferro, of Rose Hill. It was greatly enlarged by Col. George Willis, grandfather of Dr. Murat Willis, to whom the property passed.

Among other historic places in Orange should be mentioned the Barbour place at Gordonsville, which was a noted hostelry in its day, being on the main stage line to Philadelphia and New York. It was visited by John Randolph of Roanoke and Henry Clay, and in 1826 Lafayette addressed the citizens from its porch, on the Marquis' post-Revolutionary visit to Virginia. The Gordons, for whom the town was named, lived there.

Bloomingdale, near Somerset, was the home of Thomas Barbour.

Tetley, nearby, was the home of Captain William Smith, later coming into possession of Charles J. Stovin.

Bloomfield was the home of the Newmans for many generations.

Hazelhurst, near Somerset, was the home of Frank Nalle.

Walnut Hills, near Madison Mills, was the Orange residence of General James L. Kemper.

Greenfield, where are to be found some of the oldest tombstones in the county, was an old Taylor home; and Yatton, formerly called Midland, was another Taylor home which passed to Lewis B. Williams, who lived and died there. Meadow Farm was also a Taylor place.

Selma was the home of the distinguished physician, Dr. Peyton Grymes.

Retreat, formerly called Willis Grove, was the home of the Willis family, later passing to the heirs of Dr. Charles Conway.

Chestnut Hill, home of Dr. Uriel Terrell, was visited by Henry Clay and other statesmen of his period. It passed to W. G. Crenshaw, Jr.

The Taliaferro home near Rapidan came down through the Taliaferro family from a Crown grant of 1726.

Morton Hall and Lessland were homes of Jeremiah Morton, and Vaucluse was the ancestral seat of the Grymes family.

Elwood, near the Spotsylvania line, was said to have been built in 1781 by Major Churchill Jones.

Woodlawn, near Flat Run, is considerably over a century old and was built by Larkin Willis.

Orange Grove was the home of Alexander Dandridge Spotswood, great grandson of the Governor.

The second Somerset, near Flat Run, was at one time owned by two maiden ladies named Hawkins, who provided in their wills that their slaves should be freed. Certain slaves, hearing of this provision in the will, poisoned them.

Hilton and Spring Hill were James Barbour Newman and Sisson places, respectively.

Hare Forest was the home of Col. Richard Taylor, Zachary Taylor's father.

Woodberry Forest, one of the most prominent boys' schools in the South, was established by Robert Stringfellow Walker, and continued by his sons.

Many men of note have come from Orange County. Essentially it was a pioneer county in the early days and the staunchness, energy and courage of the early settlers have come down through succeeding generations. James Madison, the statesman, and Zachary Taylor, the soldier, have more or less typified the quality of the heritage of the men of Orange.

James Madison, Sr., must have been a fine specimen of Virginia citizenship. It will be recalled that he was chairman of the Orange Committee of Safety, and the committee in this county was one of the most active in the Colony in the troubled period leading up to the Revolution.

The Barbour family has been one of the most remarkable in Orange. James Barbour was one of the original Gentlemen Justices, and in a much later period there were four members of this family who attained unusual distinction.

Thomas Barbour (1735-1825) was appointed a Justice in 1768 and served for many years. He was a member of the House of Burgesses from 1772 until the formation of the Commonwealth and was a member of the conventions of 1774 and 1775. He was county lieutenant and a colonel in the Revolution. He was the father of Governor James Barbour and Judge P. P. Barbour.

Governor James Barbour (1775-1842) served in the General Assembly from 1796 to 1812, being elected Governor of Virginia in that year and serving as the State's chief executive throughout the War of 1812. He was sent to the United States Senate in 1815, serving until 1825, when he became Secretary of War. He was sent as minister plenipotentiary to England and was chairman of the convention in 1839 which nominated William Henry Harrison for the presidency. He built Barboursville and is there buried.

Judge Philip Pendleton Barbour (1783-1841), brother of the Governor, started his political career in the legislature, of which he was a member from 1812 to 1814, being elected in that year to Congress. He was Speaker of the House, resigning in 1825 when appointed United States District Judge. He was again a member of Congress from 1827 to 1830, and was a highly influential member of the convention of 1829-30, succeeding James Monroe as president of that body. He was appointed an associate justice of the United States Supreme Court by Andrew Jackson in 1836 and died in Washington.

B. Johnson Barbour (1821-1894), youngest son of Governor Barbour, was noted for his literary attainments, his eloquence and his open-handed hospitality at

Barboursville. He was for many years Rector of the University of Virginia and was greatly devoted to the cause of education. He was much in demand as an orator, one of his famous addresses being that which he delivered at the unveiling of the marble statue of Henry Clay which formerly stood in the State Capitol grounds. He was elected to Congress immediately after the war but was barred under the proscription of Reconstruction days. He represented his county in the legislature for many years.

James Avis Bartley was the author of two volumes of poems which received wide comment.

Col. Thomas Chew was sheriff of the county in 1745 and was the father of Colby and Larkin Chew, noted Indian fighters.

Col. Benjamin Cleveland was a gallant officer in the Revolution and took part in the battle of Kings Mountain.

Captain William G. Crenshaw, while he was born in Richmond and became a highly successful business man in that city, spent a large part of his life at Hawfield and died there. He married Miss Fanny Elizabeth Graves, of Orange. He was a man of great wealth and when the war broke out he raised and equipped at his own expense a battery of artillery, known as Crenshaw's Battery, which became famous. After the great campaign of 1863 he was sent by the Confederate government to England, where he rendered notable service in obtaining equipment and negotiating other assistance for the Confederacy. He remained in England until 1868 and was thereafter for many years engaged in business in New York.

Jesse Franklin was adjutant to his uncle, Col. Benjamin Cleveland, at the battle of Kings Mountain and settled in North Carolina after the Revolution. He was a member of the North Carolina legislature and was sent to Congress. He was in the Senate for two terms and was president *pro tem* of the Senate in 1805. In 1820 he became Governor of North Carolina.

Philip S. Fry was clerk from 1844 until his death fifteen years later. He was deputy clerk in 1821 and a justice in 1834.

James Gordon, although born in Richmond County, lived later in life at Germanna and was buried there. After having represented Richmond County in the General Assembly in 1781, he moved to Orange and was Madison's colleague in the celebrated convention of 1788 which ratified the Federal Constitution.

General William Fitzhugh Gordon, son of James Gordon, was born at Germanna and practiced law for a few years in Orange. He was a member of the General Assembly from Albemarle and had much to do with the passage of legislation under which the University of Virginia was established. For several sessions he was a member of the House of Representatives and was the originator of the sub-treasury system. He was a member of and took an active part in the Virginia Convention of 1829-30. He was a major-general of State militia and was known for his eloquence. He died at Edgeworth, in Albemarle, not far from the Orange line.

Roger Q. Mills, who wore the gray throughout the war, moved to Kentucky and then to Texas. He was a member of Congress from 1872 to 1892 and was Senator from 1892 to 1899.

Jeremiah Morton, who lived at Morton Hall, near Raccoon Ford, was a member of the Thirty-first Congress and as a secessionist represented his county in the secession convention of 1861.

Jackson Morton, Jeremiah Morton's brother, was United States Senator from Florida from 1849 to 1855 and was a member of the Confederate Provisional Congress.

James Newman, of Hilton, a noted agriculturist and writer, was president of the State Agricultural Society.

Gen. Thomas Sumter has been claimed as a son of Orange, but there seems better evidence that he was born at French Hay, in Hanover County, and there is a brief sketch of him in the chapter on Hanover.

James P. Taliaferro was born at Orange Courthouse, later in life becoming a distinguished citizen of Florida. As a mere boy he was in the Confederate army in the last year of the war. He was United States Senator from Florida, having been elected to that office in 1899 and re-elected in 1905.

Lewis Burwell Williams served as commonwealth's attorney of Orange for forty-nine years. He was born in Fredericksburg and was educated at Princeton. He opened a law office in Orange in 1825, where he was an influential citizen throughout the remainder of his life. He was a member of the legislature in 1833.

John Woolfolk, an able lawyer, represented Orange in the Reform Convention of 1850-51 and was a highly respected citizen.

Judge George S. Shackelford, an able attorney,

served for a number of years with ability as judge of his circuit, resigning to re-enter the private practice of law at Orange.

Judge George L. Browning, although he was born in Rappahannock County, practiced law in Orange and was elevated to the bench of the Supreme Court of Appeals of Virginia.

Judge Alexander T. Browning, who practiced law in Orange, was elevated to the judgeship of his circuit and is regarded as an unusually able jurist.

John G. Williams was for many years commonwealth's attorney for Orange.

William C. Williams, a graduate of the University of Virginia, studied law but gave up practice to serve for many years as superintendent of Orange schools. He is a nephew of John G. Williams, and there has been an extraordinary record in the Williams family. For five generations they have served as vestrymen of St. Thomas Parish.

W. W. Scott was an Orange lawyer for many years and was the historian of his county.

Albemarle County

ALBEMARLE COURTHOUSE

Albemarle County

 HUNDRED years after the first settlers arrived at Jamestown, the fertile and picturesque region now known as Albemarle County was still a wilderness. There is no evidence that Indian tribes dwelt there at the time the white men came, but it was a great hunting ground and dangerous for the pioneer white man because of the frequent inroads into the county of redskins from the north and the south.

Buffaloes still roamed in its valleys not many years before the first white men came and the country abounded in bears, elk, deer, wild turkeys, wild pigeons and other game. For many years after the whites came into the territory bounties were paid for the pelts of wolves, at the rates of 140 pounds of tobacco for an old wolf and seventy-five for a cub under six months of age. As late as 1848 Isaac Garth was paid $12 for killing an old wolf. A buffalo trail was still visible up the Rockfish River and over Rockfish Gap into the Valley.

The boundaries defined when Albemarle County was formed in 1744 embraced Buckingham, parts of Appomattox and Campbell, and the counties of Amherst, Nelson and Fluvanna, with the Blue Ridge as the western line. It was named for William Anne

Keppel, second Earl of Albemarle, at that time Governor General of the Colony.

In March, 1761, the House of Burgesses passed an act entiled "An Act for dividing the Counties of Albemarle and Louisa, etc.," in which Buckingham and Amherst were formed from Albemarle and a part of Louisa was added to Albemarle. This part of Louisa was defined as "that part of the County of Louisa that lies above a line to be run from the present line, between the said counties of Albemarle and Louisa beginning on the ridge between Machumps Creek and Beaver Dam Swamp, thence along the said ridge until the line may be intersected by an east course from the widow Cobb's plantation, and from such intersection a direct course to the line of Orange County opposite the plantation of Ambrose Coleman."

Thus that part of Fredericksville Parish which is now in Albemarle was taken from Louisa. As may be readily imagined, there was some confusion as to the boundary between Albemarle and Louisa, and there is a record in the courthouse at Charlottesville showing that at a later date a commission was named who fixed the boundary line where it is now. In the early days there was much difficulty in fixing boundary lines, for the reason that the points specified in their reckoning were so indefinite and transient. For instance, there is a record of a deed in Albemarle dated 1751 in which one of the bounds is described as a line that ran "up to the head of the branch that the Indian shot John Lawson at."

The first patents of land in Albemarle were taken out in 1727, when the present Albemarle was partly in

Goochland and partly in Hanover. Louisa, it will be remembered, was cut off from Hanover in 1742.

In 1727 George Hoomes, of Caroline County, was granted 3,100 acres "on the far side of the mountain called Chestnut," and Nicholas Meriwether was granted 13,762 acres, including the present site of Castle Hill. In 1729 Dr. George Nicholas was granted 2,600 acres on the James.

In 1730 lands were granted to Allen Howard, Thomas Carr and Charles Hudson, and Secretary John Carter was granted 9,350 acres at what still is called Carter's Mountain. Francis Eppes received land on that branch of the Hardware River still known as Eppes' Creek. In the same year Nicholas Meriwether added 4,190 acres to his already enormous holdings.

In 1731 patents were obtained by Charles Lewis, on both sides of the Rivanna, at the mouth of Buck Island Creek, by Charles Hudson and by Major Thomas Carr. The following year land, mainly along the James, was granted to Thomas Goolsby, Edward Scott, John Key and Dr. Arthur Hopkins.

In 1733 and 1734 lands were granted to Charles Lynch, Henry Wood, first clerk of Goochland, Edwin Hickman, Joseph Smith, Thomas Graves and Jonathan Clark, grandfather of George Rogers Clark, to Joel Terrell and David Lewis.

Few of these early grantees lived on their lands, but made the clearings and entered upon cultivation, which was required to perfect their titles. In many cases they doubtless sent tenants or their own servants, whom they established in "quarters." It is doubtful if there was a white man residing in Albemarle before 1730. Thomas

Jefferson said of his father, Peter Jefferson, "he was the third or fourth settler, about the year 1737, of that part of the county in which I live."

In 1735 there were twenty-nine grants, most of them in smaller tracts, to persons who meant to live on their lands. The following year Robert Lewis patented 4,030 acres on the north fork of the Hardware in North Garden.

In 1737 there were nineteen patents, including one to Michael Woods, his son Archibald, and his son-in-law, William Wallace, these lands extending to the mouth of Woods' Gap. Henry Terrell, of Caroline, was granted the tract on which the town of Batesville now stands. William Taylor received a grant of 1,200 acres on both sides of Moore's Creek. This land later passed into the hands of Col. Richard Randolph and was sold to the county by him and it is the land on which the county seat of Charlottesville was laid out in 1762.

During the decade from 1738 to 1748 lands were patented by David Mills, Dennis Doyle, Thomas Moorman, for whom Moorman's River was named, Major Thomas Carr, George Webb, of Charles City, at Webb's Mountain, Secretary John Carter, John Chiswell, William Robertson, Robert Lewis, Ambrose Joshua Smith, Samuel Garlick, of Caroline, Rev. William Stith, president of William and Mary College, and Dr. Arthur Hopkins. These grantees of land are mentioned for, with few exceptions, they were founders of families which became prominent in the affairs of the county.

The first court was held on the Scott place near the present town of Scottsville, the fourth Thursday in

February, 1745, and the following were sworn in as the first justices: Joshua Fry, Peter Jefferson, Allen Howard, William Cabell, Joseph Thompson and Thomas Ballou. The oaths taken were those of Justice of the Peace and of Judge of a Court in Chancery, and the Abjuration and Test oaths were taken, the former renouncing allegiance to the House of Stuart, and the latter affirming the receiving of the sacrament according to the rites of the Church of England. Col. William Randolph was appointed clerk, with a commission from Thomas Nelson, secretary of the Council, and Joseph Thompson, sheriff, Joshua Fry, surveyor, and Edmund Gray, King's attorney.

The county militia was organized, with Joshua Fry as county lieutenant; Peter Jefferson, lieutenant-colonel, and Allen Howard as major. The captains were William Cabell, Joseph Thompson, Charles Lynch, Thomas Ballou, David Lewis, James Daniel, James Nevill and James Martin.

The courthouse remained at Scottsville until the county was divided. A thousand acres were purchased where Charlottesville now stands from Col. Richard Randolph, of Henrico, and the title vested in Dr. Thomas Walker, as trustee, and he was empowered to sell and deed lots to purchasers. The town of Charlottesville was established by act of the Assembly in 1762, and was named for Queen Charlotte, then the bride of George III.

Col. Joshua Fry, already mentioned as one of the first justices, was afterward colonel of the regiment of which Washington was lieutenant-colonel. Col. Fry died May 31, 1754, while his regiment was on its way against the French and he was succeeded by Washington, who commanded at Great Meadows. It is impossible to say how many of Albemarle's sons took part in the French and Indian wars, but many were engaged in border warfare prior to the Revolution, and during the Revolution they played conspicuous parts, both along the Atlantic seaboard and west of the mountains.

There was a company of militia in 1758 with James Nevill, captain; John Woods and William Woods, lieutenants; and David Martin, ensign.

Members of the House of Burgesses from Albemarle were: 1745-47, Joshua Fry; 1748-49, Joshua Fry, Charles Lynch; 1752-54, Joshua Fry, Allen Howard; 1755, Allen Howard, Peter Jefferson; 1756-58, John Nicholas, William Cabell; 1758-60, Allen Howard, William Cabell, Jr.; 1761-64, Thomas Walker, John Fry; 1764-65, Thomas Walker, Henry Fry; 1765-68, Thomas Walker, Edward Carter; 1769-71, Thomas Jefferson, Thomas Walker; 1772-75, Thomas Jefferson, John Walker.

Conventions of 1775: March, Thomas Jefferson, John Walker; July, Thomas Jefferson, John Walker, Charles Lewis (alternate for Jefferson); December, John Walker, Charles Lewis.

Convention of 1776: Charles Lewis and George Gilmer, alternate for Jefferson.

Men of Albemarle were prompt to act when the Revolution approached. An independent company was formed in 1775 with Charles Lewis, of North Garden, as captain, Dr. George Gilmer and John Marks as lieutenants, and John Harvie as ensign. When Lord Dunmore stole the gunpowder from the Powder Horn at Williamsburg, eighteen of these marched to Williamsburg. In the absence of further orders, they came home, but later twenty-seven went back to Williamsburg under Lieutenant Gilmer.

A short distance east of the Rivanna River at Charlottesville was the birthplace of George Rogers Clark, the defender of Kentucky and conqueror of the Northwest Territory. His father was John Clark, son of Jonathan Clark, who had patented land in Albemarle in 1733. George Rogers Clark's mother was Ann Rogers, of Caroline, a sister of Giles, George and Byrd Rogers, all of whom owned land in Albemarle. When five years of age Clark's family moved to Caroline, having inherited property from a relative, and it was there that George Rogers Clark spent his boyhood, and it was there that a number of other brothers and sisters were born, including General William Clark.

Clark, while still a mere boy, was a surveyor, and in 1771 and 1772 made a long journey through the upper Ohio Valley and cleared land twenty-five miles below Wheeling. In Dunmore's War he was either on Lord Dunmore's staff or in command of a company, and he went to Kentucky as a surveyor for the Ohio Land Company in 1775. With the defeat of the Indians at Point Pleasant and a treaty arrangement whereby the Indians yielded all claim to the lands south of the Ohio, pioneer settlers flocked into Kentucky. Clark soon made himself a leader among them.

At this time Clark showed that he was a statesman as well as a soldier. While only twenty-four years of age in 1776, he paved the way for the recognition of

Kentucky as a Virginia County, which led to its ultimate admission to the Union as a State in 1792.

Judge Richard Henderson, who had moved in early manhood from Hanover County, Virginia, to North Carolina and had become prominent in that State, organized the Transylvania Land Company which purchased and paid for half of the present State of Kentucky. All the property between the Ohio, Kentucky and Cumberland rivers, as far east as the Cumberland Mountains, was bought from the Cherokee Indians for £10,000, or its equivalent. As a result of Clark's activities, this deed was annulled, but in compensation the State of Virginia granted the land company an area of twelve miles square, on the Ohio below the mouth of the Greene River.

In 1776, with the frontiersmen sorely in need of ammunition, and with the threat of complications in land titles, Clark and John Gabriel Jones were elected in convention as members of the Virginia General Assembly. While nominally they were members, they were in reality agents of the Kentucky people, and Clark set out upon the journey of 700 miles, most of the distance being made on foot, to petition supplies from Williamsburg. He found that the Assembly was not in session, and visited Governor Patrick Henry at his home, "Scotchtown," in Hanover County.

Governor Henry gave him a letter to the council asking that Clark be supplied with powder, which finally was done after Clark had eloquently contended that "a country not worth defending is not worth claiming." His colleague, John Gabriel Jones, lost his life in an Indian attack while trying to get the powder to Kentucky, but it finally reached its destination. Kentucky was recognized as a part of Virginia, and when the General Assembly again convened, Kentucky was organized as a county with its present boundaries.

At the outbreak of the Revolution England controlled what was familiarly known as the Northwest Territory, the region from the Alleghany Mountains north and west of the Ohio River as far as the Mississippi. The British, by bribe and otherwise, kept the Indians constantly on the warpath against the American settlers, and Clark conceived the bold idea that if the Indian outrages were to be stopped it was necessary to get at the source of the trouble and drive the British out of the Northwest Territory. The enemy had posts at Kaskaskia, on the Mississippi, at Vincennes, and general headquarters at the site of what is now Detroit.

Encouraged by Governor Henry, Jefferson, Wythe and Madison, and with a commission as lieutenant-colonel and £1,200 in Colonial currency, Clark started down the Ohio River in flat boats in May 1778, with 150 men. He stopped at Corn Island, opposite to where Louisville now stands, and established twenty families who had come with him. Here he was joined by a number of crack riflemen, such men as Simon Kenton, Joseph Bowman and other noted frontier fighters.

It is needless here to recount details of Clark's expeditions against the British forts. With few followers and poorly equipped, he surprised the garrison at Kaskaskia in June 1778. He set out for Vincennes in February 1779 and accomplished one of the boldest strokes recorded in American military history. Wading through the icy waters of the Wabash bottoms, the frontiersmen surrounded Fort Sackville, at Vincennes, and their rifles were so deadly that the British could not open the embrasures of the fort long enough to fire their cannon.

Clark's bold idea of seizing the British forts resulted in the addition of a region almost as large as the original thirteen Colonies, and made possible the Louisiana purchase and the American territorial expansion to the Pacific. The Northwest Territory would probably have been a part of Canada had it not been for Clark, and it is conceivable that the Revolution might never have been won had he not thwarted the British plan of attacking along the entire mountain front with their Indian allies while Washington was carrying on his campaigns on the coast.

Clark's remains now lie in a cemetery at Louisville, and there is a handsome monument to his memory at Indianapolis.

So much has been written of Albemarle's distinguished son, Thomas Jefferson, that it is needless here to sketch his career. He was born April 13, 1743, at Shadwell, the home of his parents, Peter Jefferson and Jane Randolph Jefferson, and was living there when the house was burned in 1770. He subsequently built and lived at Monticello, and died there July 4, 1826. It was a strange coincidence that Jefferson and John Adams died on the fiftieth anniversary of the signing of the Declaration of Independence.

His remains lie in the cemetery at Monticello and the shaft above his grave bears an inscription, written by himself, which is characteristic of the man. Ignoring the fact that he served as Governor of Virginia in the darkest period of the Revolution, was Vice-President, Ambassador to France, President of the United States, sent out the Lewis and Clark Expedition, and was responsible for the negotiation of the Louisiana Purchase, he requested that the following words be inscribed on his tomb—*and not one word more:* "Here was buried Thomas Jefferson, author of the Declaration of American Independence, of the Statutes of Virginia for Religious Freedom, and Father of the University of Virginia."

He was a man of many activities, and it is hardly probable that any other single individual exerted as widespread an influence upon American architecture as he. It was he who introduced the stately white columns, characteristic of what is usually referred to as the Early Republic architecture of this country. He designed the Capitol at Richmond, modeled after the Maison Caree at Nimes. He designed the University of Virginia, the original White House at Washington, Monticello, Farmington, Barboursville and a number of other residences, and the new style of classic architecture spread throughout the country.

James Monroe (1758-1831), fifth President of the United States, while born in Westmoreland, lived much of his life in Albemarle. His assigned reason for wanting to come to the county was to be near Jefferson, whom he greatly admired. In 1790 he bought two lots in Charlottesville and purchased the farm on which the University now stands. He resided for a short time in the house he built on what is still called Monroe Hill, then purchased the Ash Lawn property in 1793 and lived there until the termination of his second term as President. All of his properties in Albemarle were sold to satisfy his debts and he moved to Loudoun County. His remains lie in Hollywood Cemetery, Richmond.

Monroe lived an eventful life. As a lieutenant, he was wounded at the Battle of Trenton, and rose to the rank of major and afterward was a lieutenant-colonel. He studied law under Jefferson, and held the offices of U. S. Senator, Minister to France, Governor of Virginia, envoy to France to aid in the negotiation of the Louisiana Purchase, was Secretary of State, and President.

The celebrated Monroe Doctrine grew out of his statement of policy to the effect that the United States would regard as an unfriendly act any attempt on the part of European powers to extend their systems in the Western Hemisphere, or any interference to oppress, or in any manner control the destiny of governments in this hemisphere whose independence had been acknowledged by the United States.

There was a large camp of British prisoners in Albemarle from early in 1779 to late in 1780 on the north bank of Ivy Creek, the site still being called The Barracks. These British soldiers, captured in 1777 at Burgoyne's surrender, had first been sent to Boston.

Charlottesville was the objective of Colonel Banastre Tarleton in his bold raid in June 1781. With his troop of cavalry he made his way over the Louisa road in a forced march to surprise and capture Governor Jefferson, who was at Monticello, and the Legislature, which was in session at Charlottesville after Richmond had fallen into the hands of the enemy.

Tarleton stopped at Castle Hill for breakfast and for the capture of several members of the Legislature who were visiting Dr. Walker there. Meantime Jack Jouett, who was at Cuckoo Tavern, about eight miles east of Louisa Courthouse, heard the approach of Tarleton's cavalry and made a spectacular all-night ride of approximately forty miles to Charlottesville to give the alarm.

Jouett met a friend whom he sent to warn Jefferson at Monticello and then pressed on to the city to give the alarm. Tarleton's scheme undoubtedly would have been carried out had it not been for Jack Jouett's exploit. Mr. Jefferson escaped and the Legislature adjourned, the members making their way over the mountains to Staunton for their next session. Tarleton remained in Charlottesville for a part of two days and perpetrated many deeds of vandalism, including the wanton destruction of the court records. His headquarters was at The Farm, the home of Nicholas Lewis.

Jack Jouett was a citizen of Charlottesville and was probably born at Swan Tavern, conducted by the Jouetts for many years. That he was at Cuckoo Tavern in Louisa when Tarleton's cavalry rode through was not unnatural, for Matthew Jouett, in all probability his grandfather, owned land from Cuckoo all the way to the outskirts of Louisa Courthouse, and the younger Jouett was visiting relatives or looking after their landed interests.*

*The ladies of Louisa claim to have found conclusive evidence that Jack Jouett was born in that county.

As early as 1783 Jefferson was interested in establishing a grammar school in Albemarle. A charter was obtained for Albemarle Academy in 1803, but Jefferson, then President of the United States, was too busy to give his personal attention to it, and little was done until 1814, when a site was chosen. In 1816 the Legislature granted a change of name from Albemarle Academy to Central College. Members of the first Board of Visitors were Jefferson, Madison, Monroe, Joseph C. Cabell, David Watson and John H. Cocke. In 1817 land was bought from John M. Perry—the present site of the University of Virginia—and on October 6, of that year, the corner-stone of Central College was laid with ceremonies and in the presence of three Presidents of the Nation.

In February, 1818, the Legislature directed the Governor to appoint commissioners, one from each senatorial district of the State, to meet and perfect plans for a State university. They met in August at the old Leake Tavern in Rockfish Gap on Afton Mountain, with Jefferson presiding, and decided upon Central College as the site for the University, Lexington and Staunton also receiving votes, and on January 25, 1819, the Legislature changed the name of Central College to the University of Virginia.

Jefferson, who had designed the buildings for Central College, then in course of construction, enlarged his plans, and all of the original buildings of the University were designed by him and erected under his personal supervision.

The scholastic duties of the University began March 7, 1825, with forty students present at the opening.

Intended as the capstone of the public school system in Virginia, the University was governed by its board of visitors until 1904, when Dr. Edwin A. Alderman was installed as its first president.

Albemarle County and her sons certainly played their part in extending the frontiers and adding territories until the infant nation after the Revolution became the vast empire which is now the United States. The dream of the first settlers of Jamestown that they might find a short passage to the South Sea soon vanished, but nearly two hundred years later, when hardly had the echoes of the guns of the Revolution died out, there came a new vision of an overland passage to the Pacific Ocean. Men of Albemarle made this a reality.

Meriwether Lewis, of the Lewis and Clark Expedition, was a son of William Lewis, a lieutenant in the Revolution, and Lucy Meriwether Lewis. They lived at Locust Hill, near Ivy Depot, and here Meriwether Lewis was born. His companion in the famous expedition to the mouth of the Columbia River on the Pacific Coast was William Clark, a younger brother of General George Rogers Clark.

Even before the Revolution, George Washington foresaw the need of avenues of communication between the Hudson and the Great Lakes, and Chesapeake Bay and the Ohio River, and immediately after the war Jefferson manifested untiring interest in the western country.

In 1783 Jefferson wrote General George Rogers Clark that England was planning an expedition overland from the Mississippi to the Pacific. "They pretend it is to promote knowledge," he said; "I am afraid they have thought of colonizing in that quarter." Jefferson wished Clark might lead an American expedition which would get there first. The expedition never materialized.

Again in 1792, having returned from France, Jefferson sought to induce the American Philosophical Society to send a French botanist, André Michaux, across the continent. He was to have but a single companion, Meriwether Lewis, who was a friend of Jefferson, a Colonial officer and an expert woodsman. A political tangle thwarted this project.

In 1801 Jefferson became President of the United States, and it was within his power to carry out his long-cherished purpose in the West, and he began at once upon plans to send an expedition up the Missouri, across the Rockies and down by the "River Ouragan" to the Pacific.

While negotiations were going forward in Paris between Jefferson's emissaries and Bonaparte's tricky Minister Talleyrand—negotiations which resulted in tumbling the whole of Louisiana and Florida into the lap of the astonished American statesmen—Jefferson, with the utmost attention to every small detail, was completing the arrangements for the Lewis and Clark Expedition.

In May 1804 the party headed by Meriwether Lewis and William Clark started from a point a short distance above St. Louis and made their way up the Missouri. On September 23, 1806, they were back in St. Louis, having completed one of the most spectacular exploring expeditions in history.

Meriwether Lewis was immediately named as Governor of the new territory of Louisiana, and Clark also was given high honors. But Lewis did not long live to enjoy the acclaim of his fellow-citizens. He was murdered and robbed in a cabin in Tennessee while on his way east to attend to the publication of the journals of his trip to the Pacific.

In 1848 the Legislature of Tennessee erected a monument at the grave of Lewis in Lewis County, near Hohenwald, Tenn. On one of its faces is the inscription: "Meriwether Lewis. Born near Charlottesville, Va., August 18, 1774; died October 11, 1809, aged 35 years." On another face is inscribed: "An officer of the regular army. Commander of the expedition to the Oregon in 1803-1806. His melancholy death occurred near where this monument now stands, and under which rest his mortal remains."

Albemarle also played a prominent part in early transportation to the regions west of the mountains. When in 1785 the James River Company was formed, with George Washington as its first president, the dream was crystallizing that James River could be made navigable to a point where it might be in contact with water transportation in the Ohio River by means of a turnpike through Rockfish Gap.

In the rare book collection of the Library of Congress is a statement of its agents in 1805. At the time W. Foushee was president, and following were the directors: Edward Carrington, George Pickett, Robert Gamble and James Brown. It showed that from 1796 to 1804 much work had been done in the vicinity of Lynchburg, and on the Rivanna as far as Milton. Tolls commenced in 1794 and in 1796 full tolls were received. It was shown that out of the profits $2,400 annually was being paid Washington Academy (now Washington and Lee University) and in an argument opposing an outlay for expensive locks it was pointed out that it would endanger "the valuable support of education, on the state of which the freedom or slavery of a country depends."

In 1810 the Rivanna Navigation Company was chartered, to keep the channel clear in order that boats might be floated down to the James River canal at Columbia. In 1827 the stock issue was enlarged and a series of dams built, with locks for elevating and lowering boats. In the meantime Scottsville was established by act of the Legislature in 1818 and in 1824 the Staunton and James River Turnpike was commenced, with Scottsville as its river terminus.

Then came the era of the steam railroad. The little Louisa Railroad, running from Gordonsville to Hanover Junction, was chartered in 1836, permitted to extend to the docks in Richmond in 1848 and allowed to change its name to the Virginia Central in 1850. In the meantime the Blue Ridge Railroad was projected, from Mechum's River to Waynesboro. Col. Claudius Crozet was its chief engineer, and while the tunnel through the Blue Ridge was in progress, trains were moved over the mountains in Rockfish Gap on tracks laid in a zigzag manner, one of the most amazing feats of civil engineering ever accomplished. Then came the Covington and Ohio Railroad, to a point on the Ohio River, and finally all of these were incorporated into the great Chesapeake and Ohio System after the War Between the States.

Few references have been preserved in regard to the part Albemarle men played in the War of 1812, but there was a cavalry company commanded by Col. Samuel Carr, with Dr. Frank Carr as surgeon, and Achilles Broadhead commanded an infantry company. William Wirt, who commanded an artillery company on the York River in 1814, wrote that "Frank Gilmer, Jefferson Randolph, the Carrs and others have got tired of waiting for the British, and gone home."

There was much excitement in Albemarle in 1824 when the Marquis de Lafayette revisited the country where he had distinguished himself as a young Revolutionary officer. He came from Richmond in November of that year to exchange greetings with Jefferson.

At the Fluvanna line he was met by a troop of cavalry, called in his honor the Lafayette Guards. Its officers were John H. Craven, captain; George W. Kinsolving, first lieutenant; Richard Watson, second lieutenant; and Thomas W. Gilmer, cornet. They escorted the French nobleman to Charlottesville. His carriage was halted and he was addressed by William C. Rives.

There was a touching scene when Jefferson, then an octogenarian, greeted Lafayette on the lawn of Monticello. Then followed a public meeting at the Central Hotel in Charlottesville, with Thomas J. Randolph as the speaker, the procession then moving to the University, where William F. Gordon delivered an address. Dinner was served in the Rotunda, then in an unfinished condition, with V. W. Southall as toastmaster.

Lafayette then returned to Monticello with Jefferson and Madison, where he remained several days, and then was escorted by the Guards as far as Gordonsville on his way to visit Madison at Montpelier.

In addition to those already noted, brief mention may here be made of a number of men of mark in Albemarle.

John P. Ballard, descended from Thomas Ballard, who patented land prior to 1740 near the foot of Piney Mountain, established the noted Ballard House in Richmond.

James Barclay bought Monticello from Thomas J. Randolph and lived there until 1836 when he sold it to Commodore Uriah P. Levy. He became a Disciples minister and for many years served as a missionary to Jerusalem, and was author of a book called The City of the Great King.

James Black owned 600 acres on Stockton's Creek and had a tavern not far from Rockfish Gap which was visited in the Fall of 1777 by General George Rogers Clark, on his way from Kentucky to Williamsburg.

James M. Bowen, a prosperous business man, built Mirador, and his brother, Thomas Bowen, was one of the justices prior to 1850.

Nimrod Bramham succeeded William Wirt as lieutenant of militia in 1800, and in 1806 was a colonel. He was a magistrate, an active churchman, and represented the county in the Legislature in 1812.

Robert Brooks, son of James Brooks, one of the early Albemarle lawyers, for many years kept a tavern at Brooksville and was one of the magistrates. He married a daughter of James Hays. Robert Brooks, in 1818, acted as attorney for his brothers and sisters in the sale of 9,000 acres of land in Harrison County, Kentucky, and moved to Kentucky himself.

Bernard Brown, of the family which came early to Brown's Cove, was the father of three magistrates, Charles, Thomas H. and Ira B. Brown, the first two of whom served as sheriffs between 1840 and 1850.

Richard Burch, whose people purchased from Francis Jerdone 400 acres on Ivy Creek, a part of the Michael Holland tract on which Farmington now stands, was a tavern-keeper, first at Stony Point, then at Michie's Old Tavern and then at the noted Swan Tavern in Charlottesville.

When the present form of government in the State went into effect in 1777, William Cabell was the first State Senator to represent Albemarle. The office was held by a Cabell, with the exception of three years, continuously until 1830. The last was Joseph Cabell, who was a member for sixteen years.

Carr was a prominent name in Albemarle. Major Thomas Carr, of King William, started taking up land in Albemarle as early as 1730, and in 1737 owned over 5,000 acres along the north fork of the Rivanna. Most of this land was given to his son John Carr, who already held a large tract at his home Bear Castle, in Louisa. John Carr, of Louisa, first married Mary Dabney, and secondly Barbara Overton, and died about 1769. John Carr had five sons and one daughter. Thomas, the eldest son, lived in Albemarle and was father of John M. Carr, first clerk of the Circuit Court until 1819. He lived at Belmont. Dabney Carr, second son of John Carr, of Bear Castle, was a brilliant young orator and represented Louisa in the House of Burgesses in 1772 and 1773, in which latter year he died in Charlottesville while there on a visit. He presented the resolutions for a committee of correspondence for all the Colonies and was elected as Virginia's representative. He married Martha, sister of Thomas Jefferson, and his remains are interred at Monticello. Dabney Carr's son, Peter Carr, was secretary to Jefferson while President and lived at Carrsbrook. His son, Dabney Carr, was minister to Turkey in 1843, serving six years. Samuel Carr, second son of Dabney Carr, the Louisa Burgess, and Martha Jefferson Carr, was a magistrate, colonel of cavalry in the War of 1812 and member of the Virginia House of Delegates and Senate. He lived at Dunlora. Judge Dabney Carr, third son of the Louisa Burgess, practiced law in Charlottesville and after being Chancellor of the Winchester District became a judge of the Virginia Court of Appeals in 1824. He died in Richmond in 1837. Garland Carr, another member of the Carr family in Albemarle, was commonwealth's attorney from 1818 to 1829. Still another Garland Carr, who lived at Bentivar and married the daughter of Col. William O. Winston, of Hanover, was a magistrate. One of his daughters married Achilles Broadhead, who moved to Missouri and was the father of James O. Broadhead, of St. Louis, and Professor Garland C. Broadhead, of the University of Missouri. Francis Carr, son of Garland Carr, of Bentivar, was magistrate, sheriff, a physician, teacher and editor, was secretary of the County Agricultural Society and secretary of the faculty of the University of Virginia.

Edward Carter spent the latter part of his life at Blenheim and represented the County in the House of Burgesses from 1767 to 1769 and was in the House of Delegates in 1792. He was a son of Secretary John Carter, who was the eldest son of Robert "King" Carter. Edward Carter's son Robert lived at Redlands and was the father of John Carter, a lawyer and magistrate who at one time owned Farmington, later moving to Missouri.

Robert Clark, of Albemarle, was the father of Robert Clark, the first iron manufacturer in Kentucky; James Clark, who was Governor of Kentucky when he died in 1839; and Bennett Clark, the father and grandfather of two John Bullock Clarks, who were both members of Congress from Missouri and both Generals in the Confederate army.

The first John Coles came from Ireland, settled in Hanover, and married Mary Winston. His son, John Coles, Jr., settled in Albemarle on 3,000 acres of what had been the original grant to Francis Eppes in 1730. A daughter of the first John Coles, Mary, was the wife of John Payne and the mother of Dolly Madison, and a son, Isaac Coles, was a member of Congress. A number of members of the family were distinguished. Walter Coles, who lived at Woodville, was a magistrate, and was the grandfather of Dr. Walter Coles, of St. Louis. John Coles lived at Estouteville. Isaac A. Coles was a member of the Albemarle bar and was for a time President Jefferson's private secretary. He lived at Enniscorthy. Edward Coles, youngest son of the second John Coles, was private secretary to President Madison and in 1818 moved to Illinois. He

carried all his slaves with him, gave them their freedom and settled them on farms near Edwardsville. He
was the first Governor of the Territory of Illinois and
was its second Governor after it became a State.

William S. Dabney was appointed a magistrate in
1835 and was particularly useful as a member of the
county bench. His father, William S. Dabney, had
come to the county in 1803 with his wife, who was
Mary Watson, of the Green Springs Neighborhood of
Louisa. The second William S. Dabney purchased
Dunlora, the old Carr place, in 1846 and lived there
until he died. He had two sons on the University of
Virginia faculty at the same time, Dr. William C.
Dabney, of the Medical Faculty, and Walter Dabney
in the department of law.

Professor John A. G. Davis came to the county from
Middlesex and engaged in the practice of law. In
1828 he was an associate in the publication of the
Virginia Advocate. In 1830 he was made professor of
law at the University, succeeding John T. Lomax. He
died in 1840. Dr. John Staige Davis was one of his
sons.

Martin Dawson, a member of a family identified
with the county from its beginning, established himself
in business at Milton and amassed a considerable
fortune. He died in 1835 and from the proceeds of
the sale of a farm left by him, Dawson's Row at the
University of Virginia was built.

Achilles Douglass, of a family coming to the county
about 1751, was appointed a magistrate in 1796 and
was prominent in county affairs. He was sheriff in
1823.

Colonel Richard T. W. Duke of the 46th Virginia in the War Between the States was admitted to the Albemarle bar in 1849. He served his county as commonwealth's attorney and member of the House of Delegates, and was sent to Congress. His father, Richard Duke, operated the Rivanna Mills and was a magistrate and served as sheriff in 1847. Colonel Duke's son, Judge R. T. W. Duke, Jr., was a prominent Albemarle lawyer and jurist.

Marshall Durrett was a magistrate in 1796 and sheriff in 1819.

Samuel Dyer, Revolutionary soldier, became successful in mercantile pursuits and was an influential citizen. He had eleven children, most of whom emigrated to Missouri.

John Early in 1822 bought nearly 1,000 acres between Buck Mountain and Jacob's Run, and from him the village of Earlysville derived its name. He was the uncle of William T. "Buck" Early, well known lawyer and political figure.

John and George W. Eubank prospered as proprietors of taverns on the Staunton and James River Turnpike.

John S. Farrar was a colonel of the 47th Regiment in 1815, and his sister married Dr. Samuel Leake and was the mother of the distinguished lawyer, Shelton F. Leake.

Colonel Joshua Fry was born in England and educated at Oxford. On coming to Virginia he was made professor of mathematics at the College of William and Mary. He was, as hitherto noted, one of the first magistrates of Albemarle, its first county lieutenant, and its first surveyor. Washington succeeded to the command of his regiment when Col. Fry died on his way against the French on May 31, 1754, at Fort Mills, now Cumberland, Md., and he was buried there. He lived at the plantation south of Carter's Bridge later called Viewmont, which his widow sold to Governor Edmund Randolph. Joshua Fry II, grandson of Col. Joshua Fry, married the youngest daughter of Dr. Thomas Walker, of Castle Hill. He was a magistrate and member of the Legislature, late in the 18th Century moving to Kentucky.

James Garland, of Hanover, who married Mary Rice, was a magistrate in 1783 and sheriff in 1791. His son, Rice Garland, who lived at Ivy Depot on the farm later called Bloomfield, was a magistrate in 1791 and sheriff in 1811. James Garland, Jr., was killed by a sentry at The Barracks, but his widow and children moved to Amherst and were prominent.

Alexander and Ira Garrett for many years served as clerks. They were sons of Henry Garrett, of Louisa, who moved from Louisa to Kentucky in 1810. William Garrett had purchased land in Albemarle in 1764.

Thomas Garth, who first purchased land in the county in 1762 and held large properties, lived on his tract between the Staunton road and the fork of Mechum's and Moorman's rivers. He was a magistrate in 1791 and sheriff in 1807. His son, Jesse W. Garth, was commonwealth's attorney from 1813 to 1818 and served as a member of the Legislature. He moved to Alabama in 1818. Members of the family were noted horsemen.

Dr. George Gilmer, son of the immigrant to Williamsburg of the same name and profession, married a daughter of Dr. Thomas Walker and lived first in Charlottesville. He was an active patriot and played a prominent part in the earliest movements toward independence, serving as a lieutenant in the Albemarle militia of 1775. In 1777 he purchased Pen Park, noted for its hospitality, and lived there the remainder of his life. He was a magistrate, sheriff in 1787, and member of the House of Delegates. Dr. Gilmer also owned about 2,000 acres on Mechunk Creek. His daughter was the wife of William Wirt, and they lived at Rose Hill until 1800. His son, George Gilmer, was the father of Thomas W. Gilmer, noted lawyer, member of the Legislature, Governor of Virginia, member of Congress and Secretary of the Navy. He lost his life in the Princeton disaster in 1844.

General William F. Gordon, son of James Gordon, of the Rappahannock River country, was admitted to the Albemarle bar in 1809 and took a leading part in the affairs of the county for many years. He was commonwealth's attorney and member of both houses of the General Assembly, and represented his district in Congress. He was a General of militia during the period 1829-1840. His wife was a daughter of Reuben Lindsay, and they had nine children, most of whom rose to prominence.

William Harris first patented land in Albemarle in 1739 and became a man of distinction. He owned much land and established on Green Creek one of the earliest mills. The year after the county was formed he was named as one of the magistrates. He left ten children and his descendants were numerous, many of them being persons of note. John Harris, who lived at View-mont, was the wealthiest man in the county at the time of his death in 1832. Benjamin Harris, also a man of great wealth, was a magistrate in 1791 and sheriff in 1815.

Peyton Harrison in 1829 purchased Belle Grove, site of the first Albemarle courthouse at Scottsville. He was a son of Carter Henry Harrison, of Cumberland, and of the family of Benjamin Harrison, signer of the Declaration of Independence. Peyton Harrison married a daughter of Judge Dabney Carr. In 1833 he sold Belle Grove to his brother, Carter Henry Harrison, who was a magistrate in 1835 and was grandfather of Judge George M. Harrison, of the Virginia Supreme Court of Appeals.

John Harvie, a Scotchman, was one of the earliest Albemarle lawyers and was guardian of Thomas Jefferson. He first lived at Belmont, near Keswick, and owned large properties, including The Barracks and Pen Park. He was a member of the Virginia House of Burgesses and of the Continental Congress. He was appointed by Jefferson as Register of the Land Office and moved to Richmond and died there in 1807. He lived at what he called Belvidere and built a number of homes in an around Richmond, including the Gamble mansion, his death resulting from a fall from a ladder while that dwelling was being erected.

James Hays conducted a tavern on a tract including Brooksville, and John Hays likewise ran a tavern. David Hays owned land a short distance north of Batesville and was Colonel of the 47th Virginia Regiment prior to his death about 1856.

John Henderson owned land at an early date near Milton and his son, John Henderson, Jr., was a magistrate and filled the office of sheriff prior to his death in 1790. Most of the family moved to Kentucky.

William Waller Hening, who compiled the great work *Hening's Statutes at Large,* was at one time a Charlottesville lawyer. His researches led him to Richmond, where he died in 1829.

Dr. Arthur Hopkins, a leading citizen of Goochland, patented three large tracts in Albemarle, the first in 1732. His grandson, Samuel Hopkins, was lieutenant colonel of the 10th Virginia in the Revolution and a general in Kentucky in the War of 1812. For him Hopkins County and Hopkinsville in that State were named. Mary Cabell, granddaughter of Dr. Arthur Hopkins, became the wife of John Breckinridge, then of Botetourt County, who became a United States Senator from Kentucky and Jefferson's Attorney General. John Breckinridge lived in Albemarle and practiced law from 1785 to 1793, when he moved to Kentucky. His two eldest children were born in Albemarle, one of whom was the father of General John Cabell Breckinridge, Confederate officer, and Vice-President in the administration of James Buchanan.

Christopher Hudson, of Mount Air, son of Charles Hudson of Hanover and one of the early grantees of land in Albemarle, was a magistrate in 1800.

The Rev. William Irvin came to Albemarle as a Presbyterian minister in 1771 and left ten children. Among them, John Irvin was a magistrate and died in 1828; William Irvin was a member of the Albemarle bar, emigrating to Lancaster County, Ohio, where he became a judge of the Supreme Court and was sent to Congress in 1828; Thomas Irvin also went to Ohio and became a judge; and David Irvin, the youngest son, also a lawyer, was territorial Governor of Wisconsin, and afterward moved to Texas.

James Jarman, son of Thomas Jarman who obtained a grant on Moorman's River in 1762, was a magistrate in 1819. William Jarman, another son, lived near Mechum's Depot and established Jarman's Mill.

Peter Jefferson, father of the author of the Declaration of Independence, was a native of that part of Henrico which is now Chesterfield County, and came to Albemarle in 1737. He first patented 1,000 acres on the south side of the Rivanna, but wishing a better building site for his home, he bought the 400-acre Shadwell tract from his friend William Randolph, of Tuckahoe. This was the land, or a part of it, that was transferred in the celebrated deal in which figured as a consideration, "Henry Wetherburn's biggest bowl of Arrack punch." Peter Jefferson had been a magistrate and sheriff of Goochland, and when Albemarle was formed was one of the original magistrates and its lieutenant colonel. He represented Albemarle in the House of Burgesses. He and Col. Joshua Fry were employed to run the boundary line between Virginia and North Carolina, and they made a valuable map of Virginia. His wife was Jane Randolph, daughter of Isham Randolph, of Dungeness, in Goochland County. Their children were Jane, who never married; Thomas, Randolph, Mary, the wife of Thomas Bolling; Martha, the wife of Dabney Carr; Lucy, the wife of Charles Lilburn Lewis, and Ann, the wife of Hastings

Marks. Thomas Jefferson (1743-1826), whose biography is well known, married Martha Wayles, of Charles City, widow of Bathurst Skelton, and they had two daughters, Martha, the wife of Governor Thomas Mann Randolph, and Mary, the wife of John W. Eppes.

Matthew Jouett owned large acreage in Louisa County extending from about Cuckoo to the outskirts of the town of Louisa. Among the earliest court records in Albemarle in 1745 is a notice of the death of Matthew Jouett. It is believed that this was the same man, and also that John Jouett, for many years a prominent citizen of Charlottesville, was his son. In 1773 John Jouett bought 100 acres on the eastern outskirts of Charlottesville and established the famous Swan Tavern. He also owned 300 acres south of the town. His death occurred in 1802. His wife was Mourning Harris Jouett, and of his children Matthew was a captain in the Revolution and was killed in the Battle of Brandywine; John Jouett conducted the Swan for a while, then moved to Bath County, Ky.; Robert was a captain in the Revolution and afterwards an Albemarle lawyer. There is some question whether the famous Jack Jouett, who saved Mr. Jefferson and the Legislature from the British in 1781 was John Sr. or John Jr.

James Kerr was a magistrate, and was sheriff in 1793. He had come to the county from Scotland about 1762. In 1808 he sold his property and moved to Kentucky. John Rice Kerr, his son, was appointed a magistrate in 1807 and he, too, moved to Kentucky.

John, Tandy and Joshua Key, grandsons of John

Key, who patented land in the county in 1732, were all magistrates. John Key served as sheriff in 1795 and Tandy Key in 1809. John Key was an ensign and another brother, Henry Key, was a soldier in the Revolution.

James Kinsolving bought land near Mechum's Depot in 1788. His son, George W. Kinsolving, was in 1830 appointed colonel of the 47th Virginia Regiment. From this family came a number of Episcopal clergymen.

Shelton F. Leake was a brilliant Albemarle lawyer who started practice in 1838. He was a member of the House of Delegates, Lieutenant Governor of Virginia and Congressman. His uncle, Walter Leake, emigrated to Mississippi and was Senator from that State in 1817, and Governor from 1821 to 1825.

In 1836 Uriah P. Levy, a commodore in the United States Navy and a great admirer of Mr. Jefferson, purchased Monticello and became an Albemarle citizen. He had no family of his own and at the time of his death in 1862 he devised the place to the Government to be used as a retreat for sailors, and, if that plan failed, to the State of Virginia as a naval school. Both dispositions were declared invalid by the courts. In later years Jefferson M. Levy, of New York, a nephew of the Commodore, purchased the interests of the other heirs and devoted himself to the improvement of the place. Finally it passed into the hands of the association which is now caring for it and preserving it as a shrine.

Three families of Lewises lived in Albemarle. Charles Lewis, of Goochland, patented land in 1731;

David Lewis patented the tract just west of the University land in 1734; and John Lewis owned land on Totier Creek in 1741. Of the descendants of Charles Lewis, Nicholas Lewis was a captain in the Revolution. He was named for his maternal grandfather, Nicholas Meriwether. Charles Lewis was a magistrate, surveyor and sheriff and a trusted friend of Jefferson; Charles Lewis who lived in North Garden, was one of the first to volunteer at the outbreak of the Revolution. He was captain of the first volunteer company raised in Albemarle, lieutenant colonel of the first regiment formed, and afterward colonel of the 14th Virginia; William Lewis, who lived at Locust Hill, near Ivy Depot, was a lieutenant in the Revolution and died in 1780. He married Lucy, the daughter of Thomas Meriwether—one of several intermarriages between the Lewises and Meriwethers—and was the father of Meriwether Lewis, the famous explorer.

Of the descendants of David Lewis, three brothers, Micajah, Joel and James Lewis were in the Battle of King's Mountain, and the first lost his life at Guilford Courthouse. James Lewis, a son of the first David Lewis, was a Revolutionary soldier, a magistrate and a large land-owner, emigrating to Franklin County, Tenn., in 1818.

Reuben Lindsay came from Westmoreland about 1776 and was a magistrate at the close of the Revolutionary War.

Charles Lynch, believed to have been born in Ireland, who had been a magistrate in Goochland, entered land in Albemarle in 1733 and became a large property-owner. He was one of the original magistrates, a sheriff and member of the House of Burgesses. In his latter years he moved to land he owned on James River, across from Lynchburg and his son, John Lynch, was the founder of that city. Another son, Charles Lynch, was a colonel in the Revolution. It is said that his vigor in dealing with violent Tories and outlaws during the Revolutionary period gave rise to the term "Lynch Law."

Charles P. McKennie published Albemarle's first newspaper, *The Central Gazette,* in 1820.

Thomas Macon, who had come to the county from New Kent, was a magistrate until his death in 1851.

John B. Magruder came to the county from Maryland and died in 1812. Members of his family were noted millers. Benjamin H. Magruder served in the Legislature both before and after the War of the 60s. General John Bankhead Magruder was a relative.

An Englishman named Marks married Elizabeth Hastings whose son, Hastings Marks, came to Virginia. His will, recorded in Hanover in 1761, named five sons and one daughter, who settled in Albemarle prior to the Revolution. They were Peter, John, James, Hastings, Thomas and Sarah Marks, who married Captain James Winston, of Louisa. Peter Marks was a prominent citizen of Charlottesville. John Marks was a captain in the Revolution and for this service received a grant of 4,000 acres in Ross County, Ohio. Hastings Marks lived in the Ragged Mountains section and married Ann, the sister of Thomas Jefferson.

Hudson Martin, a lieutenant in the Revolution, was deputy clerk and a magistrate. He was a descendant of Captain Joseph Martin, who patented land in the county in 1745.

Charles Massie, of the distinguished New Kent family, bought the plantation Spring Valley in the southwestern part of the county, which became noted for the perfection of the Albemarle Pippin apples grown there. One of his sons, Dr. Hardin Massie, moved to Charlottesville in 1824 and was a prominent physician.

Daniel Maupin patented land on Moorman's River in 1748, and his brother, Gabriel Maupin, also lived in the county. Daniel, William and Cornelius Maupin, believed to have been grandsons of Daniel Maupin, were Revolutionary soldiers. Dr. Socrates Maupin, professor of chemistry at Hampden-Sydney College and afterwards of the University of Virginia faculty, was of this family, as was Chapman W. Maupin, who was a magistrate in 1835.

The Rev. James Maury, son of Matthew Maury and Mary Anne Fontaine, Huguenot exiles, was rector of Fredericksville Parish and lived on his farm on the border of Albemarle and Louisa. He was the complainant in the famous Parsons' Cause tried at Hanover Courthouse, in which Patrick Henry's eloquence first displayed itself. He conducted a school at his place which was attended by Thomas Jefferson. One of his sons, James Maury, was Consul to Liverpool from 1789 to 1837. Another son, Richard Maury, married Diana Minor, of Louisa, and was the father of Commodore Matthew Fontaine Maury, and grandfather of General Dabney Maury of the Confederate army.

Nicholas Meriwether, son of the immigrant from

Wales of the same name, who died in 1678, was perhaps the largest land-owner in Albemarle, also owning lands in several other counties, and he was the ancestor of many distinguished men. He was a Burgess from New Kent from 1705 to 1722 and one of the first Burgesses from Hanover, serving from 1722 to 1726. He lived on the Rivanna River on a tract extending from Moore's Creek to Meadow Creek which he acquired in 1735 and bequeathed to his grandson, Nicholas Lewis. Nicholas Meriwether died in 1744. William Douglass Meriwether, who lived at Clover Fields, was a magistrate for fifty years and was a man of wealth. He was twice sheriff, in 1801 and in 1828. Colonel Charles Lewis, Meriwether Lewis the explorer, and many other men of note trace their ancestry to Nicholas Meriwether.

William Michie, son of John Michie who was an early landowner in the county, was a man of wealth and established what is now known as Michie's Old Tavern, on the Buck Mountain road. He was a magistrate in 1791, sheriff in 1803 and died in 1811. William Michie's son, John A. Michie, was a magistrate in 1807, and his grandson, James Michie, was a magistrate in 1816 and sheriff in 1843.

John Minor, of Caroline, married a daughter of Thomas Carr, and they had eleven children, three of whom settled in Albemarle. James Minor, who built Burnt Mills, was a magistrate and died in 1791. Dabney Minor, eldest son of James Minor, was a large landowner and a magistrate. Peter Minor, another son of John Minor, of Caroline, married a daughter of Dr. George Gilmer, of Pen Park, and was appointed treasurer of the Rivanna Navigation Company in 1811. He was for many years secretary of the County Agricultural Society. A third son of the first John Minor mentioned, was Major John Minor, of Topping Castle, Caroline county, whose son, Lancelot Minor, of Minor's Folly, Louisa County, was the father of a number of distinguished sons, including Dr. John B. Minor, for fifty years the celebrated professor of law at the University of Virginia; Lucian Minor, who was admitted to the Albemarle bar in 1830 and later was professor of law at the College of William and Mary (he lived the latter part of his life near Louisa Courthouse); and Lancelot Minor, who married Sarah Winston, of Louisa, and, secondly, Mary Ann Swann, and who was an influential citizen of Amherst, living at Brieryknowne. Diana Minor, daughter of Major John Minor, of Topping Castle, married Richard Lancelot Maury and was the mother of Matthew Fontaine Maury, "The Pathfinder of the Seas."

Hugh Nelson, son of Governor Thomas Nelson, was admitted to the bar of the county in 1802. He lived at Belvoir and was Speaker of the House of Delegates, and member of Congress from 1811 to 1823, when he was appointed Minister to Spain.

John Nicholas, son of Dr. George Nicholas, of Williamsburg, who patented land in Albemarle on James River in 1729, was clerk from 1749 for sixty-six years. He married a daughter of Col. Joshua Fry. His eldest son, John Nicholas, Jr., was his father's deputy from 1792 to 1815, when the old clerk resigned. Governor Thomas Mann Randolph challenged the elder John Nicholas to a duel, and they met on Round

Top Mountain, across the Rivanna from Monticello. Nicholas fired first but missed his aim, and Randolph's bullet pierced the old clerk's hat. They made friends and John Nicholas wore the hat, with the bullet hole through it, until it was no longer wearable. Robert Carter Nicholas, treasurer of the Colony, succeeded to the James River lands of his father, Dr. George Nicholas, and three of his sons lived in Albemarle— George, Wilson Cary and Lewis. George Nicholas was a colonel in the Revolution, after the war practicing law in Charlottesville. In 1788 he was a member of the Legislature and of the Virginia convention which ratified the Constitution of the United States. In 1790 he moved to Kentucky, was active in its formation as a State, and was Kentucky's first attorney general. Wilson Cary Nicholas, the second son of the treasurer of the Colony, was a soldier of the Revolution, commanding Washington's Life Guards. He was a magistrate, represented the county in the Legislature, was United States Senator and Governor of Virginia. Lewis Nicholas, another son of the treasurer, lived at Alta Vista, west of Green Mountain, and two of his sons served as magistrates.

John Old came to the county in 1769 and operated two iron furnaces.

Robert Page bought land on Taylor's Creek in 1770, and most of his nine children went to Kentucky. Nicholas M. Page, a grandson, returned in 1829 and was a merchant at Batesville. He was a magistrate in 1841. Dr. Mann Page, son of Major Carter Page, of Cumberland, came to Albemarle in 1815 and was a magistrate in 1824.

John M. Perry in 1814 bought the land on which the University now stands, selling it in 1817 to Alexander Garrett, as Proctor of Central College. He was a large contractor. He erected many of the original University buildings, his home Montebello, and Frascati, the home of Judge Philip Barbour in Orange. He was a magistrate in 1816.

Bernard Peyton, of Richmond, about 1850 bought Farmington from John Coles Carter, and the latter moved to Missouri. Bernard Peyton lived at Farmington and was the father of Major Green Peyton, Proctor of the University of Virginia.

James Quarles, of King William, was a magistrate and was sheriff in 1783. In 1767 he had bought the Rock Hall place, which later passed to John Hunton, of Augusta, whose son, Charles B. Hunton, was a magistrate in 1791 and sheriff in 1813.

William Randolph, of Tuckahoe, Goochland County, was granted 2,400 acres on the Rivanna near the mountains in 1735, and although he was the county's first clerk, he never resided in Albemarle. His grandson, Thomas Mann Randolph, married Martha, the daughter of Thomas Jefferson, and lived at Edgehill. Thomas Mann Randolph was a magistrate in 1794, was elected to Congress in 1801, and was Governor of Virginia in 1819. His eldest son, Col. Thomas J. Randolph, was a magistrate, member of the Legislature, and president of the Farmers' Bank. Another son of the Governor, Dr. Benjamin F. Randolph, was a magistrate in 1846, and for a number of terms was a member of the State Senate. George Wythe Randolph, still another son of the Governor, was a lawyer and moved to Richmond. He was the last Secretary of War of the Confederacy. Col. Richard Randolph, of Henrico, and Governor Edmund Randolph both owned land in the county, but apparently neither became citizens of Albemarle. In 1805 Dr. Thomas Eston Randolph bought the Glenmore estate near Milton and was a magistrate in 1807. He lived later at Ashton.

Robert Rives, a successful business man of Nelson County, had a branch business at Milton and was a large landowner in Albemarle. In 1818 he bought the Boiling Springs plantation from John Patterson, of Baltimore, the consideration being $60,000, a large sum of money in those days. His son, William Cabell Rives, married Judith Walker, who inherited Castle Hill. He was one of the most gifted orators of his time. He was a distinguished member of the Albemarle bar, served in the Legislature, in the United States Senate and was Minister to France. Judge Alexander Rives, another son of Robert Rives, lived at Carleton, and was a member of both houses of the Legislature and of Congress, and was judge of the United States District Court for the western District of Virginia.

David Rodes came to the county in 1756 and was a magistrate and sheriff. He was a son of John Rodes, of Louisa, who came to Albemarle in 1749. Matthew Rodes, son of David Rodes, also was a magistrate in 1816. From this family came General Robert E. Rodes, of the Confederate army, who fell at Winchester in 1864. Clifton Rodes, another son of the first John Rodes, was a magistrate and sheriff in 1783 before removing to Kentucky. John Rodes, Jr., youngest son of the first John Rodes, was father of Captain Robert Rodes of the Revolutionary army, who was made prisoner at the fall of Charleston, S. C. He later moved to Kentucky. Captain Rodes' brother, Clifton Rodes, was a magistrate and married a daughter of John Jouett. He also moved to Kentucky. John Rodes, another brother, was a magistrate in 1807 and sheriff in 1812.

Giles, George and Byrd Rogers, brothers of Ann Rogers, the mother of General George Rogers Clark, all owned land in Albemarle, almost the entire family emigrating to Kentucky. Parmenas Rogers, son of Giles Rogers, was a magistrate in 1807 and sheriff in 1834. John Rogers, son of Byrd Rogers, was an expert farmer, and his son, Thornton Rogers, conducted a classical school at Keswick, the old Page mansion, from which came the name of the nearby Keswick Depot. Francis S. Sampson, a nephew, studied at Keswick, then at the University of Virginia, and became a member of the faculty of the Union Theological Seminary at Richmond.

Edward Scott patented land where Scottsville now stands in 1732. His son, Samuel Scott, gave bond for the erection of the first county buildings on the land of his brother, Daniel Scott.

Samuel Shelton was an early settler of Albemarle and his son, Clough Shelton, was a captain in the Revolution and was taken prisoner in the surrender of Charleston.

William Simms, who lived on Priddy's Creek in the northeastern part of the county, was a captain of militia in the Revolution.

[349]

Valentine Wood Southall, grandson of Valentine Wood and Lucy Henry, a sister of the great orator, was for many years a leading citizen of the county. He was admitted to the bar of Albemarle in 1813 and served as commonwealth's attorney from 1829 to 1850. He was a member of the constitutional convention of 1850 and also that of 1861. He was for many years a member of the House of Delegates and its speaker.

Andrew Stevenson, who was a distinguished lawyer, member of Congress, Minister to Great Britain and Rector of the University of Virginia, was born in Culpeper, but lived later in Albemarle, having married a daughter of John Coles. He owned and was living at Blenheim, the old Carter place, at the time of his death in 1857. He was buried at the Coles cemetery at Enniscorthy. His son, John W. Stevenson, was admitted to the Albemarle bar in 1834, but moved to Covington, Ky. He was Governor of Kentucky in 1867 and represented that State in the Senate in 1871.

Joseph Thompson was one of the original magistrates and was first sheriff of the county, living in the bounds of what is now Fluvanna County, which was cut off from Albemarle in 1777. All four of his sons were Revolutionary officers. Roger Thompson was a captain, and John, George and Leonard Thompson were lieutenants. In 1766, Waddy Thompson, of Louisa, came to the county, many of his progeny moving to Kentucky.

Many of the descendants of James Tooley, Terisha Turner and George and William Twyman, all early landowners in the county, moved to Kentucky.

Dr. Thomas Walker was born in King and Queen

county in 1715 and married Mildred Thornton Meriwether, the widow of Nicholas Meriwether, through whom he came into possession of Castle Hill. He was a physician by profession, but engaged in many pursuits. He was among the first Anglo-Saxons ever to stand upon Kentucky soil. In 1748 and again in 1750 he made expeditions to Southwest Virginia and Kentucky. It was he who gave the name to the Cumberland Mountains and river in honor of the Duke of Cumberland, who had recently crushed the Rebellion of 1745 on the field of Culloden. With forty-odd associates, he was granted 800,000 acres extending into Kentucky. Dr. Walker was commissary of the Virginia troops under Braddock and was present at Braddock's defeat in 1755. He was more than once named to treat with the Indians in New York and Pennsylvania and in 1778 was one of the commissioners to fix the boundary line between Virginia and North Carolina. He had the unique distinction of having successively represented Hanover, Louisa and Albemarle in the House of Burgesses, without change of residence. In 1763 he was trustee for the county in the sale of lots for the new town of Charlottesville. He died in 1794, leaving a distinguished line of descendants. John Walker, the oldest son, was an aide to Washington in the Revolution, member of the House of Burgesses and United States Senator. He was for many years commonwealth's attorney. Thomas Walker, Jr., was a captain in the Revolution. Francis Walker, who succeeded his father at Castle Hill, was a magistrate, colonel of the 88th Virginia Regiment, member of the House of Delegates and of Congress.

Captain Michael Wallace, son of William Wallace who lived near Greenwood, commanded a company during the Revolution. Adam and Andrew Wallace, sons of Peter Wallace, displayed great gallantry at the Battle of Guilford Courthouse, the latter losing his life there.

There were several families of Watsons in the county. John Watson, son of James Watson formerly of James City County, lived at Milton. He was a magistrate in 1800 and sheriff in 1825. One of his sons, John W. C. Watson, practiced law in Albemarle for awhile then moved to Mississippi and represented that State in the Confederate Senate. Judge Egbert R. Watson, another son, lived at Charlottesville and was a leading lawyer. He was judge of the Circuit Court after the War Between the States.

William Wertenbaker was admitted to the bar in 1824, but soon afterward became Librarian of the University of Virginia, serving many years.

Garrett White came to the county from Madison and was a prosperous citizen. He was a magistrate in 1806 and sheriff in 1830.

Charles Wingfield, Jr., whose home was Bellair, was a magistrate in 1794 and sheriff in 1819, but died shortly after appointment.

Henry Wood, first clerk of Goochland, was one of the early grantees of land in Albemarle. His son, Valentine Wood, was an Albemarle magistrate in 1746, but when his father died he returned to Goochland and was clerk for twenty-eight years—1753 to 1781. After his death, the family moved back to Albemarle. His wife was Lucy Henry, sister of Patrick Henry. To them may be traced the ancestry of Valentine W. Southall and General Joseph E. Johnston. Josiah Wood patented land in the county in 1741. His son, John Wood, held a commission as major until 1801, and another son, David Wood, was a magistrate in 1801. David Wood's son, Thomas W. Wood, was colonel of the 88th Regiment in 1814 and a magistrate in 1816. There were several other families of the name in the county. In 1774 David Wood came from Louisa, and three of his grandsons, Rice, Thomas and Drury Wood were lawyers, the first two serving in the Legislature. George T. Wood, born in Albemarle, was Governor of Texas 1847-49.

Michael Woods, born in Ireland, with his wife Mary Campbell came first to Pennsylvania, then ascended the Valley of Virginia and crossed into Albemarle through Woods's Gap in 1734. It is believed he was the first settler in western Albemarle, and may have been the first anywhere along the east foot of the Blue Ridge. Michael Woods had numerous descendants, many of them becoming prominent in Kentucky and throughout the Northwest.

Charles Yancey conducted a tavern, store and other establishments at what was later known as Yancey's Mills. He was a magistrate in 1796, colonel of the 47th Regiment in 1806 and was sheriff in 1821.

First Courthouse at Scottsville

The present courthouse of Albemarle at Charlottesville is the third. The first courthouse was erected by

Samuel Scott, at his own cost, with prison, stocks and pillory "as good as those at Goochland" on the plantation of his brother, Daniel Scott, about a mile west of Scottsville. This was used for seventeen years when the county was divided in 1761.

The second courthouse, on the present court green at Charlottesville, served for forty years, until it was torn down and the new courthouse erected in 1803. In 1859 a contract was let "to embellish the front with a porch and pillars," and there were other alterations in 1897.

The square was first enclosed in 1792 and a brick wall around it was built in 1811. In 1807 there was an order to repair the pillory, stocks and whipping post, and there existed a whipping post as late as 1857. The land for the courthouse square was acquired from Dr. Thomas Walker.

The courthouse for a number of years was used by various denominations for church worship. Mr. Jefferson often attended services there, bringing down from Monticello under his arm a folding seat of his own invention, which he used as a chair. This also was the meeting-place for the Legislature in 1781, when the members had to flee from the cavalry of Tarleton.

While the records between the year 1752 and 1758 seem not to have been destroyed, there nevertheless are no deeds recorded, although there are deeds for lands in Albemarle recorded both in Louisa and Goochland. In all probability citizens rebelled against going to Scottsville and recorded their deeds elsewhere to save distance.

THERE ARE TWENTY-ONE PORTRAITS

There are twenty-one portraits in the courtroom, likenesses of the following men:

Judge Archibald Stuart, Revolutionary soldier, who took part in the Battle of Guilford Courthouse as an aide to General Greene. He studied law under Jefferson and in 1788 was a member of the convention which ratified the Constitution of the United States. He was a member of the State Senate and president of that body. In 1799 he was elected judge of the General Court of Virginia and was judge of the Circuit Superior Court at its organization in 1809. He went to the Virginia Supreme Court of Appeals in 1830. He was the father of Alexander H. H. Stuart, prominent lawyer of Augusta, and a great uncle of General J. E. B. Stuart.

Thomas W. Gilmer, a son of George and Elizabeth Hudson Gilmer, was a lawyer, Governor of Virginia, member of Congress, and Secretary of the Navy. He perished in the explosion of a gun on the ship *Princeton* in 1844.

Ira Garrett was an influential citizen and clerk of the county court for thirty-eight years, having succeeded his brother, Alexander Garrett, in 1831.

Col. R. T. W. Duke commanded the 46th Virginia Infantry in the War Between the States and was a noted lawyer. He served his county as commonwealth's attorney and as a member of the House of Delegates, and represented his district in Congress.

Shelton F. Leake, son of Dr. Samuel and Sophie Farrar Leake, was admitted to the Albemarle bar in

1838 and was an able lawyer. He lived at Charlottesville. He was a member of the House of Delegates, Lieutenant-Governor of Virginia, and member of Congress.

Judge Egbert R. Watson was a son of John and Jane Price Watson and was a leading lawyer at the Albemarle bar. He was judge of the Circuit Court at the close of the war.

Judge John White served both as County and Circuit Court judge.

Daniel Harman was a lawyer of wide distinction.

Colonel John J. Bowcock commanded the 88th Regiment in the War Between the States and for many years served as magistrate, presiding justice and member of the House of Delegates. He was a son of Douglass and Mildred Blackwell Bowcock and inherited the tavern at the junction of the Earlysville and Piney Mountain roads.

George Perkins was an Albemarle lawyer of distinction.

Captain W. O. Fry, Confederate officer, was a prominent lawyer and a descendant of Col. Joshua Fry.

Captain Micajah Woods (1844-1911) was a Confederate officer and served as commonwealth's attorney for forty-one years, from 1870 to 1911. He was a fine orator and greatly admired by the citizens.

Judge Valentine Wood Southall was a noted orator and lawyer. He was a magistrate and commonwealth's attorney from 1829 to 1850. He was a member of the two conventions of 1850 and 1861 and was Speaker of the House of Delegates. He lived at Charlottesville and was a grandson of Lucy, the sister of Patrick Henry.

There is a portrait of Albemarle's distinguished son, Thomas Jefferson.

Judge John L. Cochran was a county judge.

Drury Wood (1821-1901) was a prominent member of the Albemarle bar.

R. H. Wood (1856-1928), a son of Drury Wood, also was a prominent member of the Albemarle bar from 1878 to the time of his death.

Thomas Wood, a brother of Drury Wood, was a well-known Albemarle lawyer.

Senator Thomas S. Martin, who was born at Scottsville, was for many years an influential member of the United States Senate and was a leader of the Democratic Party in his State.

William Logan Maupin (1854-1923) was for many years clerk of the Circuit Court.

Judge R. T. W. Duke, Jr., son of Col. R. T. W. Duke, was the first judge of the Corporation Court of Charlottesville and commonwealth's attorney of Albemarle for many years.

MANY STATELY HOMES

Albemarle is dotted with stately homes, only a few of which may receive brief mention here.

Edgehill was first built by Governor Thomas Mann Randolph, who married the daughter of Thomas Jefferson. Their son, Thomas Jefferson Randolph, built the brick mansion in 1828. After his death it became a noted school.

Castle Hill was built by Dr. Thomas Walker in 1765, having come in possession of the land from his wife, who was the widow of Nicholas Meriwether. Tarleton turned aside on his raid to Charlottesville in 1781 and visited Castle Hill to capture men of prominence visiting there. It is believed that had not Tarleton tarried there, Jack Jouett's famous ride to warn Mr. Jefferson and the Legislature at Charlottesville would have been in vain.

In connection with Castle Hill there arises an interesting question regarding the boundary line between Louisa and Albemarle from the year 1744, when Albemarle was formed, to 1761. Dr. Thomas Walker represented Louisa in the House of Burgesses up to 1759, then represented Albemarle from 1761 to 1775. In the conventions of 1775 he again was a member from Louisa. The dividing line was apparently vague, from the formation of Albemarle until 1761, when a special commission was named to straighten out the matter. The report of this commission is recorded in Albemarle Clerk's Office, and the findings were that the line had always been where it now is. It may have been that Dr. Walker lived in the edge of Louisa, or owned land in both counties. Certain it is that the Castle Hill home site was Meriwether property, and it has been generally supposed that he came into possession of it when he married his first wife, Mildred Thornton Meriwether.

Monticello, the home of Thomas Jefferson, is perhaps more expressive than any other home in America of the man who built it. After a checquered career after Jefferson's death, it finally passed into gentle hands and is maintained as one of the most interesting of all Virginia's shrines. It was built from Mr. Jefferson's own plans and under his personal supervision. The place is filled with interesting relics, many of them reminiscent of his inventive genius. The great clock in the front hall is operated by weights and pulleys and tells not only the time of day, but the day of the week. Preserved at Monticello is the telescope with which the aged statesman watched the progress of the work on the University from his chair on the lawn of his home. His tombstone is comparatively new, the original having been chipped to pieces bit by bit by souvenir hunters in days when Monticello was in other hands.

Keswick, a part of the Castle Hill estate, was inherited by Jane Frances Walker, oldest child of Francis Walker. She married Dr. Mann Page. For many years a school was conducted there under a long line of tutors, including James Morris Page, Thomas Walker Page, Jr., and Thornton Rogers.

The Farmington estate was once the property of Michael Holland. It was bought by George Divers in 1788 and the stately house was designed for Mr. Divers by Thomas Jefferson. The place passed by inheritance to Mrs. Isaac White, who sold it to John C. Carter. In 1853 it was sold to General Bernard Peyton. It is now one of the most attractive country clubs in the State.

Redlands was the place of Robert Carter, who died there in 1810. He was a son of Edward Carter, of Blenheim.

Pen Park was the home of Dr. George Gilmer, who died there in 1796.

Monticola mansion was built prior to the War Between the States by D. J. Hartsook, and was sold in 1887 to E. O. Nolting, of Richmond. The place was raided by Sheridan.

Enniscorthy, Woodville, Tallwood and Estouteville were all homes of members of the Coles family.

Plain Dealing was built by Thomas Staples and enlarged by Samuel Duer, Revolutionary soldier.

Other homes which may be mentioned were Colle, occupied by Mazzei, who had been brought over to adapt grape culture to Virginia. Later it was the home of Baron de Reidesei, and it furnished scenes for Ford's novel, "Janice Meredith"; Ash Lawn was the home of Monroe; Shadwell was where Jefferson was born; Mirador was the home of Chiswell D. Langhorne and home of his daughters, the celebrated Langhorne sisters.

Augusta County

AUGUSTA COURTHOUSE

Augusta County

AUGUSTA COUNTY was indeed the spearhead in the advance of Virginia civilization to the West. Not only did it lie immediately in the path of that advance, but Augusta County for a number of years included within its own boundaries all of Kentucky and the Northwest Territory. Maps of Augusta drawn in that period showed the regions which now are West Virginia, Kentucky, Ohio, Indiana, Illinois, Michigan and the western part of Pennsylvania, and the Great Lakes were on its border.

In Augusta County the tide of migration from the Chesapeake Bay country met its first counter-current, for already the Scotch-Irish had come into this area after brief sojourns in Pennsylvania, and had gained considerable foothold before the county became a county and before settlers came in from Eastern Virginia to help furnish population for enormous land grants from the Colonial Governors to wealthy citizens of their acquaintance.

The first settler in Augusta was John Lewis, a remarkable man of whom more will be said later. He came in 1732. By 1738 so many settlers had come in from Virginia east of the mountains, from Pennsylvania and from Europe that the General Assembly set aside Augusta as a county and gave it a name. But it was not until 1745 that there was set up a government for it.

The story of Augusta's settlement is as interesting as its subsequent history. Here were amalgamated several sets of hardy people who were to play an enormous part in pushing back the frontiers, beating back the French, the Indians and finally the British, and many were the families from Augusta whose descendants are scattered from the Alleghany Mountains to the Pacific Ocean.

In 1730 the Governor of Virginia granted 40,000 acres in the Valley of Virginia to a man named Isaac Vanmeter. In 1732 Joist Hite with a party of pioneers came up the valley of the Shenandoah to settle upon this grant, and with them came John Lewis, who settled and built his home about a mile east of the present city of Staunton. In 1733 the Governor issued a patent for 5,000 acres to a German named Stover further down the Valley, and in 1736 he granted William Beverley, of Essex, Sir John Randolph, of the City of Williamsburg, Richard Randolph, of Henrico, and John Robinson, of King and Queen, 118,491 acres, which included the site of Staunton and was known as Beverley Manor, the name still being retained in the modern magisterial district which was a part of it. The other grantees relinquished their interests to Beverley the day after the patent was granted.

To carry still further the picture of the land grants which had so much to do with the settlement of Augusta County, an Englishman named Benjamin Burden, who had come to America as an agent of Lord Fairfax, was granted 500,000 acres by Governor Gooch, which property extended from the southern line of Beverley Manor southward and included a large part of Augusta and Rockbridge Counties. The condition of Burden's grant was that he was to settle 100 families upon the land within ten years, and this he had accomplished in the year 1737.

In the meantime Lord Fairfax, under patent of James II, held all that part of Virginia known as the Northern Neck, and he claimed for his western boundary a line from the head of the Rappahannock, believed to have been in the Blue Ridge, to the head of the Potomac, believed to have been in the Alleghanies. Thus he claimed the lower Shenandoah Valley and, as a result, the upper, or southern, part of the Valley of Virginia was populated more rapidly than the lower, the settlers fearing complications in land titles.

Vigorous efforts were made by all of these grantees of land to induce settlement, and because of the exceptional beauty and fertility of the country, which had been glowingly described by Governor Spotswood and his gentlemen when they first visited the Valley in 1716, there was rapid migration to this beautiful area. With this brief resumé of the principal land grants as a background, the story of Augusta County may be told in detail.

John Lewis, a truly remarkable man from the North of Ireland, may very properly be called the Father of Augusta County. Not only was he its first settler, coming to the county in 1732 with his wife and four of his five sons, all of whom were distinguished officers in the French and Indian War and the Revolution, but his wisdom and personal influence had much to do with shaping the destiny of the little colony west of the Blue Ridge. He had to flee from Ireland because of his manly resistance to tyranny, made his way to Pennsylvania and there for a number of months awaited his family. They joined him in 1732 and he made his way to Augusta.

John Lewis and his descendants have played so large a part in the history of his County, State and Nation, and the story of the affair which sent him from Ireland to America is so thrilling that it should be inserted here. The following account is from the *Virginia Historical Register* for 1851 and was written by John H. Peyton from information derived orally from William I. Lewis, of Campbell County, member of Congress in 1817 and a grandson of John Lewis. He, in turn, had received it from his father, Colonel William Lewis, of Sweet Springs, who died in 1812 at the age of eighty-five:

"John Lewis was a native of Ireland, and was descended from French Protestants who emigrated from France to Ireland in 1685, at the revocation of the Edict of Nantes, to avoid the persecutions to which the Protestants, to which sect of religion they belonged, were subjected during the reign of Louis XIV. John Lewis intermarried with Margaret Lynn, also a native of Ireland, but descended of Scottish ancestors—the Lynns, of Loch Lynn, so famous in Scottish clan legends.

"John Lewis, in Ireland, occupied a respectable position in what is there called the middle class of society. He was the holder of a freehold lease for three lives upon a valuable farm in the County of Donegal and Province of Ulster, obtained upon equal terms and fair equivalents from one of the Irish nobility, who was an upright and honorable man, and the owner of the reversion. This lease-hold estate, with his wife's marriage portion, enabled the young couple to commence life with flattering prospects. They were both remarkable for their industry, piety and stern integrity. They prospered and were happy. Before the catastrophe occurred which completely destroyed the hope of this once happy family in Ireland and made them exiles from their native land, their affection was cemented by the birth of four sons, Samuel, Thomas, Andrew and William.

"About the period of the birth of their third son, the Lord from whom he had obtained his lease—a landlord beloved by his tenants and neighbors—suddenly died, and his estates descended to his eldest son, a youth whose principles were directly the reverse of his father's. He was proud, profligate and extravagant. Anticipating his income, he was always in debt, and to meet his numerous engagements he devised a variety of schemes, and among them one was to claim of his tenants a forfeiture of their leases upon some one of the numerous covenants in instruments of the kind at that day. If they agreed to increase their rents, the alleged forfeiture was waived; if they refused, they were threatened with a long, tedious lawsuit. Many of his tenants submitted to this injustice rather than be involved, even with justice on their side, in a legal controversy with a rich and powerful adversary, who could, in this country, under these circumstances, devise ways and means to harass, persecute and impoverish one in moderate circumstances.

"Lewis, however, was a different man from any who thus tamely submitted to wrong. By industry and skill he had greatly improved his property, his rent had been punctually paid, and all the covenants of his lease had been complied with faithfully. To him, after seeing all the others, the agent of the young Lord came with his unjust demands. Lewis peremptorily dismissed him from his presence, and determined to make an effort to rescue his family from this threatened injustice by a personal interview with the young Lord, who, Lewis imagined, would scarcely have the hardihood to insist before his face upon the iniquitous terms proposed by his agent. Accordingly, he visited the castle of the young Lord. A porter announced his name. At the time the young Lord was engaged in his revels over the bottle with some of his companions with similar tastes and habits.

"As soon as the name of Lewis was announced, he recognized the only one of his tenants who had resisted his demands, and directed the porter to order him off. When the porter delivered his Lord's order, Lewis resolved at every hazard to see him. Accordingly he walked into the presence of the company—the porter not having the temerity to stand in his way. Flushed with wine, the whole company rose to resent the insult and repel the intruder from the room. But there was something in Lewis' manner that sobered them in a moment, and, instead of advancing, they seemed fixed to their places, and for a moment there was perfect silence, when Lewis calmly observed:

" 'I came here with no design to insult or injure any one, but to remonstrate in person to your Lordship against threatened injustice, and thus to avert from my family ruin; in such a course I have not regarded ordinary forms or ceremonies, and I warn you, gentlemen, to be cautious how you deal with a desperate man.' This address, connected with the firm and intrepid tone of its delivery apparently stupefied the company. Silence ensuing, Lewis embraced it to address himself particularly, in the following words, to the young Lord:

" 'Your much respected father granted me the lease-hold estate I now possess. I have regularly paid my rents, and have faithfully complied with all the covenants of the lease. I have a wife and three infant children whose happiness, comfort and support depends, in great degree upon the enjoyment of this property, and yet I am told by your agent that I can no longer hold it without a base surrender of my rights to your rapacity. Sir, I wish to learn from your own lips whether or not you really meditate such injustice, such cruelty as the terms mentioned by your agent indicate; and I beg you before pursuing such a course to reconsider this matter coolly and dispassionately, or you will ruin me and disgrace yourself.'

"By the time this address was closed, the young Lord seemed to have recovered partially (in which he was greatly assisted by several heavy libations of wine) from the effects produced by the sudden, solemn and impressive manner of his injured tenant. He began to ejaculate:

" 'Leave me! Leave me! You rebel! You villain!' To this abuse Lewis replied calmly as follows:

" 'Sir, you may save yourself this useless ebullition of passion. It is extremely silly and ridiculous. I have effected the object of my visit; I have satisfied my mind, and have nothing more to say. I shall no longer disturb you with my presence.'

"Upon which he retired from the room, apparently unmoved by the volley of abuse that broke forth from the young Lord and his drunken comrades as soon as he had turned his back. After they had recovered from the magical effect which the calm resolution and stern countenance of Lewis produced, they descanted upon what they called the insolence of his manner and the mock defiance of his speech, with all the false views which aristocratic pride excited by the fumes of wine, in a monarchial government were so well calculated to inspire. During the evening the rash purpose was formed of dispossessing Lewis by force.

"Accordingly, the next day the young Lord, without any legal authority whatever, proceeded at the head of his guests and domestics to oust Lewis by force. Lewis saw the approach of the hostile army and conjectured the object of the demonstration. He had no arms but a shelalah, a weapon in possession of every Irish farmer of that period. Nor was there anyone at his house but a brother, confined to bed by disease, his wife and three infant children; yet he resolved to resist the lawless band and closed the door. The young Lord, on reaching the house, demanded admittance, which not being granted, the posse attacked the house, and after being foiled in several attempts to break down the door or to effect in any other way an entrance, one of the party introduced the muzzle of a musket through an aperture in the wall and discharged its contents—a bullet and three buckshot—upon those within, Lewis' sick brother was mortally wounded, and one of the shot passed through his wife's hand.

"Lewis, who had up to this time acted on the defensive, seeing the blood stream from the hand of his wife and his expiring brother weltering in his blood, became enraged, furious, and, siezing his shelalah, he rushed from the cottage, determined to avenge the wrong and to sell his life as dearly as possible.

"The first person he encountered was the young Lord, whom he despatched at a single blow, cleaving in twain his skull and scattering his brains upon himself and the posse. The next person he met was the steward, who shared the fate of his master. Rushing, then, upon the posse, stupefied at the ungovernable ardor and fury of Lewis' manner, and the death of two of their party, they had scarcely time to save themselves, as they did, by throwing away their arms and taking to flight.

"This awful occurrence brought the affairs of Lewis in Ireland to a crisis. Though he had violated no law, human or divine; though he had acted strictly in self defense against lawless power and oppression, yet the occurrence took place in a monarchial government, whose policy it is to preserve a difference in the ranks of society. One of the nobility (Sir Mungo Campbell) had been slain by one of his tenants. The connections of the young Lord were rich and powerful, those of Lewis poor and humble.

"With such fearful odds, it was deemed rash and unwise that Lewis should, even with law and justice on his side, surrender himself to the officers of the law. It was consequently determined that he should proceed on that evening disguised in a friend's dress to the nearest seaport and take shipping to Oporto, in Portugal, where a brother of his wife was established in merchandise. Luckily he met a vessel just ready to sail from the Bay of Donegal, on which he took passage.

"After various adventures, for the ship was not bound for Portugal, in different countries, he arrived at Oporto in the year 1729. Upon his arrival there, he was advised by his brother-in-law, in order to elude the vigilance of his enemies, to proceed to Philadelphia, in Pennsylvania, and there to await the arrival of his family, which, he learned, was in good health, and which his brother-in-law undertook to remove to America.

"Lewis, following this advice, proceeded at once to Philadelphia. In a year his family joined him and, learning from them that the most industrious efforts were being made by the friends of the young Lord to discover the country to which he had fled, he determined to penetrate deep into the American forest. He moved then immediately from Philadelphia to Lancaster and there spent the Winter of 1731 and 1732 and in the Summer of 1732 he removed to the place near Staunton in the County of Augusta, Virginia, now called Bellefonte, where he settled, conquered the country from the Indians, and amassed a large fortune."

John Lewis built his house of stone and called it

Bellefonte, because of a bold spring at that point. It formed part of Fort Lewis, and this half-dwelling, half-fortress withstood the savages until the country became sufficiently populous for the people to defy their enemies. Lewis and other early settlers showed much tact in dealing with the aborigines, and these men who might almost be called men without a country governed themselves according to the laws of common sense and handled their affairs for a number of years without any regularly constituted government.

A few years after John Lewis came to Augusta he made a trip to Williamsburg and there met Benjamin Burden. He invited Burden to come back to Bellefonte with him for a visit and the Englishman came, spending several months making himself agreeable and hunting with John Lewis' sons, Thomas, Andrew and William. On one of their hunting expeditions they captured a buffalo calf, which Burden carried back to Williamsburg as a gift to Governor Gooch. The Governor was so pleased that this gift played a large part in his granting Burden the 500,000 acres mentioned above.

Burden went abroad to obtain settlers for his grant and in 1737 returned with the 100 families required. Among them were the McDowells, Crawfords, McClures, Alexanders, Wallaces, Moores, Mathews and other founders of families which became distinguished. Because of the activities of the proprietors of Beverley Manor and the Burden grant and of other grantees, who advertised for settlers throughout the Colonies and in Europe, the number of settlements increased rapidly, which led to official action by the Colonial Government of Virginia.

Accordingly, in 1738, an act of the General Assembly provided for the establishment of two counties west of the Blue Ridge, Frederick being a sister county of Augusta. They were to include all the territory west of the Blue Ridge "at present deemed to be a part of the county of Orange lying on the northwest side of the top of the said mountains, extending thence northerly, westerly and southerly beyond the said mountains to the uttermost limits of Virginia." The "uttermost limits of Virginia" was the Mississippi, beyond which were the French possessions known as Louisiana.

It was further provided that the two new counties should remain a part of the county of Orange and Parish of St. Mark until there should be a sufficient number of inhabitants for setting up an independent government. In the act of 1738 Augusta was given its name, presumably for Princess Augusta, wife of Frederick Lewis, Prince of Wales, a daughter of Frederick II, Duke of Saxe-Gotha.

Seven years later, in 1745, the county government of Augusta was organized with the present city of Staunton as the county seat. Augusta was not reduced to its present bounds until 1790. Staunton was incorporated in 1761 and named for Lady Staunton, the wife of Governor William Gooch. The first courthouse was built in 1745 on the present court green, and the courthouse which now stands there was completed in 1837. The first clerk's office was at Port Republic and, due to its being so often traveled by the King's Attorney, Gabriel Jones, and the other lawyers, the road by the

Western Asylum through New Hope is still referred to as Lawyers' Lane.

The early story of Augusta roughly may be divided into three periods of seven years. John Lewis fled from Ireland and seven years later Augusta County was formed in 1738; in another seven years the County government was set up in 1745; at the expiration of still another seven-year period Governor Robert Dinwiddie came to Virginia in 1752, and from that time forward the story of the settlements in Augusta became much more closely connected with that of the Colony of Virginia.

The rapid settlement of Augusta is not surprising, considering the efforts which were made to induce settlement and the remarkable beauty and fertility of the region. Here were nurtured a set of men to a large extent uninfluenced by established government and church and largely free from the more objectionable traditions which had come down from feudal times in Europe. A hardy race of men developed, jealous of their liberties, self-reliant and brave to the core. Citizens of Augusta played an enormous part in the long struggles against the savages, the French, and finally the English.

The Scotch and Irish immigration to America followed the siege of Londonderry, the escape of King James to France, and the acceptance of the British throne by William and Mary. For fifty years there was an exodus of Presbyterians from Ireland to America, being lured to the new country where they might escape paying tythes to the Church of England. The Presbyterians were first to come into Augusta, and the

Colonial government of Virginia, anxious to seat a white population west of the Blue Ridge, was lenient in enforcing the rules of the Established Church upon Presbyterians and other dissenters in the Valley.

The Scotch-Irish migration to the Valley of Virginia was of transcendent importance. Most of these stern covenanters were from Ulster, in the north of Ireland just across from Scotland. An eminent historian has said of those who came to Virginia "The Scotch-Irish were so afraid of God, that this fear left in their hearts no room for fear of mortal man."

Perhaps even more important than the intermingling of blood was the kinship in spirit between them and those who had settled in eastern Virginia. When the tragedy of fratricidal war broke out in 1861, the Scotch-Irish Stonewall Jackson and J. E. B. Stuart rode on the right hand and on the left of that gentlest and greatest of the Cavaliers, Robert E. Lee.

From the Scotch-Irish of the Valley also came Gen. Samuel Houston, the Alexanders, John C. Breckinridge, Thomas H. Benton, William C. Preston, John J. Crittenden, Gen. Wade Hampton and Gen. Joseph E. Johnston, and hundreds of other men of distinction could be named. Of the same stock, but from lower down the Valley, came the two celebrated Revolutionary heroes, Col. Daniel Morgan and Col. William Crawford. The former was one of the most colorful as well as intrepid officers in the Continental Army. The brilliant career of the latter ended in 1782 when he was captured by the Indians and burned at the stake.

The first regular Presbyterian minister in the county was the Rev. John Craig, who was sent by the Presbytery of Donegal in 1739, and he ultimately became the pastor of Tinkling Spring and Augusta churches. He commenced his ministry at the Old Stone Church, on the Valley Turnpike about eight miles north of Staunton, which was built in 1740.

In the act of 1738 establishing Augusta, the Parish of Augusta also was erected, but Augusta remained a part of the Parish of St. Mark until seven years later. It seems, however, that the Church of England was never particularly strong in Augusta in Colonial times, whereas other denominations flourished. In addition to the Presbyterians, there were active congregations of Methodists, German Lutherans and Baptists. The Rev. Joseph Doddridge, D. D., an Episcopal clergyman who visited western Virginia and eastern Ohio and wrote of religious conditions there in the period from 1763 to 1783, said: "The Episcopal Church, which ought to have been foremost in gathering their scattered flocks, had been the last and done the least of any Christian community in the evangelical work. Taking the western country in its whole extent, at least one-half of its population was originally of Episcopalian parentage, but for want of a ministry of their own, they have associated with other communities."

John Wilson served as a member of the House of Burgesses from Augusta for twenty-seven consecutive years, except for a brief interim in 1754, when he was serving as a surveyor.

Members of the Burgesses were as follows: 1748-1754, John Wilson, John Madison; 1755, John Madison; James Patton; 1755-1758, John Wilson, Gabriel Jones; 1758-1765, John Wilson, Israel Christian; 1765-

1768, John Wilson, William Preston; 1769-1772, John Wilson, Gabriel Jones; 1772, John Wilson, Samuel McDowell; 1773, Samuel McDowell, Charles Lewis (Wilson died in that year) ; 1774, Samuel McDowell, Charles Lewis; 1775, Charles Lewis (killed in battle), George Matthews, Samuel McDowell.

In the conventions of 1775 were, March, Thomas Lewis, Samuel McDowell; July, Thomas Lewis, Samuel McDowell, John Harvie, George Rootes; December, Thomas Lewis and Samuel McDowell.

In the convention of 1776 were Thomas Lewis and Samuel McDowell.

The rival claims of Virginia and the French Government to the vast lands west of the Alleghanies which were then a part of Augusta County could not but lead to trouble. The French had a line of forts from New Orleans to Quebec, one of the most important being Fort du Quesne, where Pittsburgh now stands. Previous to any acts of open hostility, the English sought to strengthen their claims to the western country by throwing a large white population into it by means of land companies. The Ohio Company was granted 500,000 acres on the south side of the Ohio between the Monongahela and the Kanawha. The Greenbrier Company, with John Lewis at its head, was granted 100,000 acres on the Greenbrier River. The Loyal Company, in 1749, was granted 800,000 acres. In 1751 John Lewis and his son Andrew, who later became the celebrated general, surveyed the Greenbrier tract.

The French understood these designs and strengthened their fortifications. A company of French soldiers was sent as far south as the Miami River, and here occurred a clash in which there was bloodshed in 1752, which marked the beginning of the long contest which resulted ultimately in the loss to France of all her territories east of the Mississippi.

About the time the county government of Augusta was set up in 1745, the militia was organized, and John Lewis was colonel. This organization was in keeping with the general regulations of militia all the way from Massachusetts to Georgia. Under existing laws, the commander of the militia was required to list all males above the age of twenty-one. The men were to be thoroughly armed, and each militiaman was required to keep at his house at all times a pound of gunpowder and four of bullets. The commander was empowered to require all militiamen to go armed to their respective churches when it was deemed necessary.

When Governor Dinwiddie arrived in 1752 he saw that trouble with the French was impending and went into warlike preparations on a wider scale, determined to maintain the English claim to the country west of the mountains. Dinwiddie, in 1753, commissioned the young surveyor, George Washington, to go to the French headquarters near Pittsburg and demand that the French leave. This they refused to do, informing Washington that it was their purpose to destroy every English settlement in the West. When Washington brought his report to Williamsburg in January, 1754, Virginia proceeded to raise a regiment under Colonel Joshua Fry, of Albemarle, with Washington as lieutenant-colonel.

The ensuing clashes with the French and their Indian allies are briefly outlined here only for the reason that Augusta men played such prominent parts in them.

Col. Fry died and Washington succeeded to the command of the Virginians early in the campaign. After a victory over a French and Indian force at a place called Redstone, Washington built Fort Necessity. The enemy force of about 1,000 assaulted the fort. After nine hours of fierce fighting, the French commander sent a flag of truce, extolled the bravery of the Virginians, and offered to treat for the surrender of the place on honorable terms, which was accepted. This was known as the Battle of Great Meadows, and was fought July 3, 1753.

The British government now saw war was inevitable, and encouraged the Colonies to form a union among themselves. This was done, and a plan of action was signed by the agents of the leading northern colonies and Maryland in 1754. Early in 1755 the Colonies attacked the French at four different points, Nova Scotia, Crown Point, Niagara and on the Ohio River.

The campaign on the Ohio was under the command of General Edward Braddock, who arrived from England in February with two Royal regiments. Virginia raised 800 men to join Braddock, who arrived at Alexandria, then called Bellhaven, and appointed Washington as his aide-de-camp. Three of John Lewis' sons were in this campaign. Thomas Lewis was sent with his company to Greenbrier to build a stockade fort, while Andrew and William Lewis helped Washington in saving the remnants of the British army at Braddock's defeat. It is impossible to estimate how many more of Augusta's sons took part in this and many another bloody battle on the western frontier.

Braddock crossed the Monongahela with about 2,200 men on July 9, 1755. He fell into an ambush and was mortally wounded and his regulars were put to flight. The British and Colonial losses were estimated at 777 men killed and wounded, and had it not been for the coolness of Washington and the Virginia troops the whole force would have been destroyed. The whole frontier of western Virginia was left defenseless, and the campaign against Niagara also failed.

During this period the Indians committed unspeakable horrors all along Virginia's western outposts. In this connection the Sandy Creek expedition should be noted for the reason that so many Augusta men took part in it. The depredations of the savages were so severe after Braddock's defeat that an expedition was fitted out early in 1756 to attack the Indian towns west of the Ohio. There were 340 men under the command of Major Andrew Lewis. Among the officers were captains William Preston, Peter Hogg, John Smith, Archibald Alexander, R. Breckinridge, —— Woodson, Samuel Overton, of Hanover, and Captain David Stewart, commissary. Also there were two volunteer companies under captains Montgomery and Dunlap. The force crossed the Holstein River in February, 1756, and pushed on to Sandy Creek and continued westward, suffering untold hardships from hunger and cold, but they received orders to return before reaching their destination.

Hostilities became more and more pronounced between the French and English Colonies, and now the parent governments put an end to this unnatural state of affairs when Great Britain formally declared war against France May 9, 1756, which opened the French and Indian War, in which most of Europe, North America, the East and West Indies were engaged, and was coincident with the Seven Years War in Europe. Royal troops were sent over and Virginia contributed 1,600 men to coöperate, with Washington as colonel, Adam Stephen, as lieutenant colonel, and Andrew Lewis as major.

For another two years the French were highly successful, but in the campaigns of 1758 to 1760 the British were victorious on all fronts, with the result that Canada fell into their hands. The Treaty of Fontainbleau, agreed upon in November, 1762, ended the war.

The controversy over the western boundary line between Virginia and Pennsylvania became acute under Lord Dunmore, Governor of Virginia, and John Penn, Governor of Pennsylvania. In fact it continued until after the Revolution when the extension of the Mason and Dixon line was agreed upon by Virginia in 1784. This line had been surveyed in the period from 1763 to 1767 by Charles Mason and Jeremiah Dixon, of London. Its western extension was agreed upon in 1779 and the whole matter was settled in 1784.

The Treaty of Fontainbleau did not bring peace to the Virginia frontiers. On the contrary, the following two years were memorable for the destructive character of the war waged by the united Indian tribes of the western country with a view to extermination of the whites. They saw the English building forts far and near and realized that the time had come when they must make a last stand in defense of their country. Their plan was the general massacre of all the English settlers in the western area. Massacres were committed within the present limits of Augusta.

During the year 1763, the Augusta people organized for defense, and in August of that year Andrew Lewis was made county lieutenant—that is, commander-in-chief of the Augusta forces. William Preston was made colonel, and the following were the captains: Walter Cunningham, Alexander McClenachan, William Crow and John Bowyer. Lieutenants were John McClenachan, William Bowyer and David Long, with James Ward as ensign.

Conspicuous in what might be called Augusta's own Indian war in 1764 were the Six Nations. These, known hitherto as the Five Nations and called Iroquois by the French, were joined by the Tuscaroras, who were then living in the Carolinas. All spoke the same language. They were joined by the Shawnees and other tribes in the West, and all united against Virginia, Pennsylvania and the other Colonies. This short but bloody war was brought to a temporary close by treaty the latter part of 1764. Colonization was now encouraged, and vast land grants were made of unexplored territory all the way to the Mississippi. Officers and men who had served in the French and Indian War were entitled to bounty lands by proclamation of the King following the Treaty of Fontainbleau.

While white population increased rapidly in the following decade, atrocities on the part of both Indians and whites became so bad that in 1774 a new war broke out, with the Virginia government organizing an armed expedition to break the power of the Indians. This was spoken of by historians as Lord Dunmore's War.

Andrew Lewis, then a member of the House of Burgesses and in his fifty-sixth year, was called into conference. It was agreed that Dunmore would take command of a force at what is now Pittsburgh and come down the Ohio, while Lewis would advance by the Great Kanawha, and they would join at its mouth. Lewis then went to Staunton, named his own officers and issued a call for troops. Volunteers poured in, and they were sent off to Camp Union, on the Greenbrier, as the point of general muster.

The gallant victory of the Virginians at Point Pleasant, at the fork of the Kanawha and Ohio Rivers, is fully described in history. Andrew Lewis assumed command of the force at Camp Union and, on September 11, 1774, unsheathed the old sword he had used at Braddock's defeat nineteen years before and in the Indian war of 1763-64, and started the march to the west. After a painful journey of nineteen days through the wilderness they arrived at Point Pleasant October 1. No word was received from Dunmore, so a camp was fortified.

In the meantime the Indians were fully aware of what the two Virginia armies planned to do, and assembled northwest of the Ohio under the celebrated chieftain Cornstalk. Animated by their ancient hatred of the Virginians, whom they called Long Knives, they determined to crush first the division of Lewis and then that of Dunmore. It was found out afterward that Cornstalk was at Point Pleasant when Lewis arrived, and secretly watched the disposition of the Virginia troops.

On October 9, a message came from Dunmore that he had changed his plans, and ordering Lewis to proceed to the Indian towns on the Scioto, where Dunmore would join him. With the Revolution fast approaching, historians have not failed to accuse Dunmore of double-dealing in this campaign. It is known that even as early as 1774 the British west of the mountains were inciting the Indians against the Long Knives. It will be remembered that it was this same Andrew Lewis who at Gwynn's Island in 1776 drove Lord Dunmore, the last of the Royal Governors, from Virginia forever.

Lewis and his men, vastly outnumbered by a well-armed force of savages, fought the Battle of Point Pleasant and won it. This victory broke the power of the Indian confederacy, and it is impossible to say to what extent it interfered with the British efforts to bring over the Six Nations to their side, which efforts persisted until George Rogers Clark took Vincennes in 1779 and found papers which revealed a far-flung plan of the British to attack with their Indian allies from the West while Washington was carrying on the Revolution on the Atlantic seaboard.

So many of the officers at the Battle of Point Pleasant were from Augusta that those who are known to have served in that engagement should be mentioned.

There was a regiment of Augusta troops under Colonel Charles Lewis, brother of Andrew Lewis and one of Augusta's representatives in the House of Burgesses at the time. The captains were George Mathews, afterward Governor of Georgia; Alexander McClenachan, John Dickinson, John Lewis, son of Col. William Lewis, afterward of the Sweet Springs; Benjamin Harrison, William Paul, Joseph Haynes and Samuel Wilson.

A Botetourt regiment was commanded by Col. William Fleming. The captains were Mathew Arbuckle, John Murray, John Lewis, son of the general in command; James Robertson, Robert McClenachan, James Ward and John Stuart.

A regiment from Culpeper was under Col. John Field. There were three independent companies under Col. William Christian, and their captains were Evan Shelby, William Russell and —— Harbert. Also there was an independent company from Bedford under Captain Thomas Buford.

In accordance with Dunmore's order, Lewis broke camp on the 10th and prepared for the march west. The Virginians were attacked by the entire Indian army, made up of the pick of the northern and western confederated tribes. It is hardly appropriate here to go into the details of this highly spectacular battle.

Lewis ordered the Augusta troops to the front, under the command of his younger brother, Col. Charles Lewis. At the very outset of a furious assault on the Augusta force, Col. Charles Lewis fell, mortally wounded. The gallant Col. John Field also lost his life. Other officers known to have been killed in the fierce battle which ensued were Captains Morrow, Buford, Wood, Murray, Cardiff, Wilson and Robert McClenachan, and Lieutenants Allen, Goldsby and Dillon.

Among the Virginians in this battle who afterwards

became distinguished were Gen. Isaac Shelby, first Governor of Kentucky; Gen. William Campbell and Col. John Campbell, heroes in the Battle of King's Mountain; Gen. Evan Shelby, of Tennessee; Col. William Fleming, acting Governor of Virginia at one period during the Revolution; Gen. Andrew Moore, United States Senator; Col. John Stuart, of Greenbrier; General Tate, of Washington County; Col. William McKee, of Kentucky; Col. John Steele, Governor of Mississippi; Col. Charles Cameron, of Bath; Major John Lewis, of Monroe; General Wells, of Ohio; and General George Mathews, Governor of Georgia.

It should be remembered that as early as 1763 Great Britain began to assert a right to tax the American Colonies, and the first act with that end in view was in 1764, in the form of duties on a number of items of American consumption. This act was bitterly resented in the Colonies because it was based on the claim that they might be taxed without their consent. In pursuance of the same policy, the notorious Stamp Act was passed in 1765, and Virginia, stirred by the oratory of Patrick Henry, led the way in opposition to this measure by the adoption of Henry's celebrated resolutions against the Stamp Act by the House of Burgesses. These resolutions were warmly supported by John Wilson and William Preston, Burgesses from Augusta at the time. The controversy continued for ten years, increasing in heat, and all hope of conciliation with the mother country was at an end in 1776 with the Declaration of Independence.

Augusta saw eye to eye with her sister Virginia

[383]

counties in the movement which resulted in the Revolution. In February, 1775, the freeholders of Augusta
met at Staunton and chose Captain Thomas Lewis and
Captain Samuel McDowell to represent them in the
convention at Richmond in March of that year, with
instructions to coöperate with the other delegates in
such measures as might be deemed necessary to per-
petuate the "ancient, just and legal rights of this Colony
and all British America."

In addition to the grievances held in common with
the older counties against Great Britain, Augusta also
had seen at first hand the iniquitous traffic the British
in the West had been carrying on with the Indians, and
it is doubtful if there was a single Tory in Augusta
during the Revolution.

When the Revolution began with the Declaration of
Independence July 4, 1776, and Washington was appointed commander-in-chief of the army, the following
were among the Augusta men then, or shortly
afterward, commissioned: Andrew Lewis, brigadier-
general; colonels, William Lewis, George Mathews,
Alexander McClenachan and Thomas Fleming;
majors, M. Donovan and John Lewis. Gen. Andrew
Lewis promptly took command of the forces in and
around Williamsburg, and in that same month he commanded in the action at Gwynn's Island, Mathews
County, in which Lord Dunmore, the last Royal Governor of Virginia, was driven out, never to return.

The story of Augusta County, of course, merged
with the story of the American Colonies' fight for
independence. While her sons played their part in the
campaigns east of the mountains, they played equally

[384]

as valiant a part in the bloody encounters with the British and their Indian allies west of the mountains. But this is American history, and a very thrilling chapter, rather than the story of Augusta County.

Augusta men took part in the siege of Fort McHenry, at Wheeling, Williamson's campaign, Crawford's expedition, the second siege of Fort McHenry and the attack on Fort Rice. On the day after Christmas, 1776, Washington won the Battle of Trenton, and several hundred of the Hessian prisoners were sent to Staunton. It will be remembered that when Benedict Arnold invaded Richmond in January, 1781, the Legislature moved to Charlottesville, and with the approach of Tarleton's cavalry early in June, the members made their way to Staunton, where they convened on June 7, in the Episcopal church.

The provisional articles of peace after Cornwallis' surrender and the cessation of hostilities in the Revolution were drawn up at Paris in November, 1782, and the final treaty of peace was signed September 3, 1783. Meanwhile it was found that the confederative system of government was inadequate and in 1787 commissioners from all the States, except Rhode Island, met at Philadelphia and their work resulted in the Federal Constitution.

Although there were many Augusta families who moved to Kentucky and the Northwest Territory during and after the Revolution, many other families came into the county to replace them. Prosperity seemed particularly abundant in the period from 1840 to 1860. The Augusta Savings Bank, the first institution of its kind in the County, was established in 1848, with

Benjamin Crawford as president, Robert Cowan, treasurer, and J. Lewis Peyton, secretary.

Also in 1848 a large convention was held in Staunton with delegates from eighteen counties and the City of Richmond. This body adopted resolutions calling upon the General Assembly to appropriate funds for a railroad from "some point near the head of steamboat navigation on the Kanawha River to some point at or near Covington." Also it was resolved "that the Blue Ridge Mountains constitute a barrier to the communication between the eastern and western parts of the State, the removal of which barrier is an object of great interest to the whole Commonwealth, therefore the General Assembly ought to appropriate a sum adequate to the construction of the Louisa Railroad from the eastern to the western base," and "that the capital of the Louisa Railroad Company ought to be increased, so as to enable them to extend the road to a point at or near Covington," and "that the extension of the Louisa Railroad from the junction (Hanover) to the dock in the City of Richmond, as an independent improvement, is a measure of very great interest to a large portion of the people of Virginia now looking to that railroad as a medium of transport to market."

These objectives were consummated, and were important steps in what resulted, after the War Between the States, in the formation of the Chesapeake and Ohio System.

When President James Madison declared war against Great Britain in 1812, Augusta immediately formed a military association to devise plans for military schools in which recruits might be instructed, and when Admiral Cochran came into Chesapeake Bay and ravaged the coasts of Virginia and Maryland and the call for volunteers was sent out, Augusta was ready. The Augusta troop marched to Camp Holly, near Richmond, and then to Craney Island. Robert Porterfield, an old Revolutionary officer, was brigadier-general; John H. Peyton was chief of staff, and Dr. Williams, of Waynesboro, was surgeon. Other officers known to have been commissioned were Captains B. G. Baldwin, C. Johnson, J. C. Sowers, John Mathews, Hugh Young, Abraham Large, Christian Morris, Joseph Larew, Samuel Doake, Samuel Steele, Alexander Givens, George C. Robertson and W. G. Dudley, with James Kirke, John Sperry and John H. Peck as commissaries.

Similarly, when the Mexican War broke out in 1845, Augusta contributed a company under the command of Captain Kenton Harper, which marched to Norfolk and proceeded by water to Corpus Christi, Texas. When the war was over in 1848, Mexico having lost Texas, California, Utah and New Mexico, the Augusta troops came home after their long and arduous campaign and were tendered a dinner at Staunton by the loyal people of the county. Lieutenants in that command were R. H. Kinney, V. E. Geiger and William H. Harman.

The vast County of Augusta remained intact until 1770, when Botetourt was formed. Thereafter the formation of new counties was accelerated. The Virginia Counties of Ohio and Kentucky, and many other subdivisions of Augusta west of the mountains having been cut off, Bath County was finally formed by act of 1790 and Augusta County was reduced to its present bounds.

The county court system, which originated in Virginia as early as 1623, was not materially changed by the Revolution, and the gentlemen justices continued to preside in Augusta. Finally certain constitutional changes resulted in the substitution of a county judge for the old county court system, and in 1904 the circuit courts replaced the county courts. Other courts of wider jurisdiction had been formed in the meantime. For instance, in 1802 the Commonwealth was divided into three districts, and Staunton was the seat of the chancery court for a district extending to the Ohio River, and the first chancellor was John Brown. Also at Staunton was a common law court of which Archibald Stuart was judge, and when, in 1809, this was superseded by the Superior Courts of Law, Judge Stuart continued to preside, with John Howe Peyton as attorney for the Commonwealth.

It is a remarkable fact that two highly important inventions were perfected in Augusta within a few miles of Midway. Cyrus H. McCormick, in 1831, invented the grain reaper, and in the same vicinity in 1856 J. A. E. Gibbs worked out the chainstitch sewing machine.

As the War Between the States approached, Augusta was strongly in favor of preserving the Union, if possible, and at a mass meeting at Staunton November 26, 1860, resolutions were adopted calling upon the General Assembly of Virginia to do everything within its power to avert the tragedy of war and preserve the Union. In these resolutions were the oft-quoted words that the Constitution "is the easiest yoke of government a free people ever bore, and yet the strongest protector of rights the wisdom of man ever contrived."

The committee who drafted these resolutions were A. H. H. Stuart, H. W. Sheffey, G. K. Harper, John B. Baldwin, G. B. Stuart, John L. Peyton, John Mc-Cue, J. A. Waddell, Robert Guy, J. D. Imboden, Benjamin Crawford, G. M. Cochran, Jr., and George Baylor. It was largely through the influence of the able men who participated in that meeting that Virginia was the eighth State to secede.

Later, when the secession convention met in Richmond, John B. Baldwin, later a gallant Confederate officer, made such an impassioned plea for conciliation and the preservation of the Union that not only was a vote deferred, but, he himself was sent by the convention to Washington to confer with President Lincoln and to explain the true feelings of the Virginia people.

Shortly afterward Fort Sumter was fired on and Lincoln issued his proclamation for 75,000 troops, so Virginia voted for secession. Then the very men who had done most in efforts to avert war, flew to arms. Again, after the war, when it was seen that the cause was lost and the sooner the Union was again perfected the better it would be for all, Col. Baldwin was the leader in another mass meeting at Staunton which led to a State-wide movement for reinstatement of Virginia in the Union, a movement which went far in shielding the prostrate people of Virginia from tyranny in the years following the war.

Most of the fighting on Augusta soil was in 1864. Her sons fought with great bravery at the battles of

Mt. Crawford and Piedmont, and later in the same year came Gen. Philip Sheridan in his march up the Shenandoah Valley, after which he boasted that "a crow flying over the Valley must take his rations with him." Sheridan, with approximately 45,000 troops, continued his march up the Valley into Augusta. The Confederates tried to stem the tide of an overwhelming force at Fishersville, but were forced to retire, and Sheridan pushed on to Staunton, where all public property was destroyed, including the railroad and two factories. His cavalry proceeded to Waynesboro for further destruction. Augusta, along with the rest of the beautiful Valley of Virginia, was left in a state of almost utter desolation.

The Augusta troops in the Confederate army, with their officers, were as follows:

The Staunton Artillery: Capt. J. D. Imboden; lieutenants, T. L. Harman, A. W. Garber, W. L. Balthis and G. W. Imboden.

The West Augusta Guard: Capt. W. S. H. Baylor; lieutenants, H. K. Cochran, J. H. Waters, J. Bumgardner and W. Blackburn.

There were two companies of cavalry. One was under Captain William Patrick, afterward promoted to major; and the other was commanded by Capt. F. F. Sterrett, serving for the latter part of the war with Col. James W. Cochran, also of Augusta.

Two regiments of volunteer infantry were raised, the 5th Virginia and the 52nd Virginia. The 5th Virginia, a part of the celebrated Stonewall Brigade of Gen. T. J. Jackson and composed mainly of troops from Augusta, had the following officers: Kenton Harper, colonel; William H. Harman, lieutenant-colonel; William S. H. Baylor, major; and Captain James Bumgardner, adjutant. Captains were J. H. S. Funk, S. H. Letcher, Robert Doyle, Jacob Trevy, H. J. Williams, Captain McHenry, James Newton, Lycurgus Grills, St. Francis Roberts, Peter Wilson, George T. Antrim, James Gibson, A. W. Harman, Richard Simms, O. F. Grinnan, E. L. Curtis, James H. Waters, Thomas J. Burke and Milton Bucher.

In the Fall of 1861 Col. Harper resigned and William H. Harman was promoted to colonel. William S. H. Baylor became lieutenant-colonel and A. Koiner was made major. At the reorganization in March, 1862, Major Baylor was made colonel; Captain Funk, lieutenant-colonel; Capt. H. J. Williams, major; and C. S. Arnall was made adjutant. After the death of Col. Baylor, at Second Manassas, Lieutenant-Colonel Funk was made colonel; Major Williams, lieutenant-colonel; and Capt. James W. Newton was made major. Col. Funk was killed at the Battle of Winchester in 1864.

The 52nd Virginia was commanded by Col. John B. Baldwin. M. G. Harman was lieutenant-colonel; J. D. H. Ross, major, and John Lewis, of Bath, adjutant. The surgeon was Livingston Waddell, and assistant surgeon, John Lewis, of Albemarle. Captains were William Long, E. M. Dabney, J. F. Hottle, J. H. Skinner, Thomas Watkins, of Rockbridge, Samuel McCune, J. C. Lilley, John H. Humphreys and John Miller, of Rockbridge.

Robert D. Lilley was captain of the Augusta Lee

Rifles, with the following lieutenants: C. G. Merritt, J. B. Smith and C. Davis.

John L. Peyton was commissioned a colonel and was raising a troop early in 1861, when he was sent on a mission to England by the Confederate Government.

In addition to the family of John Lewis, whose descendants have distinguished themselves in many lines of activity in many States, brief mention may be made of a few of the other founders of prominent families who have been identified with Augusta.

Ephraim McDowell came to the County between 1735 and 1740 to be near his friend and relative John Lewis. He is credited with having built the first road across the Blue Ridge. With him came his son, John McDowell, who was Burden's surveyor and they settled on the Burden grant in what is now Rockbridge. John McDowell was killed by the Indians in 1742. From this family came Gov. James McDowell; the wife of Col. George Moffett, of Augusta, Indian fighter and Revolutionary officer; Gen. Joseph McDowell, of North Carolina; and Gen. Joseph Jefferson McDowell, of Ohio.

John Preston, a native of County Derry, Ireland, was the immigrant to Augusta and was buried in Tinkling Spring Cemetery. From his one son and four daughters are descended many men of mark. His son, William Preston, was a member of the House of Burgesses. John Preston's daughters married as follows: Col. Robert Breckinridge, of Virginia, and after his death moved to Kentucky; Rev. John Brown, a prominent Presbyterian minister of Virginia and Kentucky; Francis Smith, of Virginia, later moving to Kentucky; and the fourth married John Howard, of Virginia, and her son was a member of Congress from Kentucky and Governor of Missouri Territory.

John Campbell, born in Ireland, came to Augusta in 1733 and left two sons, Patrick and David Campbell. Among the descendants were: Gen. William Campbell, the hero of King's Mountain; Robert Campbell, an officer with his brother in the same engagement; a number of celebrated Indian fighters; and David Campbell, a judge of the Superior Court of Tennessee.

Archibald Stuart, who lived near Waynesboro and died there in 1761, also had two brothers in the County, John and David Stuart, all having been born in Ireland. Major Alexander Stuart, son of Archibald Stuart, was a Revolutionary officer and was severely wounded at Guilford Courthouse. Major Stuart was the father of Judge Archibald Stuart, of Staunton.

Joseph Bell and William Craig were among the early settlers.

John Cochran settled at Staunton about 1745.

The family of Captain James Tate, of Augusta, who was killed at Guilford Courthouse, moved to Kentucky and Missouri.

Four children of Gilbert Christian, of Ireland, came to Augusta about 1733 and settled in Beverley Manor, on Christian's Creek. Most of the family moved to Kentucky and Tennessee. Among the descendants was Gov. Allen Trimble, of Ohio.

Patrick Crawford, who emigrated from Ireland to Pennsylvania, came to Augusta about 1750.

The Rev. John McCue succeeded the Rev. James Waddell, the Blind Preacher, at Tinkling Spring church.

Peter Hanger settled in Augusta in 1750, having

come from Pennsylvania, and owned the farm which is now a part of the Staunton water-works.

Five sons of the Mathews family came from Ireland and settled in Augusta about 1739. From this family came John P. Mathews, Governor of the Territory of Oregon, and George Mathews, Governor of Georgia.

Robert and Charles Porterfield were both officers in the Revolution, the latter dying from wounds received in that conflict. Gen. Robert Porterfield came to Augusta about 1782 and left a number of descendants.

John Wayt came to the county about 1790 from Orange and was Mayor of Staunton.

Henry J. Peyton came to Augusta from another county about 1796 and was appointed clerk of the Chancery Court of the district in 1802. John Howe Peyton came to the County in 1809 as commonwealth's attorney. Both were of the Peyton family of eastern Virginia, one of the oldest in the Colony.

Judge Briscoe G. Baldwin, born at Winchester in 1789, moved to Staunton in 1809 and was elected to the Supreme Court of Virginia in 1842. He married the daughter of Chancellor John Brown, another of Augusta's distinguished sons, and from this union came Col. John Brown Baldwin, noted statesman and soldier. Col. Briscoe G. Baldwin, another of Judge Baldwin's sons, was chief of ordnance for the Confederacy.

Michael Koiner, who had settled in Pennsylvania, had a large family and two of his sons, George Adam and Casper Koiner, came to Augusta. The father joined them in 1787 and he died in the county in 1796.

Col. William Fleming, of Scotland, settled in that

part of Augusta which is now Botetourt about 1760. He raised and commanded a regiment in the Battle of Point Pleasant and was severely wounded in that engagement. For a brief period he was acting Governor of Virginia.

John Madison, first clerk of Augusta, from 1745 to 1779, lived near Port Republic in that part of Augusta which is now Rockingham. His son, Bishop James Madison, was born there in 1749. Bishop Madison was the first bishop of the Established Church in Virginia in 1785. Receiving his education in England, he was in the faculty of the College of William and Mary and became president of that institution.

Among other men associated with the outlying regions of Augusta County should be mentioned Major Samuel McCulloch, Col. Ebenezer Zane, founder of Wheeling, W. Va., Lewis Wetzel, Capt. Andrew Poe, Capt. Samuel Brady and Jesse Hughes.

All five of the sons of John Lewis, the Founder of Augusta, were distinguished men, and many of their descendants have been noted in various parts of the country. John Lewis' two daughters died unmarried.

Captain Samuel Lewis, eldest son of John Lewis, was a captain in the French and Indian War and was at Braddock's defeat. He was later distinguished in the defence of Greenbrier County from the Indians. He was the only one of the sons who never married.

Thomas Lewis was at Braddock's defeat. He had defective vision and was not as conspicuous as his other brothers in military affairs, but he was a man of much learning and an expert surveyor. He was a member of the House of Burgesses, of the Continental Congress of

1775, and of the Virginia conventions of 1776 and 1778.

The biography of General Andrew Lewis, the hero of Point Pleasant and many another engagement, is well known.

Col. William Lewis was severely wounded at Braddock's defeat. He was a practising physician, and when the Revolution broke out was commissioned a colonel. His son Thomas Lewis also was an officer, serving with Gen. Wayne's army.

Col. Charles Lewis, the youngest son of John Lewis, was serving as a member of the House of Burgesses from Augusta when he was killed at the battle of Point Pleasant.

Woodrow Wilson, World War President of the United States, was born at Staunton December 28, 1856.

William Hall, of Augusta, was Governor of Tennessee 1820-22.

Allen Trimble was Governor of Ohio 1821-22 and 1826-30.

Hamilton R. Gamble was Governor of Missouri 1861-64.

COURTHOUSE SITE UNCHANGED

The present courthouse at Staunton is on the site of the old and was completed in 1837. How many other structures which have stood on this spot since 1745 is not definitely known. The land was donated for the purpose in 1748 by William Beverley.

John Madison, the first clerk, took his books with him to his home near Port Republic for a number of years, but a clerk's office was later built at Staunton. Since the erection of the present building the east wing has been the office of the Circuit Court clerk, and the west wing the office of the county clerk.

SULLY PORTRAIT OF MARSHALL

Among the many portraits on the walls of the courtroom is one that is perhaps the most valuable picture in any courthouse in Virginia. It is a large oil painting of Chief Justice John Marshall, and is by Sully. It hangs just behind the judge's seat.

The Staunton *Spectator* of May 11, 1837, stated that "the portrait of this distinguished jurist and patriot, intended for the new courthouse, has been contracted for and is now expected daily. The artist is Mr. Sully, the gentleman who painted the admirable likeness of John Marshall which was purchased by the Common Hall of the City of Richmond."

The artist was paid $300 by the subscription of private individuals of Augusta County and Staunton, and it appears from an order of the county court May 30, 1838, that the County paid $60 to cover the cost of hanging it. In the event that the files of the Staunton *Spectator* have been destroyed, this information may be found in an article in the William and Mary *Quarterly* for January, 1930, written by Armistead C. Gordon.

The other portraits in the courtroom are likenesses of the following men, all judges and lawyers who practiced at the Augusta bar:

Marshall Hanger (1833-1912), Hugh W. Sheffey (1815-1889), James Bumgardner, Jr. (1835-1917), William McLaughlin (1828-1898), Thomas C. Elder (1834-1904), Henderson M. Bell (1826-1899), Richard P. Bell (1853-1904), Meade F. White (1847-1898), Thomas J. Michie (1795-1875), David Fultz (1802-1886), John B. Baldwin (1820-1873), John H. Peyton (1822-1898), George M. Cochran (1832-1900), S. H. Letcher (1848-1914), John Echols (1823-1896), Edward Echols (1849-1914), A. H. H. Stuart (1807-1891), Robert L. Parrish (1840-1904), A. Caperton Braxton (1862-1914), J. W. Churchman (1857-1909).

In the clerk's office: William A. Burnett (1837-1899).

SOME AUGUSTA HOMES

In addition to the many handsome old homes in Staunton may be mentioned the following homes in the county, with their builders:

Oak Grove, built about 1810 by Jacob Kinney.

Gaymont, by John McDowell.

Wheatlands, by William Poage.

Bear Wallow, by Judge David Fultz, and at one time owned by Chapman Johnson.

Selma, by Simpson F. Taylor.

Spring Farm, built by Hessian prisoners during the Revolution and added to and remodeled by Judge John Brown.

Steep Hill, by J. Lewis Peyton.

Montgomery Hall, built in 1824 by John H. Peyton from plans presented him by Thomas Jefferson.

Bellevue, by J. Emmett Guy.

Fairview Villa, by William F. Ast.

Edgegood, by Joseph P. Ast.

Killarney, by A. M. Bruce.

Glendale, by Silas Smith.

[398]

Knights of the Golden Horseshoe

KNIGHTS OF THE GOLDEN HORSESHOE

Knights of the Golden Horseshoe

N the crest of the Blue Ridge, where the beautiful Skyline Drive crosses the Spotswood Trail, there is a monument erected by the Colonial Dames of America in the State of Virginia long before the Skyline Drive was projected and before the area was made a National park.

This monument marks a spot which is important in American history, for here Governor Alexander Spotswood and his merry company of cocked-hat explorers first discovered the Valley of Virginia, crossed the mountains and claimed all that fertile territory for his majesty King George I. On their return, the Governor proposed the Tramontane Order, or the Knights of the Golden Horseshoe, and presented each of the gentlemen in his party a small golden emblem in form of a horseshoe, with gems for the nails.

Because of the jolly spirit in which Governor Spotswood and his gentlemen undertook it, the expedition has been regarded as one of the most picturesque in American annals, its more serious aspects being sometimes overlooked. At the time the French had founded Kaskaskia, on the Mississippi, Detroit, Vincennes and Mobile, and two years later Bienville founded New Orleans. Thus the English settlements along the coast were surrounded.

After the return of the party to Williamsburg, Governor Spotswood said that the purpose of his late expedition across the Blue Ridge was "to ascertain whether Lake Erie, occupying as it does a central position in the French line of communication between Canada and Louisiana, was accessible from Virginia." As a result of the expedition, he proposed to the authorities in England that he be authorized to lead another expedition to determine whether or not it was feasible to found an English post on the lakes, and thus "drive a wedge between the extremities of the French position." This second exploit was never authorized.

Unfortunately, even the names of many of the gentlemen who made the journey have been lost. There were about fifty in the party. Two companies of Rangers, consisting each of six men and an officer, and four Meherrin Indians are known to have gone. Most of the members of the cavalcade must have been of the landed gentry, referred to in that day as "gentlemen."

The names on the monument, which was unveiled September 5, 1921, are as follows:

John Fontaine, Robert Beverley, William Robertson, Dr. Robinson, —— Todd, James Taylor, Robert Brooke, George Mason, Captain Smith, Jeremiah Clouder.

Governor Spotswood, who had been a colonel under the Duke of Marlborough and was severely wounded at Blenheim, came to Virginia as Governor in 1710 and the memorable journey over the mountains took place in 1716. He was then living in the stately palace at Williamsburg, which has now been restored, and had a country place near Yorktown, and it is not to be wondered that the equipage which he took into the wilderness was as elaborate as circumstances permitted.

John Fontaine, a French Huguenot who had served as an ensign in the English army, accompanied Governor Spotswood on the entire journey and kept a diary. He and the Governor, doubtless with other gentlemen in the party and body servants who accompanied the Governor's coach, set out from Williamsburg on August 20, 1716. They crossed the Pamunkey at the present site of West Point and went from there to Chelsea, the Moore homestead in King William. A little farther along, the Governor left his carriage and they proceeded on horseback through King and Queen, Caroline and Spotsylvania, traveling by easy stages, being entertained at the manor-houses and being joined by other members of the party as they proceeded, finally reaching Germanna, in the edge of Orange County on August 24.

This was the rendezvous for other gentlemen and Rangers, and here their horses were shod—which had not been necessary in the soft sands of tidewater. They started from Germanna on the afternoon of the 29th and camped on Mountain Run. They proceeded to the Rappahannock, which they crossed at Somerville's Ford, thence by the left bank to near Peyton's Ford on the Rapidan. Here they turned south to where Stanardsville now stands, thence to the top of the mountain in Swift Run Gap, where the monument was placed, descended the mountains on the other side and crossed the Shenandoah River about ten miles north of the site of Port Republic. They called the beautiful stream the Euphrates, but fortunately the name Shenandoah survived, which in the imagery of the Indian tongue meant "Daughter of the Stars." They were back at Germanna September 10, and the Governor was back in Williamsburg September 17.

There was great rejoicing at Williamsburg over the success of the expedition and the accounts of the wonderful new country they had seen. They had called the mountain over which they had crossed, apparently meaning the whole Blue Ridge range, Mount Spotswood, and the Alleghanies were called Mount George, however, the references may have been to peaks in the Blue Ridge. The Governor specified that the requisite for future membership in the Tramontane Order was the pledging of the King's health on Mount George.

In November of that year, when the authorities of the College of William and Mary waited upon the Governor with two copies of Latin verse, their annual offering for the land held by the college under its ancient charter, these verses, written by Professor Arthur Blackamore, paid a glowing tribute to the Governor and his Knights of the Golden Horseshoe and extolled their achievement.

John Fontaine's journal describes the events of the expedition so casually, and yet so delightfully, and is so rarely found in print, that liberal excerpts from it are here given. It is the only connected story of the expedition by an eye-witness.

August 20, 1716. In the morning got my horses ready, and what baggage was necessary, and I waited on the Governor, who was in readiness for an expedition over the Appalachian Mountains. We breakfasted and at four came to the Brickhouse upon York River [Eltham, the Bassett home was near here and Col. Bassett had a tavern on this plantation across the river from West Point] where we crossed the ferry, and at six we came to Mr. Austin Moor's house [Augustine Moore's home, Chelsea] upon Mattapony River, in King William County; here we lay all night and were well entertained.

21st. At ten we set out from Mr. Moor's and crossed the river of Mattapony, and continued on the road, and were on horseback till nine of the clock at night, before we came to Mr. Robert Beverley's house, where we were well entertained, and remained this night.

22nd. At nine in the morning, we set out from Mr. Beverley's. The Governor left his chaise here and mounted his horse. The weather fair, we continued our journey until we came to Mr. Woodford's [Windsor, in Caroline] where we lay, and were well entertained. This house lies on the Rappahannoc River, ten miles below the falls.

23rd. Here we remained all day, and diverted ourselves and rested our horses.

24th. In the morning at seven, we mounted our horses, and came to Austin Smith's house about ten, where we dined and remained till about one of the clock, then we set out, and about nine of the clock we came to Germantown [Germanna, in Orange] where we rested that night—bad beds and indifferent entertainment.

For the 25th there is an account of a visit to the Governor's iron works.

26th. At seven we got up, and several gentlemen of the country, that were to meet the Governor at this place for the expedition, arrived here, as also two companies of Rangers, consisting each of six men and an officer. Four Meherrin Indians also came. . .

27th. Got our tents in order, and our horses shod. . .

29th. In the morning we got all things in readiness, and about one we left the German town to set out on our intended journey. At five in the afternoon, the Governor gave orders to encamp near a small river, three miles from Germanna, which we called Expedition Run. This first encampment we called Beverley Camp, in honor of one of the gentlemen of our party. We made great fires, and supped and drank good punch.

30th. In the morning about seven of the clock, the trumpet sounded to awake all the company and we got up. One Austin Smith, one of the gentlemen with us, having a fever, returned home. . . Two of the Governor's horses had strayed. At half past two we got the horses, at three we mounted, and at half an hour after four we came up with our baggage at a small river, three miles on the way, which we called Mine Run, becaues there was an appearance of a silver mine by it. We made about three miles more, and came to another small river, which is at the foot of a small mountain, so we encamped here and called it Mountain Run, and our camp we called Todd's Camp. . . We made six miles this day.

31st. At eight in the morning we set out from Mountain Run, and after going five miles we came upon the upper part of the Rappahannoc River. One of the gentlemen and I, we kept out on one side of the company about a mile, to have better hunting. I saw a deer, and shot him from my horse, but the horse threw me a terrible fall and ran away. . . About five miles further we crossed the same river again, and two miles further we met with a large bear, which one of our company shot, and I got the skin. We killed several deer and . . . encamped upon the Rappahannoc River. From our encampment we could see the Appalachian Hills very plain. We made large fires, pitched our tents, and cut boughs to lie upon, had good liquor, and at ten we went to sleep. We always kept a sentry at the Governor's door. We called this Smith's Camp. Made this day fourteen miles.

1st September. At eight we mounted our horses and made the first five miles of our way through a very pleasant plain, which lies where Rappahannoc River [Rapidan] forks. . . We had some of our baggage put out of order, and our company dismounted, by hornets stinging the horses. This was some hindrance, and did a little damage, but afforded a great deal of diversion. We killed three bears this day. . . About five of the clock, we came to a run of water at the foot of a hill, where we pitched our tents. We called this encampment Dr. Robinson's Camp, and the river Blind Run. . .

2nd. At nine we were all on horseback, and after riding about five miles we crossed Rappahannoc River, almost at the head, where it is very small. We had a rugged way; we passed over a great many small runs of water. . . Several of our company were dismounted, some were down with their horses, others under their horses, and some thrown off. We saw a bear running down a tree, but it being Sunday, we did not endeavor to kill anything. We encamped by a small river we called White Oak River, and called our camp Taylor's Camp.

3rd. About eight we were on horseback, and about ten we came to a thicket so tightly laced together that we had a great deal of trouble to get through; our baggage was injured, our clothes torn all to rags, and the saddles and holsters also torn. About five of the clock we encamped almost at the head of James River [the Rivanna, which empties into the James] just below the great mountains. We called this camp Colonel Robertson's Camp. We made all this day but eight miles.

4th. We had two of our men sick with the measles, and one of our horses poisoned with a rattlesnake. We took the heaviest of our baggage, our tired horses, and the sick men, and made a convenient lodge for them as we could, and left people to guard them and hunt for them. . . We were forced to clear most of the way before us. We crossed one of the small mountains this side of the Appalachian, and from the top of it we had a fine view of the plains below. We were obliged to walk up the most of the way, there being abundance of loose stones on the side of the hill. I killed a large rattlesnake here. . . We made about four miles, and so came to the side of the James River, where a man may jump over it, and there we pitched our tents . . . this camp we called Rattlesnake Camp, but it was otherwise called Brook's Camp.

5th. A fair day. At nine we mounted; we were obliged to have axe-men to clear the way in some places. We followed the windings of James River observing that it came from the very top of the mountains. . . About one of the clock we got to the top of the mountain; about four miles and a half, and we came to the very head spring of James River, where it runs no bigger than a man's arm, from under a large stone. We drank King George's health, and all the Royal Family's at the very top of the Appalachian Mountains. About a musket-shot from the spring there is another, which rises and runs down the other side; it goes westward, and we thought we could go down that way, but we met with such prodigious precipices that we were obliged to return to the top again. We found some trees which had been formerly marked, I suppose, by the Northern Indians, and following these trees, we found a good safe descent. Several of the company were for returning; but the Governor persuaded them to continue on. About five, we were down on the other side, and continued our way for about seven miles further, until we came to a large river, by the side of which we camped. We made this day fourteen miles. . . We called this place Spotswood Camp, after our Governor.

6th. We crossed the river, which we called Euphrates [the Shenandoah]. It is very deep; the main course of the water is north; it is fourscore yards wide in the narrowest part. We drank some healths on the other side, and returned; after which I went swimming in it. . . I caught some grasshoppers and fished; and another and I we catched a dish of fish, some perch, and a fish they call chub. The others went hunting and killed deer and turkeys. The Governor had graving irons, but could not grave anything, the stones were so hard. I graved my name on a tree by the river side; and the Governor buried a bottle with a paper enclosed, on which he writ that he took possession of this place in the name and for King George the First of England. We had a good dinner, and after it we got the men together, and loaded all their arms, and we drank to the King's health in Champagne, and fired a volley—the Princess's health in Burgundy, and fired a volley, and all the rest of the Royal Family in claret, and a volley. We drank the Governor's health and fired another volley. . . We called the highest mountain Mount George, and the one we crossed over Mount Spotswood.

7th. At seven in the morning we mounted our horses, and parted with the rangers, who were to go farther on, and returned homewards; we passed the mountains, and at five in the afternoon we came to Hospital Camp, where we left our sick men and heavy baggage, and we found all things well and safe. We encamped here, and called it Captain Clouder's Camp.

The old journal goes on to recite that on the return journey they made twenty miles on the 8th and stopped over night at Mason's Camp. On the 9th one of the party had a narrow escape from a bear, and they encamped on the side "of the Rapid Ann, on a tract of land Mr. Beverley doth design to take up." On the 10th, on a hill, "Mr. Beverley and his horse fell down, and they both rolled to the bottom; but there were no broken bones on either side." At twelve, "as we were crossing a run of water, Mr. Clouder fell in, so we called this place Clouder's Run." At one they arrived at a large spring, where they dined and drank a bowl of punch, calling it Fontaine's Spring. At four o'clock on September 10, they were back at Germanna, where the Governor thanked the gentlemen for their assistance in the expedition, and Mr. Mason left for home.

On the 11th, all the company dispersed, except Dr. Robinson and Mr. Clouder, and those who remained stayed at Germanna until the morning of the 13th. Governor Spotswood, a few years later, built a manor house at Germanna and resided there. They arrived at Mr. Woodford's and remained that night. On the 14th, after tarrying along the way, they reached "Mr. Beverley's house, which is upon the head of Mattapony River, where we were well entertained."

On the 15th, the Governor once more took his carriage, and in the afternoon they reached Mr. Baylor's, where they remained that night. "He lives upon the Mattapony River," wrote Fontaine, "and is one of the greatest tobacco dealers in the country."

On the 16th—"We sent the chaise over Mattapony River, and it being Sunday, we went to church in King William County, where we heard a sermon from Mr. Monroe. After the sermon, we continued our journey until we came to Mr. West's plantation, where Col. Bassett waited for the Governor with his pinnace, and other boats for his servants. We arrived at his house by five of the clock and were nobly entertained."

On the 17th of September, 1716, the Governor was back once more in Williamsburg.

There is one other contemporaneous account of the expedition, which is taken from "The Present State of Virginia", by Hugh Jones, A. M., published in 1724:

"Governor Spotswood, when he undertook the great discovery of the passage over the mountains, attended with a sufficient guard and pioneers and gentlemen, with a sufficient stock of provisions, with abundant fatigue, passed these mountains, and cut his Majesty's name in a rock upon the highest of them, naming it Mount George, and in complaisance the gentlemen, from the Governor's name, called the mountain next in height Mount Alexander.

"For this expedition they were obliged to provide a great quantity of horse shoes (things seldom used in the lower parts of the country, where there are few stones). Upon which account the Governor upon their return presented each of his companions with a golden horseshoe (some of which I have seen studded with valuable stones resembling the heads of nails) with this inscription on the one side: *Sic juvat transcendere montes;* and on the other is written the Tramontane Order."

John Fontaine's diary is the only contemporary source for the names of the men who went with Governor Spotswood. As time goes on, family papers may bring to light others, for it is generally believed that there were others than those named by Fontaine who made this memorable journey. William Russell, of King and Queen, may have gone. Later he was high sheriff of Orange, and was the father of Col. William Russell, of the Revolution. It is also possible that

Bernard Moore, of Chelsea, was of the company. He married Spotswood's elder daughter, Anne Catherine, but apparently he was too young to have made the trip.

So many confused reports have been written of those who are known to have gone, that a few notes in regard to them may not be improper here, in order that they may be identified.

Robert Brooke was the third of the name in Essex County and was the ancestor of Governor Robert Brooke and of Judge Francis T. Brooke, of the Virginia Supreme Court of Appeals. The first of the name in Essex was William Brooke, who came to Essex prior to 1650. His son, Robert Brooke, was born in 1652 and was one of the early clerks of Essex. It was his son, Robert Brooke II, who went with Spotswood.

Robert Beverley, referred to as being of Beverley Park, King and Queen County, is perhaps best known for his "History of Virginia", published in London in 1705, with a revised edition in 1722. Unfortunately his history ends with the coming of Spotswood to Virginia. The first of the name in Virginia was Major Robert Beverley, of Middlesex, who was highly influential in the General Assembly, member of the Council and in command of Sir William Berkeley's forces at the time of Bacon's Rebellion. Major Beverley came to Virginia about 1663. He incurred the enmity of the King's commissioners sent over to suppress the rebellion and was imprisoned by Governor Chicheley. Later he was again a Burgess, and when King James' representatives made an illegal request of the General Assembly to levy a tax on the Colony, Beverley was a leader in its defeat, and he was barred from holding any public office by the King.

Major Robert Beverley had three sons. Peter Beverley, the eldest, was clerk of the House of Burgesses from 1691 to 1700, when he was elected to represent Gloucester. He was speaker from 1702 to 1714, and was made a member of the Council in 1719. At various times he was treasurer of the Colony, auditor and surveyor-general.

Captain Harry Beverley, another son of Major Robert Beverley, was a justice in Middlesex in 1700 and was surveyor of both King William and King and Queen. In 1716 Governor Spotswood sent him in command of a vessel to search for pirates and Spanish wrecks. He was taken prisoner by a Spanish man-of-war and kept a prisoner seven months. He escaped from Vera Cruz and made his way back to Virginia some time prior to August, 1717. Some have said that Captain Harry Beverley went on the tramontane journey, but this is hardly probable, and the indications are that he was away at sea at the time.

Robert Beverley, who was one of the Knights of the Horseshoe, was clerk of the Council in 1697 and clerk of King and Queen from 1699 to 1702. He was a Burgess from King and Queen in 1706, and also served as a Burgess from Jamestown. He was presiding justice in King and Queen in 1718.

Captain Austin Smith lived at the falls of the Rappahannock River and was a son of Major Lawrence Smith, a prominent citizen of Gloucester. In passing, it may be pointed out that the Smith grant at the falls of the Rappahannock was one of two particularly interesting early land grants. The other was a large grant to William Byrd I at the falls of the James. These were feudal tenures. The stipulation was that the proprietors should maintain armed forces at these strategic points.

It is virtually certain that the James Taylor referred to was James Taylor, the great grandfather of General Zachary Taylor, of Orange, who became President of the United States.

The Todd mentioned is believed to have been Thomas Todd, of Essex.

George Mason, of Stafford, was the father of George Mason, the great Revolutionary statesman.

Jeremiah Clouder was probably one of the captains of the rangers.

William Robertson later lived on Black Walnut Run, in the northeastern section of Orange, and it was at his house in 1734 that the first court for Orange County was held.

Documentary information about the Dr. Robinson mentioned is not available. He apparently was the medical officer accompanying the expedition. In all probability he was the William Robinson who served with George Mason in the House of Burgesses from Stafford in 1720.

Architecture of Courthouses

Beauty was apparently a major objective with the architects of the early Virginia courthouses, and their style contrasted sharply with the architecture of private structures. The first courthouses in practically all of the counties were crude buildings of board or logs. Their cost, as revealed in the records of appropriations, was very small. There is one instance in which there was no glass in the windows until two years after the court building was erected. In a number of cases these first public buildings were built by individual citizens, at their own expense. The jails were frequently built by the sheriffs, and in many cases the clerks kept their records at their homes.

But when population and revenues in the counties increased and the people gave thought to the erection of permanent public buildings, they insisted that these buildings must be beautiful as well as useful. The few Colonial courthouses which survive are gems. An unfortunate decadence in architectural appreciation at a much later period may be traced in the alterations made by county supervisors in their efforts to gain space and save the taxpayers' money, with small regard for the appearance of the altered buildings.

Practically all of the courthouses built prior to the middle of the 18th Century showed the Georgian influence, and the idea for their stately arches may have been derived from the Colonial Capitol at Williamsburg, which had an arched passageway connecting its two wings. When John D. Rockefeller, Jr., restored

Williamsburg and it became necessary to build a new courthouse, the arched form of architecture was adopted. So far as is known, every one of the early buildings was enclosed by a brick wall, obviously to keep out straying livestock and to protect the privacy of the justices from outside noises.

The courthouse of King William County, once the courthouse of the older county of New Kent, is one of the best remaining examples of the arched form of brick building so popular in the Colonial counties. Hanover Courthouse is another. In later years almost all of the old arched courthouses were altered, and unfortunately in most cases their architectural beauty was destroyed. A favorite method of providing more space at small expense was to brick up the arches and tear out partitions. The historic courthouse of Westmoreland is now the center of a rectangular structure. In a few cases, notably in Richmond and Charles City Counties, not only were the arches bricked up, but the buildings were faced in the opposite direction.

A second form of Colonial architecture seems to have become popular as the period of the Revolution approached. Notable surviving examples are the courthouse of Gloucester, built in 1766, and the building at Williamsburg, erected in 1770. The white-columned porch of the courthouse at Gloucester was added after the Revolution. The second form of Colonial architecture abandoned the stately brick arches, but all windows were arched. The chimneys of all Colonial courthouses were tall. Many of the clerks' offices and even some of the jails had elements of beauty, and the old clerk's office at Tappahannock,

[413]

built prior to 1750, is one of the loveliest small public buildings in the State.

Almost all of the courthouses built after the Revolution were in the well-known Early Republic, or Classic form, massive white columns being the principal distinguishing feature. Many Americans persist in thinking of the white columns as being Colonial, whereas there was not a white column in Virginia until after the Revolution. Porticos with the columns have been added to some of the Colonial courthouses since the Colonial period.

Thomas Jefferson had an enormous influence upon architecture in America. He introduced the white columns into this country when he designed the Capitol at Richmond, which he modeled after the style of the Maison Caree at Nimes, a little classic temple on the outskirts of the Graeco-Roman influence before the Dark Ages. Strange to say, what is known as the Classic Revival in architecture got under way in the new American Nation before it did in Europe. In fact, the beauty of the Early Republic buildings in the United States had considerable influence upon the architecture of Europe in the early 19th Century.

In addition to the Capitol at Richmond, Jefferson designed the original White House at Washington, the University of Virginia, his own Monticello, and a number of other private residences in Virginia, and fondness for the stately columns spread throughout America. Jefferson's was a many-sided nature and in perhaps none of his personal hobbies was he more interested than in architecture.

Some of the earliest Virginia courthouses may have

been built of brick brought from England, but there has been a great misconception in regard to the importation of English brick. Undoubtedly the chimneys of some of the old dwellings were built of brick brought over in the sailing ships as ballast or as cheap cargo, and a few of the early buildings were constructed of a type of glazed brick which were undoubtedly made across the Atlantic. It is believed that some of the brick in King William courthouse were from abroad, and in the ruins of an old house in King William County were found bricks stamped A. D. 1600—seven years before the first settlers came over.

A potent reason for the prevalence of the idea that so many brick were imported was that it was customary to use the word "English" adjectively to denote elegance. There are frequent references to fine homes of "English brick", but this does not necessarily mean that the brick came from England. To this day we speak of the English mockingbird, whereas the mockingbird was unknown in England until this country was settled.

For many years it was believed that the Sir Christopher Wren building at the College of William and Mary was built of English brick, but in recent years it was found that there was a kiln nearby, and there are abundant evidences that the settlers started making their own brick at a very early period. Nevertheless, statements are sometimes heard even now that certain structures in the uplands of Virginia—even as far west as the Valley—were built of imported brick. These statements are, of course, absurd, unless they refer to isolated cases such as the construction by Major James

H. Dooley of Swannanoa, on the crest of Afton Mountain, of Italian marble, or the bringing over by Alexander Weddell of the materials of Warwick Priory and the re-erection of the building at Richmond.

The county seats in early days were even more the centers of activity for the people of their counties than they are in modern times, and the forefathers believed in making their county buildings attractive. Most of the courthouses, fortunately, have become county shrines, and from the walls of the courtrooms look down the portraits of men who deserve to be remembered by their fellow-citizens, and in many instances there are memorial tablets of more than passing interest to the present generations.

At the courthouses of all of the counties are monuments to the memory of those who fought in the gray armies of the Confederacy.

Transportation to the West

The story of transportation from Virginia to the regions west of the mountains is one of the truly romantic chapters in American history.

Whether it may be said to have had its beginning with Governor Alexander Spotswood's memorable expedition to the Valley of Virginia in 1716 might be open to question. But he discovered Swift Run Gap, and the finding of other gaps through the mountains played an enormous part in the ultimate establishment of traffic lanes. Certain it is that Governor Spotswood and his gentlemen, who were to become the Knights of the Golden Horshoe, transported their equipment through Swift Run Gap.

George Washington may properly be called the father of transportation to the West. It was an interesting subject to him both before and after the Revolution. As early as 1750, when he was a mere boy, he was engaged in surveying lands in western Virginia for Lord Fairfax and went as far as the Big Sandy River. In 1753 he was sent by Governor Robert Dinwiddie to procure information as to the hostile activities of the French, that trip taking him as far as Logstown, on the Ohio River. In his correspondence in those early years he intimated the fear that if the western territories were not given transportation to the east, they would turn to Spain, with the Mississippi as their outlet to the sea.

As early as 1765 the Virginia House of Burgesses took steps to "clear the great falls of the James." This, of course, was only a beginning, but for seventy years thereafter there were repeated and determined efforts to make the streams navigable. Even after the first steam railways were projected, there was enthusiasm over inland waterways. The mountain ranges were the big obstacles to be reckoned with, and it is remarkable how persistently the Virginians strove to overcome the problems they presented.

Immediately after the Revolution and prior to his inauguration as first President of the United States in 1789, Washington as a private citizen was particularly interested in establishing a transportation route across the Appalachians. Hundreds of families had moved to the fertile new country. He, too, believed in the extension of the waterways, and a paragraph from a letter he wrote Governor Benjamin Harrison of Virginia in 1784 urging a system to connect Chesapeake Bay with the Ohio River is highly significant:

"It is necessary to apply the cement of interest to bind all parts of the Union together with indissoluble bonds. The western settlers have no means of coming to us except by long land transportations and unimproved roads. But smooth the road and make easy the way for them and see how amazingly our exports will be increased and how amply we shall be compensated for the trouble and expense of effecting it."

The James River Company was incorporated by act of the General Assembly of Virginia at its session in May 1784, and it was authorized to receive subscriptions to its stock, with $100,000 as the maximum. Two subsequent acts are so revelatory of the character of Washington and of the esteem in which he was held by the Virginia people that they should be mentioned.

In October 1784 the Assembly presented Washington 100 shares of the stock of the James River Company, expressing the "wish in particular that these great works for its (the Commonwealth's) improvement which, both as springing from the liberty which he has been so instrumental in establishing, and as encouraged by his patronage, will be durable monuments to his glory, may be made monuments also to the gratitude of his country."

In October 1785 this act was repealed at Washington's request, and the shares were appropriated to such objects of a public nature as Washington or his heirs might direct. Washington's letter declining the gift of the Commonwealth is quoted in full in the act. In it he said, "When I was called to the station with which

I was honored during the late conflict for our liberties—to the diffidence which I had so many reasons to feel in accepting it, I thought it my duty to join in a firm resolution to shut my hand against every pecuniary recompense; to this resolution I have invariably adhered—from this resolution (if I had the inclination) I do not consider myself at liberty to depart."

He added in his letter that if it pleased the General Assembly to permit him to turn the fund vested in him to objects of a public nature, it would be his study to select those with care. Later, dividends were paid to the academy at Lexington which is now Washington and Lee University, and these were the proceeds from Washington's shares.

Washington's declining to accept compensation for his services as commander-in-chief of the American Armies in the Revolution is often cited as a mark of his patriotism. It is not so generally known that he also refused to accept a gift of shares in a legitimate enterprise in which he was deeply interested, at a time when he held no public office. It also may properly be inferred that he placed the winning of transportation facilities to the West in the same category with winning a war for American Independence.

The organization of the James River Company seems to have been complete on January 5, 1785, with Washington as its first president. It began by clearing James River for navigation and building canals around the waterfalls to connect with other streams and roads over the mountains. One of these roads was the Midland Trail, which had been surveyed under Washington's direction by General Andrew Lewis.

Among the objectives set forth in the charter of the James River Company was one to make the James River navigable for vessels drawing one foot of water to the falls from the highest point practicable, and another from the falls to build such canal or canals, with sufficient locks as would open navigation to the tidewater channel below Richmond. As the years passed, the plan developed to build canals along both the north fork (the Rivanna) and the south fork of the James, and to connect these by turnpikes over the mountains with the Ohio. The first efforts were to clear the riverbeds so that flatboats could float down.

By 1796 the company was collecting full tolls and was showing a profit, a part of which was turned over to educational purposes. Inasmuch as there was a long series of rapids from the falls of the James to the tidewater channel, considerable trouble was encountered in overcoming this difficulty. In 1810 a contract was let for thirteen locks from the basin above the falls to the tidewater channel. The Rivanna was made navigable and the Staunton and James River Turnpike through Rockfish Gap was built to connect with it. The canal along the south fork of the James was extended to Lynchburg, and eventually all the way to Buchanan, in Botetourt County.

In 1820 the rights of the James River Company were transferred to the State of Virginia, and its affairs were placed in the hands of a Board of Public Works. The State enlarged and reconstructed the canal from Richmond to Westham, at the falls, a distance of seven miles, and extended its work to Maiden's Adventure, in Goochland, a distance of twenty-seven miles. Extending navigation far up the James River, a canal of seven and a half miles was built through the Blue Ridge and the elaborate scheme was conceived of building a canal through the Alleghanies on a plan somewhat similar to that put in practice in building the Panama Canal— with locks lifting boats to an artificial lake, and other locks to lower them on the other side.

As time went on, the State built a turnpike from Covington to the mouth of the Big Sandy, 280 miles; improved the Great Kanawha from Charleston, W. Va., to the mouth of the river, fifty-eight miles; and finally built the canal through to Buchanan. It also built certain railroads, as will be shown. In March 1832 the James River and Kanawha Company was chartered, taking up the work which had been done under the Board of Public Works.

The beginning of railroad transportation from East to West was the little Louisa Railroad, which was chartered February 18, 1836, and was the immediate predecessor of the great Chesapeake and Ohio System, which was organized after the War Between the States. The Richmond, Fredericksburg and Potomac had been chartered in 1834 and in 1836 had laid its tracks a part of the way to Fredericksburg. A small group of citizens conceived the idea of building the Louisa Railroad to connect with the new north and south line at Hanover Junction. The Louisa Railroad was built from Hanover Junction westward to Gordonsville, a distance of less than fifty miles.

In 1848 the Legislature granted the Louisa Railroad permission to extend its tracks to the docks of Richmond. In 1850 its name was changed to The Virginia

Central, operating under that name until the War of the 60s, when it was almost completely destroyed. In 1865, when the smoke clouds of war had hardly blown away, the organization of the Chesapeake and Ohio was begun. It was chartered by the General Assembly March 1, 1867, and started operation under that name in 1873, having joined together other short lines and established its right-of-way through the mountains and to the Ohio River.

The second link in the present Chesapeake and Ohio System was the Blue Ridge Railroad, chartered in 1849. It was a little line of only sixteen miles, from Mechum's River, in the western part of Albemarle, to Waynesboro. It solved the old canal-builders' problem of getting through the mountains by tunneling under them. A third link in the Chesapeake and Ohio System was the Covington and Ohio Railroad, chartered in 1853.

In connection with these pioneer railroad movements it should be pointed out that an important convention was held in Staunton in 1848, with delegates from eighteen counties and the City of Richmond. This convention, more particularly referred to in the chapter on Augusta County, adopted resolutions calling upon the General Assembly to appropriate funds for a railroad from the eastern to the western base of the mountains; for an increase in the capital of the Louisa Railroad so that they might extend the road to a point at or near Covington; and endorsed the extension of the Louisa Railroad from Hanover Junction to the docks in Richmond.

The Blue Ridge Railroad was built by the State

under the supervision of that great engineer Colonel Claudius Crozet, an engineer and soldier under Bonaparte. Incidentally, he was the first professor of civil engineering at the Virginia Military Institute and was chairman of its board of visitors.

Col. Crozet built four tunnels under the Blue Ridge —an amazing feat in those early years. This was in the period from 1850 to 1853. Equally as amazing was his scheme of sending trains over the mountains of Rockfish Gap on zigzag tracks while the tunnels were being completed.

The Richmond and Alleghany Railroad was chartered by the General Assembly in its session of 1880-81 and acquired all the rights of the James River Canal interests, and the road was built from Richmond to Clifton Forge, the old towpath of the canal being used as the roadbed as far as Buchanan. The Richmond and Alleghany became a part of the Chesapeake and Ohio System in 1888.

Other railroads have been constructed, magnificent highways have been built over the mountains, and airplanes on regular schedule sail between East and West. Mechanical invention came to the rescue and simplified the difficult problems of the early Virginia pioneers in transportation, whose indomitable persistence must be admired.

Cornwallis in Virginia

When Lord Cornwallis invaded Virginia from the South in 1781, his army traversed so many of the counties mentioned in this book that it may be well here to trace his movements while within the State.

Following the defeat of the British at Kings Mountain, N. C., and the destruction of Tarleton's force at Cowpens, S. C., Cornwallis turned northward to lose heavily to the Continentals under General Nathanael Greene at Guilford Courthouse in March, 1781. So the British commander crossed the Dan River at Boyd's Ferry and marched into Virginia over the old Halifax Road toward Petersburg.

Virginia had been practiaclly defenseless against the marauding of the traitor Benedict Arnold, until Washington detached the young Marquis de Lafayette from the North to Virginia with a pitifully small force, made up largely of raw recruits. It was Washington's strategy to keep the two British armies divided. While he opposed Sir Henry Clinton in New York, Gates, and later Greene, fought the British army of the South under Cornwallis.

Governor Thomas Jefferson of Virginia was severely criticized in that period for leaving Virginia so defenseless and for impoverishing the State so unmercifully in support of the Continental armies. But Jefferson was in close communication with Washington, and not the least of his brilliant services to his State and nation was his stubborn support of the Revolution while serving as Governor of Virginia.

On May 19, Cornwallis, marching northward, was

joined by Benedict Arnold, coming south from Petersburg, in Sussex County. On May 23, the British were at Westover on the James.

Here may be said to have begun Lafayette's celebrated retreat before Cornwallis, with the latter's superior numbers. During this retreat and pursuit to the northward, both Lafayette and Cornwallis crossed many of the counties in the Tidewater and Piedmont sections of the State.

On May 28, Cornwallis camped at a spot on the Chickahominy river in New Kent county which had been occupied earlier in the same month by Lafayette. On May 29, Lafayette retreated into Hanover and crossed the river four miles north of Ashland, while Cornwallis moved a few miles to the eastward. On the following day, Lafayette crossed the North Anna and marched northward, hoping to be joined by General Anthony Wayne, who was proceeding southward to reinforce him.

Cornwallis gave up the pursuit of the young French commander and turned westward, while Lafayette continued on to the Rapidan river and was joined by Wayne. Then it was that Lafayette changed the direction of his march and he and Wayne moved southward through Orange, Louisa and Fluvanna to cut Cornwallis, who was then in Goochland, off from Albemarle county and the important town of Charlottesville.

From Goochland, Cornwallis turned east, constantly harassed by Lafayette. The British again encamped on the Chickahominy in New Kent June 21 and later made their way to Yorktown, for Clinton had sent

[425]

word to Cornwallis to make his way to the seaboard and there await reinforcements.

General Washington quickly saw the possibility of trapping the southern army in Virginia. He concentrated his forces near New York for the double purpose of concealing his intention and preventing Clinton's sending reinforcements. He had transports prepared in the utmost secrecy in the upper waters of Chesapeake Bay.

Word was received in August that the Compte de Grasse, commanding the French fleet, was on his way from the West Indies to Chesapeake Bay, so Washington conceived the plan of trapping Cornwallis with all his army at Yorktown. Leaving a force at West Point, N. Y., to oppose Clinton, Washington crossed the Hudson on August 19 and it was not until he reached Philadelphia that there was any inkling of his purpose.

By forced marches the transports were reached, and the combined American and French forces proceeded down Chesapeake Bay and up the James River and to Williamsburg. Meantime the fleet of De Grasse arrived at the mouth of York river and sent 4,000 French troops ashore to reenforce the Americans. An English fleet under Admiral Hood had followed De Grasse from the West Indies, but arriving at Chesapeake Bay and seeing no signs of the French, the British admiral proceeded on to New York for further orders. Learning the true state of affairs in Virginia, the British ships hastened back, but found the French fleet defending the entrance of the bay. After a sharp fight the British fleet sailed away, leaving De Grasse in control of the bay.

The siege of Yorktown opened September 28. Cornwallis tried to escape into Gloucester county, but his fate was sealed. He sent a flag of truce on October 17, and on October 19 the surrender at Yorktown, virtually ending the Revolution, took place.

Curious Military Punishments

America was in a woeful state of unpreparedness when the War of 1812 broke out. All through Virginia militia volunteered and there was feverish activity in training troops. There are a number of records of court martials during that period and the punishments were so unusual that one of these cases, taken from the records of Louisa county, is here qouted as typical:

CAMP CARTER, *December the 10th, 1814.*

At a court martial convened at Capt. Massie's Quarters of which Lieut. Rey is president and Ensign Penn recorder, was tried Isaiah Trent, a private in Capt. Gammaway's Company, upon the following charges and specifications:

Charge—Riotous conduct.

Specification—In that the said Isaiah Trent, a private in my Company, did on the 9th inst. kick and break the jaw bone of Thomas Jeffries, belonging also to my Company.

(Signed)   JNO. GAMMAWAY, Capt.

To which charge and specifications the prisoner pleaded not guilty.

The Court after mature deliberation on the testimony adduced find the prisoner Isaiah Trent guilty of the charge alleged against him and sentence him to remain in the guard house ten days, during which time he shall be compelled to cover the sinks every morning under the direction of a Corporal and file of men. After he has covered the sinks he shall be conducted to the parade ground in front of the 7th Regiment under the direction of the said Corporal and file of men and there be made to work an hour in digging up the stumps and leveling the ground. On the eighth day of his confinement, in the presence of the Brigade, he shall ride the wooden horse one half hour. On the ninth day, in the presence of the Brigade, he shall be put in the pillory and there remain one half hour, and on the tenth he shall be drummed from right to left of the Brigade with his crime written in large letters on labels pinned to his breast and back, and the whole time he remains in the guard house he shall live on bread and water, and finally his ration of whiskey stopped for twenty days.

(Signed)   LIEUT. REY, President.

Approved by JOHN H. COCKE, Brigadier-General.

Following is an excerpt from the sentence imposed upon another man at the same camp, dated November 30, 1814, for stabbing:

He shall ride the wooden horse tomorrow evening in the presence of the Brigade one half hour with one side of his head, one whisker and one eye brow shaved and blackened. On the next evening in the presence of the Brigade he shall be put in the Pillory and receive whilst there upon his bare posteriors fifteen cobbs, which shall be executed with a paddle made for that purpose, with a number of holes bored through the end, and he shall then be returned to the guard house and there kept fifteen days.

Officers of the Revolution

Because of the destruction of so many of the county records, accurate facts about the services of officers and men who served in the Revolution are difficult to find. Their rosters will never be complete unless the crumbling muster-rolls in the War Department and papers in the State Archives are made public.

[428]

References to them in County and State records are often indirect, being civil and not military records. Light upon the services of some of the Revolutionary officers is thrown by references to them by soldiers under their command seeking pensions. In frequent instances their names and rank are mentioned in grants of land to them for their services.

It should also be borne in mind that the Revolution lasted a long time and that the ranks of officers in miscellaneous records are not necessarily the highest ranks these officers held. While those who are mentioned unquestionably were commissioned, the following names by no means embrace all the officers from these counties:

ALBEMARLE

Colonels

Charles Lewis	William Nicholas
Reuben Lindsay	Richard Lindsay
—— Mallory	

Major

Thomas Meriwether

Captains

David Allen	Reuben Hawkins	James Quarles
Thomas Bell	William Henderson	Robert Rodes
William Brisco	John Hudson	Clough Shelton
Bezaleel Brown	Isaac Israel	William Simms
Henry Burke	Thomas James	Frederick W. Mills
John Burke	Matthew Jouett	Larkin Smith
May Button	Robert Jouett	Roger Thompson
Samuel Eddins	Mask Leake	Ralph Thomas
Edward Garland	Nicholas Lewis	Thomas Walker, Jr.
Peter Garland	Bernard Lipscomb	Daniel White
William Grayson	John Marks	James Wood
Benjamin Harris	John Martin	
Robert Harris	Thomas Martin	

Lieutenants

Nathaniel Anderson	Joseph Holt	John Piper
Nathaniel Garland	William Lewis	Joseph Thomas
George Gilliam	Judson Martin	George Thompson
George Gilmer	David Meriwether	John Thompson
William Gooch	Archelaus Moon	Leonard Thompson
John Henderson	John Nicholas	Charles Wingfield
Reuben Herndon	Lipscomb Norvell	William Woodson

Ensigns

David Anderson	John Hargis	Daniel Moseley
John Beck	John Key	John Reid
Samuel Bell	James Moore	

Adjutants

Abraham Maury   James Meriwether

Quartermasters

Peter Davie   Charles Hudson

Paymaster

Jacob Moon

AUGUSTA

Colonels

George Moffett   Thomas Hughart
Samuel Vance   Charles Cameron (1782)

Lieutenant Colonels

Sampson Mathews   William Bowyer
John McCreery

Majors

Andrew Lockridge   Alexander Robertson
John Wilson

Captains

William Anderson	Thomas Boggs	John Cartmill
Andrew Anderson	James Bratton	Michael Coger
Charles Baskins	John Brown	Robert Craven
James Bell	Patrick Buchanan	Joseph Crouch
Joseph Bell	John Campbell	John Cunningham
David Bell	Charles Campbell	Robert Davis

John Dickey
William Finley
James Frazier
John Gilmer
David Given
John Given
David Gray
Charles Hamilton
John Hamilton
Reuben Harrison
William Henderson
Thomas Hewitt
Thomas Hicklin
John Hopkins
Peter Hull
Zachary Johnson
Robert Kenny
William Kinkead

Abraham Lincoln
Francis Long
William Lowderson
William Lowther
John Lyle
John McCoy
Robert McCreery
Samuel McCutchen
John McKittrick
Andrew Moore
William Nalle
John Oliver
Joseph Patterson
John Peebles
George Pence
George Poage
Samuel Pringle
Thomas Rankin
Anthony Reader

Adam Reader
William Robertson
Alexander Simpson
John Skidmore
David Smith
Thomas Smith
John Stephenson
Ralph Stewart
Alexander Stewart
William Tate
James Tate (killed)
Paul Teter
Robert Thompson
James Timble
Jacob Warwick
Benjamin Wilson
Matthew Wilson
John Young

Lieutenants

William Allen
William Anderson
George Anderson
James Baskins
Samuel Black
George Bratton
David Buchanan
Robert Campbell
Michael Carpenter
Robert Christian Jr.
Robert Clark
Casper Clemons
Michael Coulter
James Crawford
Henry Fleisher

James Frazier
John Garner
James Gibson
Christopher Graham
Joseph Gwin
David Gwin
Nicholas Harper
Robert Harris
Jonathan Humphreys
James Johnson
Joseph Long
Richard Madison
Alexander Maxwell
William McCreery
John McCune

John McKenny
John McMahon
James Mitchell
James Poage
Samuel Rucker
Alexander Scott
Nicholas Seybert
Robert Shaw
Robert Thompson
Joseph Waddell
John Wauchub
Jacob Westfall Jr.
John White
James Young

Ensigns

Robert Anderson
Joseph Bell
Joseph Blair
Cornelius Bogart

John Boyd
Alexander Brownlee
William Buchanan
William Calbraith

Alexander Crawford
Joseph Day
James Ewing
David Gibson

[431]

James Graham
Patrick Hamilton
Abraham Hempenstall
James Hogshead Jr.
William Logan (1782)
Richard Mathews

William McClenahan
Thomas Meteer
Joshua Perry (1782)
John Poage Jr. (1782)
James Rankin
Valentine Shirley

John Smith
James Steel
Samuel Wier
David Wilson
Patrick Young

CAROLINE

Colonels

Thomas Lowry   Anthony Thornton, Jr.

James Upshur

Majors

Philip Johnson   Richard Buckner

Captains

Philip Buckner
William Buckner
Samuel Coleman
William Durritt
—— Fletcher
Robert Graham
George Guy

John Jones
John Long
George Madison
John Marshall
Anthony New
Roger Quarles
Joseph Richeson

William Streshley
Peyton Sterns
James Sutton
Samuel Temple
John Thilman
Francis Tompkins
Robert Tompkins

Lieutenants

Thomas Alcock
Gregory Boynham
John Boutwell
Thomas Broaddus
Daniel Coleman
Julius Coleman
William Collins
William Connor
Joseph Dejarnet
John Downer
Richard Durritt
Johnson Faulkner
John Fitzhugh

Duncan Graham
William Graham
William F. Gray
Thomas Guy
Thomas Hord
James Hord
John Hord
Thomas Jones
William Long
John Norment
James Rennolds
Samuel Sale
Reuben Samuels

John Thompson
George Thornton
Lewis Timberlake
Daniel Turner
Daniel Twiner
Richard Tyler
John Tyler
Jeremiah Upshur
Chilion White
Benjamin Winn
Joseph Woolfolk
Charles Woolfolk

Ensigns

Thomas Beazley
John Brame
Francis Connor
James Daniel
Thomas Ellis
John Gravatt

Thomas Hawes
Joel Higgin
David Jameson
Ambrose Jeter
James Kay
William Mitchell
Samuel Norment

Samuel Rawlins
Mungo Roy
William Samuel
George Terrell
Ambrose White
Richard Wyatt

GLOUCESTER

Warner Lewis, *County Lieutenant*

Sir John Peyton, *Colonel*

Thomas Whiting, *Lieutenant-Colonel*

Thomas Boswell, *Major*

Captains

John Hubard
John Whiting
John Billups
Benjamin Shackelford
John Willis

Gibson Cluverius
John Camp
Richard Matthews
George Booth
Jasper Clayton

Robert Matthews
William Buckner
John Dixon
Richard Billups
William Smith

Lieutenants

Samuel Cary
Richard Hall
John Foster
James Baytop
Thomas Buckner

George Green
William Sears
James Bentley
Edward Matthews
John Billups

Dudley Cary
Hugh Hayes
Churchill Armistead
Philip Tabb
Robert Gayle

Ensigns

Henry Stevens
William Davis
William Haywood
Thomas Baytop
John Fox

James Laughlin
William Bentley
Christopher Garland
Peter Bernard
John Hayes
Samuel Eddins

Thomas Tabb
Richard Davis
Josiah Foster
George Plummer
John Gale

GOOCHLAND

Nathaniel G. Morris, *County Lieutenant*

[433]

Colonels

John Hopkins   Tolley Parrish
George Payne   Robert Lewis

Majors

Richard Bibb   John Curd, Jr.

John Guerrant

Captains

Edmund Curd	Josiah Leak	Stephen Sampson
Edward Duke	Elisha Leak	Edward Smith
William George	Nathaniel Massie	Stockley Towles
Thomas Hatcher	William Miller	John Ware
Tandy Holman	Samuel Richardson	

Lieutenants

Richard Allen	Thomas Miller	Milner Redford
James Allen	James Overstreet	Thomas Royster
John Blackwell	Sherwood Parrish	David Rutherford
William Cole	Josias Payne, Jr.	Obadiah Smith
Stephen Ellis	Anderson Peers	Dabney Wade
James George, Jr.	John Perkins	James Ware
John Herndon	Charles Price	Philip Webber
Peter Johnson	Meredith Price	Solomon Williams
Walter Johnson	Nathaniel Payne	Isham Woodson
Joseph Lewis	Edward Redford	John Stephen Woodson

Ensigns

James Bennett	Major Hancock	Thomas Massie
Robert Bradshaw	Hezekiah Hanley	William McCaul
John Britt	Thomas Harding	Francis Pledge
Obadiah Britt	Nathaniel Harris	Lewis Robards
Edward Cox	Matthew Lacy	Josiah Woodson
John Guerrant, Jr.	Nicholas Lewis	

HANOVER

Captains

Thomas Nelson	John Harris
John Winston	Edward Bullock
Robert Bolling	Nicholas Hammer
John Price	Frank Coleman
Thomas Doswell	John Thompson

KING WILLIAM

Captains

Mordecai Abraham
Christopher Thompson

Mordecai Booth
Harry Quarles

KING AND QUEEN

Captain

William Richards

LOUISA

County Lieutenant
William White

Colonel
Richard Anderson

Major
John Nelson

Captains

David Anderson	George Lumsden	John Sanders
—— Bagby	Garrett Minor	—— Thompson
John Bias	—— Mosby	James Watson
John Fox	Richard Paulet	John White
Nathaniel Garland	Richard Phillips	William White
Henry Garrett	John Poindexter	James Winston
William Hughes	Samuel Ragland	Anthony Winston
Thomas Johnson	Samuel Richardson	St. Charles Yancy

Lieutenants

Turner Anderson	William Jackson	James Roberts
David Bigger	Richard Johnson	John Seay
Butler Bradburn	George Johnson	Thomas Shelton
Samuel Cole	Henry Ashton Johnson	William Smith
John Cosby	George Michie	Joseph Street
John Crutchfield	Robert Michie	Thomas Terrill
William Harris	James Michie	William Thompson
Frederick Harris	Walter Overton	John Timberlake
Samuel Henson	Hezekiah Price	Robert Wasley

[435]

Ensigns

John Brown	Joshua Hughes	Samuel Shelton
William Clark	Christopher Johnson	Peter Shelton
Samuel Dabney	William Meriwether	Joseph Thompson
Aaron Fontaine	James Moorman	Obadiah Truman
Beverley Glenn	Samuel Petis	Samuel Waddy
Forrest Green	John Ross	Lewis Walden

ORANGE

County Lieutenants

James Madison	James Madison Jr.
Zachary Burnley	Thomas Barbour

Colonel

Thomas Barbour

Lieutenant Colonels

Lawrence Taliaferro	James Taylor
Benjamin Johnson	Francis Taylor

Majors

William Moore	Ambrose Madison

Captains

Vivian Daniel	James Hawkins	John Waugh
Nathaniel Mills	Robert Miller	Robert Daniel
Robert Thomas	May Burton	Reuben Daniel
Jere White	Richard White	Bellefield Cave
Benjamin Head	Toliver Craig	Garland Burnley
George Smith	R. C. Webb	Francis Cowherd
William Buckner	Reuben Hawkins	William Campbell
John Scott	James Burton	John Sult
Zachary Herndon	Edmund Shackleford	Richard Well
Charles Bruce	Francis Moore Jr.	Philip Mallory
Richard Graves	George Waugh	David Pannill

Lieutenants

Samuel Brockman	Robert Johnson	William Young
Manoah Singleton	William Buckner	John Proctor
William Smith	George Stubblefield	Abner Porter
Benoni Hansford	Caleb Lindsay	Charles Porter Jr.
James Hawkins	Zachary Shackleford	Richard Price

[436]

Reuben Moore
James Parrish
Richard Cave
Charles Porter
Lewis Ridley
Richard Payne
William Wright
Rowland Thomas Jr.
Moses Willis

Timothy Conner
James Saunders
Thomas Chambers
John Pennill
William Burton
Thomas Forston
John Beadles
Prettyman Merry
John Scott Jr.
Lewis Willis

William Thomas
John Goodall
Zachary Herndon
Benjamin Smith
William Taylor
Richard White
William White
William Terrell
William Stevens

Ensigns

Joseph Parrish
Robert Thomas
James Head
Ambrose Burton
Thomas Chambers
Richard White
Robert Martin
Caleb Sisson

Richard Price
Moses Willis
Alexander Newman
Lewis Coleman
John Herndon
John Robinson
Thomas White
James Stevenson
William Burton

James Easley
John Dawson
James Deering
Charles Thomas
James Sleet
Thomas Bush
John Taylor
James Saunders

Court Clerks

The clerks of the courts in Virginia have been a distinguished and useful set of men. The clerkships, in many cases, have descended from father to son, and throughout the years the office has been one of dignity and influence. In many cases their names are from the best families in Virginia, and a roster of them, together with their periods of service, should not be without interest. The following were clerks from the formation of their respective counties down to recent times:

ALBEMARLE

William Randolph, 1744-1749
John Nicholas, 1749-1815 (66 years)
Alexander Garrett, 1819-1852
Ira Garrett, 1831 for the circuit court to 1852, and for the county court from 1852 to 1869.
John Carr, first circuit court clerk.
Bennett Taylor, 1871-1886
Richard W. Duke, 1886-

AUGUSTA

John Madison, 1745-1779
Alex. McClanahan, 1779-1792
Jacob Kinney, 1793-1800
Chesley Kinney, 1800-1812
Erasmus Stribling, 1812-1831
Jefferson Kinney, 1831-1858
John B. Imboden, 1858-1864
William A. Burnett, 1864-1887
Samuel Kline was nominally clerk in 1869-70 with W. A. Burnett as deputy.

CAROLINE

Benjamin Robinson, 1726-1763
Joseph Robinson, 1763-1780
William Nelson, 1780-1799
John Pendleton, 1799-1814
John S. Pendleton, 1814-1845
Robert Hudgin, circuit, 1831-1845
George W. Marshall, county, 1845-1863
Robert Hudgin, county, 1863-1887
Thomas W. Valentine, circuit, 1870-
George Keith Taylor
T. C. Valentine
E. R. Coghill
E. S. Coghill, the incumbent.

ESSEX

William Beverley, 1716-1745
John Lee, 1745-1761
John Lee, Jr., 1761-1786
Hancock Lee, 1786-1793
John P. Lee, 1793-1814
William Baynham Matthews, 1814-1830
James Roy Micou, 1830-

GLOUCESTER

(All records were destroyed in 1820 and again at the evacuation of Richmond.)
Arthur L. Davies, —1837
John R. Carey, 1837-1867
John Thawley, military appointee, 1868-1870
John S. Cooke, 1870-1887
Samuel B. Chapman, 1887-1896
A .T. Wyatt, 1896-1918
B. B. Roane, 1918-

GOOCHLAND

Henry Wood, 1728-1753
Valentine Wood, 1753-1781
George Payne, 1781-1791
William Miller, 1791-1846
Narcissus W. Miller, 1846-1868
William Miller, Jr., 1868-

HANOVER

James William Clayton, 1720-1735
Augustus Graham, 1735-1740
William Pollard, Sr., 1740-1781
William Pollard, Jr., 1781-1829
P. B. Winston, 1829-1846
W. O. Winston, 1846-1862
R. O. Doswell, 1862-1869
John R. Taylor, 1869-1904
J. A. Brown, circuit, 1907
Clarence W. Taylor, 1907-

KING AND QUEEN

(All early records destroyed)
—— Tunstall was an early clerk
Robert Pollard, about 1800-1835
Robert Pollard, Jr., 1835-1876
B. F. Taylor, 1876-

KING WILLIAM

(Early records destroyed)
Robert Pollard, 1797-1818
Robert Pollard, Jr., 1818-1842
Robert Byrd Pollard, 1842-1852
James Otway Pollard, 1852-1865
William Dandridge Pollard, 1867-1872
O. M. Winston, 1872-

LOUISA

James Littlepage, 1742-1760
John Nelson, 1760-1772
John Poindexter, 1772-1792
Nicholas J. Poindexter, 1792-1812
John Hunter, 1812-1852
David W. Hunter, 1852-1865
John C. Cammack, 1865-1870
Samuel H. Parsons, 1870-1875
    (county) 1875-1887 (circuit)
Jesse J. Porter, 1875-

NEW KENT

Chicheley Corbin Thacker, 1673-1700 (records destroyed)
Bat. Dandridge, 1800-1824
John D. Christian, 1824-1864
Bat. Dandridge Christian, 1864-1871
Edgar Crump, 1870-1887
J. N. Harris, 1887-1900
Thomas N. Harris, 1900-1927
Julian N. Harris, 1927-1935
Samuel W. Lacy, 1935-

ORANGE

Henry Willis, 1734-1740
Jonathan Gibson, 1740-1744
John Nicholas, 1744-1749
George Taylor, 1749-1772
James Taylor, 1772-1798
George C. Taylor, 1798-1801
Reynolds Chapman, 1801-1844
Philip S. Fry, 1844-1859
Philip H. Fry, 1859-

Virginia's Chief Executives

A long list of men served Virginia as Governors in the Colonial period, but not surprisingly long when it is realized that the Colonial period in Virginia was longer than has been the period of the Republic. In the span of 329 years from 1607 to 1936 Virginia was a Colony for 169 years, whereas it has been a State for only 160 years.

It will be noted that a number of men who were named as Governors never came to Virginia, but ruled through deputies, and that in a number of cases men became Governors by virtue of their office as President of the Council.

[439]

Following were the Colonial Governors, with the years in which they took office:

Captain Edward Maria Wingfield, 1607, President of the Council.

Captain John Ratcliffe, 1607, President of the Council.

Captain John Smith, 1608, President of the Council.

Thomas West, Lord de la Warr, or Delaware, 1609, appointed Governor and Captain General, but did not reach Virginia until June 10, 1610. Born in England 1577; died at sea June 7, 1618.

Captain George Percy, 1609, President of the Council. Born in England 1586; died in England 1632.

Thomas West, Lord Delaware, 1610.

Captain George Percy, 1611, Deputy Governor.

Sir Thomas Dale, 1611, High Marshal and Deputy Governor.

Sir Thomas Gates, 1611, Acting Governor.

Sir Thomas Dale, 1612, Acting Governor.

Captain George Yeardley, 1616, Lieutenant or Deputy Governor. Born in England; died in Virginia 1627.

Captain Samuel Argall, 1617, Lieutenant or Deputy Governor. Born in England 1572; died in England 1639.

Captain Nathaniel Powell, 1619, Senior Councillor and Acting Governor. Born in England; killed by the Indians in the Massacre of 1622.

Sir George Yeardley, 1619, who had been knighted and appointed Governor and Captain General in 1618, arrived in the Colony.

Sir Francis Wyatt, 1621, Governor. Born in England 1588; died in England 1644.

Sir George Yeardley, 1626, Lieutenant Governor, and in April of that year commissioned Governor.

Captain Francis West, 1627, elected Governor by the Council.

Dr. John Pott, 1628, elected Governor by the Council. Born in England; probably died in Virginia.

Sir John Harvey, 1629, Governor. Was deposed by the Council and sent to England.

Captain John West, 1635, elected Governor by the Council. Born in England 1590; died in Virginia 1659.

Sir John Harvey, 1636, arrived in Virginia with a commission dated January 11, 1635. Born in England; probably died in Virginia.

Sir Francis Wyatt, 1639, Governor.

Sir William Berkeley, 1641, Governor. Born in England about 1606; died in England 1677.

Richard Kemp, 1644, elected Governor by the Council during Sir William Berkeley's absence in England. Born in England; died in Virginia 1656.

Sir William Berkeley, 1645, Governor.

Richard Bennett, 1652, elected Governor by the General Assembly, but probably in accordance with a private intimation of the wishes of Parliament. Bennett, who was one of the commissioners sent by Parliament to subdue Virginia, brought with him sealed instructions, not to be opened until Virginia surrendered. Born in England; died in Virginia 1675.

Edwards Digges, 1655, elected Governor by the House of Burgesses. Born in England 1620; died in Virginia 1675.

Samuel Matthews, 1657, elected Governor by the House of Burgesses "until the next Assembly, or until the further pleasure of the supreme power in England shall be made known." Born in England; died in Virginia 1660.

Sir William Berkeley, 1660, elected Governor by the General Assembly. His commission from the King was dated July 31, 1660.

Colonel Francis Moryson, 1661, Deputy Governor during the absence of Berkeley in England. Born in England and died in England.

Sir William Berkeley, 1662, Governor.

Herbert Jeffreys, 1677, Lieutenant Governor. Born in England; died 1678.

Sir Henry Chicheley, 1678, Deputy Governor during Culpeper's administration, afterward acting as such during Culpeper's frequent absences from Virginia. Born in England 1615; died in Virginia 1683.

Thomas, Lord Culpeper, 1680, Governor. Born in England and died in England in 1719.

Nicholas Spencer, 1683, President of the Council. Born in England; died in Virginia 1689.

Francis, Lord Howard of Effingham, 1684, Lieutenant Governor. Born in England; died in England 1694.

Nathaniel Bacon, Sr., 1687, President of the Council. Born in England 1619; died in Virginia 1692.

Colonel Francis Nicholson, 1690, Lieutenant Governor. Died in England 1728.

Sir Edmund Andros, 1692, Governor. Born in England 1637; died in England 1714.

Colonel Francis Nicholson, 1698, Lieutenant Governor.

George Hamilton Douglas, Earl of Orkney, 1704, commissioned Governor-in-Chief for life but never came to the Colony. Died 1737.

Edward Nott, 1705, Lieutenant Governor. Born in England 1634; died in Virginia 1705.

Edmund Jenings, 1706, President of the Council. Born in England 1659; died in Virginia 1727.

Colonel Robert Hunter, 1707, commissioned Lieutenant Governor but was captured on his voyage over by the French and never came to Virginia.

Colonel Alexander Spotswood, 1710, Lieutenant Governor. Born in 1676 at Tangier, Africa, where his father was surgeon to the English garrison; died in 1740 at Annapolis, Md., when about to embark for the campaign against Carthagena, South America.

Hugh Drysdale, 1722, Lieutenant Governor. Died 1726.

Robert Carter, 1726, President of the Council. Born in Virginia 1663; died in Virginia 1732.

William Gooch (subsequently knighted) 1727, Lieutenant Governor. Born in England 1681; died in England 1751.

William Anne Keppel, Earl of Albemarle, 1737, appointed Governor-in-Chief. Died in 1754 and never came to Virginia.

Rev. James Blair, D. D., 1740, President of the Council, was Acting Governor during the absence of Governor Gooch on the Carthagena expedition. Born in Scotland about 1655; died in Virginia 1743.

Sir William Gooch, 1741, Governor.

John Robinson, 1749, President of the Council. Born in Virginia 1683; died in Virginia 1749.

Thomas Lee, 1749, President of the Council. Born in Virginia 1690; died in Virginia 1750.

Robert Dinwiddie, 1751, Lieutenant Governor. Born in Scotland 1673; died 1770.

John Campbell, Earl of Loudoun, 1756, appointed Governor General of all the American Colonies, but was never in Virginia.

John Blair, 1758, President of the Council. Born in Virginia 1689; died in Virginia 1771.

Francis Fauquier, 1758, Lieutenant Governor. Born in England 1703; died in Virginia 1768.

Sir Jeffrey Amherst, 1763, made Governor-in-Chief. Never came to Virginia.

John Blair, 1768, President of the Council.

Norborne Berkeley, Baron de Botetourt, 1768, Governor-in-Chief. Born in England 1718; died in Virginia 1770.

William Nelson, 1770, President of the Council. Born in Virginia 1677; died in Virginia 1772.

John Murray, Earl of Dunmore, 1771, Governor-in-Chief. Appointed in July, 1771, and expelled from the seat of government in June, 1775. Born in Scotland 1732; died in England 1789.

During the interregnum in 1775, from the expulsion of Dunmore to the formation of the State government, many executive functions were exercised by the Committee of Safety, the members of which were elected by the conventions. These members were Edmund Pendleton, George Mason, John Page, Richard Bland, T. L. Lee, Paul Carrington, Dudley Digges, William Cabell, Carter Braxton, James Mercer and John Tabb, elected August 17, 1775, and Joseph Jones and Thomas Walker added December 16, 1775, in place of Braxton, elected to Congress, and Mason, who declined further to serve.

Patrick Henry was the first Governor of Virginia as a State. The present constitution provides that Governors shall be elected for four years, and they are not allowed to serve two consecutive terms. It will be noted that Virginia started functioning as a State as soon as the Declaration of Independence was pronounced.

Following are the men who have served as Governors of the State, with the dates of their taking office:

Patrick Henry, 1776.
Thomas Jefferson, 1779.
Thomas Nelson, Jr., 1781 (resigned.)
Benjamin Harrison, 1781.
Patrick Henry, 1784.
Edmund Randolph, 1786.
Beverley Randolph, 1788.
Henry Lee, 1791.
Robert Brooke, 1794.
James Wood, 1796.
James Monroe, 1799.

John Page, 1802.
William H. Cabell, 1805.
John Tyler, 1808.
James Monroe, 1811 (appointed Secretary of State of the United States.)
George William Smith, 1811 (perished in the theatre fire in Richmond.)
Peyton Randolph, 1811, Senior Member of Council of State.
James Barbour, 1812.

Wilson Cary Nicholas, 1814.
James P. Preston, 1816.
Thomas Mann Randolph, 1819.
James Pleasants, Jr., 1822.
John Tyler, 1825.
William B. Giles, 1827.
John Floyd, 1830.
Littleton Waller Tazewell, resigned.
Wyndham Robertson, 1836.
David Campbell, 1837.
Thomas Walker Gilmer, 1840 (elected to Congress.)
John Rutherfoord, 1841.
John M. Gregory, 1842.
James McDowell, 1843.
William Smith, 1846.
John B. Floyd, 1849.
Joseph Johnson, 1851.
Henry Alexander Wise, 1856.
John Letcher, 1860.

William Smith, 1864.
Francis H. Pierpont, 1865.
Henry H. Wells, 1868.
Gilbert C. Walker, 1870.
James L. Kemper, 1874.
Frederick W. N. Holliday, 1878.
William E. Cameron, 1882.
Fitzhugh Lee, 1886.
Philip McKinney, 1890.
Charles T. O'Ferrall, 1894.
James Hoge Tyler, 1898.
Andrew Jackson Montague, 1902.
Claude A. Swanson, 1906.
William Hodges Mann, 1910.
Henry Carter Stuart, 1914.
Westmoreland Davis, 1918.
E. Lee Trinkle, 1922.
Harry Flood Byrd, 1926.
John Garland Pollard, 1930.
George C. Peery, 1934.

Index

INDEX

INDEX

[449]

INDEX

Hudgins, Holder, 131.
Hudgins, R. H., 19.
Hudson, Charles, 311, 337.
Hudson, Christopher, 337.
Huger, Julia Trible, 171.
Hughes, Jesse, 395.
Humphreys, John H., 391.
Hundley, John W., 135.
Hundley, Larkin, 165.
Hundley, William, 102.
Hunter, Frederick, S. C., 186.
Hunter, James, 163.
Hunter, James D., 163.
Hunter, John, 268.
Hunter, Philip Stephen, 176.
Hunter, R. M. T., 161, 165, 175, 176.
Hunton, Charles B., 347.
Hunton, John 347.
Hutchinson, Robert, 143.

I

Imboden, G. W., 390.
Imboden, J. D., 389, 390.
Irvin, David, 338.
Irvin, John, 337.
Irvin, Thomas, 338.
Irvin, William, 337.
Irvin, Rev. William, 337.
Irving, A. D., Jr., 299.
Iversonn, Abraham, 14.

J

Jackson, Andrew, 193, 255, 259.
Jackson, Gen. T. J., 104, 237, 269, 372, 390.
Jackson, William, Jr., 271.
James, 11, 363.
James, John H., 199.
James, Joseph S., 19.
James, King, 9.
Jameson, D., 94.
Jarman, James, 338.
Jarman, Thomas, 338.
Jarman, William, 95, 338.
Jay, John, 113.
Jefferson, Ann, 338.
Jefferson, Jane, 338.
Jefferson, Jane Randolph, 318.
Jefferson, Martha, 330, 338, 347.
Jefferson, Martha Wayles, 224.
Jefferson, Mary, 338.
Jefferson, Peter, 222, 223, 225, 312, 313, 314, 318, 338.
Jefferson, Randolph, 338.
Jefferson, Thomas, 2, 23, 225, 227,

251, 297, 312, 314, 318, 319, 323, 330, 336, 339, 342, 343, 347, 357, 358, 359, 398, 414.
Jeffries, J. M., 81, 137.
Jenings, Peter, 15.
Jenyngs, Peter, 15.
Jerdone, Francis, 54, 329.
Jerdone, Sarah, 54.
Johnson, C., 387.
Johnson, C. L., 187.
Johnson, Chapman, 258, 398.
Johnson, David, 261.
Johnson, Francis, 206.
Johnson, Peter, 94.
Johnson, Philip, 128, 187.
Johnson, Richard, 127, 128, 266.
Johnson, Thomas, 65, 247, 255, 258, 265, 266.
Johnson, William, 247.
Johnston, Dr. George Ben, 232.
Johnston, Joseph E., 353, 372.
Jones, Aubrey H., 163.
Jones, B. B., 60.
Jones, Catesby, 17.
Jones, Catesby apR., 20.
Jones, Charles S., 273.
Jones, Churchill, 302.
Jones, Frances, 50.
Jones, Gabriel, 370, 373, 374.
Jones, Hilary P., 91.
Jones, Admiral Hilary P., 111.
Jones, Col. Hilary P., 91, 103, 111.
Jones, Hugh, 408.
Jones, J. H. C., 126, 137.
Jones, John, 10, 187.
Jones, John Gabriel, 316.
Jones, John Paul, 114, 116.
Jones, John Thompson, 167.
Jones, Dr. John William, 260.
Jones, Maryus, 30.
Jones, Meriwether, 117.
Jones, Orlando, 50.
Jones, Mr. and Mrs. Paul, 168.
Jones, Richard, 17.
Jones, Robert, 157.
Jones, T. G., 78.
Jones, Thomas, 95, 102, 271.
Jones, Thomas Catesby, 30.
Jones, Warner T., 31.
Jones, William, 17, 31.
Jones, William apCatesby, 31.
Jones, William apW., 18, 30.
Jouett, Jack, 95, 248, 264, 321, 339, 358.
Jouett, John, 339, 349.

INDEX

INDEX

INDEX

Colophon

And so we close this book with a colophon, a custom which came into being with the very beginning of the typographer's art. From Gutenberg, Fust and Shoeffer, of Germany, through Italy's Bodoni, Holland's Coster, England's Caxton and America's own Ben Franklin the Master Craftsmen always used it. It was abandoned only when the wondrous skill of human hands had been made to surrender to the Moloch of machine and mass production.

In the Golden Age of the Arts and Crafts men knew little of barter and trade—cared less for price or pay—but wrought with unhampered genius under the impulse of a higher inspiration. When their task was over, perhaps after years of glad and untiring labor, they placed the finished volume in the hands of their liege lord as a tribute of their fealty and devotion. In the colophon they asked forgiveness that their efforts had not been more nearly perfect.

It so happens that all who have contributed in the making of this book have been able to regard their work especially as a labor of love, for in its entirety this volume is an effort to catch and preserve something of the culture and tradition of their own native Virginia.

The author is a Virginian.

The introduction is by John Stewart Bryan, publisher of *The Richmond News Leader* and President of the College of William and Mary.

The illustrations are from pen and ink drawings by Elmo Jones, Richmond artist.

The text is set in Caslon Oldstyle type and letterpress printed by The Dietz Press, Richmond publishers.

The engravings were fashioned by the Royal Engraving Company, of Richmond.

The edition was bound by L. H. Jenkins, Inc., Richmond bookbinders.

Done in the year Nineteen Hundred and Thirty-Seven.